Ramage's Prize

Also by Dudley Pope

Flag 4
The Battle of the River Plate
73 North
England Expects
At 12 Mr Byng Was Shot
The Black Ship
Guns
The Great Gamble

NOVELS

Ramage
Ramage and the Drum Beat
Ramage and the Freebooters
Governor Ramage R.N.

Ramage's Prize

a novel by
DUDLEY POPE

An Alison Press Book
Secker & Warburg · London

First published in England 1974 by
The Alison Press/Martin Secker & Warburg Limited
14 Carlisle Street, London W1V 6NN

Copyright © 1974 by The Ramage Company Limited

SBN: 436 37731 4

*Printed in Great Britain
by Richard Clay (The Chaucer Press), Ltd,
Bungay, Suffolk*

For the Georgesons,
who sailed the
good ship *Alano*
from Falmouth

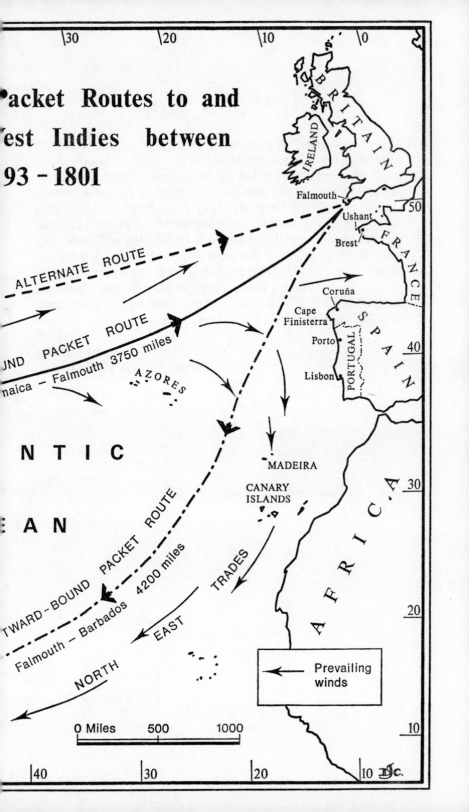

Packet Routes to and ...est Indies between ...93 - 1801

30 20 10 0

BRITAIN

IRELAND

Falmouth

50

Ushant

Brest

FRANCE

ALTERNATE ROUTE

...UND PACKET ROUTE

...naica – Falmouth 3750 miles

AZORES

Coruña

Cape
Finisterra

Porto

PORTUGAL

SPAIN

40

Lisbon

...NTIC

...EAN

...TWARD-BOUND PACKET ROUTE

Falmouth – Barbados 4200 miles

MADEIRA

CANARY
ISLANDS

30

TRADES

EAST

20

NORTH

Prevailing
winds

0 Miles   500   1000

AFRICA

40 30 20 10

10

Author's Note

This story is based on true events. Post Office packet brigs were surrendered to French privateers in the manner described because of "ventures" carried by treacherous officers and crews, and a P.O. packet was ransomed at Lisbon in the same circumstances and difficulties as the *Lady Arabella* of the story. It is worth recording that in Nelson's day mail from wartime England for the West Indies left Falmouth fortnightly and took only forty-five days to reach the most distant destination, Jamaica. Nearly two centuries later, in the age of moon walks and computers, my experience based on eight years in the Caribbean shows that surface mail from England takes sixty to ninety days to reach various islands in the West Indies.

D.P.
Yacht Ramage
Tortola, British Virgin Islands

Chapter One

Regular sleep had been impossible in the hot and windless night so typical of the hurricane season in Jamaica: the occasional slight zephyr venturing in through the window rarely had enough energy to penetrate the mosquito net and cool him. After a night when every brief doze drifted him into a wild dream, Ramage sat at the breakfast table feeling as limp as damp laundry, sipping coffee and squinting at the reality of the harsh sun reflecting into the hotel dining-room despite a latticed jalousie over each window.

He took a letter from his pocket and read it for the fifth or sixth time since a special messenger had delivered it the previous evening. Addressed to "Lieutenant Ramage, at the Royal Albion Hotel", it was signed "Pilcher Skinner", and beneath the hurried scrawl a clerk had written, "Knight, Vice-Admiral and Commander-in-Chief of His Majesty's ships and vessels ... upon the Jamaica Station".

The wording of the letter was straightforward enough, and many a young lieutenant losing his command after a hurricane ripped the masts out of his ship and drifted her up on a coral reef would have been glad to receive it. But Ramage knew that Vice-Admiral Sir Pilcher Skinner was far from being a straightforward man.

To begin with, the document was a letter, not a set of orders: in effect Sir Pilcher was making him an offer. But, he mused suspiciously, admirals do not make offers to lowly lieutenants – particularly not to one newly arrived in Jamaica, and

1

whose first official duty had been to report the loss of his ship. Apart from that, every Commander-in-Chief has his circle of favourites: young lieutenants and captains who have been serving with him for some time, and look to him for patronage, promotion and fortune.

On the Jamaica Station – notoriously the most unhealthy in the Service, where an officer bright and healthy at sunrise can be dead from the black vomit by sunset – promotion is rapid. The funeral of a young frigate captain means a favoured lieutenant is promoted and given his first command. In turn, favoured frigate captains are sent cruising in areas off Hispaniola and the Spanish Main where they are most likely to find French and Spanish merchantmen, prizes that enrich both the captains and the Commander-in-Chief, who receives a regular percentage of the prize money.

Frigate captains out of favour – or not known to the Commander-in-Chief, which for practical purposes meant the same thing and included those recent arrivals who had escorted convoys out from the United Kingdom – can expect only more convoy duty, the dreariest work in the Navy and far removed from any chance of prizes or promotion.

For what it was worth, Ramage thought ruefully, he fitted into a very special category which ensured that he would never be included in Sir Pilcher's favoured circle. To begin with Ramage's father, Admiral the Earl of Blazey, had been one of the most brilliant officers in the Navy – until a frightened government made him the scapegoat for their own stupidity. Sir Pilcher dabbled in politics, and his party supported the Government, with the result that Sir Pilcher had all the wariness of politics and politicians of someone who understood neither but hoped to profit from both. Apart from that, in late middle age, Sir Pilcher was still only a member of the lowest order of knighthood, and it was common knowledge that he thirsted for a peerage – yet that was something that would for ever evade him since it was rarely bestowed on a naval officer, and then only on a commander-in-chief following a very successful fleet action. Not even the most sycophantic officer in Sir Pilcher's circle could visualize that ever happening. But, even worse, he

2

knew Ramage not only had a title, but made a point of never using it in the Service. Ramage guessed it must irk Sir Pilcher to know that letters such as the one he was now holding should, strictly speaking, be addressed to "Lieutenant Lord Ramage".

Any one of these things, Ramage knew only too well, was enough to make him out of favour; but the last straw for Sir Pilcher was probably the fact that Ramage had come out to the Caribbean originally in command of a brig acting under the direct and secret orders of the First Lord of the Admiralty. A man with Sir Pilcher's nature would always be suspicious that hidden influences were at work.

Ramage glanced up at the tall, casually debonair man joining him at the table.

"Morning – you're up early. Couldn't you sleep?"

"Those damned mosquitoes," Sidney Yorke said viciously. "They must have found a hole in my mosquito net. I can still hear them whining in my ears. Just look!"

He showed wrists red and swollen from bites. "My ankles are the same."

"You shouldn't scratch them," Ramage said unsympathetically. "And get yourself a new mosquito net."

Yorke looked up at the coloured waiter. "Ah, there you are, Albert. Just a pot of your excellent coffee, please, and some toast. Dry toast. No, I haven't been drinking," he assured the startled man. He turned to Ramage and pointed at the letter.

"From the large and impressive seal, I don't imagine that's a love letter."

"It's been a long time since Sir Pilcher wrote a love letter."

Yorke nodded and, since Ramage obviously did not want to discuss it, changed the subject. "I've been inquiring about getting a passage back to England. Not too hopeful, though; there's no convoy for at least two months."

Ramage laughed. "There's something ironic about a ship-owner being stranded in Jamaica for the lack of a ship!"

"Since I lost mine as a result of the same hurricane that put your ship up on the same reef, you might be a bit more sympathetic," Yorke protested amiably.

"You own five more ships – why not wait until one comes in

and take over command of her? Pension off the master, or give him leave until the underwriters pay up and you can build a replacement!"

"Drink your coffee. The shipyards are on the Thames and I'm in Jamaica. A small point but relevant ... Who is likely to have any influence with the Post Office?"

Ramage shrugged his shoulders. "Are you thinking of trying to get a berth in a Post Office packet?"

"Only as a last resort."

"You've heard the news then?"

"I've heard that in the last few months most of the packets have been captured on their way back to England, and the Jamaica merchants are angry and frightened."

"Not only the merchants," Ramage said, tapping the letter beside him on the table.

Yorke sniffed contemptuously. "Perhaps if the Commander-in-Chief showed more interest, his frigates would catch these damned French privateers before they catch the Post Office packets, and honest citizens like myself could get home again. You'll be going back in a frigate, I suppose," Yorke said casually.

Ramage shook his head. "If I go, I'll probably be keeping you company. In fact, you'd better try for berths for both of us. And for Southwick and Bowen."

"Oh, I thought Sir Pilcher would be keeping you out here. And can't he find employment for a master and a surgeon?"

Ramage glanced up at the approaching waiter and Yorke waited until the man had set out his breakfast and departed before continuing. "I assumed you'd be staying here under Sir Pilcher's orders."

"I think the Admiral is already short of appointments for his own people."

"Which is a tactful way of saying that you know he's damned if he's going to deprive one of his favourites to give you a job?"

"He wouldn't phrase it so crudely. On the other hand he might find an unpleasant job that has to be done, and give it to me to avoid making one of his people unhappy."

4

After glancing at the folded letter, Yorke busied himself with his coffee and toast. He could see that whatever Sir Pilcher's letter said, Ramage was worried about it: that much was obvious. Yorke knew they had been through too much together in the past few months for Ramage to be unnecessarily secretive.

Slowly it dawned on him why he was in no hurry to arrange a passage back to England. He had spent the early years of his life at sea in one or other of the ships owned by his grandfather, and eventually commanded one of them. He'd realized later that the old man, a tyrant by anyone's standards, had given him command only when convinced that his grandson had nothing more to learn from any of the other masters; more knowledge of ships and the sea would come only from experience. So a year in command had been followed by a couple of years in the London office, learning the details of the business life of the shipowner, as opposed to the shipmaster. At the time Yorke had resented it all, but the old man had had a reason; a reason he had kept silent about even on his deathbed. It was only when the lawyers read his will that Yorke learnt that the whole fleet had been left to him: six well-found ships...

But Yorke had found the life of a rich young shipowner in London boring: mornings and afternoons spent in Leadenhall Street; the evenings a seemingly endless round of soirées and balls, where he had constantly to fend off the attentions of anxious mothers who regarded him as a good catch for their daughters. So he had gone back to sea again, commanding one of his own ships, leaving the London office to be run by trusted men. In some ways it was a lonely life – lonely because he missed the company of intelligent men of his own generation. Yet he knew only too well that in England such men either did not understand what sent him to sea or cultivated his friendship only because they considered a rich friend was a good insurance for paying gambling debts or getting credit.

Meeting Ramage in the Caribbean had been a refreshing change, and Yorke hoped a friendship had grown which would last until they reached old age. Not, he thought with a trace of sadness, that Ramage was ever likely to reach old age. Even now, only just past his twenty-first birthday, he had been

5

wounded a couple of times. He'd lost one ship (albeit a small cutter with a crew of about fifty men) in a particularly desperate affair during the Battle of Cape St Vincent. More recently he'd lost the *Triton* brig after a hurricane which in turn followed a brilliant attack on a privateer which tried to capture Yorke's own ship in a convoy of which Ramage's brig formed part of the escort. A dozen or more other episodes had led to Ramage's ship's company having a loyalty to him which Yorke knew only came from a deep respect. And you only earned the respect and loyalty of tough men-o'-war's-men by real leadership, extreme bravery and concern for the ship and the men in her.

Yet, Yorke thought, the odd thing was that on paper Nicholas Ramage, son and heir of the tenth Earl of Blazey, was far from being an ideal naval officer – or, rather, most people's idea of what one should be. He had all the obvious advantages – damned handsome, in a lean and hungry sort of way which women obviously found irresistible, and a bizarre sense of humour. He also had deep-set, piercing brown eyes which seemed to look right through you, and would endear him to few senior officers subjected to their self-assured and often chilly stare. Yet Ramage had two major handicaps: the sensitive, impatient and proud nature of an artistic person, and a lively mind and imagination. The two combined to make a young man not very amenable to the rigid, unquestioning obedience to the precise letter of an order demanded by certain types of senior naval officer.

So far, from all accounts, Ramage had been lucky. In the Mediterranean he had attracted the attention of Commodore Nelson, and a few months later at the Battle of Cape St Vincent he had made a desperate gamble which had lost him his ship but put the Commodore in the way of capturing two Spanish ships of the line and winning a knighthood. If Sir Horatio Nelson, now a Rear-Admiral, ever rose to any importance in the Navy, then Yorke knew that Ramage would have a powerful patron. But it took time for such a man to rise – if ever he did – and in the meantime young lieutenants like Ramage could have been eclipsed; thrust out of favour and left to spend the rest of their lives on half pay, fretting their hearts out for what might have been.

When Yorke had heard that Ramage's father was a lifelong friend of the present First Lord of the Admiralty, he'd assumed it would have assured Ramage plum jobs and certainly command of a frigate within the next two or three years. But no, it had meant nothing of the sort. Instead it had led, a few months ago, to Lord Spencer picking Ramage for a job where nothing would be said if he succeeded, but if he failed he'd have been sacrificed as a scapegoat in the same way that his father had been sacrificed by an earlier government.

Why then had Lord Spencer chosen Ramage? Yorke had puzzled over the question for many weeks, but now, while he sipped his coffee and tried to get enthusiastic for dry toast which even the swarm of flies seemed to ignore, he thought he knew the answer. It had been a tricky job – an impossible one, on the face of it. There was a chance that Ramage was the only lieutenant available at that moment that Lord Spencer thought stood even a slight chance of succeeding. But the Navy didn't lack bright young lieutenants. No, the answer was probably much simpler. Since Lord Spencer had known that failure would mean complete professional ruin, he'd probably cold-bloodedly chosen Ramage because if he failed he could spend the rest of his life running the family estate, wealthy if not contented, heir to one of the oldest earldoms in the country. For all too many young officers from less fortunate families, professional ruin would entail spending the rest of their lives as haberdashers' assistants.

Yorke glanced at Ramage, who was still staring at the letter. His eyes were bloodshot, his face taut and strained, and he was hunched in the chair as though thoroughly weary: not the weariness of a few hours' exertion but the weariness following months of strain. He was sure Ramage had never thought of Lord Spencer's action in that light – and to tell him would not help him at the moment. Yet ironically Ramage had successfully carried out the orders – his presence in the Caribbean proved that – but now, instead of reporting to the Commander-in-Chief with his own ship, he had had to report that the *Triton*

7

brig had been lost on a coral reef after being dismasted in a hurricane.

It didn't matter that the only ship of war that survived the hurricane had been a line-of-battle ship, that three frigates had actually sunk, that Yorke's own ship had been tossed up on the reef with the *Triton*. All that mattered was that, without a ship, Ramage was entirely dependent upon the generosity of the Commander-in-Chief, and Sir Pilcher Skinner did not view him with favour ... He could not be blamed, given the way the Navy functioned, if he just shrugged his shoulders and sent Ramage back to England ...

Which, thought Yorke as he poured himself more coffee, makes that letter folded beside Ramage's plate even more intriguing ...

"You're serious about a berth in a Post Office packet?" Yorke asked.

When Ramage nodded, the young shipowner said, "We might have a long wait. The last one is two weeks overdue, and the next due any time now, but some privateer's probably snapped her up."

"There'll be a long waiting list of passengers."

"Not on your life!" Yorke exclaimed. "Very few people are so anxious to get to England that they want to risk their necks before it's known what's happening."

"What do 'they' suspect is happening?" Ramage asked quizzically.

Yorke grinned. " 'They' are positive there are just too many French privateers, and 'they' include Mr Smith, the Deputy Postmaster-General, who is in charge of Foreign Mails. I spent half an hour with him yesterday trying to arrange a passage."

"Presumably you'll have the whole packet to yourself."

"No, I didn't even get round to asking the fare. There are simply no packets. And all the Navy's fault, if you listen to the Deputy Postmaster-General. He blames the Navy entirely – or Sir Pilcher, anyway."

Ramage grimaced, irritated at finding himself making excuses for Sir Pilcher. "What does Mr Smith expect – a frigate to escort each packet?"

8

"No, just more frigates patrolling the more obvious places where privateers can seize the packets after they sail from here."

"I can't imagine privateers lurking in *obvious* places, can you?"

Yorke signalled to the steward to bring more coffee and turned to Ramage. "To be quite honest, I can't imagine them finding and capturing one packet after another in the middle of the Atlantic either ... Perhaps an occasional one. No, I'm sure they're capturing them just as soon as they get through the Windward Passage – within a couple of days of leaving here, in other words; just as soon as they pass out of the Caribbean into the Atlantic."

"Give Sir Pilcher a little credit," Ramage protested mildly. "He has a standing patrol across the Windward Passage and well out into the Atlantic, and no privateer's been sighted anywhere in the area for weeks."

"You seem well informed. Have you any theories?"

"No, none at all." Yorke noticed that Ramage's eyes glanced down at the letter before he added, "I wish I had."

"Has anyone?" Yorke asked flatly.

Shrugging his shoulders, Ramage said ruefully, "If he has, he's keeping quiet about it in case Sir Pilcher gives him the job."

"What job?" Yorke asked innocently.

"The job of delivering the mail," Ramage said as the steward brought Yorke more coffee. "Albert, I think I'll have some more, too. It's the best I've ever tasted. What's the secret?"

The coloured man smiled happily. "A pinch of salt in the pot, sah."

"Just salt?" Yorke asked doubtfully.

"Nuthin' else, sah," the steward said solemnly. "The beans must be fresh ground, of course."

When the steward had gone back to the kitchen, Yorke said casually, "Any news from Admiralty House?"

"Nothing definite," Ramage said, his eyes again dropping to the letter.

9

"Any hint as to whether you're in or out of favour?"

Again Ramage shrugged his shoulders and, after a minute's hesitation, passed the letter to Yorke. "Sir Pilcher sent this last night; I can accept or refuse."

Yorke's brow wrinkled as he unfolded the sheet of paper. "Is that usual – having the option, as it were?"

Ramage shook his head. "On the contrary, it's –" He broke off, not wanting to influence Yorke's reaction.

The other man read slowly and finally glanced up. "Interesting."

"You think so?" Ramage asked sarcastically, for once irritated by Yorke's flippant manner.

"Interesting, significant – and suspicious."

"Suspicious?"

"Yes. I don't know quite what it is, but I don't like the option. Surely admirals don't give lieutenants options, do they?"

Ramage shook his head. "I've spent most of the night trying to guess what's behind it."

Yorke stirred his coffee. "I begin to wonder why Sir Pilcher almost labours the point that you have the option. Let's go through the letter slowly."

He spread the letter on the table and ran his finger under the first few lines. "Well, after all the usual routine phrases, he tells you that there have been heavy and unexpected losses among the Post Office packets coming from England and returning. 'Unexpected'? Any clue in that word?"

"That struck me, too, but I don't think so. There were very few losses in the first years of the war; now they've suddenly increased. Obviously it was unexpected..."

"Very well, he goes on to say that increased frigate patrols off the coasts of Cuba, Hispaniola and Puerto Rico prove that far from there being more French and Spanish privateers, fewer than half seem to be operating this year compared with last. Do you believe that?"

Ramage smiled. "In the previous couple of years, frigate captains made small fortunes from head money alone. Privateers have large crews, and at five pounds a head, plus prize

10

money ... There's no doubt the French and Spanish in the Caribbean are now short of both ships and men for privateering."

"In the Caribbean," Yorke emphasized, "and perhaps for a few hundred miles out into the Atlantic. All right," he said in response to an impatient gesture from Ramage, "we'll leave privateers based in Europe out of it for the moment. Now, Sir Pilcher says that while he has no reason to think the packets are being lost on this side of the Atlantic, he has decided to make an investigation ... that seems reasonable enough. However, he goes on to say, he is extremely short of ships, but 'because you are at present unemployed by virtue of having lost the *Triton* brig', he is prepared to place the investigation in your hands 'as an alternative to you returning to the United Kingdom'."

Yorke read the passage again. "It's rather like blackmail."

"No, he's quite right. I haven't a ship now, and the court of inquiry into the loss of the *Triton* has cleared me of blame, so there's nothing more to be done about that. If Sir Pilcher has no appointment for me, I return to England. That's the routine."

"It still seems odd," Yorke persisted. "I can't believe he's so short of ships that he can't spare anyone else to make this investigation. It's obviously the most urgent job he and the Navy face! It's not just Jamaica that's affected: there's Barbados, Grenada, St Lucia, St Vincent, Martinique, Antigua, Tortola – dozens of 'em! The whole West Indies must be in turmoil, cut off from England in both directions, yet he ..."

Ramage nodded wearily. "Exactly! I can imagine him passing the job to the captain of one of his 74-gun ships, and giving him three or four frigates as well. Or even choosing one of his favourite captains and sending him off with a couple of frigates. But ..."

"But you can't see why he'd pick a lieutenant who commands nothing more than a cabin trunk. Neither can I. This sheet of paper," Yorke said, holding up the letter contemptuously, "doesn't tell a tenth of the story. When do you have to give your reply?"

Ramage took out his watch. "In an hour's time, and I'm damned if I know what to say."

"What's in favour of accepting?"

Ramage picked up one of the heavy knives on the table and balanced it horizontally on a finger. "Nothing really, except that it might be amusing to try to find out what is happening to the packets – assuming Sir Pilcher is merely being silly, not cunning."

"Suppose he is being cunning and there's something else involved?"

"I hope I'll find out in time to get out of it."

"That means you'll accept?"

Yorke spoke so sharply that Ramage glanced up in surprise. "You think I should refuse?"

Ramage did not hide his disappointment when Yorke nodded. Despite the vagaries of the letter, he had hoped that somehow it would get him back to sea again. The heat and smell of Jamaica and the noise and bustle of Kingston were little to his liking. Moreover the heavy social pressures brought on eligible young officers by anxious mothers seeking matches for their dumpy daughters drove most young men to the rum bottle before long.

But now Yorke was grinning. "Refuse – and then wait. See what else the old boy has to offer!"

"Bargain?" Ramage exclaimed, obviously horrified.

"Now, now! Don't use those nasty tradesmen's words. There must be a good reason why Sir Pilcher wants you to undertake this job, when he has dozens of other officers to choose from. Once you know why he picked you instead of some post-captain, you'll be in a better position to make up your mind."

There was much in what Yorke said: he needed to know Sir Pilcher's motives. "But supposing he's being straightforward? It's unlikely, but what then?"

"Up to you," Yorke said banteringly. "It looks as though we're all stuck in Jamaica until the packets start getting through or a convoy assembles in a couple of months. If you want to go home in a packet you'd better solve the mystery!"

Ramage glanced at his watch and said as he slipped it back in his pocket, "I'd better get along to Admiralty House."

"Present him with an ultimatum," Yorke said.

"*Force majeure*," Ramage said, "it's quicker and more certain than negotiation."

Chapter Two

Ramage was thankful the large waiting-room at Admiralty House was cool and comfortably furnished; probably one of the coolest spots in Kingston since Jamaica was already sweltering in what promised to be the hurricane season's hottest day so far. There was hardly a breath of wind, and Ramage pitied any captain under orders to sail – it would be a case of out boats and tow...

The white-painted jalousies over the windows let in sufficient light while their slats threw striped shadows on the walls and kept out the sun's harsh glare. The floors were cool marble and four rattan armchairs were grouped in the middle of the room round a small, highly polished baywood table whose legs stood incongruously in shallow, metal trays of water: part of the constant war waged against white ants in the Tropics.

The ceiling was high, adding to the sense of coolness, and there was a large portrait in a wide, matching gilt frame, carefully hung in the precise centre of each of three walls. Ramage saw that the one opposite the window, like the centre panel of a triptych, was of Sir Pilcher Skinner, with – presumably – his plump wife on the wall to his right. Was the young woman on the other wall a daughter?

All the artist's skill with brush and pigments could not conceal the fact that Sir Pilcher's legs and neck were too short for his plump body, nor disguise the fat and sagging cheeks eventually tapering and merging into several chins which sat on his lace stock like slices of wet bread. He was depicted standing

14

four-square on the quarterdeck, his uniform a splendid array of blue, white and gold, left hand resting on the hilt of his sword and right hand holding a telescope tucked under his arm. Few people, however, would think the pinkness of the cheeks came from the rays of a setting sun; that colour and texture of watered silk came only from owning a good cellar and employing a chef who took a pride in his work.

Yet the face was curiously cheerful; Sir Pilcher looked like a man who could enjoy a good joke almost as much as a well-roasted saddle of lamb or a fine claret. The artist had been clever (and for Ramage it redeemed an otherwise undistinguished portrait) in catching the Admiral's eyes.

Although the eyes could be humorous on occasion, Ramage guessed that they could also be as shifty as a dishonest moneylender's when Sir Pilcher was being forced into making a decision or taking responsibility. Yet with no fleet in the Caribbean, making minor and mostly administrative decisions was his only major task.

Ramage touched the letter in his pocket, as if seeking some link between the paper and the portrait staring fixedly at him. If he accepted, his orders would be drawn up with extreme care by a man who wanted to get the most done while assuming the least responsibility. Sir Pilcher wanted a lowly lieutenant to find an answer (which had presumably eluded the resources of the Post Office and several ministers of state in Whitehall) but at the same time was giving him no authority. The Admiral was no fool, and Ramage guessed that the letter represented the first time he had ever given a mere lieutenant the option of backing out; of politely declining. If Sir Pilcher thought he was being magnanimous (which was unlikely) to the mere lieutenant it was rather like staring cross-eyed into the muzzle of a highwayman's pistol on Blackheath and being given the option of "Your money or your life!"

The rattan of the chair squeaked in protest as Ramage stretched back. The captain, who had been the sole occupant of the waiting-room when Ramage arrived, was now with the Admiral, and since he commanded the *Hydra* frigate, which had arrived from England only a day or two ago and was about to

15

sail again, Ramage was going to have a long wait.

He wriggled his feet: the heat made them swell so that his long boots were tight and uncomfortable. He noticed the Royal Albion Hotel's shoeblack had expended a lot of energy on them, but not much skill; the leather was lacklustre – the fellow had not learned to use the minimum of polish and a bit of spit.

Let's sit comfortably in Admiralty House and look at everything from Sir Pilcher's point of view, Ramage thought to himself. Sir Pilcher owed absolutely nothing to Lieutenant Ramage; on the contrary. From Sir Pilcher's point of view...

"Ramage," a smooth voice said at the door, and he turned to see Henderson, a thin man wearing a clerical collar who seemed to combine the roles of Sir Pilcher's chaplain and secretary. "The Admiral will see you now."

The chair creaked as if in relief as Ramage stood, straightened his stock, gave the scabbard of his sword a tug and wished he had drunk less coffee: it was swilling around in his stomach, now unpleasantly chilly and uncomfortable. He was nervous; there was no denying that. For all his offhand talk to Sidney Yorke, the fact remained that the word of a British admiral could end a young lieutenant's career as effectively as a whole broadside from a French ship of the line.

Clack, clack, clack – he found himself treading heavily on the marble floor. Whistling in the dark, Ramage? Trying to keep your spirits up? Don't forget, Sir Pilcher may simply be putting out an anchor to windward: he knows a great deal about the working of the collective mind of Their Lordships...

The portrait was good: as he looked at the subject again Ramage realized that he had underrated the artist, who had been as subtle as he dare while still being sure of getting his fee. The Admiral rose from behind his desk in a movement halfway between the majestic and the ponderous, and pointed to rattan armchairs grouped round another small table, a replica of the arrangement in the waiting-room.

"Ah, my boy, let's sit here and be comfortable," he said affably.

16

He motioned Ramage to one side of the table and sat down opposite in a chair which groaned loudly in protest.

"I've been giving Captain Jeffries of the *Hydra* frigate his orders: he sails for Antigua in a couple of days, lucky fellow."

"Indeed, sir?" Ramage said politely. The Admiral's voice was curiously squeaky considering the bulk from which it emerged.

"Taking Admiralty orders and all the routine paperwork. Absurd not being able to entrust anything to the Post Office. There's talk of the Admiralty having to use the King's ships instead ... and I'm so short of frigates. Damnably short."

Ramage nodded, guessing that most of Sir Pilcher's frigates were out cruising, combining the hunt for privateers with the hunt for prizes, to bring a double profit to Sir Pilcher: a tactical profit of fewer enemy ships, and a cash profit since he received an eighth of all prize money. Jamaica was the biggest money prize the Admiralty had to offer: two years in command of the station in wartime made an admiral as rich as a nabob who had spent a lifetime in India.

"Mr Dundas," Sir Pilcher said, as though thinking aloud. "An impetuous man."

But a powerful one, a startled Ramage thought to himself. As His Majesty's Secretary of State for the War Department and one of Mr Pitt's closest friends, Henry Dundas can afford to be impetuous since his drinking partner is the Prime Minister.

"Yes, an impetuous man. He has just ordered all his general officers out here to send duplicate and triplicate – *triplicate* – copies of dispatches and routine reports by merchantmen sailing home in different convoys. He passed a duplicate of this order to the Prime Minister, who sent copies to both Lord Auckland and Lord Gower. Never could understand why they have Joint Postmasters-General," he sniffed. "*And* a copy to the First Lord of the Admiralty. Most uncalled for, in my opinion."

But most effective, Ramage noted, guessing that Sir Pilcher's soliloquy was an oblique way of leading up to the letter. After staring at the empty chair next to Ramage for a minute or two

17

without speaking, Sir Pilcher focused his shifty eyes on him.

"Well," he asked, "you've read my letter?"

"Yes, sir."

Ramage realized that he still had not finally made up his mind how to answer the inevitable question: now he was facing the Admiral the decision that he thought he had reached with Yorke at breakfast seemed wrong.

"Think you stand a good chance of finding out what's happening?"

"No, sir," Ramage said lamely.

Sir Pilcher's jaw dropped into the folds of his many chins. "No?"

Obviously it was not the answer Sir Pilcher had expected, and he groped in his pocket as he recovered from his surprise. Eventually he extricated a blue-enamelled snuffbox and snapped open the lid.

"Why not?" the Admiral demanded, glowering at the brown powder in the box, a podgy finger and thumb poised ready to take a pinch.

"There's not enough information to go on, sir: the packets are disappearing somewhere in scores of thousands of square miles of ocean."

"They can't just *vanish*."

"So many privateers, sir," Ramage said vaguely, deliberately trying to avoid being put on the defensive and making specific objections which the Admiral could pin down and dismiss with an airy wave of the hand.

Sir Pilcher shook his head violently, the flesh of his face swinging from side to side as if about to break loose from the bone. "There might be more to it than privateers," he said mysteriously.

Ramage remained silent, realizing that his refusal had fallen flat.

"Much more," the Admiral said, his voice dropping conspiratorially.

"I had no idea, sir; you didn't mention it in your letter."

"Secrecy, my dear boy: you realize what all this means, don't you?"

18

Unsure if the question was rhetorical and wary of the querulous note in Sir Pilcher's voice, Ramage said nothing.

"It means, my dear Ramage, that because so many packets are being captured, London is cut off from the rest of the western hemisphere. *Completely cut off!* Can you imagine it? In the middle of a war, Whitehall can't send a single order to any admiral or general overseas – let alone to Governors and those sort of people – and be sure it'll be received unless it's sent in a ship of war. The War Office is cut off from the Army out here, the Admiralty isn't receiving my dispatches and I'm not getting their orders; and not a single merchant in England or the West Indies can send or receive an order or a remittance. Both war and trade are at a standstill – and have been for months..."

"I see, sir," Ramage said, feeling some comment was necessary.

"Just think of the Admiralty and War Office not receiving regular dispatches from their commanders-in-chief for weeks and months. Imagine the confusion when they finally get one and find it refers to matters raised in three preceding dispatches they've never received. And the dreadful position commanders-in-chief are in when they suddenly get instructions referring to previous orders and plans which never reached them. The *Hydra* brought out triplicate copies – *triplicate*," he repeated pettishly, "of all Admiralty and War Office orders going back five months. It doesn't do to think of what's happening at the Navy Board and all the other offices: it'll take months to find out which reports and requests of mine they've received and which have been lost..."

Sir Pilcher broke off and shuddered, apparently overcome by the enormity of scores of clerks being deprived of the hundreds of reports and forms which might have been sunk in the Atlantic in weighted mailbags to avoid them falling into enemy hands.

Ramage conjured up a picture of London as the head of a body deprived of most of its limbs: an order from the head in London was incapable of provoking even a twitch of a muscle in the limbs of Jamaica or Martinique, Barbados or Antigua ... if the losses spread, what of Canada and Gibraltar, the Peninsular and the Mediterranean? Every frigate and smaller vessel in the Navy would have to be clapped into service just delivering and collecting official mail, let alone dealing with the correspondence of merchants all over the world. Cargoes not shipped until they were paid for; urgently needed provisions, cordage, sails, powder and shot for the King's ships not sent because the Navy Board, Ordnance Board and the dozen other offices never received requests and reports ... He felt something approaching sympathy for the portly admiral sitting opposite him and staring fixedly at a snuffbox. The French had (perhaps accidentally) suddenly discovered a way of paralysing Britain. True, the opportunity had always been there, but surely the French didn't have enough ships to comb the oceans picking out Post Office packets?

As if reading Ramage's thoughts, Sir Pilcher tapped his nose knowingly. "You know the only thing that's going to stop the losses?"

When Ramage shook his head the Admiral said, with the air of a man revealing a great secret, "We've got to use our brains: we have to out-think those French rascals!"

"Surely having some frigates would help," Ramage said lamely.

"Not at this stage. Later, perhaps, when we know what's going on. No, my boy, we – I mean the Admiralty, the Post Office and myself – can't act until we get the answer to one particular question." He paused, and Ramage was reminded of an actor savouring the climax of his best role.

"Do you know what that question is?" Sir Pilcher asked, and his face fell when Ramage nodded.

"I think so, sir."

"Oh, you do, eh? Out with it then; out with it!"

"Well, sir, I understand there are fewer French privateers at sea now than last year, and they're capturing fewer merchantmen. So why are fewer privateers capturing more packets? If that is what is happening."

The look of admiration on Sir Pilcher's face was quickly replaced by one of irritation. "Exactly. That's the question, and what's the answer, eh?"

Ramage shrugged his shoulders; the tone of the Admiral's voice told him that no one else had found it, either. "Any officer investigating the losses is going to need a great deal of information before he'd even dare to make a guess, sir. He'd almost need to be able to see into the mind of the enemy."

Sir Pilcher gave a deep sigh, as if relieved to find someone who agreed with him. "Between you and me, Ramage, that's just what I've hinted in my dispatches to the First Lord. Still, can't say it aloud, can we!" His fingers were still poised over the snuffbox but his earlier agitation had vanished. "Well, Ramage, what about it?"

"Information about losses so far, the way the packets operate...?"

"All taken care of," Sir Pilcher said airily. "The Deputy Postmaster-General here in Kingston has all those sort of details."

His tone implied that they were trivial but that – well, Ramage wondered, that what? He was probably being stubborn (Sir Pilcher would call it mulish), but he felt he was being led along blindfolded. And why had *he* been chosen? If the situation was as desperate as Sir Pilcher said (and he was certain the Admiral was not exaggerating) surely it was a job for a senior captain on the Jamaica station: someone like Captain Napier of the 74-gun *Arrogant*, who could ask for three or four frigates if he found he needed a small squadron to root out privateers.

Yet Sir Pilcher had made great play of that "one particular question", as though the real job of destroying the privateers, whatever it was, could not be done until someone had served up the answer on a plate. It made sense – providing the losses conformed to some special plan. Find out what the plan was, and then move quickly to wreck it. Supposing the losses were pure chance; privateers encountering the packets at random? Then no answer existed, and a lot of time would be wasted looking for it.

Ramage was deliberately avoiding looking squarely at his own particular question, but it was nagging at him like toothache. All right, he thought grimly, take a good look at it this time: Why has Sir Pilcher chosen me? He dislikes me – no one makes a secret of that. He has a couple of dozen favourite lieutenants he wants to get promoted and given their own commands, yet none of them was given the job. He has at least a dozen young frigate commanders, low on the list of post-captains but high on his patronage list, any one of whom he would like to single out for special praise in a dispatch to the First Lord.

The Cabinet has told the Admiralty to halt the losses, the First Lord passed the word to Sir Pilcher, and Sir Pilcher has picked Lieutenant Ramage. It was a damned odd sequence, because if Ramage succeeded, the process reversed itself: Sir Pilcher would have to give him the credit in a dispatch to the First Lord, and the First Lord would probably mention his name to the Cabinet. All of which, he thought cynically, would be most gratifying to an admiral, let alone a mere lieutenant, since it would probably result in the lieutenant getting instant promotion.

He looked across at Sir Pilcher, who was still staring fixedly at the enamel snuffbox. You're up to something; there's not the slightest doubt about it. Why haven't you chosen your favourite lieutenant to reap this golden harvest? Or your favourite young frigate captain? Is it because you know there'll be no harvest to reap? That all you will be able to report to the First Lord, and the First Lord to the Cabinet, is abysmal failure? Ramage watched Sir Pilcher's hands for a few moments, saw their slight trembling, and was sure that the Admiral believed the mission was impossible.

Still, it was worth fishing around a bit more to try to be sure why Sir Pilcher had chosen him before he finally refused the job. Ramage decided to bait a hook and lower it gently over the side into what were palpably deep waters.

"The *Hydra* frigate, sir," Ramage said tentatively, "she brought out the latest news from London about the packet losses?"

"Of course – Lord Spencer sent her because that's the only secure way of passing orders these days."

"Did the First Lord make any suggestions, sir?" Ramage

congratulated himself: the diffident note in his voice was perfectly pitched.

"Suggestions? My dear boy, the First Lord doesn't *suggest* things; he gives *orders*."

Gently does it, Ramage told himself, the hook is baited and the fish is swimming close to it. Just a little twitch should be enough.

"I hope I'm not being impertinent, sir, but did the First Lord specify a particular officer for this – ah, this task?"

"A particular person? I have *my* orders from him, naturally," Sir Pilcher said, his eyes never moving from the snuffbox, into which he was peering with all the absorption of a fortune-teller gazing at a crystal ball. Was he being evasive?

"But no particular officer was named...?"

"His orders to me cover the point."

As soon as he saw Sir Pilcher was not taking the bait, Ramage found himself losing both patience and interest. Sir Pilcher's reasons for choosing him were still far from clear and Ramage was damned if he was going to get mixed up in the old man's chicanery. Now's the time to withdraw gracefully, he told himself.

"Well, sir, since you've been kind enough to give me the option of – well, travelling home as a private individual instead of ... ah, receiving fresh orders..." He patted the letter in his pocket as if overcome with nervousness.

It took Sir Pilcher two or three seconds to realize that Ramage was declining. Instead of glaring at him, the Admiral's eyes flickered up for a moment and then resumed their watch on the open snuffbox, as though a solution would crawl out of the brown powder and nestle in the palm of his hand if only he waited long enough.

"Great pity, Ramage, a great pity. You've thrown away a splendid opportunity to distinguish yourself."

"May I ask, sir –"

"Damnation, boy, you're turning it down, aren't you?" Sir Pilcher interrupted angrily, finally snapping the snuffbox shut without using it. "Do you expect me to let you read the First Lord's orders to me?"

23

Since he had nothing to lose, Ramage could not resist saying, "If you would be so kind, sir."

The Admiral's eyes swung round and focused on Ramage in shocked surprise, his face blotching and his Adam's apple bobbing like a buoy breasting a flood tide. Suddenly he took a deep breath and abruptly stood up, waddling over to his desk. Assuming he had been dismissed, Ramage had grasped the arms of his chair to get up when he saw the Admiral open a drawer and take out some papers. He turned and came back, handing them to Ramage.

"Second page," he growled as he sat down heavily. "Third paragraph. Read from there, and be quick about it."

Ramage hurriedly skimmed the words, half expecting the Admiral to change his mind and snatch the letter back.

"... losses of packets became so heavy..." Lord Spencer had written. "... Cabinet ordered a new investigation at Falmouth ... but the Inspector of Packets appears a stupid man ... his report reached no conclusions and is useless ... Lord Auckland has sent all details of the losses on the Lisbon and West Indies routes to the Deputy Postmaster-General at Jamaica...

"... I have no need to impress upon you the seriousness and urgency of the situation ... Cabinet has instructed the Admiralty to investigate and halt the losses ... I must entrust this to an energetic, young officer with an alert and questioning mind who is unafraid of taking risks or responsibility ... urge upon you to give him the widest latitude and suitable cooperation ... My choice would be Lieutenant Ramage of the *Triton* brig, who will by now have arrived at Jamaica with Rear-Admiral Goddard's convoy ... He has an unfortunate penchant for acting on his own initiative ... but in no way do I insist if your choice of an officer differs from mine ... In London we find the circumstances of the losses so puzzling, I can give you no guidance of how the investigation should be carried out ... But it *must* succeed..."

Sir Pilcher's hand was outstretched and Ramage gave him back the letter. While the Admiral folded the pages along their original creases he said crossly, almost pettishly, "It so happens

24

that my choice *does* differ from his Lordship's."

At once Ramage guessed what Sir Pilcher had intended. By offering Ramage the job in writing and making it seem impossible of achievement, he had hoped Ramage would refuse. Lord Spencer would eventually be told that Ramage had declined the appointment – which would be the truth, though far from the whole truth – and it would then go to whichever favourite Sir Pilcher had in mind. He would have effectively covered himself against Lord Spencer's phrase, "but in no way do I insist if your choice of an officer differs from mine ..."

Ramage knew only too well that such a remark from the First Lord was little more than politeness, put in almost routinely, so that a commander-in-chief would not complain about undue interference from the Admiralty. Yet it would be a brave – and foolhardy – commander-in-chief that ignored it even if his own choice did differ. If the commander-in-chief's man failed, the First Lord would listen to no excuses, pointing out that his own recommendation had been ignored ...

Sir Pilcher was well aware of all that; indeed, he was already one step ahead, since the whole difficulty would be removed if the wretched Lieutenant Ramage could be manoeuvred into refusing the appointment. Every officer could refuse an appointment; it was a vastly different thing from refusing to carry out an order. But Ramage knew he must step warily in dealing with someone like Sir Pilcher.

Then Ramage suddenly remembered Sir Pilcher's obvious disappointment when he had declined – when he'd done what he assumed the Admiral hoped. No, Sir Pilcher was not trying to manoeuvre him into refusing. Hell, it simply did not make sense.

"If your choice differs, sir, I would naturally much prefer ..."

"There are other factors," the Admiral said, waving away objections with a flabby hand.

"I'm afraid that quite unwittingly I've put you in a difficult situation, sir," Ramage said smoothly. "Obviously you would prefer to give these orders to an officer you know, and in whom you have trust – and for whom," he said with a slight emphasis, "you can ensure the cooperation of everyone on the station."

As the Admiral's hooded eyes lifted to stare at him, Ramage realized the advantage of dealing with someone like Sir Pilcher: he was so ruthlessly determined to look after his own interests – which ultimately meant keeping in with the First Lord – that, after a certain point, tact and circumlocution were quite unnecessary. Once it was clear what was being bought and sold, Sir Pilcher was quite happy to sit down and drive a hard bargain.

"Well?" the Admiral snapped. "What about my letter?"

"It's in my pocket, sir," Ramage said innocently.

"Indeed? Ramage, I don't give a damn where it is: you know what I mean!"

Now for the bargaining, Ramage told himself, suddenly realizing that, irrationally, he now wanted the job of solving the mystery of the vanishing Post Office packets.

"Lord Spencer mentions 'widest latitude and suitable cooperation . . .', sir."

"Well?" the Admiral growled suspiciously. "It doesn't mean giving you a ship o' the line and half a dozen frigates, you know."

Ramage was thankful for the Admiral's angry exaggeration, since it made his next request sound trivial. "Although obviously I don't know how the investigation will proceed, sir, I'd like to count on having some of my officers and men."

"*What* officers and men?" Sir Pilcher snapped. "You don't have a ship now."

"Some of those who were with me in the *Triton*, sir."

"They've already gone to the *Arrogant*. She's very short."

"I'd need only a dozen or so."

"Oh, very well."

"When does the *Arrogant* sail, sir?"

"Not for a week or so. Give me a list and I'll warn Captain Napier."

"Thank you, sir."

"So you'll do your best to catch these beggars?"

Sir Pilcher was suddenly anxious, almost pleading, as if he'd taken off a grim mask he'd worn for bargaining. Ramage was immediately puzzled again, and felt a chill of fear. Had he fallen into some trap? At first the Admiral had seemed disappointed that he'd declined the job; then the moment Ramage discovered that Lord Spencer had recommended him, the Admiral had apparently contradicted himself by making it abundantly clear he would have chosen another officer. Now, he was anxious for Ramage to succeed.

To give himself time to think, Ramage took his hat from his lap, carefully placed it on the chair beside him, and then tugged at his coat, as though feeling too hot. Quickly he tried to think of all Sir Pilcher's possible motives, but only two factors stood out.

First, it's an almost impossible job, and for all his protest that "my choice *does* differ", Sir Pilcher obviously wants to avoid giving it to one of his favourites, who would then be saddled with failure. Second, the wily old man can see in the uncertain mist of the future an angry Cabinet blaming the Admiralty for the failure, and an equally angry Admiralty blaming Sir Pilcher.

While the Admiral would not be able to avoid all the blame, Ramage realized Sir Pilcher was neatly covering himself: he had just told Ramage – and presumably would hint at it in a subsequent dispatch to Lord Spencer – that he personally would have chosen someone else, but since the First Lord had suggested Ramage, he had felt himself bound to accept the recommendation. That left the Admiral in a happy position whether Ramage eventually reported success or failure.

Oh yes, he thought wryly, in a way it is a trap; but the job presented a challenge he found himself increasingly reluctant to ignore.

"I don't know about 'catch them', sir," he said warily. "I can't do much with a dozen men and no ship. Your letter mentions only 'inquiry', though I noticed Lord Spencer refers to 'halting' the losses."

"But I haven't a suitable ship to give you, blast it," Sir Pilcher protested, the earlier querulous note creeping back into his voice. "Absolutely nothing. If I had, you'd be welcome to

27

her. You need something as slippery as these packets – or as slippery as they're *supposed* to be."

Now Sir Pilcher was speaking the truth: there was no suitable ship on the station. At least, since Ramage had not the faintest idea what he was going to do, he did not know what type of ship he would need: fast and lightly-armed or slower and heavily-armed.

"Very well, sir. If you'll excuse me, I'll start off by seeing what I can find out from the Postmaster."

Sir Pilcher did not bother to hide his relief.

"Fine, my boy, fine. You have a splendid opportunity to distinguish yourself; quite splendid. Every one of my lieutenants will envy you," he said heartily, confirming Ramage's suspicions. "If you can put a stop to all this wretched business, the Cabinet will hear about you, I assure you."

And if I don't, Ramage thought sourly, they'll still hear about me.

The Admiral stood up. "Now, I have your final orders here ready – just give me a moment to sign and date them." He waddled to the desk, scribbled and then handed them to Ramage. "You'd better glance through them before you leave."

Ramage read the few lines.

"You are hereby required and directed to inquire fully into the recent heavy losses among Post Office packet vessels between the West Indies and the United Kingdom, the details of which you have already been apprised, and having determined beyond any manner of doubt the reason for these losses, and if possible halted them, you are at once to deliver a written report, to me if the conclusion of your inquiries is reached within the limits of this station, or to my Lords Commissioners of the Admiralty if in Home or distant waters..."

Chapter Three

Before seeing the Deputy Postmaster-General, Ramage went to Government House to call on the Governor's secretary in his large and immaculately tidy office. Thankful to be sitting down in a cool and friendly room, Ramage chatted for a few minutes, politely refused a rum punch and then asked if he could borrow a copy of the *Royal Kalendar* for ten minutes.

The secretary was a few years older than Ramage and obviously assumed that any visitor had a favour to ask of the Governor. He looked relieved when he gave Ramage the small, thick volume. "Want to see how your name is rising up the Navy List?" he asked jovially.

Ramage laughed. "Progress is so slow that I need look only once a year!"

The *Kalendar* listed nearly everyone employed in Government offices at home and abroad, and gave many other details ranging from the ships of war in commission to the names of the staff of the City of London Lying-in Hospital. The information about the General Post Office (ranging from the fact it was "Erected by Act of Parliament, 27 December 1660, Lombard Street" to a list of nearly two hundred offices open for the delivery and collection of the Penny Post) covered eight pages.

Ramage saw that the political leadership was divided between two Joint Postmasters-General, Lord Auckland and Lord Gower, each of whom received a salary of £5,000 a year. The Secretary, Francis Freeling, received £500 a year – hardly overpaid. Except, he noticed in another section, Freeling was also the "Principal and Resident Surveyor", at £700 a year, which gave him a total of more than that received by an admiral...

He ran a finger down the rest of the names and was surprised at the number and variety of jobs listed. They ranged from the receiver general to the superintendent and surveyor of mail-coaches; from the Postmaster-General's chamber-keeper to the deliverer of letters to the House of Commons (at 6s 8d a day – presumably he starved when the House was not in session).

The Post Office, in effect, was split into two sections, the Inland Letter Office and the Foreign Letter Office. The former employed four dozen sorters and more than a hundred letter-carriers (at fourteen shillings a week), but was far less complex than the Foreign Letter Office, whose comptroller was paid £700 a year – not much less than Sir Pilcher Skinner.

Twenty letter-carriers presumably delivered the incoming foreign mail to the Lombard Street sorters, and carried the bags of outgoing foreign mail to the various ports to be loaded on board the packets – to Falmouth for the West Indies, Lisbon and America; Weymouth for the Channel Islands; and Harwich for Hamburg.

There were five "mail ports" abroad and each had its Post Office agent (among them "J. Smith, Deputy Postmaster-General of Jamaica"), while elsewhere there were postmasters. And as he read their names, Ramage began to feel uneasy: the number of places listed brought home the enormity of the orders he had been given – from Quebec and Halifax at one end of the Atlantic to Surinam, Demerara, Tobago and Barbados at the other; from Hamburg and Lisbon on one side of the Atlantic to New York and Jamaica on the other.

He pictured the packets sailing from Falmouth to deliver bags of outward mail at all these places and collect the inward, and realized the Cornish port was the centre of a giant cobweb, the lines reaching out thousands of miles across the Atlantic. Not straight lines, but lines gently curved as they met trade winds, bent sharply as they rounded continents and islands, and sometimes forced back on themselves by gales and storms. Quebec, Halifax and New York were three thousand miles

30

across the often stormy North Atlantic, much of it against strong headwinds; to Barbados was more than four thousand miles in a long dog-leg sweep past Spain and the west coast of North Africa, passing close to Madeira and the Canary Islands before picking up the North-East Trades for the long run across the Atlantic to a landfall at Barbados, with three hundred miles on to Antigua and another nine hundred to Jamaica. Another packet sailed a similar route towards Barbados before turning south-west for Demerara and Surinam, on the continent of South America.

So much for the routes. He found his interest quickening as he came to the ships themselves. The *Kalendar* gave a list of "His Majesty's packet boats, with their stations", and beside each one was the name of her commander. There were twelve packets given for "W. India and America", but seventeen commanders were listed. Five had blanks against their names – had their packets been captured? But, Ramage groaned inwardly, some of the packet people had let their patriotism swamp their imagination – one packet on the Lisbon and three more on the Hamburg route were named *Prince of Wales*, and two called *King George* were listed under Hamburg. The only way of distinguishing them was by the names of their commanders.

Finally, reluctant to leave the coolness of the secretary's office to go out into the scorching sun and noisy, dusty streets for his visit to the Deputy Postmaster-General, Ramage turned over another page and glanced at the "Postage of simple letters in British pence". From Falmouth to any port in North America or the West Indies cost twelve pence, plus the inland postage to Falmouth. Thus a letter from London to New York or Jamaica cost eight pence to Falmouth and another twelve pence to cross the Atlantic. Sending a letter between the West Indies and North America – a part of the way round the edge of the spider's web, as it were – cost four pence.

Well, anything more he was to learn about the Post Office would have to come from Mr Smith. He gave the *Kalendar* back to the Governor's secretary, once again refused a rum punch, borrowed a pencil and some paper to make some calculations and left, tucking the papers in his pocket.

31

The Deputy Postmaster-General of Jamaica was a man with a mania for tidiness. Although the enormous outer office looked like a cross between a counting house and a warehouse, with sorters working on the local mail at a long bench along one wall and the canvas mailbags hanging from hooks along another, Mr Smith's own room was as neat as a column of printed figures.

He worked at a large, square, mahogany table on top of which smooth pebbles held down piles of papers whose edges fluttered in the breeze coming through the jalousie at either end of the room. The piles were spaced out with geometric precision, as if the pebbles were chess men.

On top of each pile under the weight was a neatly written label indicating what it contained, and a scrutiny of the labels showed the scope of Mr Smith's work. The largest pile was marked *"Inward packetboats – lost"*, and next to it was *"Outward packetboats – lost"*. Another large pile contained *"Complaints – from committee of West India merchants"*, and next to it, *"Complaints – from private citizens"*. Yet another said simply, *"From Lombard Street, miscellaneous"*. Directly in front of him was a small pile which said: *"From Lord Auckland"*.

In contrast to the neatness of his table-top, Smith was a large, gangling man with heavy features and large hands seemingly too clumsy to handle papers: they were, in size, the hands of a labourer. Yet Smith not only had one of the most coveted jobs in Jamaica – in peacetime, anyway – but he did it supremely well. He had it and, despite the influence and patronage of other claimants, held it because without him the Post Office's foreign section in Jamaica became chaos.

Unmarried, and with a widowed sister in Cumberland as his only relative, he lived for the mails. Until recently his life had had a series of fortnightly peaks. Every two weeks – in normal times – the packet arrived and he went on board to meet the commander, inspect the sealed bags of incoming mail, sign for them and supervise their removal on shore to his office before arranging for the outgoing mail to be brought out and stowed on board.

He was meticulous in having the mail sorted quickly – and equally meticulous in refusing to allow anyone but Post Office employees to be in the sorting-room while it was being done. The early days when impatient folk protested that his predecessor always allowed them to wait there for it were now long past.

He was equally meticulous in having the commander to dinner on the night the packet arrived. Although in any case he enjoyed the company of the lively Falmouth men, the long chats over glasses of rum punch after the meal also meant that he kept himself well informed about everyday events in England. Also the commanders had few problems, whether concerning their youngest sons, maiden aunts or their ships, that they did not discuss with him. Over the years he had become a distant uncle to most of the sons and daughters of the commanders, and his ambition when he retired was to live in Falmouth and enjoy the company of the large and closely knit "packet families".

His closeness to the commanders, and his meticulous habits, meant that at this moment his world was chaos: Smith was now a man with a job but almost no work. There were no bags of foreign mail to be officially sealed and labelled – no one was writing letters to England now, not until the *Kingston Chronicle* announced that a packet had at last arrived. And then, Smith thought gloomily, everyone possessed of pen and paper will write a score of letters and the commander will start complaining about the bulk ...

Still, Lord Auckland in a letter sent by the *Hydra* – instinctively he tapped the paperweight holding it down – had written reassuringly. It was not normally Lombard Street's policy to get involved with other Government departments – they were usually so lamentably disorganized – but from what he could see (reading between the lines, anyway) the Cabinet had decided that action over the heavy loss of packets was now up to the Admiralty. He was pleased and flattered to note that Lombard Street had seen (at last) that Jamaica was the real centre of the Foreign Mails on this side of the Atlantic, despite the claims of that damned agent in New York. Obviously the

Admiralty agreed, but anyway Lord Auckland assured him that Sir Pilcher Skinner had been given orders to put one of his best officers in charge of a complete investigation.

Smith moved a paperweight half an inch to stop a particularly thin sheet from flapping too irritatingly in the breeze. Well, Sir Pilcher was a meticulous man, and the Deputy Postmaster knew he could rely on his choice of officer. There were two 74-gun ships in the harbour, each commanded by a senior captain. Presumably one of them would be given the job, and there were plenty of frigates. For the first time in weeks, Smith began to nourish a hope that his orderly world would return...

Smith took out his watch. He'd wait another hour before leaving for lunch, although for all the good he was doing sitting here he might just as well have accepted Mrs Warner's invitation to her picnic. He admitted she frightened him a little. Although she was quite one of the most comely widows in Kingston, her constant invitations were embarrassing: people gossiped and chattered and all took it for granted that even a well-chaperoned young widow had only marriage in mind if she entertained a bachelor to dinner more than a couple of times in the year.

Someone was knocking at the open door, and he glanced up to see a young naval officer standing there. Ah, news from Sir Pilcher! That was the advantage of being a commander-in-chief; you had plenty of young fellows to run errands for you.

"Mr Smith?"

The Postmaster nodded.

"My name is Ramage. Sir Pilcher sent me."

Again the Postmaster nodded affably, waiting for him to deliver the letter, or whatever it was from the Admiral.

"About the packets," the lieutenant said, coming right into the room.

This was rather irregular: Sir Pilcher was not the man to send verbal messages.

"What about the packets, pray?"

"Sir Pilcher said you could tell me about them. You have a letter from him, I believe?"

"No. At least, telling me what?"

"That I would be calling on you."

"Wait a moment."

Smith waved Ramage to a chair and bellowed: "Dent! Come here, Dent!"

A moment later an elderly clerk appeared at the door.

"Are there any letters for me?"

"Only this one, sir," Dent said, holding it up nervously.

"Give it to me! When did it arrive?"

"A couple of hours ago, sir; came by messenger."

"Then why the devil – oh, go away!"

Smith looked across at Ramage. "I'm sorry. It's from Sir Pilcher – give me a moment to read it."

He looked at the right-hand corner of the table for a paper-knife, extricated it from under a pile, and opened the letter with the precision of a surgeon. He read it twice, folded it again and reached out, his hand hovering between the labels "*Outward packets – lost*" and "*Inward packets – lost*". Finally he tucked it temporarily under "*Lord Auckland*", mentally noting that he would write a fresh label later.

He thought for a moment, and then looked up at the lieutenant. He's only a youngster, he thought crossly; obviously one of Sir Pilcher's favourites. There's no disguising that the Admiral's one major fault is pushing his favourites and giving them quick promotion. It wouldn't matter if half of them weren't young ninnies. This one doesn't look as much of a ninny as the usual run, but a *lieutenant*! Damnation, with the foreign mails at stake a rear-admiral would not be too much, even if his only task was to ask questions.

There were dark rings under the lad's eyes: late nights, heavy drinking, wenching ... Sir Pilcher's young lieutenants never seem to have done much fighting: those two scars over his right eyebrow – slipped with a glass of wine in his hand no doubt, or fell out of some trollop's bed: they aren't deep enough to be wounds.

Yet, Smith admitted to himself, the youth's eyes were intelligent enough: brown, deep set and almost frightening. He was handsome, too, if you liked that thin-faced aristocratic type:

35

high cheekbones and a hard, firm chin.

The lad was looking at him, and Smith found himself feeling uncomfortable, as if he had been thinking aloud. A curious power seemed to surround the lieutenant, as though his body was merely the covering for a powerful spring. Smith found it hard to understand why a lad like this was content to hang around as one of the Admiral's lackeys.

"Forgive me, Lieutenant," Smith said finally, "I was pre-occupied. All this is a great worry to me."

"To everyone," Ramage said politely. "Would you care to ...?"

"Yes, of course. Now, what do you want to know?"

Ramage shrugged his shoulders.

"Everything! How the Packet Service is organized ... How frequently the packets sail ... The routine for loading mails ... How long the voyage usually takes ... Who actually employs the commanders ... Does the Post Office own the ships ..."

Smith threw up his hands. "But what's all that got to do with Sir Pilcher finding out how and why the packets are being captured?" He was conscious of Ramage's eyes boring into his brain.

"Then tell me, Mr Smith," he said gently, "where do you think I should start finding out 'how and why'?"

"Well, my dear fellow, that's your affair!" Really these young men had precious little sense of responsibility!

"Suppose it was your job, Mr Smith. Where would you start making your inquiries?" Ramage persisted, taking a piece of paper from his pocket and unfolding it. "For example, the distances involved are quite considerable. Roughly 4,200 miles from Falmouth to Barbados, 300 up to Antigua, and another 900 on to Jamaica. From Jamaica back to Falmouth – well, let's take it from the Windward Passage. That's about 3,750 miles, depending on the wind."

Smith tapped the table impatiently. "I'm quite aware of the distances across the Atlantic Ocean, Lieutenant."

"Ah, but are we really concerned with *distances*, Mr Smith?" Ramage's voice was bantering now, and Smith wondered hurriedly why there had been such emphasis on the

36

word. "We are trying to find something in the Atlantic Ocean, Mr Smith, so aren't we really concerned with *areas*?"

When the Postmaster nodded warily, Ramage said: "I hope you'll take my word for it that, because of the uncertain direction of the wind, a packet could sail some 250 miles either side of the regular route. In other words a packet on its way from Falmouth to Barbados could be lost in a rectangle measuring 4,200 miles by 500 miles. That" – he glanced at the paper – "is an area of more than two million square miles."

Smith said nothing.

"We'll ignore the leg from Barbados to Antigua, and say that for the 900 miles from Antigua to Jamaica the packet could be twenty-five miles either side of the direct course," Ramage continued. "A rectangle 900 miles by fifty comprises 45,000 square miles."

Smith was now jotting down the figures, and Ramage paused for a moment. When he saw the Postmaster had stopped writing he said: "Now for the voyage home from Jamaica. It's roughly 3,750 miles from the Windward Passage to Falmouth, and allowing the 250 miles either side of the direct route gives us nearly two million square miles. For the round voyage, Falmouth, Barbados, Antigua, Jamaica and back to Falmouth, we get" – he glanced at the paper again – "a total of more than four million square miles. Four million and twenty thousand, to be exact," he added: Smith was a man who would like exact figures. He waited while Smith wrote them down.

"Now, in good conditions a lookout at sea might sight a ship at ten miles – it'd be unlikely, but I'll be generous with the figures. That means he is looking from the centre of a circle twenty miles in diameter and scanning an area of about 300 square miles. Since a packet can be lost anywhere in more than four million square miles of ocean, I admit it's only of academic interest to divide it by the 300 covered by the lookout, but – I'm using the precise figures now – the answer is 13,400. Tell me, Mr Smith," Ramage said quietly, "where would *you* start your investigation?"

Smith smiled amiably, already regretting his sharp tongue. The lad was right, and he was prepared to admit it. "I'd start right here, Lieutenant, sitting in that very chair and asking me questions!"

As if to emphasize his change of heart he removed three paperweights and put the "*Outward Bound – Lost*" and "*Inward Bound – Lost*" piles of paper in front of him, with "*Auckland*" on top. Tapping them, he said: "All that's known about the losses is written here."

"Yes," Ramage said gently, "but first I want to know how the Packet Service functions."

The question still puzzled Smith: his whole life had been so wrapped up in the Service he could neither credit that there could be people who knew nothing about it nor really know how to begin describing it.

"The packets," Ramage prompted. "How long does the average passage take?"

"Forty-five days out to Jamaica, via Barbados, and thirty-five days back, sailing direct."

"Who actually owns the ships?"

"They're owned individually, usually by the commanders – by the commanders and their business associates, in some cases."

"And the Post Office charters them?"

"Yes, Lombard Street hires the ships."

"And the crews?"

"They are employed and paid by the Post Office: the commander and the entire ship's company."

"Even if the commander owns the ship?"

"Yes, he's paid a monthly wage as well as the charter fee."

"Who stands to lose if a packet is captured? Or pays for repairs if she's damaged in action?"

"The Post Office pays. Of course, the conditions are all set down in the original charter agreement, but in effect the Post Office carries the insurance."

"How many packets serve the West Indies?"

"Normally there are sixteen – that's the number needed to maintain a regular fortnightly service."

"And the losses in the whole war so far?"

"Thirty-two. Not all of them bound to or from the West

38

Indies, of course. Twelve were lost in the first four years of the war. After that there was a lull, although towards the end of '97 three more were lost in a month. Then losses were irregular – until this year. We've lost nine so far, all West Indies packets."

"Where do the replacement packets come from?"

"Several new packets are building to Post Office specifications," Smith said, "but we are having to hire temporary vessels to make sure we have ten available."

"This year's losses – you have details?"

Smith sorted through his pile of papers and extracted one sheet.

"Here's the list."

Ramage saw that the *Princess Royal* had been lost in February from the Leeward Islands, the *Cartaret* from Jamaica homeward-bound in March, the *Matilda* also in March from Falmouth for the West Indies, three more in May, all homeward-bound from Jamaica, and two outward and one homeward-bound in June.

"You don't have the actual positions where they were captured?"

Smith shook his head. "The only information sent to me is given there."

"Out of nine, five were homeward-bound from Jamaica," Ramage said, slowly scanning the neat writing, "one homeward-bound from the Leeward Islands, and only three outward-bound from Falmouth..."

"That is correct," Smith said.

"Seems strange," Ramage mused, reading the list again.

"What does?"

"So many lost on the way back."

Smith shrugged his shoulders. "Easier to catch 'em going back – that's obvious!" Really, he thought, the youngster looks sharp enough but he doesn't seem to know much about the way these damned French privateers lurk around the islands!

"Why is it easier?" Ramage asked, his voice disarmingly innocent.

"Well," Smith said pompously, "far be it from me ... But obviously the privateers just hang around the Windward Passage! Probably waiting in the southern Bahamas."

Ramage folded the list and tapped the table with it. Quite reasonably, Smith was assuming the losses were due to privateers, yet assumptions at this stage were dangerous. "But they don't know the date a packet is likely to sail from here, do they?"

"Of course not! I hardly know myself until the last moment. It all depends when one arrives."

"So if they wanted to be sure of catching the Falmouth-bound packets, privateers would have to patrol all the obvious places all the time?"

"Obviously," Smith said, with something approaching contempt in his voice. He's recovering from the effect of those millions of square miles, Ramage noted wryly.

"But surely the mails bound *for* Jamaica would be more valuable? Anyway, no less valuable."

Smith shrugged his shoulders; the young fellow seemed to be asking questions just for the sake of it.

"The Jamaica packets," Ramage said. "They all come here from the Leeward Islands after calling at Barbados and Antigua. None comes direct from Falmouth?"

Smith nodded.

"So in effect we can picture two highways," Ramage said, running a finger along the table-top. "One goes from Falmouth across the Atlantic to Barbados, up to Antigua, and then right across the Caribbean to Jamaica, and the Jamaica packet sails along that, delivering and collecting mail at the various islands until she arrives here in Kingston about forty-five days after leaving Falmouth. The other runs north-east from Jamaica up through the Windward Passage between Cuba and Hispaniola and out into the Atlantic and back to Falmouth and is used by the homeward-bound packets which take about thirty-five days to reach England."

Smith nodded. "That is so," he said patronizingly.

Ramage flicked some specks of dust off the hat resting on his lap.

"But I still don't understand why privateers would concentrate on the homeward-bound packets," he said almost absentmindedly. "It would be so much easier to capture them between here and Antigua..."

"Nonsense!" Smith snapped. "It's hundreds of miles from here to Antigua. The Windward Passage is almost in sight of Jamaica."

"Ah," Ramage said dreamily, "but the poor privateersmen would starve if they relied on capturing only homeward-bound Post Office packets..."

"But they don't!" Smith protested. "There are plenty of small merchantmen and local schooners and droghers – they're being captured all the time."

Ramage shook his head. "No, they're not; that's what is so puzzling."

"What? Don't argue with me! Ask Sir Pilcher – the privateers snatch up almost anything that isn't in convoy," Smith said angrily, lifting up and putting down the smooth pebbles he used as paperweights.

"There's nothing for me to argue with you about, Mr Smith," Ramage said calmly. "Let's take it point by point, and you'll see what I mean. I'm sure we agree that at this moment there are probably dozens of small ships sailing alone between here and, say, the Leeward Islands?"

When Smith nodded impatiently, Ramage continued: "So if you commanded a French privateer you'd reckon to capture a few on that route? Of course," he said when Smith nodded again. "But you agree that, in contrast, the only ships that go up through the Windward Passage into the Atlantic are in heavily escorted convoys – which privateers rarely dare tackle – or homeward-bound Post Office packets?"

"My dear fellow, that's elementary; everyone knows that!"

"But that's why I'm so puzzled, Mr Smith. Why should privateers hang around the Windward Passage – where they risk running into one of Sir Pilcher's frigates – knowing the *only* prize they are likely to find is an occasional homeward-bound Post Office packet? Why not cruise between Jamaica and the Leeward Islands where – as you've just pointed out – there are

41

always plenty of coasting vessels, as well as the occasional Jamaica-bound packet?"

When Smith said nothing, Ramage continued: "A French privateer captain gets rich by capturing coasting vessels laden with cargo which he can sell. With all due respect to the Post Office, a packet is a poor prize – a privateersman isn't interested in mail, which I presume a commander would in any case throw over the side before capture. All the privateersman gets is another ship whose only value is her speed, not her cargo or her carrying capacity. He'd find it hard to sell such a ship here in the Caribbean, so if he can't get enough men to fit her out as another privateer, a packet is hardly worth the bother of capture. Certainly not worth the bother of waiting, possibly for weeks, somewhere out there beyond the Windward Passage."

Ramage was now examining the inside of his hat, as though speculating whether he needed a new one, but in fact giving the Postmaster time to absorb what he had been told. Smith was staring at his pile of papers, his hands pressed flat on the table. He looked, Ramage thought sympathetically, like a doting husband unexpectedly confronted with evidence of his wife's unfaithfulness.

"It doesn't make sense," Smith whispered. "It must be a coincidence – yes, that's what it is, Lieutenant, it's a coincidence. You wait, the next packet they capture will be inward-bound; you'll see, she'll be taken between Antigua and here."

"Perhaps," Ramage said briskly, "but we can't afford to wait to find out. And the odds are against it, Mr Smith. Your own figures show that."

"Aye, they do," Smith admitted reluctantly. "I'd noticed the high homeward-bound losses, naturally, but I never thought about the privateers' motives ... You're sure of all that? What does Sir Pilcher think?"

"I don't know what Sir Pilcher thinks, but if I commanded a French privateer, I'd cruise between here and Antigua."

"Ah, that's what you might think, young man," Smith said, as if suddenly he had found a flaw in Ramage's reasoning that allowed him to reject the whole argument. "But if you'd ever commanded a ship you'd think differently."

42

"I've commanded a ship for more than two years," Ramage said quietly. "A few months ago I captured a couple of privateers off St Lucia and, more recently, a large privateer that made a night attack on the last convoy that came in..."

Smith looked up sharply. "My apologies," he said. "I've heard all about that last one – I didn't realize you were ... Is that why Sir Pilcher...?"

Ramage shrugged his shoulders and grinned, knowing that at last Smith would trust his judgement. "The nearest he can get to turning a poacher into a gamekeeper? I don't know, but", he added, choosing his words carefully, "since you and I are the only people who've commented on this odd pattern of losses, it might be an idea if we kept it to ourselves for the time being."

Smith, flattered at being given such unexpected credit, although still far from sure of the significance of the pattern, gave a broad wink.

"Now," Ramage said, "you were saying that the Post Office employs and pays the crews of the packets. Do you happen to know how the French treat the men when a packet is captured? Are they dealt with in the same way as Royal Navy men?"

"No, the French have been very fair. They usually exchange them within six weeks or so – a commander was telling me only a few months ago that he was back in England within eight weeks of being captured. Now the poor fellow's a prisoner again."

Ramage nodded sympathetically. Six weeks ... the prisoners must have been taken direct to France; there would not be time to get them to Europe from the Caribbean. Was that significant? Or was Smith referring to isolated cases?

"Now, Mr Smith, imagine a letter written by – well, a London merchant to his brother here in Kingston. What happens to it between London and here?"

Smith sat back in his chair and relaxed: he was on familiar ground now, and beginning to understand why Ramage found the background as important as the foreground.

"Well, it'd probably be posted in Lombard Street, right in the City of London. It'd be sorted into the Jamaica bag. The bag – when it was full, or was due to catch a particular mail,

43

since one sails every two weeks – would be sealed. Then it would be taken by coach to Falmouth."

"And then?"

"There it would be handed over to the Post Office agent, who is in charge of all the Falmouth packets. There'd be many bags for the West Indies – at least half a dozen for each particular island. In the meantime the packet would be ready on its mooring, fully provisioned and with the commander and crew on board. The agent would see the mails loaded and properly stowed."

"And then the packet would sail?"

"Well, before she actually sailed the searcher would go on board."

"Searching for what?"

"In case any seaman is carrying his own private cargo!"

"Of what?"

"Well, you know seamen. They try to bring out a few small items. They call 'em their ventures: leather goods, like boots and shoes, small bales of cloth for women's dresses – oh yes, and cheeses: they get a good price for cheeses!"

"Since you say they get a good price, Mr Smith, what does the searcher actually do? Just confirm that the men have their ventures?"

"My goodness no! His job is to *stop* them carrying anything!"

"But he's not always successful?"

"I don't think he's too strict: the men have been carrying ventures for so many years that it's become a tradition. The profit supplements their pay."

"But it's forbidden?"

"Oh yes – by a statute of Charles II, as a matter of fact."

Ramage stopped himself commenting that for the sake of discipline a regulation that was not enforced ought to be rescinded, and asked, "After the searcher has left, then what?"

"Well, the passengers are always embarked by now, of course, and the agent has had the mails brought on board. Then he musters the ship's company, gives the commander any last-minute instructions, and bids them a safe voyage. Oh yes, he also checks the trim of the packet, to make sure the mails have been properly stowed, so the ship isn't down by the bow or stern – that sort of thing."

"And then the packet sails for Barbados – whatever the weather?"

"She sails at once, as long as she can carry a reefed topsail. You can get out of Falmouth in anything but a south-easterly gale – but you know that well enough."

Ramage nodded: obviously that was why the Post Office had chosen Falmouth in the first place. "And then what happens to that letter?"

"Well, it gets carried to Barbados first. The packet then calls at two or three of the Windward and Leeward Islands delivering and collecting mail – Antigua would probably be the last – and then comes across the Caribbean direct to Jamaica."

"Where that letter comes under your care."

"Yes, indeed," Smith said grimly. "I meet the packet with the Customs Officers and the doctor, take off the bags of inward mail, and bring them here, where they are sorted again and delivered."

"What happens to the packet and the crew?"

"The commander provisions the ship, the men are allowed a few hours on shore – they all have Protections, of course, so they don't have to worry about press gangs – and then the packet is ready to sail again, when the fresh mails are loaded."

"Now," Ramage said slowly, "imagine the brother here is replying to the merchant in London."

"Well, it's much the same story in reverse, really, except that when the packet sails from here, she doesn't go back across the Caribbean: she goes out to the north-east, touching only at Cape Nicolas Mole on her way through the Windward Passage into the Atlantic and then direct to England."

"Why the different route?"

"Well, she has already delivered all the inward and picked up the outward mail at the other islands on her way to Jamaica."

"So apart from touching at the western end of Hispaniola, Jamaica is the last port of call before England?"

Smith nodded.

"And your searcher," Ramage asked. "Is he as diligent as the one at Falmouth?"

"No more and no less."

Ramage nodded in turn. "These ventures – do the officers...?"

"I hope you're not asking me officially. As Deputy Postmaster-General, I have no knowledge of any ventures in any packet. Between you and me, I think the officers also regard themselves as badly paid, and the little profit they might make – well, it balances the books without costing Lombard Street anything."

"I'd like to ask a question addressed to you, not the Deputy Postmaster-General," Ramage said. "Do you have any suspicion at all of what might be going on?"

"None," Smith said emphatically. "If I had, I'd tell you. I've thought of every possibility – from spies in the Department to passengers seizing the ships..."

"Treason?"

"Out of the question. The commanders and crews are eventually exchanged, and Lombard Street would soon hear. Anyway, the commanders own the ships. They have everything to lose."

"And when they are exchanged and get back to England, nothing they report has given Lombard Street any hint?"

"Nothing. The story is always the same: my last communication from Lord Auckland" – he patted the pile of papers – "makes the point again: each packet was overtaken by a privateer and attacked and forced to surrender after sinking the mails."

Ah, thought Ramage, so we do know for certain that it is privateers...

"Casualties must be quite heavy."

"No, I'm thankful to say they aren't. The commanders have orders to run, not linger and fight: that's a long-standing policy established by Lombard Street: the packets rely on their superior speed."

"Hardly superior, surely, if so many are captured?"

Again Smith shrugged his shoulders. "I am merely telling

you the Post Office's policy, Lieutenant. The West India merchants, for example, think otherwise: they want the packets more heavily armed, so they can fight back."

"But Lombard Street doesn't agree."

"No. They prefer the policy of a speedy escape."

I wonder, Ramage thought, how many packets have to be lost before Lombard Street admits its policy is wrong? He asked, "Who specifies the size and type of ship? I've noticed most of them are similar."

"They were of different designs before the war: whatever the contractors – which usually meant the commanders – wanted. Then Lombard Street specified that they should be the same design – 179 tons burthen, with a ship's company of twenty-eight men and boys, and armed with four 4-pounders and two 9-pounder stern chasers. And small arms, of course."

"Not much against a privateer."

"No, but remember that the instructions to the commanders are, in effect, 'Run when you can; fight when you can no longer run; and when you can fight no longer, sink the mails before you strike.' "

"Tell me, Mr Smith, since the 'run when you can' policy has obviously failed, why hasn't the Post Office tried larger and more heavily armed ships?"

"The Post Office doesn't want to be a party to privateering!" Smith said, smiling. "Early in the war there was some trouble because a few of the packet commanders were not above going after a prize themselves – and Lombard Street couldn't allow such risks with the mails."

"One last question," Ramage said. "When is the next packet due?"

"Using the forty-five-day passage rule, she was due here yesterday. If she hasn't been taken I'd expect to see her at the latest within the next seven days. But I'm not hopeful; in fact I'm refusing to accept mail or passengers for her."

Ramage stood up and thanked Smith. He had the curious feeling that there was a clue in all the information he'd been given, but discerning it was like trying to recall details of a half-remembered dream.

47

Chapter Four

That evening Ramage sat out on the terrace of the Royal Albion Hotel with Yorke, comfortably sleepy after a good dinner and, like most people in Kingston at that time, waiting for the offshore breeze to set in for the night and give the first relief from the sweltering heat they had endured all day. The palm trees were alive with the buzz of tiny frogs and mosquitoes whined; moths of all colours and sizes battered themselves against the glass of the lamps.

"You don't feel like changing your mind about the Governor's Ball?" Yorke asked. "There's still time..."

"It's too hot," Ramage said drowsily. "If it's anything like last night, the offshore breeze won't set in at all. That damned ballroom turns into an oven even with half a gale blowing through it. Anyway, I've had my share of trying to make conversation with planters' dumpy daughters."

"Come now, don't blame the poor girls; the moment their mothers heard that Lieutenant Lord Ramage had arrived in Jamaica they knew the season's most eligible bachelor was within their grasp: tall, dark and handsome, two romantic scars won in battle, wealthy and the heir to an earldom ... what more could a mother – let alone a daughter – want from life?"

"My friend," Ramage said, "unless you use all your energy in spreading a story that I'm a notorious rapist and the family estate is mortgaged to the butler whose daughter my grandfather recently deflowered, I'll drop the hint that not only is that young shipowner Sidney Yorke so rich that he lends small fortunes to nabobs at one per cent, but that his main reason for coming to Jamaica is to find himself a wife."

"Your ruthlessness appals me," Yorke said cheerfully, and glanced round to see if anyone was within earshot. "Well, you've been suitably mysterious all through dinner, so now you can tell me what's happening."

"I have a new job – acting as Neptune's Postmaster, I think."

"Ah – so you accepted! Why was Sir Pilcher being so generous?"

Ramage pointed across to the door from the dining-room where two men stood looking out across the terrace. "Here are Southwick and Bowen," he said, waving to attract their attention. "They might as well hear about it at the same time."

Edward Southwick was a stocky man in his early sixties, with flowing white hair and a cherubic pink face. If he was wearing long vestments and holding a crozier in his hand, Ramage thought to himself, he could pass for an amiable bishop calling to exorcize the hotel terrace of jumbies. Certainly no one looking at him now would guess that he was never happier than when leading a boarding party with his enormous meat-cleaver of a sword in his hand – preferably against absurd odds. Ramage had a deep affection for the old man who had been master of each of the two ships Ramage had commanded in the past two years. He treated the seamen like a group of wayward schoolboys, and Ramage with a quiet loyalty that made nothing of the fact that his captain was young enough to be his grandson.

The man with him was perhaps ten years younger, tall with a stoop, but walking with an air of authority. An almost haggard face marked him as recently recovered from a severe illness. It was unlikely that many of the wealthy patients who had once flocked to his fashionable surgery in Wimpole Street would recognize him now. Since they had last seen him, James Bowen had changed from being one of the finest surgeons in London to a pathetic wreck needing a bottle of gin to get him through the day and whose nights were a private hell of drunken fears.

Shame had finally driven him to quit his practice and go to sea. A Navy short of surgeons did not quibble about his drinking habits and sent him to the *Triton* brig, commanded by Lieutenant Ramage and bound for the Caribbean.

But Lieutenant Ramage, responsible for the lives and wellbeing of a ship's company of seventy-five men and bound for one of the unhealthiest stations in the Navy, was far from pleased that circumstances had brought him a drunken surgeon. With Southwick's help, he had ruthlessly cut off the man's alcohol and systematically nursed him through the horrors of *delirium tremens*. By the time they arrived in Barbados, Bowen had sworn never to drink again and had proved himself to be a witty and cultured man, as well as a superb chess player. Southwick, instructed by Ramage to play chess with Bowen to keep his mind occupied during the worst part of the cure, had unexpectedly turned out to be a good player.

The two men pulled up rattan chairs and sat opposite Ramage and Yorke.

Ramage gestured at the board and box which Bowen held in his lap. "I didn't mean to interfere with your chess."

"Southwick isn't in the mood, sir."

Ramage looked inquiringly at the Master, who grinned. "He's beaten me six times in the last three evenings, so I'm not sacrificing anything! It's time I got back to sea; this idle life is rotting m' brain!"

To Ramage's surprise, Bowen asked: "No news of a ship yet, sir?"

"Not exactly, but I called you over to hear the news I was just about to give to Mr Yorke."

He saw that Southwick's face had fallen. Like the surgeon, the Master knew that he would not get a ship if it was left to the Commander-in-Chief; their only chance lay in Ramage obtaining a command and asking for them.

"I haven't got a ship, but I've got an appointment. What it'll lead to, I don't yet know."

Quickly and briefly he told the men of the orders he had received from Sir Pilcher, and then described the information from the Deputy Postmaster-General about the lost packets. He purposely told them only the facts of the losses, and when he finished he said: "Well, has anyone a theory?"

Yorke and Southwick both spoke up together, and the Master gestured to Yorke, who said: "I was puzzled by the number of homeward-bound packets that are lost. I'd have expected most of them to have been captured between Antigua and here."

Southwick agreed. "I was going to mention the same thing, sir. Those lost on the way home – were the majority captured on this side of the Atlantic, in mid-ocean, or as they approached the chops of the Channel?"

"The Postmaster doesn't know the positions – the Post Office in London didn't bother to tell him. He seems to think most were taken on this side of the Atlantic – the moment they'd cleared the Windward Passage, to hear him talk – but I doubt it. For one thing, the crews are exchanged too quickly for them to be taken this side, carried to Guadeloupe, sent to France and then exchanged. That alone makes me certain packets are taken towards the end of the voyage."

"It sounds logical," Yorke said, "especially since they are exchanged in – what, about eight weeks, didn't you say?"

Ramage nodded. "It seems amazingly quick to me, but the Postmaster didn't seem to think there was anything unusual about it. Maybe there's some sort of arrangement with the French Government so that the Post Office men get special treatment."

"I can't see us getting a ship out of it," Bowen said gloomily. He turned to Yorke. "Looks as if Southwick and I will be travelling back to England with you."

"I'd better start polishing up my chess," Yorke said. "I have plenty of time, though; the next convoy isn't due to leave for seven or eight weeks..."

The four men sat in silence for several minutes, each engrossed in his thoughts, until finally Southwick said bluntly, "I'll be damned if I see where you start, sir. Seems to me a job for the whole Channel Fleet; can't see what good can be done this side of the Atlantic."

"Ah, Southwick, you're an honest fellow," Yorke said, tapping the Master's knee. "But just think back. The Post Office referred the problem to the Cabinet, and the Cabinet turned it over to the Admiralty. And the Admiralty – I hope I'm not being too unfair to Lord Spencer – were as puzzled about where to start as you. Then they realized that since so many West Indies packets had been lost, they could get rid of the problem by passing it over to the Commander-in-Chief in Jamaica ... Am I right?" he asked Ramage.

Since he had not told them that Lord Spencer had named him especially – as well as passing the whole problem to Sir Pilcher – Ramage contented himself with a suitably cynical laugh and the comment, "I'm sure that's how the Admiral views it!"

But as he sat with the three men, he found himself wondering if the Post Office and the Board of Admiralty had considered the homeward-bound losses significant: Lord Auckland had not mentioned it to Smith: Lord Spencer had made no comment to Sir Pilcher.

"Magic," Yorke said suddenly. "The French are using magicians. Wouldn't surprise me to hear the Ministère de la Marine has had a hot press out for them for the past couple of years."

"Aye," Southwick said, "it must be something like that. It'll be my birthday in a month or so, and since I could have fathered both you young gentlemen I'm not saying how old I'll be. But if you'll forgive me for saying so, sir," he said to Ramage, "this story of the Post Office packets is the weirdest yarn I've heard, an' I've heard a few in my lifetime!"

Yorke was tapping his teeth with a thumbnail. "So the Post Office compensates the owner if a packet is lost," he said, almost to himself.

When Ramage nodded, Yorke commented: "So no underwriters are involved?"

"I doubt it. You know more about marine insurance than I, but I can't see the Government reinsuring on the open market."

"Nor can I; they'd have to pay a pretty premium! And I have a feeling that before paying out underwriters would ask more pointed questions than the Inspector of Packets, who is probably an underpaid quill-pusher who has never been to sea."

"He hasn't," Ramage said. "I checked that with Smith. It's purely an administrative job. He has the book of rules and makes sure everyone abides by them."

"But what questions could he ask?" Southwick ran a hand through his white hair. "No one doubts the packets are captured by privateers; no one's suggesting they sink, because the lads are exchanged."

"True enough," Yorke admitted, "but are there really that number of privateers on either side of the Atlantic?"

Ramage shook his head. "I doubt it very much. In fact Sir Pilcher has had a frigate at one end or other of the Windward Passage continuously for the past two years, and for the past twelve months they've sighted almost nothing."

"There's only one way of finding out what goes on," Southwick said bluntly, "and that's to man a packet with proper fighting seamen, not these Post Office gentlemen raised on a bread-and-milk diet of running away. You take command, and we all sail for England..."

"That's a damned good idea!" Yorke exclaimed. "I'll come as a passenger."

All three men were looking questioningly at Ramage who smiled grimly and shook his head. He had reached that conclusion long before leaving Smith's office, but he had no hope of persuading either the Commander-in-Chief or the Deputy Postmaster-General to agree.

"My last question to Mr Smith was 'When is the next packet due?'"

"And what was his answer?" Southwick growled.

"His exact words were, 'Using the forty-five-day passage rule, she was due here yesterday.'"

"That doesn't necessarily mean she's lost," Yorke pointed out. "Bad weather, light winds..."

"No, I agree," Ramage said, "and Smith gives her up to a week. But he's not accepting any passengers or mail..."

"Look on the bright side," Bowen said cheerfully. "If she comes in, you really don't think Sir Pilcher would agree – and

53

give you three dozen former Tritons to man her?"

Ramage shook his head again. "The knight's move," he said enigmatically. "It's the only way to find out what's happening, but ..." He thought for a few moments, then said: "I can get the men – Sir Pilcher has already promised me a dozen Tritons without knowing what I wanted to do. But the Post Office would never agree ..."

Yet another idea was forming vaguely in Ramage's mind; a possible improvement on the one that formed in Smith's office. "You're serious about going back in a packet?" he asked Yorke.

"Not in an ordinary one," Yorke said emphatically. "After what we've just heard I'd sooner wait and go in a convoy. If you can get your hands on one, that'd be different."

The idea was now slowly taking shape, like a buoy emerging from a fog bank. "We might all four be passengers."

"What – you wouldn't be in command?"

"Perhaps not. After all, we don't know what happens, do we? It might be better to have a normal packet sailing in the normal way. With a few passengers – us, and perhaps some others."

"What, no Tritons, sir?" Southwick was shocked. "The four of us wouldn't stand a chance."

"A packet has – by Post Office regulations – a ship's company of twenty-eight men and boys ... that includes the commander, master and mate."

"But even so, sir ..."

"But if a dozen of her men were given a few hours' leave and didn't return by sailing time ... and the Navy offered a dozen seamen to help out ..."

"By Jove," Yorke said gleefully, "that's it!"

"As far as the Post Office commander and the rest of the crew are concerned, they'd be just a dozen seamen taken at random from one of the King's ships. That wouldn't seem odd because the chance of finding a dozen merchant seamen in Kingston at half an hour's notice is nil – particularly if one or two of the ships o' war had sent out press gangs a few hours earlier ..."

"Lack of secrecy, that'd be our best ally," Yorke said. "Make a great fuss if the packet comes in – be sure the newspaper announces it, and so forth – so that the French will hear."

Ramage nodded slowly. "We might even use the newspaper to reveal – accidentally, of course – when she's due to sail."

"Aye," Southwick said, "have the Postmaster announce that all letters for England have to be at the Post Office by nine o'clock in the forenoon on a certain day. That'd warn anyone who was half awake that she's sailing by noon."

As they talked, Ramage became convinced that the idea was not only a good one, but the only one likely to bring results. Then Yorke caught his eye and said flatly:

"You suspect treachery, don't you?"

The words reached into Ramage's mind and jogged something: something lying there since the visit to Smith's office but which still refused to emerge. "I'm not sure. At the moment I suspect everything – and nothing."

"But as you've just outlined it, you're covering yourself against it."

"Of course, but treachery from any direction, not just on board the packet."

Southwick was shaking his head. "It'd have to be treachery on board all the packets lost so far," he said. "I can't really..."

"No, I suppose treachery doesn't seem likely," Yorke admitted. "But privateers nabbing packet after packet doesn't seem likely either."

"What happens if the packet doesn't come in?" Bowen asked, in his usual down-to-earth manner.

"We'll have to think again," Ramage said with a lightness he did not feel.

"All that chess," Southwick muttered. "She has to come in..."

Ramage had just washed, shaved and dressed next morning before going down to breakfast when a knock at the door revealed a lugubrious servant who handed him a letter with the announcement that it had just been delivered by hand. As he

55

fumbled in his pocket for a coin and gave it to the man, Ramage noticed the Post Office seal on the letter.

It was from Smith and said: "The lookout on Morant Point has sent word that a vessel believed to be the packet was sighted to the south-east at daybreak, and I'm hastening to pass on the good news to you."

Ramage sat on the bed, feeling strangely excited. The lookouts at Morant Point, at the east end of Jamaica, had seen enough packets not to be mistaken: Smith's "believed" was probably no more than a bureaucrat's inability to write anything definite.

One thing is certain, he thought bitterly. Although persuading Sir Pilcher to agree to the plan would be very difficult, Smith would never agree. The natural reluctance of a bureaucrat, and Post Office pride, made it dangerous even to suggest it. Dangerous in case Smith's refusal resulted in a definite order from Sir Pilcher forbidding it ... He went along to Yorke's room, banging on Southwick's door as he passed and calling him to join them.

Yorke was having trouble shaving. "This damned strop," he grumbled. "My hand slipped and I've almost cut it through!"

Southwick chuckled. "Take your chance with the hotel's barber!"

"Prefer to shave myself," Yorke said crossly, "it's part of the ritual of waking up!"

"You gave a hail, sir," Southwick prompted Ramage.

"They've sighted the packet."

"Well I'm damned!" The Master ran his hand through his flowing white hair like a shopkeeper demonstrating a mop. "I thought the French had got her."

"You're going off to Sir Pilcher?" Yorke asked.

"Once she's anchored. I'd sooner be able to point to her than talk to him of a ship that's out of sight."

Yorke nodded approvingly. "That's a good idea. Out of sight makes it – well, abstract almost. By the way, should I dash down and see Mr Smith about a passage?"

"No, I'll arrange all that. Incidentally," Ramage added, "I

56

must warn you that it'll cost you fifty guineas and you provide your own food as well as bedding."

"Food? Why on earth does the passenger supply food?"

"I don't know," Ramage said, "and nor does Smith. It's an old tradition, though food is provided outward-bound. If it's any consolation, the fare back to Falmouth is four guineas less than the fare out!"

"The whole thing intrigues me," Yorke said, busily lathering his face. "The packets for Lisbon, Gibraltar and Malta provide food each way."

"Each way," Ramage said, "but Smith tells me the fare homeward from Gibraltar costs ten guineas more than outward, and from Malta it's five guineas extra."

"Tradition, too?"

"No – he says victuals cost more in Gibraltar and Malta than Falmouth."

Yorke snorted. "More likely they know they have passengers on board at pistol point!"

"Don't you charge more in your ships?" Southwick asked.

"No fear. Same either way. And we provide food and bedding."

He wiped the razor and began shaving, his voice distorted as he stretched the skin of his face. "By the way, I've been thinking of your passenger idea. I can see a disadvantage."

"That I end up in England?"

"Yes. You might end up in England and have nothing to report to the Admiralty."

"I know, but I don't think it matters."

"Doesn't matter? But surely –"

"The only place I'll find the answer is at sea in a packet, that's for sure. And being at sea in a packet means departing from one place and arriving at another."

"Still –" Yorke began doubtfully.

"At least it'll mean a packet got safely back to Falmouth," Southwick said.

"And you'll have had a quiet voyage playing chess with Bowen," Ramage said.

Southwick's face dropped as if he was suddenly seeing the

packet's progress across every minute of latitude and longitude as a game of chess with the doctor.

"I'll put up a silver cup," Yorke said. "'The Western Ocean Trophy'. The winner is the man with the most games as the packet enters Falmouth."

"I'll add fifty guineas," Ramage said. "How's that for encouragement."

"Fine, sir," Southwick said gloomily. "Trouble is, it'll only encourage Bowen, not me."

Ramage was talking to the Deputy Postmaster-General in his office when a clerk brought word that the packet had just been sighted passing Fort Charles.

"Do you want to come out with me?" Smith asked.

Ramage shook his head. "No – for the time being I'd prefer it if no one on board the packet knew that there's an investigation under way. You haven't mentioned to your staff ..."

"To no one."

"Good, but find out what you can from the commander – if he saw privateers, has news of more losses and so on."

"She left Falmouth before the *Hydra* sailed," Smith pointed out. "Six days before. And she's come via Barbados."

"Of course," Ramage said, irritated that he'd forgotten. "So they'll have no hint that..."

"None at all." Smith looked at him shrewdly. "You know, Lieutenant, you sound as if you suspect them!"

Ramage was thankful that he had decided not to take Smith into his confidence.

"No – after all, they're one of the packets that *hasn't* been captured! And what would a packet crew gain by being captured?"

He spoke in a casual voice but watched Smith, who was sorting his inevitable piles of papers as he answered. "Gain? Why, nothing! In fact everything to lose – remember their little ventures that so shocked you."

Indeed, Ramage thought, ten guineas invested by a seaman in ventures would be more than six months' pay for these men

58

and more than a year's pay for a man serving in one of the King's ships.

"What is the pay of a commander?" he asked, almost thinking aloud.

"Nothing lavish – eight pounds a month."

"Only eight pounds?" Ramage exclaimed. It was within a few shillings of his own pay, and lieutenants in a first-rate received seven pounds.

"Yes – but don't forget the Post Office is also paying him to charter his ship. I don't know the rate. And the passengers' passage money – that's paid to the commander."

"So his wages are not much more than a token."

"I suppose you could look at it like that. If he can't sail on a voyage because of illness he receives his pay – against a physician's certificate, of course."

"Who would then command the ship?"

"The master. No packet is allowed to sail with less than a master in command. A fairly recent ruling."

"They had sailed with less – before the ruling?"

"Occasionally," Smith admitted.

"Does a packet often sail with only the master in command?"

"Not too often. One or two commanders suffer from ill-health," Smith said uncomfortably.

"But the Post Office knows about them."

Smith nodded. "They take steps, where they can."

"So such a commander gets his pay and can make his profit from the charter money without stepping out of his house?"

"Yes," Smith admitted angrily, "but see here, Lieutenant, I don't reckon your inquiries into privateering give you a right to criticize the Post Office!"

"I'm not criticizing," Ramage said coolly. "I was merely asking you to confirm something you've just said. If you choose to interpret your own statements as criticism, well..." He shrugged his shoulders.

"I'm sorry," Smith said quickly, "I'm a sight too touchy. Fact is, these losses are getting on my nerves. If only you realized what's at stake."

59

Ramage's eyebrows lifted, and Smith said: "Communications. Without them London is – well, like a giant without arms and legs!"

Was that all he meant? Ramage wished he could be sure.

"I must see about the boat," Smith said. "You're sure you won't come out with me?"

Ramage shook his head.

"When shall I – er, tell you what the commander has to report?" Smith asked.

"Why don't you dine with me at the Royal Albion?"

"I'm afraid I can't," Smith said apologetically. "It's a custom of mine to dine the commander the night he arrives."

"Ah yes, so you told me. The newspaper?"

"I'll arrange all that. Tomorrow's issue of the *Chronicle* will announce today's arrival and warn everyone that the mail closes at nine o'clock the following morning."

"If you're dining the commander tonight why don't we meet tomorrow morning? Breakfast at my hotel? Say seven o'clock?"

Chapter Five

Sir Pilcher Skinner had been vastly relieved when his secretary brought in the news from Morant Point that the packet had been sighted. Relieved and surprised, since he had already presumed her lost. Still, it was a relief to know she had sailed before the *Hydra*, so there would be no unexpected or unwelcome official business in the mails; just private letters, and now he was a widower he found himself taking less and less interest in family or friends. It was unfortunate that his daughter had not found herself a husband but he had long since given up worrying about it.

He pulled out his watch. Eleven o'clock already and Henderson had put out a pile of reports for him to sign, so that they could be sealed and sent home in the packet. As he reached for his pen he reflected crossly that although the Admiralty had given him few enough ships for the station, from the paperwork one would guess he had ten times more than the Channel Fleet.

The Channel Fleet: he shivered at the very thought of it. Jamaica suited him well enough: a splendid climate – although it could be a bit too hot in the hurricane season – and the most comfortable quarters the Navy had to offer. And prize money – by jingo, the prize agents here must be making enormous profits, judging by the fees they charged for their dabblings.

He glanced at the top report, scribbled a signature and put the page to one side. He glanced up. Now Henderson was back again. There was no peace for a commander-in-chief, al-

61

though he shouldn't really complain since the fellow did a splendid job.

"Lieutenant Ramage, sir. Says it's important."

"Important!" Sir Pilcher snorted. There wasn't a lieutenant in the Navy List who didn't think whatever he was doing was important. "Well, what's he want? He has his orders."

"He wouldn't disclose the substance of it, sir."

Disclose the substance of it! Only Henderson could use a phrase like that. Half the time he sounded like a superannuated judge.

"Oh very well, send him in."

Why can't the boy just go away and carry out his orders? Run into some damned silly little problem, no doubt; scared of taking any responsibility and determined to shove it on the Commander-in-Chief's shoulders. That seemed the ambition of every officer on the station – and every blasted quill-pusher in the Admiralty, too, including the First Lord!

Henderson announced Ramage.

"Ha! What now, my boy?"

"The packet, sir."

"Yes? She'll be anchoring shortly. Surely you don't want my permission to board her?"

"Not board her, sir."

Now what did he mean by that emphasis on "board"? He's a deep one, this lad. "Just because one packet's got through I hope you don't think..."

"Oh no, sir. I had a proposal –"

"You've got your orders; just carry 'em out!" Wouldn't hurt to shake him up a bit, Sir Pilcher decided.

"Very well, sir: I just wanted to warn you of possible repercussions."

"Repercussions? What the devil are you talking about?"

"I'm proposing to sail in her."

"I should think so. You won't find out what's going on by lounging around Government House!"

"And take Southwick and Bowen – the former master and surgeon of the *Triton* – and a dozen men with me."

"A dozen men? *Seamen?*"

"Yes, sir. You were kind enough to warn Captain Napier to keep some Tritons available."

"My goodness! You're not expecting the Admiralty to pay their passage money, are you?" The lad's up to something; that's for sure, Sir Pilcher decided. Why on earth doesn't he just take a passage himself and – oh well!

"Mine, Southwick's, sir, and the surgeon, Bowen; not the seamen."

"Very well, I'll allow you three, just berth, bedding and victuals. No wines and spirits. But the seamen – are they to be guests of the Post Office?"

"In a way, sir. I want to exchange a dozen of them for a dozen of the packet's men."

It was a good idea, but the Post Office would not like it – the protests would be endless. How to lodge the dozen Post Office men left in Kingston, and then crowding them all into the next packet, and no doubt the commander would demand a victualling allowance for them – oh no!

"I'm sorry, Ramage, it's out of the question."

"It's our only chance, sir."

"*Your* only chance," Sir Pilcher corrected. "You have your orders."

"Yes sir, but – with respect – I can't tackle a privateer by myself!"

"Your orders don't say that you should: you're supposed to inquire, not fight."

"The First Lord mentioned 'halting the losses', sir."

"See here, Ramage, you weren't supposed to see that letter: I exceeded my authority in showing it to you. Forget all about it. And don't plan to fight privateers, either."

"But that's been the trouble, sir. I think we're going to find at least some of the packets have been taken by small privateers: ones from which they could have escaped if they had had the wish."

"That's absurd! You've no grounds for saying that. These privateers carry scores of men."

"Just so, sir. And they're not that fast. They're crammed with men and guns. They can dodge frigates most of the time because they're slippery to windward, but I can't see how they can catch so many of the packets, which are designed for speed."

"Well, they do, and that's that."

Ramage knew he had nearly lost. There was only one more chance. "But if I arrive at Falmouth, sir, I can't help feeling his Lordship will think I've just taken passage in the packet to get home."

"I shouldn't worry about that; you stand a dam' good chance of ending up a prisoner in France." Damn, he shouldn't have said that: it was just the opening the boy wanted.

"Exactly, sir: but with a dozen of my own men, we'd stand a good chance of escaping a privateer."

"What the devil can a dozen men do?"

"They might – er, encourage the rest to do something."

That was true enough; if the Post Office men were shy of the smell of powder, at least men picked by Ramage would stiffen 'em up a bit.

"Very well, if you can get the Postmaster to agree to using a dozen of your men..."

"Thank you, sir." Ramage tried to make sure he would remember the exact phrase Sir Pilcher had used.

If the Postmaster agrees, Sir Pilcher thought to himself, that's his affair. Whatever happens after that is the concern of the Joint Postmasters-General. It won't hurt those lofty fellows in Lombard Street to have their share of responsibility; they're a sight too free in trying to push it on to other people's shoulders.

Sir Pilcher relaxed as Ramage left the room. The Postmaster would never agree to the lad's crazy plan, but if he did ... He shrugged his shoulders. Really, when the Cabinet decided to pass the responsibility to the Admiralty, they had absolutely no idea what it meant in practice.

Once outside Admiralty House, Ramage paused in the blazing sun and scribbled down Sir Pilcher's phrase, "Very well, if you can get the Postmaster to agree to using a dozen of your men." He folded the paper carefully and put it in his pocket.

The Deputy Postmaster arrived punctually at the Royal Albion next morning, and even before he sat down at the breakfast table Ramage thought he detected a change in the man. Was it nervousness? Apprehension? His movements seemed jerky; the fingers of his big hands opened and closed, as if he was unsure of himself.

After the usual greetings both men remained silent until the waiters had served them and moved back to stand by the kitchen door, as though on guard. As Smith began eating, Ramage asked: "What news, Mr Smith?"

"About as bad as it could be. Seems that Lord Auckland delayed the *Lady Arabella*'s departure so she did leave after the *Hydra*. His Lordship tells me that news came in that two Lisbon packets have been lost, and the packet due from here didn't arrive in Falmouth, either."

"And news of the war?"

"Nothing fresh. The French hold out in Malta, though Sir Horatio Nelson has a squadron at Naples and is blockading them. The Czar of Russia is showing more signs of friendship with this man Bonaparte. But no great battles – you knew about Luneville, of course?"

Ramage nodded: the Austrian defeat meant the end of Britain's last ally; from now on she was alone in the war against France and Spain. "The Lisbon packets," he said, helping himself to more fried bacon. "Any pattern? Where were they lost?"

"No pattern," Smith said. "At least, Lord Auckland did not mention any, except that they were homeward bound. One was taken within sight of Porto, so she'd barely cleared Lisbon. The other was only fifty miles from the Scillies."

"The weather?"

Smith wrinkled his brow, obviously casting his mind back over Lord Auckland's letter.

"The first one – light winds. The second – yes, it was blowing more than half a gale from the east, because one of the privateer's boats capsized."

More than half a gale from the east. Ramage could picture the packet beating up to the chops of the Channel when she

65

sighted the privateer. Yet she should have been able to turn
and run . . .

"What were the casualties in the packets?"

"None in the first," Smith said miserably, as though he knew
only too well that it belied any serious attempt to avoid capture, "and one wounded in the second, according to the French
newspapers."

"But they managed to sink the mails before hauling down
their flags?"

"Oh yes – there's not been a single mail taken by the enemy
yet."

"Not one that's been reported, anyway," Ramage said
sourly, buttering some toast.

"I resent, that Mr Ramage: quite uncalled for." Yet Smith's
voice carried no conviction.

"We need to be realistic," Ramage said sharply. "A captain
in the Royal Navy surrendering his ship in half a gale with only
one man wounded would face some very unpleasant questions
at the court of inquiry."

"How can you say that? You've no experience of surrendering a ship."

"I have," Ramage said, passing the toast rack to Smith.

"With more than one wounded, I presume."

"Yes, two-thirds of the ship's company dead or wounded,
and the ship sinking," Ramage said coldly. "More tea?"

"I'm sorry," Smith said contritely. "Was that your first command?"

"I started off the battle as the fifth lieutenant. The captain
and the rest of the officers were killed before it ended. I took
command because I was the senior officer left alive."

Ramage could have said much more, but decided against it.
How could he explain to a Postmaster that he was contemptuous of the French and Spanish habit of firing a single broadside *pour l'honneur du pavillon* before surrendering? It was a
charade, a fraud, a polite gesture. Any captain who gave a
damn whether he had fired a single broadside (taking care to
cause no casualties, for obvious reasons) or surrendered without firing a shot was only slightly less a fraud than the men

66

who accepted such a code of behaviour.

"The Scilly Isles one," Smith said. "You feel she should have put up more of a fight?"

"No, since I wasn't there I couldn't make a judgement. But I'm certain she could have made a greater effort to *escape* – after all, the Post Office has told commanders to run when they can, and with half a gale from the east the whole Atlantic was open to her."

"I wondered about that," Smith admitted.

"Well, what did you hear last night from the commander of the packet?"

"Captain Stevens reports a completely uneventful voyage of forty-three days. He sighted two frigates south-west of the Scillies, and then nothing until he met a British sloop-of-war east of Barbados."

"Has he any ideas – or suspicions?"

Smith shook his head. "He says there are so many enemy privateers around that the packets are bound to be captured."

"Yet he came through safely – and saw only British warships."

"It's only the exceptional case that gets through these days."

"I know," Ramage said soothingly. "Captain Stevens is probably upset over the losses anyway."

"Philosophical, I should say."

"Yet the other commanders and masters must be friends of his – after all, they're probably all Falmouth men."

"Yes, but he tells me the French are still regularly exchanging prisoners fairly quickly."

Ramage signalled to a waiter and ordered more coffee for himself and tea for Smith.

"So Commander Stevens is not much help."

"I'm afraid not. Have you – er, made any plans?"

"Yes, and I want to discuss them with you."

Smith leaned forward attentively, pushing aside a plate.

"I'm proposing to sail in this packet," Ramage said.

"I rather anticipated that."

"And I'll need three other berths: four in all."

"Very well: that leaves six remaining."

"Have any Naval officers applied?"

"No: eleven Army officers, and nineteen planters and businessmen."

"Who were the Army officers?"

"A captain of the 31st Foot – and a lieutenant from – oh dear, I can't remember all the regiments."

"Could you give a berth to the one that seems the steadiest and leave the others empty?"

"Of course," Smith said eagerly. "That'll be the captain from the 31st, name of Wilson. By the way, don't forget you have to provide your own food and bedding."

"I haven't forgotten Captain Stevens makes a profit from me of fifty guineas without having to provide a slice of bread or a pillow-case." A sudden thought struck him. "I presume that we pay when we arrive in Falmouth?"

"Oh no! You settle with me on behalf of the captain before the ship sails!"

"Why?" Ramage asked flatly. "Tradition?"

"No – the commanders insisted on that as soon as the packets started being captured. I think they like to send the drafts home by a merchantman in convoy: it's safer than having it on board the packet and risking capture."

"The gallant commanders can't lose," Ramage said sourly, and then regretted the remark. Smith flushed but said nothing.

"When are the passengers supposed to board?"

"When do you propose she sails?" Smith asked, and the tone of his voice assured Ramage that the Postmaster now accepted his authority.

"Would noon the day after tomorrow be normal?"

"Quite normal. If you'd asked me, that's when I'd have suggested. It gives Captain Stevens enough time to provision the ship."

"And give his men some shore leave," Ramage said casually.

Smith grinned. "Yes – a few hours to dispose of their ventures."

Ramage realized he should have remembered that that alone would have ensured the men came on shore.

"Well now," Smith said affably, as a waiter set down a tea-

68

pot and a coffee-pot, "can you and your people be on board by nine o'clock in the morning? Your baggage can be stowed and you'll be settled in before she sails."

"Excellent," Ramage said. It would fit in perfectly with his timetable, and give him time to look over the packet and her crew before she sailed.

"The packetsmen," Ramage added casually. "How is their leave arranged?"

"Captain Stevens usually gives half of them a few hours the first day, and half get the night on shore."

"A dozen men at a time – oh well, they have Protections, too, lucky fellows; they can enjoy themselves without worrying about a press gang picking them up!"

Chapter
Six

His Majesty's packet brig *Lady Arabella* was on the special Post Office mooring right in front of Kingston itself, and the following evening four seamen were watching her from a waterfront bar. They had moved one of the two tables in the tawdry saloon to a spot where they could get the best view, tipped the potman lavishly and told him to stay away until they called him.

The bar was otherwise empty; in fact it was unlikely that three dozen seamen could be found in all the bars within two hundred yards of Harbour Street and not ten more in all the brothels. The reason was simple – the same four men had visited a few of the bars earlier and mentioned that there would soon be a hot press out because one of the ships of the line had just received sailing orders. It took only a few minutes for the word to spread among the men who belonged to the few merchantmen in the anchorage, and they vanished like summer mist at sunrise.

Now the only seamen in the city's bars were those with Protections tucked in their pockets or money belts. Some Protections, issued by the Admiralty, declared their holders to be protected from being pressed because of their jobs – ferrymen, for instance, who were often disabled seamen for whom a Protection was the nearest thing to a pension they were likely to get. Other Protections had been issued by the Government of the United States – or, rather, its Customs officers – and declared their bearers to be American citizens.

Although the documents issued by the Admiralty were rare,

the American Protections were comparatively common: the Customs officer in any American port readily issued one to any man who swore on oath that he was an American citizen. There was nothing to prevent a man collecting one in each of a dozen different ports, and then selling the other eleven at a handsome profit. British seamen considered a change of name a small price to pay for immunity from the press gangs.

One of the four men sitting at the table owned a genuine American Protection which was probably unique in Kingston that day because it truly described its owner as an American citizen: Thomas Jackson, a lean man with a cadaverous face and receding sandy hair, had indeed been born in Charleston, South Carolina, forty years earlier, and thus became an American at the age of twenty. The document – with the American eagle printed right across the top and signed with a flourish by "James Bennett, Collector of Customs for Charleston" – was now yellowed and foxed by tropical heat, creased and stained at the edges with salt water.

Thomas Jackson had carried it with him for more than three years, a genuine document which would stop a press gang hauling him on board a British warship or ensure that an American consul would subsequently secure his release. Yet for more than three years Thomas Jackson had served in the Royal Navy, and for most of that time he had been the captain's coxswain. For nearly two years his captain had been Lieutenant Ramage, and between the two men, so different in rank, age, temperament and background, existed that indefinable bond between men who have shared the same dangers and know that a French roundshot did not care whether it knocked the head off an earl's heir or the son of a Carolina woodsman.

Two of the other men, Stafford and Rossi, had served with Lieutenant Ramage for the same length of time; only the fourth, a coloured seaman named William Maxton, who came from Grenada at the southern end of the Windward Islands, was a comparative newcomer.

Will Stafford was a true Cockney, having been born in Bridewell Lane. He was now twenty-seven years old and stockily built with a round and cheery face and curly brown hair.

An observant onlooker might have been puzzled by his delicate hands (the skin now coarsened by hauling on ropes) and a habit of rubbing thumb and forefinger together, as though feeling material. Before being swept into the Navy's net Stafford had been a locksmith, not a tailor, and he made no secret of the fact that much of his work on locks had been done by his sensitive fingers at the dead of night, unrequested and unpaid, though rarely unrewarded.

Alberto Rossi, nicknamed Rosey by his shipmates, was correctly described in muster books as having been born in Genoa and was twenty years old, plump and black-haired with flamboyant good looks. Like many Genovesi, Rossi spoke good English: hundreds of men from that great seaport had to seek employment in the ships of other nations because there were too few ships flying the flag of the Republic of Genoa, which had recently been occupied by the French and renamed the Ligurian Republic. Rossi maintained a bantering reticence about his reason for signing on in a British ship of war that happened to be in the harbour, although admitting it was the fastest and certainly the safest way of leaving the city without being asked embarrassing questions.

Although the other three had formed a tightly knit group under Jackson's leadership, and many times had risked their lives with their captain, they had accepted Maxton when he joined the ship because of his cheerful intelligence. In turn, Ramage had come to realize that he could rely on the quartet. In common with most of the men of the Royal Navy they gave their loyalty not to a flag or a vague ideal, but to an individual they could respect. It was a spontaneous and natural loyalty; not the loyalty demanded by the harshly worded Articles of War.

"Jacko," Stafford said suddenly, glancing round to make sure the potman was out of earshot, and wiping the perspiration from his forehead with the back of his hand, "make sure I stay sober."

"Don't worry."

"But I do. I worry all the time. Just supposing these beggars don't come on shore from the packet. Say they don't get leave?"

"They will," Jackson said reassuringly. "You saw the first half going back on board twenty minutes ago."

"Aye, and three sheets in the wind, the lot o' them! Supposin' the captain decides he don't want the rest of his men blind drunk, and belays their leave?"

"Then we'll go on board and pull 'em out like winkles. Got a bent pin?"

Rossi tapped his mug of beer. "Seriously, Jacko, is a good question. *Accidente* – everything depends on it!"

"It's a good question all right," the American said calmly, "but if they don't get leave and come on shore, we can't do anything: it's as simple as that. You saw the first half had their run on shore, just like Mr Ramage said, so why should anything stop the second half? There's plenty of time for them to get their twelve hours before the *Arabella* sails at noon tomorrow."

"All right," Stafford conceded, "let's say they're here and we've got 'em all stupid drunk. Where's this bleedin' crimp supposed to meet us, so we can hand 'em over to him?"

"Down the other end of Harbour Street. At the Sign of the Pelican. He owns it."

"Can we trust him?"

"Yes, he's got only half the money and doesn't get the rest until morning. And I swore Maxie would slit his throat if he tried any nonsense."

"But a dozen drunken packetsmen," Stafford persisted. "Where the 'ell is he going to lock 'em up safe?"

Jackson sighed. "He's got a small building out the back like a big cell. Has a mahogany door on it two inches thick and a padlock as big as a melon. They'll be half drunk by the time we invite them along to the Pelican, and there it's free drinks on us. As they pass out we pass them out to the crimp who locks 'em up in his cell. I had a good look at it – they can shout until their tongues wear out and no c e'll hear them."

"Like a purser's storeroom," Stafford commented, "only he sells seamen to shipmasters!"

"And then?" Rossi prompted Jackson.

"With all the packetsmen locked up for the night we sleep at

73

the Pelican, and the other eight of our lads join us with their seabags. Then at nine o'clock tomorrow morning we lurk around the landing stage and wait for the word from Mr Ramage to go out to the *Arabella* and take the packetsmen's places."

Stafford shook his head doubtfully. "I don't like the idea of trusting that crimp."

"Don't worry about him," Jackson said contemptuously. "He'll do anything for money, and I've got it. He doesn't get the other half until we leave the Pelican to board the packet, and he's only to keep that cell door locked until he sees her sailing out past Fort Charles. Why, he's doing this sort of thing all the time, only usually he has to find the drunks to lock in his cell. Then he has to drag 'em off to a merchant ship that's short of men, get them signed on and collect his money from the captain before they've sobered up. I bet he's selling a couple of dozen men a day once a convoy starts forming up here."

"Is just kidnapping," Rossi exclaimed angrily, his accent becoming more pronounced. "Is a crook, this crimp!"

"Sure it's kidnapping," Jackson said calmly, "and it goes on in every port in the world. It's selling seamen to shipmasters, just like a chandler sells rope and candles. But every seaman knows the minute he sets foot in a bar that if he gets drunk the ladies of the town will get his money and the crimps or a press gang will get his body. It's the same in Genoa, isn't it?"

"No, is worse," Rossi said soberly. "Too many seamen and not enough ships, so you lose your money after getting a knife between the ribs."

"I'd sooner take me chance with a crimp," Stafford said complacently. "But Jacko, ain't what we're doing a bit sort of – well, irregular? We must be careful not to do nothin' that'd get Mr Ramage into trouble."

"Don't worry," Jackson said soothingly, "I've got my orders from Mr Ramage himself, and the money to pay off the crimp and buy some beer. Just rem mber that, as far as the packetsmen are concerned, we've just een paid some prize money and want to enjoy ourselves."

"Yus, but wot 'appens when we get on board the packet? Are we supposed to sign on?"

"*Mama mia!*" exclaimed an exasperated Rossi. "Is not bright today, eh Staff?"

The Cockney looked shamefaced. "It's the heat. I'd sort of worked it out like that, I just wanted confirmeration."

"Confirmation," Jackson corrected out of habit.

"An' I got it. 'Ow much drinkin' money did Mr Ramage give us, Jacko?"

"Officially, he hasn't given us any, and if anything goes wrong just remember we haven't even *seen* him: we've just got shore leave from the *Arrogant* and that's that."

"Is a boat," Rossi said, suddenly pointing towards the *Lady Arabella*. A local boat was leaving her, crowded with men, and the heavily patched lugsail was being hoisted. Soon the boat was reaching quickly towards the jetty.

"Come on, Jacko!"

"Sit down, Staff: we aren't going to welcome them at the jetty and give 'em the freedom of the city; we'll find them in a bar in fifteen minutes or so."

"Supposing they split up?"

"We'll keep an eye on them."

But an hour later four very worried seamen came back to the same table in the saloon, their shirts soaked in perspiration, and ordered themselves drinks.

"We're in trouble now," Stafford muttered gloomily. "What'll Mr Ramage say?"

"They vanish – poof!" Rossi said, disbelief in his voice, "and is getting dark."

"Why were they all carrying bags?" Jackson mused. "Large bags. Not their seabags, though; bags with something special inside. Listen, you three, I'm going to report to Mr Ramage; he's waiting at the Royal Albion."

He was back within ten minutes, walking jauntily.

"Ventures!" he said contemptuously. "Seems all these packetsmen are really budding merchants. They bring out goods to sell here – boots, shoes, wines and cheeses – I ask you, *cheeses* – and take back things that are difficult to get in England, and sell them in Falmouth."

75

In the cardroom at the Royal Albion next morning Southwick and Bowen were having a leisurely game of chess, the Master now regretting that he had refused the surgeon's offer of an advantage of two bishops.

Bowen shook his head reprovingly. "The centre of the board, Southwick; always try to dominate the centre of the board."

"I know," Southwick snapped, "you've told me enough times, but all I can say is it's easier said than done."

"Are you looking forward to our cruise?"

"Not much," Southwick said. "Don't like sitting round idle, especially on board a ship."

"Let someone else worry about sailing the ship for a change. I'm looking forward to the company of you and Mr Ramage without one or other of you constantly bobbing off on watch!"

"Aye, it'll be a nice enough voyage in that sense."

"But not in the other sense, though."

"No," Southwick said. "Trouble is, we don't know what we're looking for."

"Getting the dozen former Tritons on board the packet – Mr Ramage's method seems a trifle – er – unorthodox."

"No choice," Southwick said, lifting a bishop carefully, and then hastily putting it back. "Has to be a little unorthodox when they give him these rum jobs. I tell you this, Bowen: I'm dam' sure the Admiralty couldn't make up its mind whether to give the job to an admiral with a squadron or a junior officer..."

"Or Mr Ramage," Bowen said cheerfully. "He makes a nice compromise."

"Check," Southwick said triumphantly.

Bowen glanced at the board, moved his knight, and looked up again. "Best choice they – you see what you did, don't you? Good – they ever made."

Bowen rolled a pawn along the table-top. "You know, Southwick, potentially Mr Ramage is a fine chess player. Curious, he makes brilliant moves when he's using his own life – and other people's. Yet sit him behind a chessboard and he gets lost..."

76

"It's a matter of concentration," Southwick said. "Nothing concentrates your thoughts better than knowing you'll get killed if you don't do the right thing. But sitting behind a chessboard – well, he's probably thinking of a dozen different things while his opponent decides on a move."

"I suppose so," Bowen said. "For me, I can think only with a chessboard in front of me." He moved his queen. "Check, I think; possibly even checkmate. You see, Southwick, you don't concentrate either."

"How can I, when you're jabbering all the time," an exasperated Southwick exclaimed. "Anyway, it's not 'mate'."

Bowen pointed to his knight.

"Oh blast it," Southwick said. "I hate knights. I like straightforward moves; none of this hoppity dodging about business." He looked at his watch. "Hmm, time we began moving."

Ramage was in his room and finding it strange to be out of uniform. He was thankful that he and Yorke were the same build – more or less, anyway. A tightness across his shoulders warned him to be careful lest a seam split, and that Yorke was narrower-chested. But he had excellent taste and a good tailor, so borrowing his clothes for the first day or so on board the *Lady Arabella* was a pleasure.

Yorke reached over and gave the stock a slight twitch. "You're listing to starboard a trifle."

"It's your damned tailor," Ramage grumbled, "he's sewn in a list."

"When we get on board," Yorke said, "we are – well, ourselves as it were?"

"Completely. We all know each other. The only thing is you don't know any of the ex-Tritons – Jackson, Stafford and the rest of them."

Yorke grinned. "I'm glad we'll have those rascals with us. They're reassuring. Wish we had all the rest of them."

After rapping on the door Southwick called from the corridor: "Bowen and I are just leaving, sir. Your carriage will be ready in a couple of minutes – they're putting up your baggage now."

Chapter
Seven

Yorke and Ramage climbed on board His Majesty's packet *Lady Arabella* to find Southwick and Bowen on deck talking to a sombre and lanky man with a thin, cadaverous face who immediately came over and introduced himself.

"Gideon Stevens, gentlemen, owner and commander of the *Lady Arabella*: welcome on board."

Ramage, realizing Stevens had been expecting him to be in uniform and now could not distinguish them, introduced himself and Yorke.

Stevens' voice was soft, almost ingratiating. "The steward will show you to your cabin, gentlemen. Your baggage will be hoisted on board in a moment or so. I hope you'll be comfortable."

The small cabin that Yorke and Ramage were to share was panelled in dark mahogany and smelled stuffy; at least one of the previous occupants had smoked cigars and the stale, cloying aroma still clung to the furnishings. The covers on the berths, the cushions on the two chairs and the carpet were all a dull, deep red.

"This plum colour – it just doesn't go with polished mahogany," Yorke grumbled.

"Doesn't show the dirt either," Ramage pointed out. "Don't forget Captain Stevens has to safeguard his profit."

"Ninety-nine per cent of the fare, I should think," Yorke said acidly. "And why the devil didn't the steward open the skylight to air the cabin?"

The saloon was large, combining a dining-room and drawing-room in one, and the passengers would spend much of their time in it when they reached the colder weather to the north. It was also panelled in dark mahogany, matching the long dining-table. A heavy oil-lamp hung in gimbals at each end of the cabin; a big brass stove at the forward end warned them that once they were through the Windward Passage it would get a degree colder every day.

Ramage and Yorke had just finished inspecting the saloon and noting that the green corrosion on the brass of the lamp and stove fittings indicated a lazy steward, when a ruddy-faced, stocky young Army officer walked in and, stopping in front of Yorke, barked: "You Ramage?"

"No, this gentleman is."

"How d'y'do: I'm Wilson, 31st Foot."

He had an open, round face, the mouth almost hidden by a blond moustache a shade lighter than his hair, which was already thinning. Ramage liked his straightforward bluffness and after a minute or two left him talking to Yorke as he went back up on deck to find Southwick deep in conversation with the commander.

"Ah, sir," Southwick said. "Mr Stevens was saying how much he liked the brig rig."

"It's ideal," Ramage said agreeably. He'd enjoyed commanding the *Triton* brig, and for a moment pictured her wreck now lying on the coral reef near Puerto Rico. He glanced round and added: "Particularly with a small crew."

"That reminds me," Stevens said, pulling out his watch, "I gave a dozen men leave last night. They're due back – why, half an hour ago!"

He turned away, excusing himself and calling: "Harry? Pass the word for the Bosun! Oh, there you are. Where are those men? They're half an hour adrift. And damnation, here's Mr Smith's boat with the mails. He'll want to muster the ship's company as soon as the mails are stowed. Harry, get yourself on shore and find the men!"

He turned back to Ramage, "I can't understand it. Never had trouble before."

"I heard there was a hot press last night," Ramage said casually. "Just about cleared the streets of Kingston."

"They've got Protections."

"They can be stolen..."

Ramage watched Stevens nibbling at the idea, picturing his seamen drinking themselves insensible on the local rum ... crimps or doxies relieving them of their cash and their Protections (much more valuable than money) ... the drunken men being seized by the press gang and sobering up under guard in one of the ships of war anchored close by...

"Harry! Changed my mind!" Stevens shouted. "You'd better stay on board and get the mails below. Send Our Ned to find the men."

He turned back to Ramage. "Bad time to have men coming back late: the Agent musters the ship's company, then we're off. Still, mayhap Our Ned will find them. He's the Mate's son."

He turned away again. "Fred!" he bellowed, and when a small, grey-haired man came over he said, "Mr Ramage, this is the Mate, Fred Much. He's Our Ned's dad."

Much shook hands, and then said to Stevens: "What'll we do if Our Ned can't find 'em?"

"Let's wait until he comes back a'fore we start fretting," Stevens said curtly, and Ramage sensed there was little love lost between the two men.

When the Deputy Postmaster-General came on board, Stevens at once took him down to his cabin. The paperwork must be formidable, Ramage thought; Smith was carrying quite a bulky bag.

Meanwhile Fred Much, with a list in his hand, was supervising the men, using a net sling and the stay tackle to hoist the mail on board. The heavy canvas bags, each with its mouth closed by a thick draw-string, the knot of which was secured with a lead seal, were lined up alongside the hatch coaming. When seamen in the boat called that the last one was coming up, the Mate sent a boy for the Captain.

Stevens came back with Smith, who held out his hand to the Mate for the list. He consulted it and began to walk slowly along the row of bags. Ramage noticed that each had a three-figure number stencilled on the side, and Smith was comparing the numbers with those on the list.

Finally he folded the paper and walked back. "All there, Mr Mate?"

"Aye aye, sir."

"Satisfied, Captain?"

Stevens nodded. "I'll sign for 'em, Mr Smith. Right, Fred, get 'em below and pass the word when they're stowed."

As the Captain and the Postmaster disappeared into Stevens' cabin again, Yorke and Southwick walked over to Ramage and Southwick said wryly, "Might be different owners, but the paperwork seems about the same!"

"And the problems, too!"

"You mean the men overstaying their leave, sir?"

"Yes," Ramage said, raising his voice slightly and winking at Southwick. "Not unknown in the Royal Navy, eh, Southwick?"

"Indeed no; but believe me, sir," he said, his voice heavy with disapproval, "I'd never have given men leave within a few hours of sailing! Not in the present circumstances."

The Mate could hear them clearly and Ramage hoped that the conversation would be reported to Stevens. Yorke had seen Ramage's wink and gave a rasping cough. "No, most unwise, and I've a damned good mind to tell Stevens so. Particularly unwise since, for safety's sake, we must sail as soon as possible. Why, I'm sure a French spy's telescope is watching us at this very moment."

One by one the bags were lowered into the hold, and Ramage could hear them being dragged about. Then there was banging, thumping and cursing as the men hauled shifting boards into position, lashing them so that the bags could not slide around as the ship pitched and rolled.

Finally the Mate passed the word that all the bags were stowed, and Smith climbed down into the hold. He was back on deck within a couple of minutes and with a curt "Good, batten down then" to the Mate, returned to Stevens' cabin.

Ramage had seen another man – who had boarded with

Smith – wandering about the ship, peering into various corners. "The searcher," he murmured to Southwick.

Southwick surveyed the man, whose clothes were obviously intended for a much fatter person, and who walked with a curious gait, swinging his left arm in unison with his left leg but keeping his right arm rigidly at his side, as though holding up his trousers.

"He can search as much as he wants," Southwick commented, "but he looks to me as though he's completely lost."

At that moment Smith came back on deck, followed by Stevens. Both men were flushed and angry and Smith said abruptly, without bothering to turn his head: "You sail at noon, Captain, whether they come back or not!"

"But how can I? We've barely enough men to handle the ship in heavy weather, thanks to Lombard Street's meanness. And I'm supposed to beat off privateers – with a handful of men and boys. I'm short of the Master, too, since he's sick in Falmouth. No sir, we don't sail."

Ramage knew this was the moment he had been waiting for and walked casually over to join the two men. "Mr Smith – I hope I'm not interfering, but I can't help thinking that some of Mr Stevens' men might have 'run', or been picked up by a press gang."

"They most certainly have *not* deserted," Stevens said emphatically. "Perhaps got themselves beastly drunk, but they'll be back!"

"But I can't allow you to wait, Captain; I've already made that quite clear," Smith said firmly. "I couldn't even in peacetime – you know full well the packet sails as soon as the mails are on board. In the present circumstances it's most important you sail before the French get the word..."

"But I daren't," Stevens almost wailed. "A dozen men short of my complement! I'll lose the ship for sure."

"Might I suggest Sir Pilcher Skinner?" Ramage said smoothly.

"Sir Pilcher?" Smith repeated. "What – how could..."

"A dozen well-trained seamen from one of his ships ... if it meant the packet could sail at once. Particularly in view of all the circumstances..."

"Oh no, I couldn't do that," Stevens protested. "Not sail with Navy men!"

"Why not?" Smith demanded. "I'll remind you the Post Office has hired your ship; that's why she's called 'His Majesty's packet brig *Lady Arabella*'. His Majesty has chartered her and pays the wages, Captain. And I am his agent. Yes, Mr Ramage, that seems a very good idea."

"I'll go on shore at once and see what I can arrange," Ramage said. "A dozen men, eh?"

Stevens nodded reluctantly.

"Topmen?"

"If you can get them."

"We can try!"

An hour later Ramage returned with a dozen seamen, led by Jackson, and ordered them to line up in front of Smith, who sat waiting at a small table under the quarterdeck awning with the muster book, a pen and ink in front of him. There was no sign of Captain Stevens.

Swiftly Smith questioned the men: full name, age and nationality; where born and when; rating. When he had written the details in the muster book he dismissed the men and turned to Ramage.

"Is there a receipt you want me to sign?"

Ramage shook his head. "No, there's no need," he assured Smith.

"Well, thanks very much; you've got me out of a very difficult situation. I'm sure Captain Stevens will be grateful, once he's given the matter some thought. Now I just have to muster the rest of the ship's company, and then you'll be under way."

With the muster complete, the dozen new men given their positions in the watch bill, and the searcher reporting lugubriously that he'd found nothing, Smith finally shook hands with the Captain, took his farewell of the passengers and climbed down into his boat.

Stevens then turned to the Mate: "Well, Fred, let's see what jail bait the Admiral has sent us."

His tone was so vicious that Ramage turned to see Stevens

watching him. Let's hope we make a fast passage, Ramage thought; Stevens is going to be poor company. Ramage took only a few more minutes to realize that Stevens was unsure of himself; that his crude behaviour might be due to nervousness. But why? Was he always like this? Was he rattled because of his dozen missing men? Plenty of questions, but no answers yet.

The *Lady Arabella*'s men were energetic but obviously poorly trained; so much so that the dozen former Tritons seemed out of place among them, moving faster although in a strange ship, anticipating the next order, working together – and keeping silent. At one point Ramage noticed Southwick beginning to fidget as some of the packetsmen began discussing Stevens' order to let fall the maintopsail.

By the time the mooring had been dropped and the brig was passing out of the harbour, Ramage had the impression that Stevens was too indulgent, treating the men as part of a large and wayward family of which he was a benevolent uncle. There was an easygoing atmosphere which should have made for a happy ship, albeit slack and badly handled, yet Ramage sensed undercurrents – glances between packetsmen, a wink here and a sly grin there, a contemptuous shrug of the shoulders and movement of eyebrows. There was nothing definite that he could point out to Yorke, but he was sure that Southwick had also noticed it.

Perhaps he was comparing the packet with all the ships he had served in? Such slack discipline would be fatal in a man-o'-war, where orders had to be given and obeyed instantly even though, in a gale or in battle, men might be killed. If they were allowed to debate orders, there would be occasions when they might be reluctant or slow to obey. Ramage remembered the *Triton* brig, both in battle and in the hurricane which had swept her masts by the board, leaving her a helpless hulk. No man had ever hesitated – nor had it ever occurred to Ramage that one might ... Was this, he wondered, why packets were being lost? Not because the packetsmen lacked courage, but simply because they lacked discipline – what one might call "fighting discipline"?

84

That evening as Yorke, Southwick and Ramage walked the deck for some exercise before dinner, the sun was just dipping below the horizon astern, while to the north lengthening shadows were turning the mountains of Jamaica a soft blue-grey. The *Lady Arabella* was making good time against a falling Trade wind, stretching south-east with a long tack and then taking a short tack inshore.

Southwick had been speculating if they would find an off-shore wind at nightfall, or whether it would back north-east as they rounded Morant Point, the easternmost tip of Jamaica, and head them as they began the long haul up to the north-east to make the Windward Passage.

The sea was already flattening; spray no longer flew up over the bow, and the wet, dark patches on the foot of the headsails were fading as the canvas dried. The brig's earlier sharp pitching had settled into an easier ridge-and-furrow motion, like the flight of a woodpecker.

Once round Morant Point, there would be no land until the brig began to pass through the Windward Passage between Cuba and Hispaniola, the western end of which looked on the chart like the head of a grotesque, open-mouthed fish trying to bite the eastern end of Cuba. Cape Dame Marie formed the lower lip; Cape Nicolas Mole the upper.

The three men walked in silence, turning inwards as they reached the taffrail and tramping forward until they were abreast the main shrouds, where once again they turned and headed aft.

There were two men at the helm, and Much was on watch. Captain Stevens had stayed in his cabin once the brig was clear of the harbour, and the only other seamen on deck, apart from a lookout, were those Much called up from below when the time came to tack.

Ramage sensed that Much was not popular with the men. Quietly spoken, small and grey-haired, the Mate gave orders clearly, without any hectoring or bullying, and Ramage was puzzled by the men's resentment – that seemed the only explanation of their attitude.

With the sun now below the horizon, Ramage felt a slight

chill in the air, and knew that in half an hour Much would be kept busy sail-trimming in a faltering breeze.

"Ah, Mr Wilson!" Yorke said suddenly, gesturing to the Army officer as he came on deck. "Join us in our promenade."

"Delighted, delighted. A mile before dinner; that's my rule. Stops me getting fat."

"Why not walk half a mile and eat half as much?" Ramage asked lightly.

Wilson shook his head and fell into step beside them. "Much obliged for the suggestion, but it don't work."

Intrigued that a flippant remark should be treated so seriously, Ramage asked why not.

"Food's not the problem," Wilson said. "Porter's my trouble. Have a disgusting passion for it. Drink too much and get fat. Not drunk, you know; just fat."

"Do you, by jove," Yorke said sympathetically. "Have you tried watering the porter?"

"Tastes ghastly, my dear fellow, absolutely ghastly. Tried everything. Best walk a mile."

The four men lapsed into silence for a few minutes, regularly turning and retracing their steps each time they reach the taffrail or main shrouds.

"Think we'll meet the Frogs?" Wilson asked suddenly.

Yorke glanced at Ramage, who said, "There's always a chance."

"More than a chance from what I hear."

"What have you heard?" Ramage asked politely.

"Post Office losing three packets out of four. Hardly any mail getting across the Atlantic. Chaos at the Horse Guards, so my colonel says: can't send reports to London or receive orders. Dam' funny, says I."

A whimsical thought struck Ramage. "I hope you're prepared if we do meet the French," he said lightly.

"Oh yes – make ready, present, fire! Yes, by Jingo, I'm ready; even brought m' own powder and shot."

Ramage had his answer, but the soldier's manner stopped the conversation. He was one of those unfortunate people combining a limited brain with a forceful manner who unwittingly

86

strangled almost any attempt at small-talk.

Yorke's silence showed he had reached the same conclusion, but he eventually devised an escape. After an inward turn that brought them facing forward again, he said, "Well, that's our mile for today – we're going to have to leave Captain Wilson to march on alone."

"Dam' short mile," Wilson commented cheerfully. "Mine's longer. I'll see you at dinner."

Down in their cabin, Ramage said, "That was brilliant!"

"What a bore the man is. But probably a good soldier, for all that."

"He might come in useful," Ramage muttered. "I wonder whether we should tell him more."

"I shouldn't bother," Yorke said. "Just wait until something happens. He needs ten seconds notice, no more and no less. More would worry him and less would get him fussed."

As Ramage opened a drawer and took out a clean shirt, Yorke said, "Do you think Smith will say anything to Sir Pilcher about the Tritons?"

Ramage shrugged his shoulders. "I'll try not to stay awake tonight worrying about it."

"I should hope not, but what did you tell Sir Pilcher?" Yorke persisted.

"Nothing. On the day he gave me my orders – and that was before the packet was sighted – I said I might need some men, and he agreed to me having a dozen former Tritons. Later he said I could use them in a packet if the Postmaster agreed."

"So...?"

"So when a dozen of the packetsmen overstayed their leave, you heard me suggest to the Postmaster that a dozen seamen should take their place."

"But you told Smith you were going on shore to ask Sir Pilcher for them!"

"No I didn't," Ramage said emphatically, "I was very careful about the words I used. I said to Smith, 'Might I suggest Sir Pilcher Skinner ... a dozen well-trained seamen from one of his ships ... if it meant the packet could sail at once. Particularly in view of all the circumstances.'"

"You seem to have learned that by heart."

"I had! The point is that I was careful not to suggest that anyone *asked* Sir Pilcher. I'd already arranged for the dozen Tritons to be sent on shore from the *Arrogant*, and given them their orders. Sir Pilcher had given permission for me to use them on board the packet – if Smith agreed. Well, Smith agreed, so I'm completely covered as far as Sir Pilcher is concerned, and frankly I don't give a damn about Smith. Anyway, he not only accepted the men but signed 'em on himself!"

"But the packetsmen – how could you be so sure they'd overstay their leave?"

"Seamen get drunk," Ramage said vaguely. "You know that perfectly well."

"Curious how Jackson and his men were waiting for you on the quay, though!"

Ramage glanced up in alarm. "How did you know that? You couldn't see from on board, could you?"

Yorke roared with laughter. "So you have a guilty conscience! No, that was just a guess. You fell for it, though."

Ramage began to untie his stock. "Don't play tricks like that," he said. "My nerves won't stand it!"

Yorke put a hand on his shoulder, his face now serious. "You take the most devilish risks at times. You're lucky to have people like Jackson and Southwick." He paused for a moment. "And Stafford and Rossi and Maxton ... and Bowen ... the whole damned lot, come to think of it. Do you realize those men would do anything for you, and damn the consequences?"

Ramage looked sheepish. "I suppose they would – I've never thought about it."

"You should," Yorke said, a harshness creeping into his voice. "You should, in case one day you ask too much."

"They've all risked their lives half a dozen times for me," Ramage said defensively. "You can't ask more than that."

Yorke shook his head. "You're wrong. You're asking more if you ask an honest man to lie on oath."

"We've thirty-five days or more to argue that point, so leave it for now," Ramage said, pulling off his shirt. Neither man

88

spoke again as they changed their clothes.

When they went through to the saloon a few minutes after the gong had sounded for dinner and joined Bowen, Southwick and Wilson, they found only five places had been set. Mr Much was on watch, the steward said; Mr Farrell, the surgeon, was ill in his bunk, and Captain Stevens always dined alone in his own cabin.

Chapter
Eight

When the *Lady Arabella* finally reached the western end of Hispaniola and beat into Cape Nicolas Mole to make her one stop before stretching north into the Atlantic, there was only one frigate at anchor. While the mail was being brought out, Captain Stevens had himself rowed over to her, returning half an hour later to announce to no one in particular that she had been patrolling the Windward Passage and as far out as Great Inagua for the past two weeks without sighting any privateers. However, he said, there were the usual rowing galleys skulking in and out of the inlets round the coast, waiting to catch someone in a calm, so they had better keep whistling for a good wind.

Within three hours of arriving the packet was under way again, heading north through the Windward Passage to pass the island of Great Inagua before reaching out into the Atlantic. Stevens chose the difficult Crooked Island Passage rather than tackle the Caicos Passage, which usually turned into a beat dead to windward in the teeth of the Trades.

The route was a fitting one for a ship leaving the Caribbean, Ramage thought to himself, combining all the beauty of the Bahamas with most of its dangers. As the packet beat her way through, zigzagging against a brisk breeze blowing out of an almost garishly blue sky, the deep mauve of the ocean turned light blue near any of the many banks before changing to dark green over a rocky bottom or light green over sand. Brown patches warned of rocks with only a fathom or so over them;

90

brown with yellowish tinges told of coral reefs.

Flying fish came up as silver darts to skim a few inches above the sea, rising over crests and dropping into troughs with effortless grace and rhythm; occasionally a shoal of small fish glittered in the bright sun as they leapt out of the water for a few moments in a desperate attempt to escape from some darting predator. What seemed to be a line of dark bottles on top of a low sandy cay suddenly moved as pelicans, drying themselves in the sun, decided that the packet frightened them and hoisted themselves into the air at the end of a long, ungainly run.

The islands themselves varied from Great Inagua, fringed with reefs, low and flat except for a few hills, and the home of pink flamingoes, to Crooked and Acklins Islands, forming a great bight with rolling hills and growing so many herbs that Columbus had referred to them as "the fragrant islands".

Everyone on board the *Lady Arabella* knew that once the last of the Bahama Islands dropped below the horizon there would be no more land to sight until the packet reached the chops of the Channel, more than three thousand five hundred miles to the north-east.

Up forward, the dozen Tritons were beginning to settle in. The packetsmen's initial resentment that a dozen of their shipmates had been left behind in Kingston was beginning to wear off – or, rather, was being aimed at Captain Stevens and the Mate.

Just before supper on the fifth day out from Cape Nicolas Mole, Jackson, Stafford and Rossi were sitting on the foredeck with one of the packetsmen.

Stafford said: "You was born in London."

The man grinned. "Islington. Me dad took me down to Falmouth when I were a nipper."

"Thought so," Stafford said. "See, Jacko, I recognized 'is accent."

"So did I," Jackson said ironically. "How do you like Falmouth, Eames?"

"Well enough. Busy when a packet arrives or sails, and nice and quiet the rest of the time."

"How long have you been in the *Arabella*?"

"Just this voyage. I change about."

The idea of changing ships at will was so strange to a Royal Navy man that Stafford said, "Just think of that! Why change, though?"

Eames shrugged his shoulders. "I squeeze another voyage into the year."

"How so?" Jackson asked.

"Well, the *Arabella*'s hard put to make three round voyages in a year, counting docking time, repairs and so on. I like to make four."

"Why? Don't you get paid just the same when she's docked?"

Eames avoided Jackson's eyes. "Oh yes, we get paid just the same. It's just that some of us like the hot weather." He gave a little giggle. "And all the sunshine makes the money grow."

Jackson looked puzzled. "Doesn't make mine grow," he grumbled.

"Ah," Eames said knowingly, "you've got to know what to plant – aye, and where to reap."

"I'm a sailor, not a farmer!"

"Ah," Eames said. "An' that's the difference!"

A call for all hands stopped Jackson asking him any more questions, and when Stafford grumbled later, Jackson said quietly, "We don't have to rush things; it'll be a month before we get back to England."

While Jackson and Stafford talked with the packetsman, Ramage was making his first visit to Captain Stevens' cabin. Although they had met on deck several times and chatted briefly about the weather or the day's run, Stevens had ignored the passengers until, five days out from the Mole, he invited Ramage to his cabin for a drink before dinner.

"My apologies for not asking you sooner," he said, gesturing to a small settee built athwartships against a bulkhead. "Here, let's push that box out of the way so there's more room for your feet."

The box was one of two small wooden crates crudely made of unpainted wood, the heads of the nails already rusting, and from the ease with which Stevens moved it, its contents were light. As if guessing his thoughts, Stevens explained: "Tobacco – some really choice Jamaica leaf. I usually bring a few pounds back for a friend that appreciates it. Have to be careful where I stow it because it absorbs the smell of things like spice – or bilgewater!"

"Now," he said, opening a locker to reveal a row of bottles sitting snugly in a fitted rack, "What's your pleasure? Whisky, rum or gin – and I still have some fresh limes left."

With the drinks poured, Stevens sat back comfortably in his chair. The cabin was fitted out in the same dark red used throughout the rest of the accommodation, but Ramage noted that the joinery had been done with great skill and the mahogany carefully selected to make the best use of the grain pattern.

"I was 'pologizing for not asking you along sooner," Stevens said conversationally. "Fact is, I always find getting clear o' the Windward Passage a great worry these days. Always was a worry, with those currents setting right across the banks, but nowadays, with the privateers..." He shrugged his shoulders expressively.

"We were lucky," Ramage said noncommittally, puzzled by Stevens' curious mixture of deference and apology.

"We were, too; I don't remember when I last came through without sighting a sail and having to make a bolt for it."

"Always French privateers?"

"Ah, I wouldn't be knowing," Stevens said smoothly, "I never wait to find out!"

"I hear Falmouth has been unlucky lately."

"Aye, it's been a disastrous twelve month," Stevens said, the "a" broadening with his Cornish burr.

"But you've been lucky so far."

"Depends what you call lucky. I've been taken twice in three years, if you call that luck."

"But –" Ramage stopped, waving his hand round the cabin to indicate the ship.

Stevens smiled patiently. "The first time, the Frenchies exchanged me and m'crew, and the agent in Falmouth – I suppose it was really the gennelmen in Lombard Street – chartered another ship for me while a new one was a'building. Got taken a second time – towards the end of the third voyage in the chartered ship – and exchanged again. After that I stood by at the yard until the new ship was ready – and this is the lady."

"Nice ship," Ramage said politely.

"Nice enough," Stevens said cautiously. "Me and the builders are having a falling out, though – a little matter of some bad wood they slipped in while I was a prisoner." He finished the rum in his glass and glanced up at Ramage. "No need to mention that to anyone, mind you, else the Inspector at Falmouth will want me to start rebuilding the ship."

"Nothing serious, then," Ramage said casually.

"No, just a bit o' soft wood here and there in the counter," Stevens said equally casually but putting down his glass in a way that showed that was all he had to say on the subject.

"You've managed to keep the same ship's company through all this?"

"Almost. Fred Much is still the Mate, and Farrell's the surgeon. Same Master, but he stayed behind sick for this voyage, and the same bosun. A few of the seamen shift about."

"You're lucky to be exchanged all together," Ramage commented. "And so quickly."

"Aye. Reckon the Frenchies know we b'aint fighting men; not like you Navy fellows."

"You were homeward-bound both times?"

Stevens nodded. " 'Bout four hundred miles out."

"How do they treat prisoners?"

"Mustn't grumble. Never got beyond Verdun – that's the big prison depot. Let out on parole. Lodged with the same family both times."

"Most of the packetsmen get sent to Verdun?" Ramage asked.

Stevens nodded. With a curious mixture of pride and apology he said, "Fact is, packetsmen get special treatment. Verdun's got plenty of prisoners from merchant ships who've been there three or four years. Plenty of packetsmen, too; I met five other commanders, the last time. We were all exchanged together."

"Do you have to pay the French a ransom?"

Stevens shook his head, then said, "Leastways, the commanders don't. Maybe the Post Office does, though I never heard tell of it."

Ramage felt cramp beginning in one leg but the second box prevented him from straightening out. Stevens jumped up immediately. "Here, let me shift it out of your road."

As he rubbed the knotted muscles, Ramage noticed that the second box was heavier than the first, and Stevens grunted as he pushed and tugged at it.

"A few presents for the folk at home," he explained as they both sat down. "And something for the troachers, too."

"Troachers?"

"You a Cornishman and you don't know troachers?" Stevens was laughing but as if to avoid more questioning he picked up Ramage's half-empty glass. "This is looking a bit stretched; I'll freshen the nip." From then on, Stevens talked only of the Caribbean, and Ramage knew the evening would yield little else of interest.

In the saloon, Bowen had finally persuaded the *Arabella*'s surgeon, Farrell, to play chess. Yorke and Southwick sat round the table watching as the two men placed the pieces on the board. After five moves it was obvious that Bowen had at last found an opponent worthy of him.

"You play often?" Bowen asked.

Farrell shook his head. "Last time was in prison."

"Prison?" exclaimed Southwick before he could stop himself.

"Oh – a French one!" Farrell said. "As a prisoner of war. I was out on parole, really."

"What's it like?" Yorke asked sympathetically. "Being a prisoner, I mean."

Farrell moved a pawn before answering.

"Depends which depot they take you to. Some are worse than others. I've been lucky."

"How long before you were exchanged?"

"Six weeks the first time, nine the next."

"Oh – you've been taken twice?"

"Yes – with Captain Stevens both times."

"Were the casualties heavy when the privateers attacked?" Bowen said with apparently clinical interest.

Farrell shook his head. "It's your move," he said pointedly. "We've got weeks to talk and weeks to play chess. Let's not be doing both at once."

Late that night, sitting on their bunks in the darkness, Ramage and Yorke compared notes. When Ramage said that Stevens had been captured twice, Yorke commented, "The surgeon was with him. I don't think there were many casualties either time. Farrell dodged the question when Bowen asked him."

"I'm beginning to think the story is the same for all the packets – capture, exchange, new ship ... Lucky that the French exchange the whole ship's company, instead of a few men at a time."

"Is that usual?" Yorke asked.

"It seems so for packetsmen. For the Navy it's certainly different – a single British lieutenant against a French one, and so on."

Yorke rubbed his chin miserably. "The fact is, we don't know much more than the day we left Kingston."

"I didn't expect we should," Ramage said. "We shan't find out anything important until a privateer's masts lift over the horizon!"

"That reminds me, I haven't the faintest idea what the French do about exchanging passengers," Yorke said ruefully. "I'm beginning to regret my enthusiasm: I should have sailed in the next convoy."

"Nine weeks to wait."

"Better wait in Kingston than a French prison."

"Cheer up," Ramage said. "You needn't worry about privateers for another two or three weeks."

"Oh!" Yorke exclaimed. "Well, you might have told me sooner: ever since we dropped the Bahamas astern I've been lying awake in my bunk just fretting..."

"Sorry – I've only just worked it out for certain."

"Worked out what?"

"That most of the homeward-bound packets *must* be taken towards the end of the voyage."

"Why so certain now? I know we suspected it, even though Lord Auckland forgot to mention it, but..."

"Both times Stevens was captured on the way back and taken to the depot at Verdun and paroled. The last time he met five other packet commanders. They all seem to end up at Verdun. If they'd been taken near the Caribbean they'd have ended up in Guadeloupe."

Both men stretched out on their bunks, and as Ramage pulled the sheet over himself he began to feel depressed. He knew that, despite what he had told Yorke, he had been hoping to hear or see something on board the *Arabella* that would transform all the disconnected facts dancing around in his mind into a regular pattern, like cementing chips of coloured marble into a mosaic. Stevens' reference to Verdun only confirmed what he had already guessed. Yet there was something odd about the way Stevens referred to being captured. Was there a hint of evasiveness? Was Stevens secretly ashamed of something and afraid that if he said too much he would reveal a guilty secret?

There was a gentle tapping at the door. Quickly he slid off the bunk and turned the handle.

"Jackson, sir," a voice whispered.

"Come in, I'd given you up!"

A moment later the American was in the cabin, shutting the door silently behind him.

"Mr Yorke's awake in the other bunk."

"Evening, sir," the American said. "Is it–?"

"Don't worry," Ramage assured him. "Mr Yorke and I have just been talking about it. Have you–"

"Sorry, sir, I'm really reporting that I've got nothing interesting to report. Just one or two odd things..."

"Out with them!"

"Well, most of the men stay in the same ship. But although each packet makes three round voyages to Jamaica in a year at the most, some of the men change ships to get in an extra voyage."

"Why?" Ramage asked.

"Haven't been able to find out yet, sir; the chap I talked to was very mysterious. But I'll wager he makes a lot of money out of it."

"Ventures," Yorke whispered. "The more you venture, the more you gain!"

"Ventures!" Jackson repeated, clearly angry with himself. "That's what the fellow must have meant when he said he made the extra voyage because he liked the sunshine – 'it made the money grow'!"

Slowly the *Lady Arabella* worked her way to the north-east. The hour glass was turned regularly, the log was hove twice a day and the ship's speed noted along with the courses steered. Stevens made a great ritual of the noon sight – apparently he had turned it into something of a mystic rite which normally impressed the passengers. The *Lady Arabella* crossed the invisible line of latitude at 23 degrees 27 minutes, marking the Tropic of Cancer, the northern boundary of the Tropics, and each day the temperature continued to drop slightly.

The drop was almost imperceptible; one night Ramage, accustomed to sleeping naked on his bunk to keep cool, wished he had a sheet to cover him; a couple of nights later he used it. Five days later he thought of a blanket, and the very next night pulled it over himself for an hour or so round three o'clock in the morning. That day the heavy canvas awning which had sheltered the after deck from the scorching sun of the Tropics was finally taken down, rolled up and stowed below.

The only thing that did not change was the diet: the food the passengers had provided for themselves was not very varied, since there had been little time to look around, and the packet's cook was neither skilled nor imaginative enough to do anything more than boil or roast whatever he was given. The fruit lasted well: limes and oranges were shrivelling but still yielding juice after two weeks; stalks of bananas cut at varying stages of greenness were ripening in succession.

Like the fruit, the chess contest was ripening. Playing against a tougher opponent had sharpened Bowen's skill; now Farrell

98

had to fight hard for his increasingly rare victories. But more and more Bowen preferred to play against Southwick, with the result that Farrell was becoming remote. It was difficult to decide whether the passengers unconsciously edged him out of their circle or he withdrew of his own accord, but the reason was simple enough: he was an appallingly bad loser.

Each defeat at Bowen's hand led to Farrell holding an hour's inquest on the game: an hour spent describing and justifying, in almost excruciating detail, why he had made various moves. In the end, it seemed to Ramage, Farrell was always satisfied that he had proved he could only have lost because Bowen had been guilty of duplicity, if not of actually moving the pieces while Farrell was not looking.

The man's behaviour was inexplicable because Ramage could not credit that anyone could take a game of chess – or any game, for that matter – so seriously. He once commented to Yorke that if one got down to Farrell's level, the game became a business. Yorke pointed out that there Farrell had failed: from the beginning, despite cajoling and sneers, Bowen had refused to play for money. Farrell's disappointment had been obvious – at first, anyway, until Bowen found his stride and began to win more often than he drew or lost.

For Ramage much of the tedium of the voyage was removed because it gave him a chance of making a leisurely study of the personalities of several different men – Farrell, Captain Henry Wilson, Mr Much the Mate and his son Our Ned. Stevens was not worth much effort: he was a typical close man who, having made a little money, regarded the world with suspicion and divided it into two sections – the part which could make him further profit, and the part which might cost him money.

The sea, ships and seamanship had very little interest for Stevens, and far too much was left to the Mate. Stevens rarely seemed to reach any decision in the instinctive way of a true seaman: when he gave the order to reef, for instance, Ramage felt that he was applying some formula, or dredging his memory for a precedent. Yorke finally summed up Stevens: "He's a greedy man who long ago reckoned that owning and running a Post Office packet would make the most money in the shortest possible time. That's why he's not running a lead mine or a rope walk in Bridport."

The Mate's son, Our Ned, was the type of young man that, if he was serving in a ship commanded by Ramage, would have been transferred at the first opportunity. He was small and slim; his face was long and narrow with the eyes close together, two small brown buttons which had a tendency to glance uneasily from side to side. Perhaps it was just the shape of his mouth, but to Ramage he always seemed to be smirking secretly when he spoke to anyone: as though he was the possessor of some secret, or the speaker was being laughed at by people standing behind him. But for all that, he was probably the most useful man in the packet's crew. He knew nearly as much as his father – whom he treated alternately with patient affection and near-mutinous derision.

The Mate was a lonely man who lived in a private world; a world limited to the hull, sails, masts and spars of the *Lady Arabella* and occasionally lit by Our Ned. It was hard to define the Captain's attitude towards him – at various times Ramage had seen signs of irritation, awe, fear and respect. The Mate's attitude towards Captain Stevens was harder to discover because he spoke rarely, but both Ramage and Yorke agreed that it was based on contempt. It was as though Stevens had some guilty secret which the Mate knew about, disapproved of, but could do nothing to change.

Just as the Mate's world was the ship, Captain Wilson's world was the Army and, Ramage thought, at times just the barrack square. During every waking moment Wilson's life was drill and manoeuvre: his every remark was littered with military expressions. For Wilson nothing turned, it wheeled; nothing was passed, it was outflanked. Distance was range; going on deck for fresh air was making a sortie. Yet the blond-moustached captain had a clear if limited brain, even though he tended to see problems with the same deceptive clarity as the instructions in a drill book: if the enemy is behind that hill, you outflank him by this manoeuvre.

Once clear of the Tropics, the *Lady Arabella* ran into ten days of light, variable winds in which the packet tacked and wore two or three times an hour in order to steer not just in the direction they wanted to go but to avoid heading back towards the Bahamas.

After the variables came a gale and a sudden drop in temperature. It lasted five days, and the five passengers spent most of the time in the saloon playing cards or chess, or else lying in their bunks reading, wedged in by pillows and cushions against the rolling of the ship that tried to pitch them out.

On the afternoon of the last day, as the cloud began to break up and the wind to lessen, Yorke tossed aside the book he was reading and sat up in his bunk.

"You don't fret much about privateers these days."

"I'm taking some leave," Ramage said. "It expires in a couple of days' time."

"Why then?"

"I think we'll find we have to start watching for privateers from then on."

"Two days, eh?" Yorke said slowly. "Neither one nor six, but two. I admire your precision."

Ramage grinned. "Geography. I reckon the majority of privateers from St Malo, Rochefort, Barfleur and such ports patrol no farther out than six hundred miles."

"Why that magic figure?"

"Well, each prize they take must be sailed back to France with only a small prize crew who have to dodge British patrols – and British privateers, too. They'd be lucky to average five knots. Six hundred miles – five days' sailing – seems far enough!"

Yorke waved a hand in agreement. "I'm glad you think like a privateersman!"

"I wish I could: our necks might depend on it!"

"They do, too. Tell me, now we've been on board nearly a month, d'you think this was the best way of carrying out your orders?"

Ramage made a face. He'd spent many a sleepless hour in his bunk asking himself that question. "Too early – or too late – to say. Ask me again as we pick up the mooring in Falmouth."

"That's how I feel," Yorke said ruefully.

"So far," Ramage admitted, "even if we don't know much more than we did in Kingston, I'm still convinced the only way anyone will ever find the answer is to be on board a packet."

"I wonder," Yorke mused. "One privateer capturing one packet and sending her in with a prize crew – what can that really tell you? It's happened twenty or thirty times already and the Post Office discovered nothing!"

"If I knew, obviously I wouldn't be here," Ramage said briskly. "But we know what to look for and what questions to ask. The gentlemen in Lombard Street are land animals. They can only make guesses."

"Are the French really interested in the mails?" Yorke persisted. "Are they trying to get hold of them? Cut communications, perhaps?"

"No. I've thought a lot about that," Ramage said, "but the commanders all report sinking the mails before surrendering. Although I can't imagine them saying otherwise, I believe them. If not, we get into the realms of treachery, and it's too widespread for that. I doubt if the French have got one bag of mails so far. Anyway, if they were trying to cut communications, would they rely on privateers? I doubt it."

"Then I can't understand why the French bother with packets: no cargo to sell; just the hull."

"A fine hull, though: fast and well built. Just the sort of ship to fit out in St Malo and send to sea again as a privateer!"

"Yes, but not a very profitable capture – compared with the value of cargoes. I've carried cargoes in the *Topaz* worth ten times what the ship was insured for."

"Agreed, agreed," Ramage said. "But you're forgetting the most important thing: obviously a privateer takes what comes along: one day it's a *Topaz* worth twenty-five thousand pounds with her cargo, the next day it's the *Lady Arabella* worth – how much? Six thousand pounds?"

"You could build her for that. But, my friend, you're also forgetting something."

"And that is?"

"That twelve months or so ago the packet losses suddenly

increased by several hundred per cent, while the losses of merchantmen stayed the same."

Ramage shook his head. "No, I haven't forgotten. That's the puzzle. That's why we're passengers in the *Lady Arabella*!"

Chapter
Nine

Stafford looked at the bags of spices, picked one up, shook it and then sniffed. "Nutmeg, eh? Yer mean to tell me there's money in a bag o' nutmegs, Wally?"

The seaman nodded. "Cost me two shilluns in the Windward Islands, they did. I'll get five pound in Falmouth – mebbe ten if I give 'em to the troachers."

"Poachers?" Stafford exclaimed.

"No – troachers. They're the old women who take our stuff to sell out in the villages. They go from house to house. Probably get a shillun each for nutmegs." He fondled the bag lovingly. "Troachers is best for things like spices. The profit comes in selling 'em one at a time."

"What about rum?" Jackson asked.

"Oh, merchants is best for likker."

"Why's that? Why not house to house?"

"Merchants are more used to arrangin'," the seaman said vaguely.

"Arranging?"

"With the Customs, an' all that sort of thing."

"All helps pay the rent," Jackson said. "Must double your pay."

"*Double* it?" the seaman exclaimed indignantly. "You've got a pretty daft idea of how much we get paid! That lot there" – he waved at the bags of spices – "and me drop of rum will make the same as five years' pay. An' me outward freight's already made me that – with the money coming home safe in the next convoy from Jamaica."

"Supposing the *Arabella* is taken?" Jackson asked.

"Don't matter," the seaman said airily. "All this is insured."

"You say a packetsman's pay is bad?" Stafford asked.

"Well – t'aint as bad as what you chaps get, but it's bad enough. The Captain gets only eight pounds a month."

"Pore fellah," Stafford said sarcastically. "But a couple of 'undred pounds of ventures will help – he carries ventures, I suppose?"

The seaman nodded. "And we carry passengers, too. You've seen 'em. Fifty guineas each – that's what they've paid the Captain. Clear profit for the skipper – stands to reason!"

"My 'eart bleeds for you pore men," Stafford said sourly, trying to provoke the seaman.

"We take risks, though," the seaman said defensively. "Look how many packets have been lost in the last year."

"Think how many of the King's ships have been lost, too," Jackson said, "and they have to stand and fight."

"Well, we have to run from the Frenchies – that's orders from Lombard Street," the seaman said angrily. "We're just carrying the mails: we ain't men-o'-war – neither us nor the packets."

"Easy now," Jackson said soothingly, "no one's blaming you; we're just talking. Come on, I'll help you pack up these spices again. Thanks for showing us. We don't have to worry about the strange smell now!"

That night, Jackson slid into Ramage's cabin and reported the conversation.

"Making a profit equal to five years' pay?" Ramage repeated incredulously.

"That's what he said, sir. And that's on this venture alone. He's already made that on the one he took out, and the money goes home on the next convoy."

"But what does he get paid? More than our seamen, anyway. Say a pound a month. Five years' pay is –"

"Sixty pounds," Yorke said in the darkness. "So his profit is one hundred and twenty pounds on a round trip – providing he gets the inward-bound venture back safely."

"Doesn't matter, sir," Jackson said. "It's insured."

"The venture is?" Yorke asked sharply.

"So the fellow said."

"Is this seaman the same chap that told you about making four voyages a year?"

"The same, sir."

Yorke sighed. "And I don't suppose he can read or write..."

"He can't," Jackson said glumly, guessing the point Yorke was going to make.

"He can't, eh? Well, let's not forget he's making four hundred and eighty pounds a year ... How does that compare with the Royal Navy, Nicholas?"

Ramage thought for a moment. "A third less than the captain of a first-rate like the *Victory* or the *Ville de Paris*, and twice as much as the master," he said. "Exactly five times as much as Southwick was paid as master of the *Triton* brig," he added bitterly.

"Not bad for a man who can't read or write," Yorke said ironically.

"Well, sir," Jackson said, "I'd better be getting back before anyone spots my hammock is empty."

After the American left the cabin, Yorke said softly to himself, "An assured market, free freight and no risk: a merchant's dream, my dear Nicholas, and one that comes true only for seamen in a Post Office packet!"

"Not just the seamen," Ramage said. "What about the mate and the captain? I wonder how much they venture?"

"Well, the captain gets paid eight times as much as a seaman – that's about the figure, I think – and we can be sure he ventures in proportion, although he only makes three voyages a year. Eight times the seaman's £480 – hmm, that's £3,840, which is only £160 less than the Prime Minister is paid."

"And £840 a year more than the First Lord of the Admiralty," Ramage added.

"And no risk!" Yorke said. "That's the beauty of it."

"You're envious of the insurance," Ramage said lightly, trying to erase the bitterness in his mind.

"I most certainly am! These packetsmen are backing a horse so that *they* win whether the horse wins, loses or drops dead."

Suddenly Ramage felt goose-pimples spreading over his body in the darkness. The water was swilling past outside the hull; the whole ship was creaking, as it had done since it rounded the east end of Jamaica. But, for the first time, he did not hear it. He heard only his heart beating, and the faint echo of Yorke's voice saying: "... *whether the horse wins, loses or drops dead.*"

It was absurd, but it had all the beauty of a simple plan. After a few minutes he relaxed and began to feel sleepy.

Next morning Ramage went up on deck to find seamen checking over the *Lady Arabella*'s storm canvas, and was reminded that in Europe it was now halfway between autumn and winter. Curious how one never referred to winter and summer in the Tropics, only the hurricane and the dry season. Hurricane season if you were a sailor, rainy season if a soldier.

He shivered. The temperature was still dropping steadily, like water from a leaking roof: the days when the thermometer moved leisurely between eighty and eighty-five degrees were memories. In a week he would be thankful if it went above sixty-five. Sixty-five! In the Caribbean the *water* temperature rarely dropped below eighty...

Yorke joined him standing aft at the taffrail, watching the *Lady Arabella*'s wake as she dipped and lifted her way over the swell waves. The sky was overcast and Stevens had not been able to get a sight the previous day. With the ship close-hauled there was enough wind to ensure that the helmsmen could not overhear their conversation.

Yorke prodded one of the two brass 9-pounder stern-chase guns with all the hard-bitten contempt of a horse coper. "We need a lot more of these 'Post Office guns'!"

"Instead we have those miserable 4-pounders..." Ramage gestured to the two guns each side. "Punt guns at best. Useful against wild duck."

"How can we fight?" Yorke asked. "Judging by the losses, we aren't fast enough to run, so the point is of more than academic interest now!"

107

"If we fight," and Ramage purposely emphasized the first word, "we just keep steering away from a privateer: keep her astern and bang away with these 9-pounders. They should carry farther than a privateer's bow-chasers. And we'd hope she hadn't any long 9-pounders on her broadside."

"It'd be suicide to let her get a broadside into us," Yorke commented.

Ramage nodded. "Calls for some smart tacking and wearing! Still, there might be a heavy sea running."

Yet like most events at sea, Ramage mused, it was impossible to dogmatize. Firing a broadside from a heavily rolling ship could be like shooting at snipe from the back of a runaway horse, yet a well-trained and cool gun's crew firing on the broadside would probably do more damage than a badly trained, excitable crew firing a stern-chase gun in the same conditions.

But for all that a couple of well-served stern-chase guns – particularly these long-barrelled "Post Office guns" – were like a kick from a mule's hind legs: very effective as long as the ship could keep stern-on to the enemy target. And that in turn meant the enemy (unless she had a good margin of speed) could only approach bow-on, and none of her broadside guns could be brought to bear.

If the enemy had a good margin of speed she could of course approach from astern and then range alongside; if only a slight margin she could suddenly turn away at the last moment, firing her broadside guns in turn as they bore. He knew that was what a large privateer would probably try to do to the *Lady Arabella*. It required skilful gunnery: the enemy gunners would see the target in their sights for only a second or two as their ship swung. On the other hand, every shot that hit was potentially more effective because a ship's transom and bow were very vulnerable compared with her sides: a shot smashing through it could sweep the whole length of the ship below deck, possibly damaging the rudder, steering gear or the masts below deck. Raking a ship, firing into her end on, whether through the transom or bow, was the most destructive method of attack.

108

Presumably that was why the Post Office equipped each packet with two 9-pounders as stern-chase guns: given the "turn and run" instructions, they were the best defence for a fleeing packet, since she could rake her pursuer.

Although the long barrels of the 9-pounders gave them the extra range, their very length and weight made them less useful as broadside guns because they were more difficult to handle: apart from the extra weight, they had to be run in farther so the men could get to the muzzle for sponging and loading. That in turn meant more room was needed, and the gun had to be hauled farther to run it out again ready to fire. All this meant more time.

Ramage guessed that in specifying long guns for stern-chase, the Post Office was gambling that any ship attacking a packet was likely to be a privateer, and the average privateer (they hoped) would be slower and armed with more but smaller guns, since privateers favoured close-range action. Smaller guns with shorter barrels certainly meant much less range, but they also meant easier handling, a higher rate of fire and more grape and canister shot fired into the victim. For the weight of one of the long 9-pounders, a privateer could probably fit a couple of 4-pounders. More than double the rate of fire but perhaps half the range ... That was why a highwayman preferred a brace of pistols, with a range of only a few paces, rather than a musket that could bowl a horse over at fifty yards: the highwayman's potential victim would be in a carriage only a few feet away.

Ramage knew only too well that privateer tactics were completely different from usual ship-to-ship actions: two lines of battle ships or frigates would fight it out with broadsides, and usually one would try to board the other only after she was badly damaged.

But privateers carried very large crews: one the size of the *Lady Arabella* would have more than a hundred men on board. Nor were they ordinary men: instead of being paid wages they were usually on a "share-of-the-profits" basis. At worst they were licensed pirates, regarding prisoners as an inconvenient nuisance. At best – well, little better than pirates.

All too often one heard of a privateer running up the "bloody flag", the red flag that meant they would give no quarter; no prisoners would be taken, and the wounded would be slaughtered and tossed over the side with the men already killed. Few ships of war showed any mercy to a privateer: to avoid one escaping, a ship of war would not hesitate to "give her the stem", ramming the vessel to make sure of sinking her.

"Do you think Stevens ever exercises his guns' crews?" Yorke asked quietly.

Ramage shook his head. "We know he hasn't this voyage. I'll tell Jackson to find out."

That night, as the two men sat in their cabin after supper, Yorke came back to the subject. "If we meet a privateer...?"

Ramage sighed: it was a question he had been turning over in his mind since before they left Kingston, and Yorke had not missed the significance of his earlier reference to "*If* we fight..." Still, there was no point in keeping his thoughts secret. "I can't decide."

"You mean you won't fight?"

"Well," said Ramage carefully, "I'm trying to leave the welfare and safety of you and our splendid soldier friend out of the calculation..."

"Agreed, and no ill feelings."

"Thanks," Ramage said wryly. "The reason is simply that my orders are to find the cause and halt the losses."

"I know that!" Yorke did not try to keep the impatience out of his voice.

"Well, can you tell me the point at which I'll find the 'cause'? What happens on board when a packet is attacked by a privateer—"

"She surrenders," Yorke interrupted. "Even the Post Office knows that much!"

"Maybe she does. Maybe she tries to escape. Maybe she's boarded. Maybe the privateers shoot the rigging away. We don't know for sure."

"There are the reports of the commanders who were captured and exchanged."

"Oh yes – but were they speaking the truth? Although we

110

haven't seen any of the reports, we've no reason to think they weren't – but we don't know for sure."

"What's all this to do with whether or not we fight?" Yorke demanded impatiently.

"The short answer is, the other packets didn't have three extra officers – five if we include you and the gallant Captain Wilson – and a dozen well-trained seamen from one of the King's ships."

"Perhaps that's why they were captured!"

"Exactly. And that's why I'm damned if I know whether we'll fight or not. If we drive off a privateer, what will we find out about the 'cause'? We might get a completely distorted picture. So far we can only guess at what's involved – you once said it must be magic! Well, our very presence – helping with the fighting, I mean – might stop the magic working."

"It might also stop the *Arabella* being captured – I've no wish to have my throat cut by a privateersman."

"Leaving aside the sanctity of your throat for a moment, isn't that the point? If I'm going to find the answer, wouldn't it be best to let Stevens do what he'd do if we weren't here? And we watch?"

"Who," Yorke said with heavy sarcasm, "reports your finding to My Lords Commissioners of the Admiralty after the privateersmen have cut your throat?"

"They haven't cut packetsmen's throats, but anyway I've gone over all that so many times – lying here early in the morning, while you snore in your bunk..."

"Do you want my advice?"

"No," Ramage said emphatically. "Most certainly not; your advice would coincide with what I'd like to do. And what I'd *like* to do would probably stop me carrying out my orders."

"You think I'm going to advise fighting?"

"Aren't you?"

"No. I speak with all the wisdom culled from forebears who have spent a thousand years soaking up good whisky and eating tons of porridge."

"Speak before those ancient Scots turn in their graves!"

"My advice coincides with what you've decided without realizing it: not to make up your mind until we meet a privateer. Her size, the weather, her position, the way Stevens and his men react: all these will affect the issue."

Ramage nodded. "I've been telling myself I'm afraid of a definite decision, but–"

"That *is* making a definite decision," Yorke interrupted. "You've decided that the proper decision can't be made until the situation occurs. Until a privateer attacks, in other words. That's definite enough!"

"I'm blaming myself for letting you risk your neck. You should have waited for the convoy."

"Thanks," Yorke said sourly. "I get scared from time to time, but the fact is I came in the hope of seeing some action. Can you imagine how boring it is commanding a merchantman in a convoy? Leading ship in the fifth column ... two cables from the ship on either side, one cable from the next astern ... week after week ... And planters and their wives as passengers, the men sodden with rum and quarrelsome by suppertime and the women frozen in embarrassment..."

"At least you have the company of frozen women. In a ship of war..." Ramage said unsympathetically.

"What have you told Southwick and Bowen?"

"About an attack? Nothing so far."

"Supposing it doesn't happen?" Yorke asked, beginning to undress and pulling his nightshirt from under the pillow. "Just to cheer ourselves up!"

"Well, when we get to Falmouth I see you into the London carriage, and sail again in the next packet for Jamaica."

"Stevens seems fairly cheerful," Yorke said casually. "At least, he isn't as worried as I'd have expected."

"No, I'd be happier if he was more worried." And that, Ramage thought, is something I've only just realized. All the packetsmen on board the *Lady Arabella* know the odds are heavily against them reaching Falmouth safely, yet only Much seems at all worried. And only Much is unpopular ... Impossible to think why there should be any relationship between the two facts, yet the *Lady Arabella* seems to be a ship full of contradictions.

"I'm sleepy!" said Yorke. "If this weather holds, we should be in Falmouth a week from today."

"Or St Malo," Ramage said soberly. "It might be an idea to sew some guineas into the padding of our coats – just in case. Living out on parole is probably expensive..."

"Parole!" Yorke sniffed. "They'll never allow *you* parole! For all the trouble you've caused the French so far, it wouldn't surprise me if they've put a price on your head!"

Chapter Ten

On the following Sunday, when Stevens told the passengers in his usual abrupt manner that there would be Divine Service at eleven o'clock, Ramage had the impression that Sundays would be ignored if Stevens had his way, but that the Mate forced him to conform.

Certainly at the services on the previous Sundays, Mr Fred Much had read the lesson with all the fervour of a revivalist preacher and sung the hymns with a loud and surprisingly good tenor voice. Our Ned also had a good voice, but after watching the Mate's son for a few minutes at the first service, Ramage was reminded of the word unctuous.

Ramage glanced at the mirror and gave his stock an impatient twitch. It annoyed him to have to change into uniform but Southwick and Wilson made a point of it, and at least it gave the cloth an airing – the weather was still humid and warm enough to make mildew grow quickly. He clipped on his sword, picked up his hat and went on deck.

The *Lady Arabella* was running up to the north-east before a brisk quartering wind, an all-plain-sail breeze from the west with billowing clouds startlingly white in the early autumn sunshine. The seas rolling eastward were the deep blue of the broad ocean and stippled with just enough white horses to emphasize the irregularity of the waves.

He watched as two seamen carried up a small table and set it down just forward of the binnacle box. A short length of line hung down from the underside of the table-top and one of the men passed the end through an eyebolt in the deck, heaved down taut and made the rope fast so that as the ship rolled the table could move only a few inches. A third seaman walked up with a Union Flag which he carefully draped over the table. The altar was now ready.

Mr Much carried out a large brass-bound Bible – Ramage, standing aft by the taffrail, guessed it was the Mate's own copy – and placed it carefully on the table. He then turned and spoke to one of the seamen, who immediately went towards the Captain's cabin. He returned a few moments later, said something to the Mate, and then went on to call the ship's company aft for church. As soon as the men were grouped round the altar, freshly shaven and hair combed and tied in neat queues, Stevens appeared in white nankeen trousers and a dark grey coat, with his usual Sunday black hat perched squarely on his head. He had a weary gait which reminded Ramage of a sad prelate who had long ceased trying to placate a nagging wife.

Yorke and Southwick were waiting on the starboard side, and they were now joined by Wilson and the *Lady Arabella*'s surgeon, Farrell, who stood a few paces apart. Bowen was conspicuously absent – there was more than a hint of the free-thinker about Bowen, and in the past Ramage had often been shocked by some of the surgeon's comments. Yet if he was honest he had to admit they sometimes left him trying to find answers to disturbing questions. In fact, he thought sourly, he'd spent most of the last month trying to find answers to a different but equally bewildering variety of questions.

As he stood watching, left hand on the hilt of his sword, Ramage recalled, with a nostalgia that knotted his stomach muscles, all the many Sundays when he had conducted the service in the two ships he had commanded. The toothless John Smith, who usually stood on the capstan with his fiddle, playing some cheerful forebitter as the men heaved on the bars to weigh the anchor, would suck in his cheeks and crease his forehead in a frown of concentration as he sawed out the music of a hymn, and the ship's company would sing with gusto. When he first went to sea, Ramage suddenly remembered, his father had told him that he would find Divine Service was a ship's weather glass: if the men did not sing with their hearts in it, he should look for a defect in the captain or officers.

Stevens stopped abaft the table, clasped his hands behind his back, and slowly stared round the ship's company.

The wind hummed in the rigging; the downdraught from the mainsail curving down from high over their heads was chilly and flapped the edges of the Union Flag draped over the table. The *Lady Arabella* rolled with a ponderousness belying her elegant name as the seas swept up astern and passed under her: Ramage was reminded of a plump fishwife on her way to market. But for all that, it was a comfortable roll; regular enough that the men could balance without effort.

There was a heavy thump every two or three minutes as the packet's bow punched into a larger sea, showering up a sparkling spray which the sun scattered with rainbow patterns before it hit the deck and dribbled aft along the scuppers in prosaic rivulets of water. Almost without realizing he was doing it, Ramage braced back his shoulders: a bright and brisk day like this made up for a score of others when the sky was low with scudding grey clouds and wind drove rain and spray in blinding squalls.

After looking round at the ship's company – resentfully, it seemed to Ramage, as though conducting the service took him away from other more important work – Stevens removed his hat with a flourish, and everyone followed suit.

Catching sight of Southwick's flowing white hair, now fluffing out in the wind, Ramage saw the look of stern disapproval on his face: a ship's company standing round on deck as though on a quayside waiting for a ferry was obviously not the old Master's idea of the way Divine Service should be conducted.

Handing his hat to the nearest seaman, Stevens took a pair of spectacles from a pocket and put them on with great deliberation. He then took a prayer book from another pocket and, after giving a cough intended to get the men's attention, opened it.

At that moment the lookout at the bow shouted excitedly: "Sail – ho! Sail to loo'ard on the starboard bow!"

116

Ramage immediately watched Stevens. The man tossed the prayer book on to the table, removed his spectacles and thrust them into his pocket before taking his hat back from the seaman. But he did not do what everyone on deck but Ramage had done instinctively as soon as the lookout hailed – look over the starboard bow.

Stevens turned back to the binnacle box, opened the drawer beneath the compass, took out his telescope, and strode over to the aftermost gun on the starboard side. He climbed up to balance himself on the breech, but before looking through the telescope he turned and called, "Run up our colours, Mr Much."

He waited to see two seamen getting ready to hoist the big ensign before putting the telescope to his eye.

Puzzled at what he had seen, Ramage hurried to the main shrouds, unclipping his sword and handing it to Jackson. As he swung into the ratlines he saw Yorke perched halfway up, and as he scrambled up to join him he saw Southwick hurrying across the deck, obviously having run down to his cabin to collect his telescope.

Yorke moved to make room for Ramage, pointing without saying a word. On the horizon Ramage saw two tiny white rectangles, like visiting cards standing on end at the far side of a dark blue tablecloth. The hull of the ship was still hidden from sight below the horizon; only the masts and sails had lifted above the curvature of the earth.

But one glance told him all he needed to know. The ship was not square-rigged; she was a two-masted schooner carrying fore and aft sails. She was hard on the wind on the larboard tack, and she was steering an intercepting course. Miracles apart, there was only one thing she could be.

By now Southwick, puffing slightly, was beside him on the ratlines and turning to face outboard. He took one look at the horizon and gestured with the telescope. "I needn't have bothered to get this!"

"Our lookout must have been asleep," Yorke commented. "How many guns do you reckon she carries?"

"A dozen 4-pounders. These privateer schooners rely on boarding," Ramage said.

117

"She's dam' fast: we'll have a sight of her hull in a minute or two."

Ramage took Southwick's telescope, adjusted the focus – he had used it so many dozens of times he could do it automatically – and with an arm through a ratline he balanced himself against the *Arabella*'s roll and put the telescope to his eye.

The schooner showed up with almost startling clarity in the circular lens: the lower part of her sails were dark where flying spray kept them soaking wet. Suddenly a long, low, black hull lifted for a moment under the sails like a distant whale, and then sank below the horizon again. He glanced down – they were perched about thirty feet up in the ratlines. From that height you could see the horizon at about six and a quarter miles. Again a random wave lifted the privateer's hull momentarily above the horizon, and he saw the spray slicing up from her stem. Hard to count, but half a dozen gun ports?

The privateersmen had been wide awake: from well down to leeward they had sighted the packet, estimated her track and hardened in sheets to steer an intercepting course ... all this had gone on even before Stevens had removed his hat.

Automatically Ramage began converting what he could see into a mental diagram. The *Lady Arabella* was running northeast before a quartering westerly wind, and the privateer was beating to windward on the larboard tack, making good a course somewhere between north-west and nor'-nor'-west. When I come to describe it later to Gianna, Ramage thought irrelevantly, the *Arabella* will be a coach thundering down a long straight road. The privateer will be a highwayman galloping along another road coming diagonally from the right. Unless Stevens does something about it, both coach and highwayman will meet at the crossroads.

The privateer is not travelling along her road as fast as the *Arabella,* my dear, since she's beating to windward, but that doesn't matter because the French have less distance to travel to the crossroads: it is about six miles away for the *Arabella*, but less than three for the privateer.

But how, Gianna will ask, with that quizzical wrinkling of

her brow, could the *Arabella* escape? And I will smile reassuringly: her fastest point of sailing was with the wind on the beam, so we immediately turned northwards to put the wind on the beam – taking a turning on the left, in other words, leaving Johnny Frenchman over on our right and well down to leeward: so far to leeward he could never beat up to us before nightfall. We would have no trouble dodging him once it was dark. By making a sudden and drastic alteration of course, at daylight on Monday morning there would be nothing to see on the horizon ...

Ramage was brought back to the present with a jerk as both Yorke and Southwick shouted at him, pointing down at the afterdeck, where he saw Stevens standing with a hand cupped behind his ear as if to hear the answer to a question.

"He just asked what you make of her," Yorke said sarcastically. "Apparently thinks it might be Westminster Abbey on the horizon."

Ramage handed the telescope to Southwick and cupped his hands.

"Carries no more than a dozen guns. About six miles away."

"What nationality?"

Ramage turned to Yorke in startled disbelief. "Is he joking?" When Yorke shook his head Ramage shouted: "She's a French privateer schooner on an intercepting course: you'd better turn northward a bit sharpish, Mr Stevens, or she'll be on you within the hour!"

"Are you sure, Mr Ramage?"

Was Stevens a fool or a knave? The most stupid seaman in the Post Office Packet Service – indeed, the youngest cabin boy – knew that such a schooner hard on the wind steering an intercepting course in this part of the Atlantic could only be an enemy privateer.

"I am absolutely certain, and so are Mr Yorke and Mr Southwick. It's time you bore up, Mr Stevens; you've lost a mile to leeward already!"

"Can't act hastily," Stevens called back fretfully. "We'd soon be at the North Pole if I bore up every time we sighted a strange sail."

Southwick nudged Ramage and growled: "First sail we've seen for weeks! You give the order, sir: the Tritons will make sure it's carried out."

Ramage took the telescope again without answering. The privateer was hull-up over the horizon now – an indication of how fast the two ships were converging. She was long, low, black with white masts, and sailing fast; well-heeled to the west wind but pointing high. Almost continuous sheets of spray were flying up from her stem and sweeping aft over the foredeck. She looked sleek and graceful, her sails well cut and well trimmed. Her captain was obviously expecting the packet to turn north and was making sure his helmsmen did not lose an inch to leeward.

As he returned the telescope to Southwick, Ramage remembered Stevens' unhurried, unsurprised behaviour when the lookout hailed. Was he a completely unimaginative man who naturally acted slowly in an emergency? Was that why privateers had twice before captured his ship? Surely not – even the slowest-witted of men must have learned a lesson by now.

Ramage was puzzled, and because he was puzzled he was uncertain what to do. That black-hulled privateer and its crew of a hundred French cut-throats could represent certain capture for everyone in the *Arabella* and possibly death for some. The *Arabella*'s choice of escape or capture depended on Stevens' whim, not on the orders given by the captain of the French privateer: it depended on how soon the packet bore up and escaped to the north.

Yet the capture of the *Arabella* might somehow reveal why many (if not all) of the previous packets had been captured. That was the only reason why the *Arabella* was graced with the presence of Lieutenant Ramage. The devil take it, he told himself angrily, I've talked over the possibility enough times with Yorke and Southwick in the past few weeks. Talked, yes, and there's the rub: it's the old story of looking in the cold light of dawn at an idea born in the warm and mellow glow of a late evening's conversation.

Very well, the *Arabella* might be captured. The privateer might be able to get up to her before night came down. Even

120

if she did not, she might outguess the *Arabella* and find her in the darkness. "Might" should have been the key word, but the way Stevens was behaving it could be a certainty.

Ramage glanced down at Stevens, trying to guess what was passing through the man's mind, and saw he was talking to the Mate. Suddenly Much waved towards the privateer and made an angry gesture at the starboard side 4-pounders, his head jerking like a pigeon's from the violence of his words. Even from a distance it was clear to Ramage that Stevens' features were strained and his whole body tense, as though gripped by pain.

Then he saw the Surgeon walking aft towards the two men. A mediator – or an ally for one of them? Much saw him coming and repeated the gestures, only this time talking to Farrell, who stopped a couple of paces away as though the Mate was threatening him. For a few moments the men seemed silenced by the violence of Much's words; then all three began talking at once, their hands waving wildly. Although the wind carried away their words, their quarrel was obviously a bitter one.

"Like hucksters haggling in the market," Yorke commented.

"What's the Surgeon doing there?" Ramage murmured, thinking aloud.

"It's like watching a play without hearing the actors. My guess is that Mr Much wants to bear up, but fight if it becomes necessary; the gallant Captain can't make up his mind; and the noble sawbones wants to surrender without ceremony."

"Aye," Southwick growled, "that's my reading of it."

"It's about what one would expect," Ramage commented. "I wonder who ... Come on, it's time we joined the party: we're losing a quarter of a mile to leeward every couple of minutes..."

With that he climbed down the ratlines and, walking towards Stevens, reminded himself that the packet captain knew nothing of the real reason why he was on board. Stevens had no inkling that the chance that brought the privateer in sight had made Ramage the key figure in a secret investigation ordered by the Cabinet. As far as Stevens and his officers were concerned, Ramage was just another anxious passenger, and for the moment he must remember to play that role.

All three men stopped talking as they saw Ramage approaching.

"Ah," Stevens said, a reassuring smile trying to struggle across his face but getting lost round his mouth. "Well, Mr Ramage, a pity one of your frigates isn't up to windward, eh?"

"The laurels are all for you to win," Ramage said cheerfully. "I'm sure you'd begrudge having to share them!"

The smile vanished completely. "Well, Lieutenant, she's a big ship..."

"Yes, but smaller than the *Arabella*, I fancy."

"Oh no! Why, she's pierced for eighteen guns!"

"Rubbish!" Much snapped. "Might be pierced for ten and carrying eight."

Stevens swung round angrily to face the Mate. "I'll thank you to hold your tongue, Mr Much. Just remember I'm the owner of this ship as well as the commander."

"Aye, I'm aware of that," Much said bitterly, "and I rue the day I ever signed on with you again."

The Surgeon took a step nearer. "Steady, Much, steady; I've warned you of the risk of getting too excited; overheating the blood can be fatal." He turned to Ramage. "You mustn't take too much notice of him, Mr Ramage: he's overwrought. He refuses my offers of medication."

"*You* hold your tongue," Much said with a quietness belying his tone. "It's caused too much trouble already."

Ramage waited, trying to discern in the bickering phrases the original causes of what were obviously long-standing and bitter differences which had come to a sudden climax when the privateer hove in sight. *Was* Much in fact overwrought, and Farrell and Stevens trying to calm him down? *Was* it some mania that had set Much apart from the rest of the *Arabella*'s officers and crew? Although Farrell was a poor specimen when seated at a chessboard, he might well be a good doctor. Ramage was angry with himself for having been on board so long without knowing the answers. He felt a gentle pressure from Yorke's elbow.

"Well, Captain, can we offer ourselves as a gun's crew?"

Yorke asked with polite enthusiasm. "Or would you prefer us to have musketoons? You'll outsail that fellow, of course, once you bear up to the north" – he waved airily towards the privateer – "but we might as well be prepared."

It was smoothly done and Ramage was grateful: Stevens had been told once again that the *Lady Arabella* should now be stretching off to the north, leaving the privateer down to leeward, and that his passengers took it for granted that in the unlikely event of the packet being overtaken they would fight.

"Most civil of you to offer, Mr Yorke," Stevens said quickly, "but I hope it won't come to that. I know Mr Ramage is also anxious that we should bear up, and although it won't help us much I was about to do so when I had to calm down Mr Much. Well, we mustn't waste any more time," he added, like a schoolmaster regaining control of an unruly class, "we'll turn north – see to it, Mr Much."

Even before Stevens had finished speaking the Mate was shouting the orders that sent men running to sheets and braces, ready to trim the sails as the brig altered course.

Ramage turned away with a feeling of relief: it had taken too long for Stevens to decide to turn north – they were at least a mile nearer the privateer by now, a valuable mile lost when yards might count by nightfall – but at least the damned man was at last doing something.

Suddenly the whole horizon lifted and sank again as the *Arabella* heeled: the helmsmen had put the wheel over and aloft blocks squealed as the yards were braced round and the sheets hardened in to trim the sails with the wind just on the beam.

Slowly the privateer seemed to slide aft along the horizon as the *Arabella* turned, finally ending up just forward of the beam, steering an almost parallel course four or five miles to leeward. Almost parallel, Ramage thought grimly. Almost, but not quite: parallel lines never meet. But because the privateer could sail closer to the wind than the *Arabella*, the ship's courses were converging slightly. As he would explain later to Gianna, continuing the coach-and-highwayman analogy, the highwayman's road was four or five miles away on the right,

123

converging gradually on the coach's road, but with luck they would not meet until after nightfall.

As he stood with Southwick's telescope watching the privateer's narrow hull, the unrelieved black glistening wetly and the foot of every sail dark from the spray, Ramage felt the worry over Stevens' behaviour slowly ebbing away. In its place the excitement and tension of action was gradually seeping in, like a fire slowly warming a room. He lowered the telescope to find Yorke standing beside him.

"Happier now?" the young shipowner asked.

"Hardly happier. Less unhappy, perhaps."

"How so?"

"I'd be happy if I was in the *Triton* brig so I could run down and capture that chap!"

"There's no satisfying you. Just be happy that Stevens eventually did what you wanted."

"Did what *he* should have done from the start," Ramage said impatiently. He glanced round to make sure no one else was within earshot and then said with a quietness that did not hide the bitterness in his voice, "I hope I never get orders like these again. It's ridiculous – I have to chase up Stevens to do the obvious thing so that the *Arabella* isn't captured, but it's beginning to look as if capture is the only chance I'll have of carrying out my orders. If I succeed in one thing I fail in the other."

"All very sad," Yorke said lightly, "but I can't see Their Lordships – of the Admiralty or the Post Office – thanking you for helping one of His Majesty's packet brigs get captured!"

When Ramage continued looking glumly at the distant privateer Yorke added, a more serious note in his voice, "Don't despair of capture too soon: when you've a spare moment, cast an eye aloft. Southwick's prowling round the binnacle as though he'd like to strangle the helmsmen."

A quick glance round the ship confirmed Yorke's warning – and jolted Ramage into realizing he had been so absorbed in his own problems that his seaman's ears had stopped functioning: instead of the sails being tautly flattened curves, every seam straining with the pressure of the wind, they looked like heavy curtains hanging over a draughty window, the luffs fluttering.

"What the devil is Much up to?"

"He's been exiled to the fo'c'sle," Yorke said heavily. "The Captain has the conn."

"But ... just look ..."

"That's what I mean: don't despair too soon!"

"And for all that, we must be sagging off a point or more!"

"More, I suspect" Yorke said sourly.

"Have you or Southwick said anything to Stevens?"

"No. Much was just getting the sheets hardened in when Stevens began an argument with him. I couldn't hear what was said, but then Much was sent forward."

"What orders did Stevens give the helmsmen?"

"Didn't say a word while I was there: just left them to it. Much had told 'em to steer north, but when he went forward they just let her sag off. They don't seem to give a damn."

"Do we start seamanship lessons for Stevens?" Ramage growled.

"You're just a passenger, Mr Ramage," Yorke said with mock sarcasm. " 'We don't want any of these smart Navy gentlemen interfering with the Post Office Packet Service!' "

"I can hear him saying it," Ramage said miserably.

"What are you going to do?"

"Join Southwick and just stare at the compass: see if Stevens can take a hint. Come on!"

He walked over to the low, wooden box that was the binnacle and, standing to one side, looked at the compass. The lubber's line representing the ship's bow was on north-by-east and the card was still swinging towards north-north-east.

Ramage turned slightly and looked directly at the two helmsmen, one standing each side of the wheel.

"She's a bit heavy on the helm, eh?" he asked sympathetically.

"Aye, she is that!" one of the men grunted. "Very tiring, sir."

Stevens had been standing aft by the taffrail and now walked up to Ramage, but before he could speak Ramage said, "These

125

men are tired, Captain; perhaps they could be relieved?"

Stevens stared at the two men, who avoided his eyes and gave a half-hearted heave at the spokes of the wheel.

"Are you tired?" he demanded.

"Ain't complainin'," the nearest man said. "The gennelman was axing if she's 'eavy on the 'elm."

"Very kind of the Lieutenant to inquire," Stevens said heavily, "and I know you men appreciate it. But" – he turned to Ramage – "'tis a strict rule in any ship I command that no one talks to the men at the wheel."

"So I see," Ramage said sharply. "I'd expect someone to tell them to get back on course."

"They are on course," Stevens said smoothly.

Ramage looked down at the compass.

"They're steering north-by-east."

"Well?"

"They should be steering north."

"By whose orders, pray?"

"Yours, I should hope!"

"When I want your advice I'll ask for it, Mr Ramage," Stevens said acidly. "Until then I'll continue as my own navigator."

With that he walked back to the taffrail and stood facing aft, as if absorbed by the sight of the *Arabella*'s wake.

Ramage eyed the two helmsmen, who had an almost triumphant look in their eyes. Perhaps they were just pleased at seeing their captain snub a naval officer. He turned to Southwick and said casually, "It'd be interesting to see what sort of course they steer, eh?" The Master nodded, and Yorke followed Ramage as he walked back to the starboard side.

Yorke had lost his flippant manner; his left hand was rubbing his chin as though tugging at a goatee beard.

"When I look at that damned privateer I hear the prison gates at Verdun creaking open."

"Stop looking, then," Ramage said unsympathetically, putting the telescope to his eye. He counted five gun-ports. Four-pounders? Probably, for a schooner that size, and double-fortified too, so they can be packed with grape or canister shot without fear of bursting. But a count of guns, the *Lady Arabella*'s single broadside against the French schooner's, hardly gives a true picture: Johnny Frenchman's strength lies in the horde of a hundred or so privateersmen who, at this very moment, are arming themselves with pistols, cutlasses, tomahawks and pikes, and waiting eagerly for the moment their schooner crashes longside the *Arabella* so they can swarm on board and overwhelm these Falmouth men.

Why north-by-east? Why not north? With the wind on the beam and the sails trimmed properly the *Arabella* would be romping along. But steering a point or more to the east of the sensible course, and with the yards braced up so the wind was spilling out of the sails – why, if Stevens had been waiting to meet a pilot cutter and wanted to waste an hour without heaving-to, he would do just what he was doing now.

"Excuse me, sir," Southwick said, "they're steering more than a couple of points off course. Never a bit above nor'-nor'-east, and often down to nor'east-by-north . . ."

"Very well," Ramage said, but Southwick did not return to the binnacle; instead he stood there, as if waiting for orders, and Ramage knew the old Master felt the time for action was fast approaching. It was, and Ramage knew it. But what action? And against whom? First, he had his orders from Sir Pilcher to find out how the packets were being captured. Carrying out those orders comes before anything else, he told himself yet again, and I've already decided that being on board a packet when it's actually captured might be the only way of getting the answer.

But the *Arabella* – unless I can do something about it – is going to be captured just because Stevens is a fool. Perhaps a knave as well. Being on board the *Arabella* when she's captured because her captain hasn't the wit to keep her up to windward isn't going to give me any answers. If poor seamanship is the only reason why all the other packets were captured, then I have the answer now: all I need do is seize the *Arabella* – and with the dozen Tritons and surprise that would be easy – and drive her hard. Even if Stevens has lost us too much to leeward to let me . . . he dismissed the rest of the train of thought: he was confident he could avoid capture.

So by tonight, he told himself the *Arabella* could be safe, and I'd be able to start writing my report to the Admiralty. Just poor seamanship. "Judging by Captain Stevens' behaviour when the *Arabella* sighted a privateer, none of the packet commanders knows how to sail his ship with the wind on the beam, let alone close-hauled..." Their Lordships would give a derisive laugh, and because of their disbelief Lieutenant Ramage would spend the rest of his life on half pay. And no wonder. It did not sound a very plausible explanation.

So what could he do? Force Stevens to bear up? If he refused, Ramage would have to take over command of the ship. He did not give a damn about the furious complaints the Post Office would make to the Admiralty, but the problem was simple: if he did take over the *Arabella* it would not help him to carry out his orders. All he would know was that Stevens was not fit to command anything.

What a mess, he thought bitterly. Sir Pilcher was wiser than he knew when he kept his favourites out of range of this job.

"Well?" Yorke asked. "You've been staring at that privateer for three minutes. You've sighed five times and rubbed the scars on your brow twice. By now your plan must be ready, and Southwick and I await your orders."

Ramage shook his head miserably. "No plan, no orders ... I just wish to God I'd never lost the *Triton*; then I wouldn't be here."

"Now, sir," Southwick said soothingly, "why don't we just get to windward of Stevens and put a warning shot across his bow? Just close enough to give him a shock: might do him a world of good."

Ramage shrugged his shoulders. "It's about all we *can* do. We're just outraged passengers making a formal complaint. Remember that. Passengers, nothing more."

Even before he finished speaking, Yorke was striding aft to where Stevens still stood at the taffrail. Ramage noticed he was now wearing a cutlass. In fact several men now wore them. But Stevens had not sent the men to quarters yet ... He remembered he had not yet retrieved his sword from Jackson and saw

128

the American waiting near by. Taking the proffered sword he did up the clips and hurried aft to join Yorke and Southwick.

Stevens was now looking apprehensive, his face creased into the worried, almost sycophantic expression of a grocer seeing his three best customers coming to complain about the quality of some of his goods, but not yet sure exactly what the complaints would be.

Passengers, Ramage reminded himself; we're just passengers. As he reached Stevens he gestured towards the privateer (startled to see how close she now was) and said, "I thought we'd have shown her a clean pair of heels!"

"Not a hope" Stevens said dolefully.

"We were six miles to windward when we sighted her. The *Arabella* looks a fast ship," he said contemptuously, "but whoever designed her must have used a haystack for a model."

"Aye, 'tis true," Stevens said, still in a doleful voice. "She's not as fast as she looks."

Yorke suddenly appeared at the other side of Stevens and said crisply, "If I owned this ship I'd be ashamed!"

"How so, Mr Yorke?" Stevens was not provoked. His voice was still sad, like a professional mourner's.

"I'd be ashamed at the way she's being sailed, and I intend telling Lord Auckland about it, too."

"I can't set any more canvas, Mr Yorke; I haven't the hands to furl when the privateer gets to close quarters."

"*When?* That's putting the cart before the horse," Yorke said, his voice taking on a distinct edge. "If you'd spent a couple of minutes sail trimming and then kept a sharp eye on the helmsmen, that privateer wouldn't have got within five miles of us, and we'd lose her once it's dark. Why, it's not too late even now."

"I wish 'twas so," Stevens said lugubriously, "I've no wish to be a prisoner again."

"Then put better men at the wheel," Yorke snapped. "Those two are steering a couple of points to leeward all the time."

"Oh, you're mistaken, Mr Yorke, indeed you are; this ship won't hold up to windward like that fellow." Stevens waved towards the privateer. "Designed for close-hauled work, those Frenchmen."

"Bah!" Yorke exclaimed. "Captain Stevens, it's my duty to remind you of your duty towards your passengers. You're not taking the proper steps to safeguard us. Why, you haven't sent the men to quarters yet. Look, every gun is still secured!"

Well spoken, thought Ramage: Yorke's protest was just the sort a passenger would make. But at that moment he heard Captain Wilson's heavy footsteps clumping along the deck behind them.

"I say, Yorke my dear fellow," Wilson said hotly, "that's demned insulting, don't you know? I've complete faith in Captain Stevens. We're ready to stand to our guns the moment the Captain gives the word. You'll see, we'll give our French friends a run for their money!"

"Nonsense!" Yorke said angrily. "You don't seem to realize that all this is like a dispatch rider not putting spurs to his horse when he's chased by a squadron of enemy cavalry."

"Oh, come!" Wilson exclaimed.

"Listen, you know as much about the sea as I do soldiering," Yorke said abruptly. "I wouldn't presume to tell you how to lead your company into battle, but you can take my word for it that this ship is being sailed badly. Because of Captain Stevens, that privateer will be alongside us inside a couple of hours. We're just drifting, not sailing. Would you hobble a racehorse? *That*'s what's going on, Captain Wilson, among other things, and if you doubt my word, ask Mr Ramage and Mr Southwick!"

Ramage realized that Yorke was deliberately provoking Wilson as a means of stirring up Stevens, but he didn't want Yorke to go too far: the way things were going the privateer might be trying to get alongside in less time than Yorke estimated, and Wilson's cheerful aggressiveness would be welcome. "Gentlemen," he said, "instead of bickering we ought to be listening to Captain Stevens giving us our instructions ..."

Yorke glanced at him admiringly: neatly done, the shipowner thought to himself, very neat indeed. And he noticed Ramage was again rubbing one of the scars on his right brow, a sure sign that he was concentrating hard.

Stevens coughed and straightened his back. "I – er, well, you can see we turned away a few minutes ago..."

His voice trailed off when he realized several pairs of eyes were watching him closely.

"My orders," Stevens said lamely, a whining note in his voice, "they tell me to run from an enemy when I can, and when I can't run any longer, then to surrender – after sinking the mails."

"Forgive me," Ramage interrupted. "I probably misunderstood you. I thought the Post Office instructs its commanders first to run, then fight when they can run no longer, and sink the mails only when they can no longer fight. *Then* surrender."

"Of course, Lieutenant, of course! That's what I meant," Stevens said hurriedly.

"Very well," Ramage said crisply, "but so far you haven't sent the men to quarters. Your guns are still secured, the magazine locked, not a musket or pistol issued, boarding nets not triced up and the mails aren't up on deck in case you have to sink them ... What exactly have you done so far, Mr Stevens, apart from buckling on that cutlass?"

Stevens was both embarrassed and on the defensive now, as though Ramage was asking him if his wife had ever cuckolded him. "Now, now, Mr Ramage," he said chidingly, "don't let us be impetuous. Coolness in action, Mr Ramage, I'm a firm believer in it; you'll learn in time how important it is."

Ramage flushed with anger at the crudeness of Stevens' remark, and decided it was time to regain the initiative. "I agree, Captain," he said coolly. "Although I doubt if you've ever fired a shot in action, despite surrendering twice, I can assure you from experience that your theory is correct."

Ramage jumped in surprise as someone standing behind him gave a sudden bellow of bitter laughter. He turned to find Much who, looking directly at Stevens, said contemptuously, "Impetuous!"

Stevens now gave Ramage the impression of a man not only under great strain, but who had a lot to conceal, like a clerk in a counting house just before his books were checked. But to be fair, Ramage told himself, a clerk might be worrying that some arithmetical error could cost him his job, not scared that a fraud he had perpetrated would be discovered. Whether the clerk was honest or fraudulent, the symptoms could be the same.

"Yes, Mr Mate, impetuous!" Stevens said, as if trying to re-assert his authority.

"We don't have too much time," Ramage said, gesturing at the privateer. He then pointed at the boat hanging across the packet's stern. "Isn't it time we cut this adrift? It's going to interfere with the guns."

"I'm the Master of this ship, Mr Ramage."

"Yes, you mentioned that earlier," Ramage said pointedly, "but since you've let the ship sag off to leeward, we'll have to fight, and repelling an attack eventually gets down to aiming and firing guns. And I assure you" – Ramage pointed over the beam – "that she'll soon be within range, thanks to the course you've been steering."

"Get the mails on deck, Mr Much!" Stevens ordered, ignoring Ramage. "And look lively about it."

Ramage turned away, noting that Farrell had joined them but not said a word so far. As he walked to the mainmast he saw that the men at the wheel were still letting the ship sag off to leeward, and Stevens had given them no fresh orders, nor sent men to the sheets and braces. Yet perhaps he was pressing Stevens too much – or causing the pressure, anyway. The man was getting even more nervous, but left in peace for a few minutes he might possibly start making the right decisions. He might yet decide to fight.

Jackson and Stafford, as if anticipating the approaching climax, were standing where they could see any gesture Ramage made – even a raised eyebrow. Yorke and Southwick, moving a few feet away from Stevens, were watching the seamen hauling bags of mail on deck and placing them just abaft the aftermost gun on the lee side. From there it would be easy to pitch the bags out through the port.

Three men came up with several pigs of iron, and Much took the neck of the nearest bag, cut off the lead seal and untied the

132

knot of the line holding the bag closed. He put in two of the iron weights and retied the line, then took the next bag. There were twenty-three bags, Ramage noticed, and painted on the canvas were the large numbers that Smith had so carefully checked in Kingston. Finally all the bags were weighted with iron bars and, after ordering a seaman to guard them, Much walked over to Stevens and said loudly, "Your mails are ready to go!"

Stevens ignored the emphasis on "Your" and said quietly, "Thank you, Mr Much, and I see you've put a sentry over them. Excellent!"

Yorke caught Ramage's eye and joined him by the mainmast. "What's he going to do? Fight or surrender?"

"Who knows?" Ramage said. "It's like trying to shovel smoke. I wish we knew more about the Mate."

"A very religious man, obviously," Yorke said. "Probably one of Mr Wesley's followers – they're pretty numerous in Falmouth. He might regard Stevens as a sinful man."

"Or a villain," Ramage said.

"And all the time he might be just a fool. But" – Yorke looked round, and lowered his voice – "I think he's mightily influenced by that crafty surgeon."

"Yes, it's a pity Bowen hasn't been able to get much out of the fellow."

"Chess isn't a talkative game."

Ramage pointed over the starboard quarter. The privateer, well heeled under a press of canvas, was now almost bows-on, her hull gently seesawing as she drove up and over the swell waves in a graceful but powerful movement reminding Ramage of the ridge and-furrow flight of the woodpecker. With sheets eased and a flowing white moustache of bubbling water at her bow, she must be near her maximum speed.

Half an hour ago the *Arabella* and the black-hulled privateer had been well separated, although steering courses that slowly converged. But now the privateer, racing along under a skilled captain, had seen the *Arabella* gradually sagging down to leeward so she would soon be in the privateer's path and perhaps a mile ahead. After that, Ramage noted grimly, unless Stevens

133

can be forced to act, it will be only a matter of minutes before she ranges up alongside to windward with the *Arabella* at her mercy.

"Come on," he said to Yorke, "she looks very nice but she reminds me of the gates of Verdun prison. It's time we gave Stevens some more encouragement."

Stevens was watching the privateer with all the horrified fascination Ramage had once seen in a rabbit stalked by a weasel.

"She'll soon be within gunshot," Ramage said cheerfully.

"Ah, Mr Ramage. Gunshot eh? These guns won't do any good. You're thinking of those 12-pounders you have in frigates."

Ramage decided it was time for frankness.

"Mr Stevens, quite apart from the fact that none of your passengers wishes to be captured, are you going to continue disobeying your orders?"

"What orders, Mr Ramage?" Stevens said in the same doleful voice he used earlier.

"To fight when you can no longer run."

"But we're still running, Mr Ramage."

"With your sails badly trimmed, Mr Stevens."

"Oh, so the Royal Navy is teaching me my business, eh?"

"If you think the sails are trimmed properly, then you need some lessons," Ramage said abruptly. "Now, can we be told why you haven't sent the men to quarters?"

"No point, Mr Ramage; our shot would never reach her!"

"We can but try."

Stevens shrugged his shoulders and then said, as though placating a child who was scared of the dark, "Very well, I'll send the men to quarters if it'll make you feel any better Mr Ramage. Much" – he turned forward and shouted to the Mate – "send the men to quarters!"

Ramage began rubbing one of the scars on his brow, struggling to control his anger, and a moment later felt Yorke's hand on his other arm, gently pulling him away.

"Steady," Yorke murmured when they were out of earshot. "Just listen a moment: this fellow's acting out a play!"

"What on earth do you mean?"

134

"Well, so far we've thought he hasn't known what the devil to do next, but now I'm dam' sure that not only has he done exactly what he wanted so far, but he knows exactly what else he wants to do."

Ramage turned and stared at him. "You realize the significance of what you're saying?"

"Yes," Yorke said soberly, "and I've a fancy the same thought has crossed your mind, too."

Ramage nodded as he looked around the *Arabella*'s deck. "They all seem to know the routine..."

The men were obeying Much's order, but judging by the almost lethargic way they were moving about preparing for action, the prospect of a few score screaming French privateersmen leaping on board was not filling the packetsmen with the spirit of butchers; indeed, Ramage noted, they looked more like complacent grocers. But was he misjudging the men because he was more used to the cheerful bustle and controlled excitement of a man-o'-war preparing for battle?

Mr Much now had the men casting the lashings from the guns, overhauling train tackles, removing tompions and scattering sand on the deck to prevent men's feet slipping. Just enough spray was coming over the weather bow and washing aft along the deck to make it unnecessary for men to sprinkle water on the planking to douse any stray grains of powder and to stop the sand blowing away. Other men were opening a large wooden chest and taking out heavy, bell-mouthed musketoons as well as regular muskets. An opened case of pistols stood near by and two seamen, each with an armful of cutlasses, were going round the guns, calling to the men to collect their weapons.

There was little disciplined movement about the men at the guns – obviously they were rarely if ever exercised at quarters. And while there was no sign of excitement, there was no sign of fear, either. Surely there should be one or the other?

Yorke nudged him. "Come on, let's collect our musketoons, and a brace of pistols too!"

As they walked towards the arms chest Ramage once again looked at the privateer over on the starboard quarter, heeled over as her captain tried every trick he knew to work his ship up to windward. He pictured him watching the luffs of the great fore and aft sails and keeping his men working at the sheets, taking advantage of every gust to steer a few degrees closer to the wind – the old trick of "luffing in the puffs" – like a conductor determined to get the best out of his orchestra. By contrast, the *Arabella* now seemed to have even less life in her. He glanced up at the set of the sails, and then at the helmsmen, who avoided his eyes.

"Stop daydreaming," Yorke said. "Just look at our soldier friend!"

Wilson was standing at the arms chest with Bowen, busily loading musketoons. A dozen or more muskets, obviously already loaded, rested against the side of the chest.

Ramage said nothing. Instead he looked at the privateer for a good half a minute. Now he could make out the details of her rigging, which meant she was a mile away, perhaps less, and closing fast. The combination of the packet sagging to leeward and the privateer working her way up to windward meant she was almost sailing in the *Arabella*'s wake. And at a guess she's sailing a couple of knots faster. In half an hour or less, she'll be alongside...

To carry out my orders, Ramage told himself once again, I should do nothing. The complete answer to the Admiralty's question is hidden somewhere on board this damned packet. And I'm pretty sure I have half the answer already. Not neatly worked out, admittedly, because there's no time to sort out the significance of everything that's happened since the privateer lifted over the horizon. Between now and the time she catches us and makes us all prisoners, something must happen that provides me with the other half of the answer.

But what the devil can happen that I can't predict now? She'll range alongside, send over a swarm of boarders, and that will be that. As a prisoner, how can I get the information to the Admiralty? What about the next year or two – or three or four – in a French prison? I've gone over all this dozens of times since we left Jamaica, and I decided what to do. I decided I would let myself be taken prisoner if necessary. Lying comfortably in my bunk at night or sitting in an armchair talking with Yorke, the decision was easy and seemed to be the right one.

Now, staring at the privateer – which previously was only an abstract idea – it's damned obvious I'm wrong: utterly and completely wrong.

I am wrong for three reasons – all of them blindingly obvious now that black hull is slicing along in our wake. First, even the most obsessive gambler would not bet tuppence that I'll be alive a moment after those privateersmen swarm on board, so the chances are Their Lordships will never hear what I have found out so far – albeit a mixture of observation, conjecture and suspicion. Second, even if I am taken alive I will not be able to get the word to the Admiralty from a French prison. And third, what more can I find out in the time it will take that privateer to get alongside – half an hour, perhaps – that I don't know now?

All that thinking while lying in my bunk did not allow for one thing. It was the only mistake I made – but it was enough. I never suspected Stevens would behave like this. He has, and so have the rest of the packetsmen. That is half of the answer to the Admiralty's question. And half a loaf is better than no bread – providing the half gets to the Admiralty.

By the time he turned back to Yorke and Southwick his mind was made up. There was no time to get Sir Pilcher's letter and wave it under Stevens' nose: words weren't going to help now, whether written by a commander-in-chief or the First Lord of the Admiralty. Speed was the only thing that might save the *Arabella* – speed and surprise.

"Keep close to me," he told the two men, and walked over to the binnacle. He glanced down at the compass and then at the luffs of the sails. "Steer north," he snapped at the helmsmen, "and God help you if you let her get half a point off course."

Before the startled men could say a word he turned to Southwick. "You have pistols? Good – watch these men. If they don't obey you, shoot them."

He looked round for the Mate and saw him standing by the mainmast.

"Mr Much," he called, "As a King's officer I'm relieving

Captain Stevens of his command. Get those sails trimmed properly!"

Motioning Yorke to cover Stevens, he bellowed, "Tritons! Stand by Mr Much!"

As he turned to go to Stevens at the taffrail he saw the man glancing round wildly. Suddenly Stevens snatched the cutlass at his side and, holding it high over his shoulder, ran to the starboard main brace to try to slash through the heavy rope so that the main yard would swing round out of control.

Ramage leapt towards him and a moment before Stevens could wield the cutlass, managed to trip him. As the Captain toppled forward his head banged the bulwark and he crumbled to the deck.

Ramage tugged his sword from the scabbard and, not sure whether or not Stevens was still conscious, stood over him.

"Captain Stevens, you are charged with treason. I am assuming command of this—"

An urgent warning yell from Yorke made Ramage turn in time to see the Bosun only a couple of yards away, eyes bulging, and leaping at him with a cutlass held high in the air and already beginning a great downward chopping movement aimed at Ramage's head.

A blur of impressions: perspiration beading the man's upper lip and forehead, knuckles white as he gripped the cutlass handle, the absolute silence except for the pad of his bare feet and hoarse breathing.

The parry of quinte, Ramage thought almost irrelevantly as automatically he swung his sword blade up almost horizontally just above the level of his head, bending his left knee slightly, and thanking God the man had never been to a fencing master.

A moment later the cutlass blade hit Ramage's sword blade with an arm-jarring clang and slid sideways until it caught the guard and glanced off clear of his body.

The heavily built Bosun had put all his strength into the blow and the cutlass, deflecting off Ramage's sword like an axe blade glancing from a tree trunk, made him swing round to his left and stagger two or three paces.

It took him only a couple of seconds to recover. Ramage just had time to see Southwick and Yorke coming to his help and shout to them to keep clear before the Bosun, with a bellow of rage, was coming at him again, cutlass upraised for another chopping attack.

Again Ramage's blade flashed up almost horizontally, covering his head in the classic parry of quinte, but with the guard slightly lower than the point. Again the Bosun's cutlass clanged down, slid along the blade, hit the guard and glanced off. And yet again the Bosun spun to his left, off balance from the force of the blow.

As the man staggered Ramage put out his right foot and tripped him. The Bosun fell on his face and a moment later Ramage slapped him across the buttocks with the flat of his sword.

"Let go of that cutlass and get up," Ramage snapped. "This isn't a nursery."

With that he deliberately turned his back on the man. The packetsmen might put him down as a cool fellow; the former Tritons might think it bravado; but the fact was that slapping the fellow across the backside was so ludicrous he was afraid he would burst out laughing, and Southwick's pistols covered him.

"Very neat," Yorke said quietly. "I thought he'd got you."

"He learned swordsmanship by chopping logs," Ramage said. He looked round the ship. "The Captain and the Bosun have had their turns with cutlasses. Anyone else?"

Southwick waved a pistol in each hand. "Let 'em try," he rumbled. "I'd have winged that fellow but you were both in line from where I stood."

Ramage signalled to Jackson. "See to Captain Stevens. You'd better fetch the surgeon – oh, there you are, Farrell. Why the devil aren't you attending to Mr Stevens?"

He gestured to Jackson. "Leave the Captain: get these stern-chasers loaded and run out."

"Boarding nets?" Yorke asked.

One look at the privateer provided the answer. "No time for that now. I want you to take charge of the mails. I don't want to dump them unless I have to, but use your own judgement: don't risk leaving it too late."

By now Jackson had half a dozen Tritons casting off the lashings securing the stern-chase guns and he came up to Ramage.

"Magazine's locked up, sir."

"What?" Ramage exploded. "Are you sure?"

"Bosun's just told me the Captain still has the key."

"But Captain Wilson had powder for the muskets and pistols."

"Aye, sir," Jackson said patiently, "but the magazine was locked again. Captain's orders."

"Very well," Ramage said, and looked round for the Mate, noting the sails were now setting perfectly and Southwick had resumed his watch at the wheel. The Mate was nowhere to be seen.

"Pass the word for Mr Much," Ramage told Jackson, and walked to where Farrell was bending over Stevens, who had recovered consciousness and was sitting on the deck with his back against the carriage of a gun and clutching his black hat, whose crushed brim revealed the force with which his head had hit the bulwark.

Stevens looked up and said weakly, "It's mutiny; you've taken my ship. You'll pay for today's work, Mr Ramage."

"Give me your word you'll take the proper steps to avoid capture, Stevens, and you can have her back."

Farrell straightened his back. His eyes were hard and full of hate; words came like the sharp strokes of a scalpel.

"A King's officer, eh? A Frenchman's bullet doesn't care whether it lodges in the head of a King's officer or a cabin boy."

"Or a surgeon's," Ramage said coldly. "But attend to your bandages, Farrell. Get below to the saloon, where you belong. Take Stevens with you if he wants to go. But get below: if I see you on deck again I'll have you put in irons."

Ramage was still holding his sword in his right hand and tapping the deck with the point. Farrell held his eyes for a moment and quickly looked away. He glanced down at Stevens: "I'll be at my post in the saloon if you want me."

As soon as he left, Ramage said to Stevens, "Give me the key to the magazine."

140

"I don't have it."

"Where is it, then?"

"I don't know."

"It's in one of your pockets," Ramage said contemptuously. "I'll have a couple of men tear every shred of clothing off you unless you hand it over now."

Stevens knew he meant it and wriggled until he could get his hands into a coat pocket. He reached up with a heavy bronze key. Ramage took it and found Much waiting.

"You sent for me, sir?"

"Yes – I want a steady man for the magazine. Then stand by for some smart sail handling. I'm going to use the stern-chase guns until they try to range up alongside. Then we'll give them a broadside and wear round smartly. After that we'll see how things stand."

Ramage saw tension in both Much and Stevens. Oh no, he thought, don't say I've misjudged Much; don't say he is one of Stevens' creatures after all ...

Much pointed at Jackson and his crew preparing the stern-chasers. "You can't use those, sir: you'll have to rely on the 4-pounders."

Ramage's eyebrows rose. "Why not, pray?"

"Well, you see the –"

"Much!" Stevens interrupted sharply, "watch your tongue! There'll be a day o' reckoning in Falmouth ..."

Ramage glared down at the Captain. "You tell me, then, and be quick about it!"

"The eyebolts won't hold the breechings when they recoil," Stevens said hurriedly, his eyes on Ramage's sword. "There's a bit o' rot there. Just dig into the wood with that sword o' yours if you don't believe me."

"He's right, sir," Much said, "When the guns recoil they'll run wild and kill your fellows. Here, I'll show you."

"Don't bother," Ramage said, knowing the two men would not lie about something that could be disproved by walking a couple of paces, and suddenly remembering that Stevens had long ago mentioned trouble with the builder over some green wood. "Well, carry on, Mr Much: get every fraction of a knot out of this ship. Where were you, by the way?"

Much took two long-barrelled pistols from his belt: ornate guns which looked well cared for. "I went to fetch these. Had to load 'em."

Ramage nodded and Much went to join Southwick at the binnacle.

The privateer was half a mile away: perfect range for the stern-chasers. And, Ramage thought ruefully, apart from being a good target, she was a beautiful sight, with her black hull glistening. He could just distinguish the muzzles of her guns on the lee side: the way she was thrashing along, the starboard scuppers must be running deep with water.

So much for my idea of wearing round after firing a broadside: she'll attack from to leeward because her larboard side guns are dry: there'll be no risk of priming powder being wet in the pans...

"Secure both those guns," Ramage said to Jackson. "We can't use 'em. I want the broadside guns loaded with grape and canister, and spread the Tritons among the guns' crews. At least one per gun. Jump to it; we've only minutes left."

Captain Wilson was talking to Yorke, and when Ramage walked to the taffrail to look once again at the privateer the soldier came over to him.

"Owe you an apology, Ramage," he said abruptly.

"Accepted, Wilson; you weren't to know."

"Feel a fool. Yorke's been telling me about—"

"Quite!" Ramage said hastily, knowing Stevens could probably hear. "All your barkers are ready?"

"All loaded and issued to the men," he said cheerfully. "And a barrel full of extra ones" – he pointed to an up-ended cask forward of the mainmast from which the muzzles of several more muskets protruded.

"Good – you stand by them: there'll be some hot work in a few minutes."

"We'll show 'em!" Wilson declared as he marched forward.

"Sorry," Yorke said quietly, "I had to tell him some of it because he was just about to point one of his musketoons at you and force you to hand the ship back to Stevens."

142

The prospect was so ludicrous that Ramage burst out laughing. "Can all this get any more complicated?"

"We might end up with the French on our side," Yorke said lightly. "At least they haven't tried to kill you yet."

"They'll be a bit more skilful than the Bosun, once they get a chance!"

"It's a blow about the stern-chasers. Much was speaking the truth. I believed him anyway but checked and the wood is ripe all round the bolts."

"I saw you prodding. Just look at Johnny Frenchman," Ramage said with sudden savageness. "Perfect target – dammit, we're hardly pitching. It'd be shooting at a sitting bird, and with a bit of luck we might have fetched one of her masts down."

"I wonder why she hasn't given us a round or two from her bow-chasers – she must have 'em."

"Why bother? Her captain can see how fast he has been overtaking us. He's probably puzzled why we've suddenly come up a couple of points and done some overdue sail trimming, but he's not going to risk damaging our masts. He's certain he can catch us, and he wants to be sure his prize crew can sail the *Arabella* to France."

"What do you –" Yorke began and broke off, looking over Ramage's shoulder. Ramage turned to find Stevens standing there, white-faced and a hand on the taffrail for support.

"I ... I'm sorry," Stevens said, his voice low, and his tone contrite. "I'm afraid I ... er, gave way to panic."

"*Eventually* gave way to panic," Ramage said coldly, "hence the bruise on your head. It's the previous hour that you'll have difficulty explaining away to the Post Office."

"I'm ashamed," he said in his familiar doleful voice. "I was weighed in the balance and found wanting, but I hope the good Lord in his wisdom will forgive me."

"Speaking for myself," Yorke said sourly, "I'm damned if I do. Thanks to you we all stand a good chance of marching into Verdun prison in a couple of weeks' time."

"But Mr Ramage is in command now," Stevens sneered. "It's up to him whether we escape or surrender."

Yorke took a step towards him and said, his voice hard, "Quite true, Stevens. But just you remember that with the privateer less than a mile away, the first thing Mr Ramage did on taking command was to get the sails trimmed and the ship on a proper course. The second was to stop you cutting the main brace. And the third was to send the ship's company to quarters. There are plenty of witnesses, Stevens, and that evidence alone would be more than enough to see you hanged at Tyburn for treason."

"Ah, how right you are," Stevens said contritely, but obviously not alarmed at the thought. "Mr Ramage, in the few minutes we have left please tell me what I can do to help save ourselves."

"Keep out of my way," Ramage said uncompromisingly, and turned back to Yorke. "We haven't gained much. If we'd had the ship going like this at the start we'd have kept to windward until after nightfall. As it is, we've put off the attack by a quarter of an hour."

"So what do you propose doing?"

"Not much choice. Our French friend is all ready to board us. That means dozens of men on his deck waiting with cutlasses and pistols, and many of them probably half drunk by now..."

"And all getting in each other's way!"

"Exactly! We can take advantage of that by making her tack and wear a few times. Force her on to the starboard tack, for instance, so all the larboard side guns get drenched. Do a few unexpected things so all those boarders are thoroughly confused."

"You make it sound easy," Yorke said gloomily, "but what unexpected things?"

Ramage could see that Jackson now had all the *Arabella*'s 4-pounders loaded, and from the positions the men were standing, he had made a former Triton the captain of each gun. Much was marching up and down the deck, watching the luffs of the sails, and Southwick stood four-square at the binnacle, a pistol in each hand and, from the way the helmsmen were hold-

144

ing the wheel, ensuring both men steered better than they had ever believed they could.

"Just look at her," Ramage said. "She's heeling so much she can only use her weather-side guns. That means she's got to attack us from to leeward. Very well, the moment she begins to draw up alongside to starboard – just as her first gun will bear – we suddenly tack. Our turn away to larboard should take her completely by surprise so we're off on the other tack before her captain can sort out sail-trimmers from boarders."

"If we don't, he'll rake us. This transom" – Yorke gestured the width of the *Arabella*'s stern – "will look like a torn fish-net."

"And so will you and I," Ramage said.

"Supposing we *do* take him by surprise," Yorke said doubt-fully. "Then what? Eventually he tacks and draws alongside again. You won't catch him twice with that trick."

"After that we make it up as we go along. Dangerous to have a rigid plan in a situation like this; you have to keep your mind flexible."

"I'll be thankful to keep a flexible head on my shoulders," Yorke said, the light tone in his voice showing he agreed with Ramage's plan. "Just look at her thundering along! Her skip-per knows his job, blast him."

"Let's hope he's shipped the usual bunch of murderous land-lubbers who are handier at waving a cutlass than hauling on a sheet. Anyway, keep an eye on things here: I'm going to give Southwick and Much their orders."

Walking forward to join Southwick at the binnacle, Ramage saw that the Bosun was working again, his cutlass back in its scabbard, obeying Much's orders. But it was risky relying on him: Jackson had better take over his functions.

It took only three minutes to give Southwick, Much and Jackson their instructions. Both Much and Southwick assured him the helmsmen were converted to the idea of steering an exact course, so he was able to use the combination that had always worked so well in the past; he remained free to watch the enemy and exploit every tactical opportunity, simply giving Southwick the briefest orders. Southwick would remain at the

145

conn, giving orders to the helmsmen and passing sail orders to Much. Jackson's job would be to supervise the guns, making sure the guns' crews worked fast, and shifting men around if there were casualties. Ramage gave him strict instructions to fire at the privateer's rigging in the hope of sending a mast by the board. Yorke would deal with the mailbags. That left Wilson. It took only a minute to tell the soldier he was free to open fire with his musketoons as soon as the enemy was in range, using Bowen and any men Jackson could spare temporarily from the larboard guns.

As Ramage walked aft to rejoin Yorke, Southwick said quietly: "Do you want a man to keep an eye on Stevens, sir?"

"No – I can't trust a packetsman and can't spare a Triton. I'll tell Yorke to watch him."

At the taffrail Yorke was watching the privateer, which had by now closed the gap to four or five hundred yards, sailing in the *Arabella*'s wake as though the packet was towing her. Stevens, standing by himself on the larboard side between the taffrail and the aftermost gun, occasionally gave the privateer a disinterested glance and looked round the *Arabella*'s deck with a curious detachment, as though aloof from all the activity.

Now, Ramage told himself, we just wait. There's Stafford acting as captain of the aftermost 4-pounder on the starboard side, and Rossi at the forward one. Maxton looked cheerful enough in command of the forward gun on the larboard side, and a young Scot named Duncan had the after one.

Yorke saw Ramage looking at the four guns and commented, "They seem to get smaller every time I look at them!"

"As long as they don't get fewer! But," he added ruefully, lowering his voice, "I don't think I'd have taken over from Stevens if I'd known these stern-chasers were unusable. I was betting on them to chip off some of the Frenchman's paint..."

"Rubbish!" Yorke said. "You're like a wild Irishman: you couldn't stay out of a fight whatever the odds!"

"We haven't much choice, anyway. About five minutes to go."

"If that."

"I think you'd better send those bags of mail to Father Nep-

146

tune. Use this larboard after gun's crew. Duncan!" he called, "You and your men are under Mr Yorke's orders for a few minutes."

Stevens began walking forward, unhurried but obviously recovered, and carrying his battered hat. He had picked up his cutlass and it hung from the wide leather belt slung over his right shoulder.

Now Ramage could see a crowd of men perched on the privateer's bowsprit. Something glinted in the sun – a cutlass being waved, and he imagined the stream of threats and insults its owner was hurling at the *Arabella*.

Yet there's something odd about all this, he told himself. No privateer captain in his right mind would sail along the wake of a potential prize which he knew had two 9-pounder stern-chase guns. The *Arabella*'s pair may be useless, because of rotten wood round some ring bolts, but the captain of the privateer doesn't know that. All he knows is that his bowsprit is pointing down their barrels and they haven't fired at him. It's as though he knows they will not. Is that the reputation the Post Office packets have among the privateers? It seems the only possible explanation. But not every damned packet captured up to now could have had rot round the ring bolts of the breechings!

Having so much to think about has at least stopped me from getting frightened ... Not frightened of being killed, anyway, but this weird ship of fools leaves me feeling as though I've spent a long and chilly night in a haunted church.

The *Arabella*'s jogging along nicely: plenty of way on her to carry her round when I give the word to tack. If anyone makes a mistake and we get caught in stays...

Here she comes ... bearing away half a point to get out of our wake and ready to range up alongside. Those men perched along the bowsprit like vultures on a branch must be soaking wet from the spray. God, what a crowd – cutlasses, boarding pikes, tomahawks, not one of them has shaved for a month. One of them is bending over being seasick – or vomiting up an overdose of brandy.

Sudden puffs of smoke from her weather bow: the wind whipping the smoke away. Faint popping. They'll be lucky if a musket ball hits the *Arabella*'s mainsail! Plenty of heads showing along the weather bulwark now and some enthusiastic fellows climbing up the ratlines ready to drop on board as soon as that black hull crashes alongside.

"Mailbags have all gone."

"Thanks. Duplicates and triplicates of all Sir Pilcher's dispatches – just think of it!"

She's going to come on to a parallel course – now! Forty yards to leeward. Just the range for 4-pounders. Her bowsprit will begin to overlap us in a couple of minutes. Just time to let Stafford and Rossi have a crack at her with their 4-pounders before we tack.

"Jackson! I'm going to bear away for a few seconds so you can use the starboard side guns. Stafford, Rossi – stand by! Get those guns trained as far aft as possible. Aim for the masts and don't fire until your guns bear!"

A three-point turn should do it. Bear away, fire, up with the helm and then tack. That should surprise the beggars!

"Stand by for a three-point turn to starboard, Mr Southwick. No sail trimming: bear away, and then bear up the moment the second gun's fired."

There are Wilson and Bowen tucking themselves in by the main shrouds. Those musketoons won't hurt the French but they'll keep the lads' spirits up: nothing like the banging of one's own powder to induce bravery...

Thirty men perched on that bowsprit and one of them still being sick. Aye, wave those cutlasses and cuss and swear, but you're going to get a shock in a moment ... Tip of the bowsprit has another twenty yards to go. Neat patches in that mainsail. The gaff jaws are chafing the mast badly. Bottom clean – just some weed on the copper sheathing. One sheet ripped off near the stem – probably hit a floating log.

Ten yards ... plenty of new rope up there: she must have had some successful cruises. Fifty or more heads along the bulwark. Is that the captain standing up on the bulwark right aft? No wonder that fellow is sick – the bowsprit's rising and falling twenty feet. Five yards. That might be your last retch, *mon ami*. What's Gianna doing now? My right shoulder aches – the muscles probably jarred by the Bosun's cutlass.

"Bear away, Mr Southwick; three points to starboard! Steady, Stafford – give 'em one for the Lord Mayor of London! Rossi, I'd like to tell the Marchesa you brought the foremast down!"

And the Tritons shouting their heads off! Bow beginning to swing – round she comes – don't overdo it, Southwick old chap. Damn, we're going to shave that bowsprit off! Wilson's musketoon – and a man's fallen off! Southwick's steadying her up...

The aftermost gun gave a bronchitic cough, followed a moment later by the forward one. The carriages rumbled back in recoil as smoke swirled away in a thick oily cloud.

"Helm up, Mr Southwick!"

But the Master had anticipated the order while Stafford and Rossi bellowed at their men to hurry with the reloading. And now the *Arabella* is turning fast, away from the privateer. In a few moments her stern will be pointing at the row of 4-pounders.

Ramage found himself staring at the muzzles: for many moments, until the *Arabella*'s bow swung across the eye of the wind, and the yards were hauled and the sheets trimmed on the other tack, he had nothing to do but wait.

Suddenly the muzzle of the privateer's aftermost gun winked red and smoke streamed along the afterdeck and curled over her taffrail. A sharp twang showed that one of the grapeshot had hit something metallic on board the *Arabella*; solid thuds told of hits on wood. But there were no shouts and screams of wounded men; no whiplashing of parted rigging.

Then the privateer had passed, still thrashing her way northwards while Southwick and Much took the *Arabella* away to the south-west.

Ramage turned to Yorke, who was staring over the starboard quarter at the privateer's stern and saying, "You did it! It worked!"

"We were lucky," Ramage said, "but –"

He broke off as he saw Stevens gesticulating. Suddenly half a dozen or more packetsmen left the guns, cutlasses in their

149

hands, and ran to the sheets and braces.

Much grabbed Stevens by the throat and both men toppled over, struggling violently. Southwick shouted something at the helmsmen and, as the one bolted away from the wheel, pointed his pistol at the other.

"Stop them," Ramage bellowed at the top of his voice and, drawing his sword, ran at the man chopping into the main brace. Within seconds individual fights between packetsmen and Tritons were going on all over the *Arabella*'s deck, but before Ramage reached his man the main brace parted with a bang and the huge yard began to swing. Forward Ramage could see the forecourse flapping and the fore yard swinging with no brace to control it.

As the *Arabella* lost way and her bow paid off, the whole ship out of control, Ramage saw the privateer had tacked and was steering straight for them, dropping her mainsail at the same time. And that is that, he thought bitterly; Stevens has won: he must have whispered his orders to the Bosun while they were aft here with Farrell, and the Bosun passed them on to the rest of the packetsmen.

It would take half an hour or more to get the slashed rigging repaired, and –

He jumped sideways, sword raised, startled by something overhead; something large which fluttered down out of the sky. Then he saw Farrell standing by the ensign halyard, cutlass in hand, watching the flag settling on the deck in an untidy heap in the classic signal of surrender.

There was a stream of hoarse Italian and a moment later Rossi had flung Farrell to the deck, jumping on his stomach before pouncing on him with his hands round the surgeon's throat.

"Tritons, Tritons, lay aft all you Tritons," Ramage shouted, but Yorke was shaking his arm.

"Wait a minute or two," Yorke hissed, "let our chaps settle their accounts."

"I don't want unnecessary bloodshed," Ramage snapped, "we've enough trouble as it is."

Southwick came aft, driving a stumbling Stevens before him,

followed by Jackson and Much. The Captain was holding his throat and breathing in hoarse, convulsive gasps; the Mate was dusting the wet sand from his clothes. Ramage noticed that as the Tritons came aft, the packetsmen were grouping round the Boatswain on the foredeck. A bloodcurdling yell from just behind him made Ramage spin round. Rossi, sitting astride the surgeon, had the blade of a knife pressed down on the surgeon's throat, and from the jumble of Italian Ramage realized the Surgeon was being given a few seconds to say his prayers before the blade cut down.

"Rossi! Don't kill him!" Ramage seized the seaman's shoulder. "Leave him – he'll swing from a gibbet before long."

As he stood up Ramage knew it was improbable. The privateer was now lying hove-to a hundred yards to windward of the crippled packet.

"Any casualties?" he asked Southwick.

"A packetsman lying dead by one of the guns, and one or two cut. Stevens here has a sore throat, sir, and –"

"He's lucky to be alive to enjoy it," Much said angrily. "That man" – he pointed at Jackson – "stopped me finishing my job."

"There are a lot of unfinished jobs," Ramage said, looking at Stevens and down at Farrell, "but we'll all be prisoners in a few minutes." He turned to the group of Tritons and gestured to include Much, Yorke and Wilson. "Thanks – but for our friends we'd have beaten our enemies!"

Chapter Eleven

The privateer was the *Rossignol* schooner of St Malo, armed with ten double-reinforced 4-pounder guns, manned by ninety-three Bretons, and at sea for seventeen days. As wild-eyed and raggedly dressed men swarmed over the *Lady Arabella*'s bulwarks from three boats, Ramage was reminded of a horde of starving rats running into a granary.

Few were seamen and most were drunk – that much was obvious the moment they jumped on deck – but they were highly skilled looters. They stripped the passengers' and officers' cabins of valuables in a matter of minutes. To begin with, Ramage did not understand the men's haste in the cabins until he realized they were all from the leading boat.

One of the first on board from the second boat was a man who hastily introduced himself as the *Rossignol*'s Mate and, after formally taking possession of the *Lady Arabella*, he dashed below with four men following him, pistols in their hands.

A minute or two later a shot was fired. Yorke and Ramage looked at each other in alarm. Was it Bowen? Southwick and Wilson were on deck. Then there was a second shot, and suddenly two dozen frightened privateersmen ran up on deck and went forward, where they stood like a group of naughty schoolboys.

They were followed by the French Mate, who immediately began shouting at them in a fury, his cutlass sending splinters flying as he slashed at the forebitts to emphasize each word.

"What the deuce is he saying?" Yorke exclaimed. 'His accent is too much for me!"

"Breton," said Ramage, and began translating. "He's cursing the men for looting ... Says they were forbidden to go below – no need for it since the prize surrendered ... The dead man – he knows the dead man was the ringleader. They can regard that as punishment for them all ... Next time the Captain will make examples and hang every fifth man."

"Hm, so the men are only just under control," Yorke commented as the Frenchman finally stopped talking. "Thank goodness we have Jackson!"

As soon as the privateer hove to and hoisted out boats, Ramage had run below to Stevens' cabin to find the private signals and destroy them, and the American seaman had joined him. "You're all going to lose your watches and rings and everything for sure when they board, sir," he said. "If you'd all like to give me your valuables, there might be a sporting chance of seeing them again, unless they transfer us."

Yorke and Southwick had already handed over their watches and rings without, as far as they could see, anyone noticing: all eyes were on the privateer. Jackson had slipped away as unobtrusively as he came, and now, looking at his left hand, Ramage wondered if the privateersmen would think of checking. His whole hand was suntanned, except for a thin band of white skin on the little finger where his signet ring had been.

With the looters under control and remaining on the foredeck, the French officer went back to Stevens again. Ramage watched the Falmouth man tensely. What would he say? There was a dead packetsman lying on the foredeck, but as far as the French were concerned he could have been killed in the brief action with the privateer. The one or two packetsmen wounded by Tritons had their cuts bandaged by now. If Stevens had any sense he would keep his mouth shut and let the Frenchman assume it was a normal surrender.

Ramage suddenly wondered if – as far as the Frenchman was concerned – it *was* a normal surrender. Stevens (and Farrell: he was sure of that now) had wanted to surrender without

153

even trying to evade the privateer, which had ignored the *Arabella*'s stern-chasers. Would Stevens now explain to the French that the single broadside from the *Arabella* was due to an interfering naval officer? Did Stevens or Farrell know – or had they guessed – that Ramage was under Admiralty orders to investigate the losses?

He would soon have the answer: if they knew, then Ramage was a threat to them, and a word to the privateer captain would ensure that he had already seen his last sunset.

The Frenchman gave Stevens a slight bow and smiled. "Forgive me," he said in good English, "my men were overzealous. Now, Captain, your papers: certificate of registry, manifests – everything."

"We were carrying mails."

"That is all?"

"Was all," Stevens said significantly.

The Mate shook his head. "My Captain isn't going to like that. I thought I saw you pushing bags through the ports. All that chasing after an empty ship! Have you a surgeon on board?" he asked suddenly.

"Two," Stevens said. "The ship's surgeon and a passenger."

"Good, one of our officers is ill. I'll take the ship's surgeon back to the *Rossignol*. Now, get your papers and come as well. But first, tell your Mate to start getting these sheets and braces repaired." He waved at the yards swinging noisily overhead. "Tell them to make a good job of it – we have a long way to go."

Ten minutes later Stevens, still clutching his battered hat, and Farrell, his clothing torn from Rossi's assault, were on their way to the *Rossignol*, which had remained hove-to up to windward. Ramage noticed the privateersmen on board the *Lady Arabella* stayed on the foredeck. Their officer's threats had been effective. In the meantime Much set the men to work furling the sails before beginning the long and tedious job of splicing the sheets and braces.

An hour later the boat returned with the Mate and another Frenchman who sat on a thwart wrapped in a blanket, and who had to be helped on deck. After he had been taken below the French Mate came back on deck to demand, "Who is Mr Much?" When the Mate stepped forward he said, "Your captain and the surgeon are staying on board the *Rossignol* as prisoners. You are responsible for the *Lady Arabella*'s men. I see you've made a start on the repairs. Now, point out Mr Bowen."

"He's below."

"Fetch him!"

As soon as Much left, the Frenchman turned to the group of passengers and then looked at a list in his hand.

"Tell me your names." As each of them spoke, he checked them against his list.

"Ramage – which is Ramage? Ah – you know what your name means in French? The song of the birds, that is '*ramage*'. No, perhaps 'music' is better. A suitable prisoner for the *Rossignol*, eh?" He laughed softly. "Well, Captain Stevens says you can speak for the passengers. You are prisoners, of course. You will stay on board this ship, which I am going to sail back to her new home port."

"Might we ask where that is?" Yorke asked.

The Frenchman smiled: he was under thirty, small and well built, blue-eyed with curly black hair and the spare, strong face typical of a certain type of Frenchman.

"St Malo, the home of the corsairs."

"The men of Dunkerque will argue about that," Ramage said.

"And Brest, too," the Frenchman said, "but they are wrong! *Alors*, Mr Bowen?"

The surgeon stepped forward.

"Your colleague Mr Farrell is incompetent, so you have a patient awaiting you in the saloon, Mr Bowen. He is our – how do you say – accountant. Not purser – almost an *agent* for the owner. He is very ill. He did not have confidence in Farrell. So now it is your responsibility that he reaches St Malo alive."

Bowen glared at the Frenchman. "I'm responsible only for the treatment, not the original sickness. If your friend is dying ..."

"The responsibility is yours. He must live. He is the *armateur*'s son."

"I'll do my best," Bowen snapped. "But as far as I'm concerned he gets the same treatment whether an able seaman, an admiral or the son of an *amateur*."

"*Armateur*," the Frenchman corrected, "but I understand; you are a man of ethics. We too believe in equality. Indeed, you may have heard of our Revolution," he added dryly.

With that he looked round at them. "You are all officers, I see" – he waved his list – "and it's up to you whether you complete your journey in comfort, or in irons. If you give me your *parole* . . . otherwise you will be locked up."

Ramage shook his head, and the others murmured, "No . . . no parole . . ."

Again the Frenchman shrugged. "Then I regret, gentlemen, that I must assume you'll try to recapture the ship, so you'll be locked up as soon as I select suitable cabins. I'll introduce myself: Jean Kerguelen. My brother Robert commands the *Rossignol*. Now, my men will finish the splicing and then we can get under way."

While he had been talking, the privateersmen had been herding the *Lady Arabella*'s crew below, searching each man carefully before he went down the hatch. Kerguelen called to one of the men, and said politely to the group of Britons, "You have refused your parole, so please submit to be searched."

Ramage felt the seaman's nimble fingers and thought that they were more interested in finding valuables in pockets than pistols or knives. After much argument among their captors, they ended up in the passengers' cabins: Kerguelen decided it was easier to guard them there than anywhere else, much to the annoyance of some of the privateersmen, who had obviously been looking forward to a comfortable voyage back to St Malo.

Ramage and Yorke were locked in their original cabin but had Southwick and Bowen as well, so the four men would have to share the two bunks, two chairs and the cabin sole. As soon as Bowen joined them half an hour later, Ramage looked up expectantly.

"An *armateur*," Bowen said as the sentry slammed the door and locked it again, "is a backer, the man who puts up the money to finance a privateering voyage."

"I know that," Ramage snapped and then, remembering Bowen had earlier mistaken the word for "amateur", added, "He can also be the owner, or manager."

"Well," Bowen said, "the sick man is his son."

"So Kerguelen said. What's wrong with the fellow?"

"It's hard to say. A fever. He is very debilitated."

"You can cure him?" Ramage asked.

"I don't know, but Kerguelen's silly threats don't make a scrap of difference."

"I know that; I was just curious."

"There's a strange attitude towards the agent," Bowen said. "As though the men like him well enough, but are suspicious."

"The backer's son and the accountant – a glorified purser," Ramage said. "No ship's company likes the purser. They probably think this fellow is the backer's spy, put on board to make sure they don't cheat."

"By the way, sir, I had to treat Much."

"Oh, what's wrong?"

"He had a quarrel with one of the Frenchmen. Ended up with a tap on the head from a pistol butt."

"Badly hurt?"

"I don't think so. With these cases, though, it's sometimes difficult to be sure about damage to the cranium – often several hours pass before anything manifests itself."

"And then what?"

"Collapses, pallor, heavy perspiration..."

"Supposing that happened to Much: where would you nurse him?"

"There's nowhere," Bowen said, "apart from the cabin he's sharing with Wilson."

"It would be more convenient to have him in here, wouldn't it?"

Bowen saw Ramage wink and smiled: "Yes, sir. Much more. Do you want me to arrange it?"

"I badly want to have a chat with our Mr Much. A suitable

157

collapse and a request to Kerguelen should do the job."

Southwick was scratching his head and Ramage guessed that the locked door with an armed sentry outside was affecting the old Master, who asked, "What do you reckon our chances are of being recaptured, sir?"

"Very slight, if these Frenchmen can handle her properly. Sounds as though they've finished the splicing. They'll have her under way soon."

Breakfast next morning was a piece of bread – the Navy's euphemism for tough biscuit – and a bowl of thin watery onion soup whose only merit was its temperature. Yorke was the first to finish his bowl. "I wish I'd soaked this bread a lot more: I'm sure they've chosen the hardest for us."

Ramage offered his bowl. "Pop it in there for a few minutes; that'll soften it."

"I suppose what annoys me most is that we're paying for their food."

There was a banging on the door and the key turned in the lock. "Here," Ramage said to Yorke, "grab your bread; they're probably collecting up the bowls."

But it was Kerguelen, who came into the cabin and said to Bowen, "Go with the seaman outside: that Mate of yours has collapsed."

As the surgeon left, Kerguelen sat down on the bunk. "You are comfortable?"

Ramage smiled wryly. "Let's say we appreciate you asking the question!"

Kerguelen was tired: his sallow skin had the grey waxiness of strain and weariness.

Yorke asked conversationally, "You and your brother are having a successful cruise?"

The Frenchman made a face. "My comrades in other privateers seem to have cleared the game from the fields. You are only our second prize in more than two weeks."

"My condolences!" Yorke said ironically.

The Frenchman gave a half bow and grinned. "Yes, and you were the more welcome."

"Why?"

"The first was small – little more than a drogher – and gave us bad news."

"Might one ask...?" Ramage said.

"Your Channel Fleet is at sea. There seems a possibility of an attack on Brest."

Ramage felt there was more to it than that – at least as far as Kerguelen was concerned. "And so...?"

"And so we are going to have to stay out of the Channel and the Bay of Biscay for a while."

"You don't mean..."

"No, don't worry, I won't spend a month lying-to in the Atlantic! We haven't enough provisions for that. No, I'm going to Lisbon. It'd be a pity to return to St Malo with empty holds, small as they are in this wretched little ship. Thanks to your blockade, France is very short of just about everything needed to fit out ships. You saw the new rope in the *Rossignol*? That's from our first prize. So a few tons of rope and canvas from Lisbon will be very welcome in St Malo. Fetch a high price, too."

"Also thanks to the British blockade," Ramage said.

"Ah, of course! But we won't sell all of it: we'll re-rig this ship, make a new suit of sails, and send her to sea privateering. She's just fast enough – and your frigates will recognize her as a packet brig and who knows, perhaps they won't be too inquisitive. Anyway, you'll be able to spend a month or so looking at Lisbon – from the anchorage, of course!"

"Why a month or so?" Yorke asked.

"Until we hear your Fleet has returned to Plymouth. How long do you think it will stay at sea, Mr Ramage?"

Ramage shrugged his shoulders. "Your guess is as good as mine, since neither of us knows what the Commander-in-Chief's orders are."

"*Alors*, we'll sample the hospitality of the Portuguese."

Lisbon, Ramage thought; the capital of the only neutral country on the Atlantic coast. He could just imagine the face of the Post Office agent there when he saw not the Lisbon packet from Falmouth coming up the river with the latest mails but

159

the Jamaica packet flying a French Tricolour. Would there be a chance to escape? He pictured himself climbing over the side in the darkness and swimming through the murky water of the Tagus...

One of the guards came into the cabin and whispered to Kerguelen, who stood up and excused himself. "This Mate is apparently very ill – your surgeon wants to see me. I would like to stay and talk, but..."

When he had gone and the door was again locked, Southwick said, "Coincidence, that, sir. Almost as though Much had heard what you were saying last night."

"I'm just hoping he's not badly hurt. A broken skull could be fatal."

Yorke said, "This fellow Kerguelen: he's a cut above what I'd expected."

"Several cuts above," Ramage said. "But his men..."

"Sweepings of the jails," Southwick said. "I'd –"

The key turned in the lock and the door opened. Kerguelen waved Southwick to one side and two seamen carried Much into the cabin and put him in one of the bunks.

"You change places," Kerguelen told Southwick as Bowen entered the cabin, clutching a bag of surgical instruments and his chessboard. "You go to the Mate's cabin next door, and he stays here: then the surgeon is with him all the time."

The Master left the cabin and Kerguelen said, "It is best, eh?"

"Pity he was hit."

"Pity? He's lucky to be alive. Usually we take very few prisoners. But your captain surrendered so swiftly, you can thank him for your lives."

"Are you always so generous?" Ramage asked curiously.

Kerguelen shrugged his shoulders. "Yes – if a ship surrenders without firing a shot. But usually only these Post Office vessels do, so we can afford to be generous."

"You speak good English," Yorke said as Ramage digested the fact that the packets had a reputation among the privateers.

"My mother even better."

Yorke nodded. Only an English parent or long residence in

160

England could give an accent such polish. Kerguelen looked at Yorke and Ramage, and said coolly, as if warning them against attempts to recapture the ship, "I also understand the English character quite well."

Bowen said, "If you'll excuse me," and Kerguelen moved to let him bend over Much, who was lying inert on the bunk, his head and brow swathed in bandages.

"Tell the sentry if you want anything." With that Kerguelen left the cabin and the door was locked once again.

"How was that?" Bowen whispered. "No sooner said than done!"

"What happened?"

"Much had the same idea or, rather, he wanted to pass the word that he had to talk to you."

"Is he badly hurt?"

As Bowen began to reply Ramage saw Much open one eye and wink.

"Yes," Bowen said loudly. "It was a savage attack. The patient will be unconscious for several hours, I fear. I suggest a game of chess while we wait."

Ramage looked startled but Bowen pointed to the door and mimed a sentry listening at a keyhole. Yes, an hour's chess would probably be enough to lull even the most ardent eavesdropper. Bowen took out the board and box of pieces, explaining they were among the few items the privateersmen had left behind in his cabin, and held out both fists. When Ramage touched the left, Bowen opened his hand to show a white pawn.

"You start," he said. As soon as they had set the pieces out on the board, Ramage gingerly moved the king's pawn.

"That move is a great comfort to you and Southwick, sir," Bowen said, "and I can guess your next will be to advance the queen's pawn two squares."

Ramage nodded. "What's wrong with that?"

"Nothing, nothing at all," Bowen said cheerfully. "Only chess is a game of the unexpected; of bluff and attack, long-term trap and quickly exploited opportunity. It's truly the game for you, sir, but you play it like the vicar's wife sipping

161

something she half fears will turn out to be a devil's brew!"

"I have an advantage over the vicar's wife," Ramage said heavily. "I *know* it's a devil's brew!"

An hour later, with the game only a third played, Yorke was sitting with Ramage and they both struggled to defend against Bowen, who seemed possessed of a dozen each of bishops, rooks and knights, most of which had the gift of becoming invisible until the last moment.

Ramage pointed at Much, and signalled to Yorke and Bowen to make conversation. He went to the Mate and bent over him, whispering, "Well, Mr Much?"

"I'm sorry to impose myself on you gentlemen –"

"Don't worry about that," Ramage said. "We were trying to arrange something like this."

"Oh?" Much was startled. "Why, sir?"

"I wanted to talk to you."

"What about, sir?"

"Probably what you want to talk to me about," Ramage grinned reassuringly.

"Ah – yes, well, it's complicated."

"You didn't agree with the way Stevens handled the ship?"

"Indeed I did not!"

"And we weren't really *trying* to get away?"

"Certainly not! We –"

Ramage held his fingers to his lips: Much's voice was rising in proportion to his indignation.

"– we *could* have got away, but the Captain's mind was made up long ago to surrender if a Frenchman's topsails lifted over the horizon. If not this voyage, then the next."

"Why?" Ramage gestured to Yorke and Bowen, who had stopped talking, fascinated by what Much was saying. As soon as they began talking again, discussing the game, Much said, "It's all insurance. On the ship and on the ventures. You know what ventures are, sir?"

Ramage nodded.

"Well, everyone carries them. Captain, surgeon, seamen, the two boys. You really do know what ventures are?"

"Leather goods, cheeses, lace, French wines..."

162

"Yes, things like that outward-bound. And mostly tobacco, spices and rum for Falmouth. Well, they insure their ventures for the round voyage, out to Jamaica and back."

"And back? Why – they sell them out there, don't they?"

"They sell them out there, yes; but nearly all the packets are captured on the way back, aren't they, sir?"

Again Ramage nodded. "I still don't understand, though. Presumably they buy more ventures out there to bring back, so they've lost if the packet is captured."

Much shook his head violently and then winced. "Phew, that hurts! No, sir, let's take an example, Seaman Brown buys £100 of ventures in Falmouth. He insures them out to Jamaica and back, because – so he says, anyway – he may not be able to sell them in the West Indies and would have to bring them back. But he insures them for £400.

"Right, his costs before leaving Falmouth are £100, plus the insurance premium. He gets to Jamaica, and sells the ventures for maybe £200. That's a profit of £100. He gets a draft for £100 and gives it to someone in a merchantman to bring back : a merchantman sailing in convoy. So he knows the £100 profit will get to Falmouth safely."

Much reached up and gingerly pushed up the bandage a fraction of an inch.

"Then he can use the remaining £100 to buy more ventures in Jamaica to sell in Falmouth for £200, which means another £100 profit. Once his draft arrives from Jamaica he has a profit of £200, less the insurance premium."

"Yes, and a one hundred per cent profit is excellent," Ramage said patiently, "but supposing the packet is captured?"

"Ah," said Much, "I was describing what *used* to happen – up to a year or two ago, just so's you understand the system. But nowadays our Seaman Brown is a lot smarter. Let's start again in Jamaica, Mr Ramage. Our seaman has just sold his ventures for £200. He can do one of two things : either send all the money back in a merchantman, or keep some of it – say £25 – for more ventures. Can you guess which he'll do?"

Ramage shook his head, excitement creeping over him as he

realized that at last he was on the verge of discovering –

The key grated and the door swung open without warning and Kerguelen came in. Ramage, bending forward to hear Much, sat up abruptly and was so startled he snapped at Kerguelen, "What do you want?"

It was Kerguelen's turn to be surprised. "I just came to see if Mr Much has recovered. I see he has."

"Just enough to tell me what happened," Ramage said indignantly. "Barbarism, M. Kerguelen, sheer barbarism!"

"You're all alive," Kerguelen said briefly. "Most privateersmen would regard that as barbaric: dead men tell no tales – and cause no problems."

"It can work both ways," Ramage pointed out. "Privateersmen get captured, too."

"True. How is this fellow?" He waved to Much.

"Time," Bowen interrupted. "The patient needs time."

"Well, he has two or three days before we get into Lisbon. After that – who knows?"

"Will you let us go in Lisbon?" Yorke asked hopefully.

Kerguelen shook his head. "Alas, no; I wish I could. Unfortunately I need you with me all the way to France."

"Why?"

"As my insurance," Kerguelen said with a disarmingly frank smile. "Privateersmen are always a little sensitive about their necks. If I was unfortunate enough to be captured, having you with me..."

"Oh quite," Yorke said breezily, tapping the table with one of his pawns. "It's just that the thought of being locked up in a French prison is..."

"Not very agreeable," Kerguelen agreed. "Quite so – I spent a few months as a guest of the British in the prison at Norman's Cross. You know it?"

"I don't know a soul in Huntingdonshire," Yorke said airily, bringing a smile to Kerguelen's face, "although I'm told the hunting is good."

Ramage knew the largest prisoner-of-war camp was now at Norman's Cross, although there was talk of building a great new stone place at Princeton, in the middle of Dartmoor. "The

164

hunting could not have been very good if M. Kerguelen escaped!"

"I had an advantage with my English," Kerguelen said. "I travelled by coach. No one hearing me speak thought I was a 'bloody Frog'."

"No," Yorke said with a grin. "You might almost pass for an Englishman!"

"Almost?"

"Almost," Yorke said firmly. "We're your prisoners, don't forget."

"For the last few minutes I did," Kerguelen said gracefully. "However, if you'll excuse me..."

With that he left the cabin and they heard the key turn in the lock.

"We were in Jamaica with Seaman Brown's £200," Ramage reminded Much, "and deciding whether he'd send it all back in a merchantman or send back £175 and risk the privateers by spending £25 on more ventures."

"Well, you've probably guessed that he'd spend £25 and send the rest home. But you can't guess why?"

"No," Ramage said. "I was trying while Kerguelen was here."

"He gave you a clue," Much said cryptically.

Ramage wrinkled his brow. "Kerguelen only said he couldn't free us in Lisbon because we were his insurance..."

"That's it, sir, insurance! Don't forget that before Seaman Brown left Falmouth he'd insured his £100 worth of ventures for £400 for the outward *and return* voyage. So his £25 worth of new Jamaica ventures are still insured for £400. Of course, the underwriters don't know he's already sold the ventures he brought out and that his draft for £175 is safely on board a merchantman."

At last Ramage saw what was happening. "And when the homeward-bound packet is captured Seaman Brown loses his £25-worth of new ventures but claims for and collects the whole £400 from the underwriters because he says he was bringing back the original ventures."

"Exactly! As soon as he's exchanged, Seaman Brown goes back to Falmouth to find the £175 draft from Jamaica and collect £400 from the underwriters. He deducts the £25 spent on lost ventures and the original £100 investment, and finds he has a profit of £450 ..."

"All for six or eight weeks in a French prison."

"Yes, and Seaman Brown can comfortably manage at least two such voyages a year. One voyage out lasts forty-five days and thirty-five days back, plus about twenty days' waiting. That's one hundred days, plus six weeks as a prisoner. So Seaman Brown makes the round voyage, is captured and back in Falmouth before six months is up. Time enough to do it again so that by Christmas – if he's captured a second time – he's made a clear profit of £900 on the year at no risk."

"And at all times his ventures were insured ..." Yorke commented quietly. "Where would he get the original £100?"

"That's not difficult. He'd have started as a boy, taking out goods for some Falmouth merchant on commission. Ventures have been carried for many years, Mr Yorke ..."

"How can he be sure the packet will be captured?"

"He can't be absolutely sure," Much said, "but he *can* be sure – unless he's sailing with one of the very few commanders who'll have nothing to do with it – that his packet will surrender if a privateer is so much as sighted. It's not only seamen involved, Mr Yorke: mates, masters and commanders, too."

"Supposing the packet isn't captured," Ramage asked.

"Well, his £25 venture will still make him £50, and he has the £175 draft from Jamaica."

"And if the ship's taken on the way out?"

"Seaman Brown loses £100-worth of ventures and collects £400 from the underwriters as soon as he's exchanged. That's a profit of £300 in less than three months. Believe me, Mr Ramage, Seaman Brown can't lose!"

"I can see that," Ramage said ruefully. "But why has all this spread so quickly in the last year or so? The war's been on a long time!"

"It took a couple of years for the men to be certain the French would always exchange them without long delays."

"Yes, that also puzzles me: seamen – whether merchant or from the King's ships – usually wait years."

166

"The French – I'm ashamed to say this, Mr Ramage – the French exchange packetsmen quickly because they know they won't fight: they want the men back at Falmouth and off in another packet to surrender again. That way the French Government knows it's disrupting the mails, and it makes sure of a regular supply of prize packets," Much said bitterly. "They like the ships to use as privateers – fast, well built, most of them new, and captured without damage; no shot holes in the hull."

"Yes, the packetsmen, privateersmen and the French Government all get handsome profits. It just chafes across the back of any honest Briton posting a letter," Ramage said bitterly, "not to mention Government business. Downing Street, the Admiralty and the War Office all cut off from governors, ships and troops because of the greed and treason of a few score men. A few score Englishmen who've done what the whole French Fleet have failed to do..."

The four men sat silent, each lost in his thoughts. Finally Ramage asked the Mate, "Why are you telling me all this, Mr Much? Don't you risk having your throat cut?"

"The risk is there all right, but supposing you were in my place? What would *you* do?"

"Don't you venture?"

"Indeed, I don't," Much exclaimed angrily. "'Tis more vicious than drink – apart from being against the regulations – and 'tis treason, too."

"But you've sailed with Captain Stevens a long time," Ramage said pointedly.

"Aye, to my eternal shame, and I know you wonder why I've done nothing before this. Yes, I've sailed with him a long time, and his father before him. A commander for many years, the old man, and with his dying breath he asked me to stay on as Mate with his son Gideon. I was so upset with the sight of the old man dragging his anchors for the next world that I promised. I kept that promise until yesterday, when Gideon broke his solemn word to me. I think the old man knew he had a bad streak in him; many's the time I heard him round on Gideon and say money wasn't everything in this world; but Gideon reckoned it was..."

Much's voice faded as he roamed alone with his memories, and finally Ramage brought him back to the present. "What started the quarrelling between you and Stevens after the *Rossignol* was sighted?"

The Mate sighed. "That I should be talking like this of the old man's son. Well, the fact is the Captain – I'll call him Gideon, so we don't get mixed up – has done this twice before. I was wrong to stay with him – but I'd promised the old man. Still, before we left Falmouth this last time, I'd had enough. I made Gideon swear he'd never do it again. But the Master – he felt the same as me – didn't believe him and reported sick, so he didn't sail with us. Me – well, I thought Gideon would stand by his word and I signed on again, seeing I'd promised his father, God rest his soul."

"Why didn't the Master believe him?"

Once again Much tried to ease the bandage round his head. "Because he knows how desperately Gideon wants a new ship," he said simply.

"But the *Arabella*'s almost new," Ramage exclaimed, and a moment later remembered the rot round the eye-bolts of the stern-chase breechings, and the vague remark Stevens had made the evening they had drinks together.

"Yes, she's almost new," Much said, "but the builder was sharper than Gideon: while Gideon was a prisoner that last time, seems the builder used a lot o' green wood in the stern, and most of it's gone rotten already. It'd cost a pretty penny to rip it out ... And Gideon reckoned that rather than pay for repairs out of his own pocket he'd sooner have those gentlemen in Lombard Street buy him a new ship – they paid for the *Arabella* of course, because the last one was captured. And Gideon would spend another year – on full pay – supervising the construction."

"Yes, but what the devil does Stevens get out of it?" Ramage objected. "He loses charter money and passenger fares ..."

"Aye, he'd lose that, but he gets a brand-new ship. Apart from the rot, there's a year or so's depreciation written off just like that!"

Yorke, who had been listening as best he could while carrying out a conversation with Bowen, turned to Ramage and said quietly, "Believe me, Nicholas, as a businessman I can assure you that even if he takes two years to build the new ship he'll make a far greater profit than if he'd been at sea. In effect, he's gained – well, I'd guess a third or half of his original investment."

"I can see the temptation is enormous. But the risk of discovery..."

"It's been going on for four or five years, much longer than over-insuring ventures," Much said, "and the Post Office suspects nothing. They think it's because there are swarms of French privateers at sea."

"And we know there aren't," Yorke commented. "No wonder the Admiralty are puzzled: I'll bet their frigates don't sight that many!"

Ramage decided to keep his own orders secret: Much seemed quite satisfied at opening his heart – or was it purging his soul? – to a King's officer.

"Did they think they could always keep this a secret – the ventures frauds and the new ships?"

"The new ships, yes: the commanders keep their mouths shut, and who could actually prove anything anyway? There's no secret about carrying ventures – it's been going on for years, and when the Post Office tried to stop it last year the men went on strike: you probably remember it. Lombard Street kept quiet about the reason, but it was ventures. The over-insuring – well, that's something else! That's a secret all right – why, if the underwriters got so much as a hint..."

"But why hasn't the Post Office suspected something?" Ramage persisted. "Surely they question the commanders when they're exchanged? Don't the commanders face a court of inquiry when they lose a ship, like we do? I've gone through three so far!"

"Oh yes; it's a routine business. As soon as he gets back to Falmouth from France, the commander goes to a notary and swears a 'protest' like any other shipmaster, and delivers that to the Post Office Agent. Then a committee – made up of other packet commanders – sit to question him, and that's that.

Obviously his brother commanders aren't going to stir up any mud! Sometimes the Inspector of Packets comes down from London, but" – Much shrugged his shoulders – "he's a man who neither sees nor hears evil."

"So that's it," Ramage said. "But you haven't explained why Stevens broke his promise."

"It's Farrell," Much said angrily. "I could see that damnable Surgeon was persuading – or threatening, for he's a wicked man – long before we reached Kingston. It's my belief the Surgeon's carrying very high insurance on his ventures."

"But how can the Surgeon threaten him?"

"On behalf of the ship's company. When they get back to Falmouth, moorings could get cut in the night and the ship drift ... she could catch fire ... spring a leak ... Bear in mind, sir, the Post Office only pays out if she's lost due to enemy action."

"Don't forget Stevens wanted a new ship anyway," Yorke muttered. "It'd be enough to persuade an owner. Probably wouldn't seem like treachery or treason: simply safeguarding his interests by submitting to blackmail by the officers and crew. And getting a new ship into the bargain."

Ramage rubbed the scars over his right eyebrow. "I can see that. Wouldn't make any difference in court, of course; it's still treason and Stevens would be hanged."

"Hanged!" exclaimed Much. "Oh my God, what have I done?"

Ramage said nothing and Yorke and Bowen turned back to the chessboard.

"Hanged ..." Much whispered. "I told him it was sinful; I warned him before we left Falmouth ..."

After a few minutes, Much said to Ramage, "I'm still glad I've told you, sir; I didn't want to meet my Maker without telling someone what's happening to the mails. It seems so dangerous for the country ... I could go back to the other cabin now and let Mr Southwick come back here again."

"No, you'd better stay here for a day or so. We might think of more questions," Ramage added vaguely.

"I'll tell you something, Mr Much," Yorke said bluntly.

"That fellow Stevens deserves to swing. More blameworthy than the Surgeon."

"Oh, sir!" Much said, deeply shocked. "Farrell is a real rascal."

"Make no mistake," Yorke said, "Stevens is more blameworthy because he's the captain. The Surgeon's simply a dirty little rogue. Picking pockets, poaching, treason – it's all the same to him. But not to Stevens; he knows the difference. That's why the Post Office pays him to command. You must understand that. Leaders get paid not for the work they do but for the responsibility they bear. Whatever happened on board the *Arabella* was Stevens' responsibility."

The Mate nodded numbly. Ramage saw that for all Much's concern and soul-searching he was only now realizing the full extent of the damage done to the Post Office by the greed of short-sighted men. There was just one important question left – after he had the answer to that, Ramage knew he'd carried out his orders, and his remaining duty was to stay alive long enough to report to the Admiralty. "Tell me, Mr Much," he asked, "are you sure the packetsmen – both seamen and commanders – aren't deliberately seeking out privateers and surrendering?"

"No, definitely not. All it boils down to, Mr Ramage, is that they've covered themselves in case they do meet one."

Ramage said quietly, "Yes, but they make much *more* profit if they're captured, Mr Much. Treason pays them a far higher dividend than doing an honest job."

Much held up his hands helplessly. "But they've enough sense not to kill the goose that lays the golden egg."

"Supposing the Royal Navy took over delivery of the mails?" Ramage asked out of curiosity.

"That's what I mean," Much said. "The packetsmen won't risk that. Anyway," he added, "the one time a Navy cutter took the New York mails she was captured on the way back."

171

Chapter Twelve

When Ramage first thought of the idea the *Arabella* was running fast in the darkness, the sea sluicing past the hull planking only a few inches from his head and sounding like a cataract. It was not the proverbial flash of inspiration; rather that as he was lying sleepless in his bunk Ramage found the idea had arrived in his mind like a cat coming unobtrusively into a room and waiting to be stroked.

Since he was no stranger to weird ideas thought up during pre-dawn bouts of sleeplessness, he turned over on to his back to consider it again. Ten minutes later he knew there was nothing wild about it, nor did it leave anything to chance, and there was only one real "if". He eased himself out of the bunk and shook Much, who was sleeping deeply and snoring gently. He was awake in moments, whispering, "Whassermarrer?" at someone he could not recognize in the darkness.

"It's Ramage. Tell me, how much do the Post Office pay out to the owner when a packet is lost? What's the cost of building?"

"Phew" – Much sat up, rubbing his head – "give me a moment to wake up properly, sir. Now, let me think – the *Halifax, Westmoreland, Adelphi* ... Yes, about three thousand pounds."

"Thanks," Ramage grunted, and as he turned back to his bunk Yorke spoke from the chair he had drawn in the chairs–cabin sole–bunk lottery with Ramage and Bowen. "Why the sudden interest at this time o' night, Nicholas? Going to make

Kerguelen an offer for the *Arabella*?"

"Yes," Ramage said shortly. "Like to take a half share?"

Ramage heard the chair creaking as Yorke sat upright and said, "Yes."

"Make it a third, sir," Bowen said sleepily, "and I'll take a third."

"Congratulations – not many men can raise three thousand pounds in twenty seconds before dawn out in the Atlantic," Yorke said banteringly. "Now you can tell us how you propose buying the ship."

"Don't misunderstand me," Ramage said. "Three thousand pounds is the Post Office figure. She may be worth six to the French."

"So you are likely to dun Bowen and me for another thousand each, eh?"

Ramage asked the Surgeon, "Can you stand two—"

"Three, if need be," Bowen interrupted, "but no more than three, though."

"Wish I could put up something," Much said miserably. "I've got seven hundred pounds in the Funds, an' that's all, but you're welcome to it."

Ramage leaned over and patted the man's shoulder in the darkness. "Don't start fretting: if all this works, Mr Yorke will buy us out and may offer you a job as well!"

"I certainly will," Yorke said cheerfully. "I can use a good mate in one of my ships."

"Oh dear me!" Much exclaimed, completely overwhelmed. The inadequacy of the words brought home to Ramage the extent of Much's self-control: few men would have been able to resist some blasphemous expression of surprise and pleasure.

"Don't let's declare any dividends yet," Ramage reminded them. "First we have to persuade Kerguelen to sell; then we have to agree on a price."

"If nothing else, he'll drive a hard bargain," Bowen said. "We aren't in a particularly strong position," he added ruefully.

"Stronger than you might think," Ramage said. "Depends on how much of a gambler Kerguelen is."

"Gambler, sir?" Bowen exclaimed, making no attempt to disguise his surprise.

"Yes. He knows he has only a fifty-fifty chance of getting back to St Malo from Lisbon without being captured. Eight or nine hundred miles. Don't forget the Channel is an enormous funnel: the closer you get in, the narrower it is, and the Navy is always watching. Ships are converging on it from all over the world, and apart from patrolling frigates, warships are returning. And plenty of British privateers are out looking for ships such as this – French prizes trying to get back to the Channel ports."

"But he could increase the odds in his favour by sneaking into Brest," said Yorke gloomily. "Save himself a hundred miles. Or Bordeaux."

"No," Ramage said, "from Lisbon he'll head for St Malo – once the Channel Fleet's back in Plymouth. Apart from pride, he'll make for his home port because he'll have rope and canvas in the hold. In St Malo he knows all the officials, and he and his brother probably have a proper base there for fitting out prizes."

"All the more reason why he won't agree to sell," Yorke said. "This packet's fast; she's just the right size for a privateer: easily handled, well-equipped –"

"And her whole stern so rotten we'll be lucky to make Lisbon, let alone St Malo," Much said lugubriously.

There was complete silence in the cabin for a full minute.

"The *whole* stern?" Ramage repeated incredulously.

"The whole stern," Much said. "You can punch your fist through the archboard; the last dozen feet of the stringers and shelf are soggy like a bad potato. Don't even dare think about the deadwood; the rudder's hanging on by faith."

"How long have you known all this? The extent of the rot, I mean."

Much waited a minute or two before answering and Ramage wished he could see the man's face.

"I've known we had some rot for six months – I mentioned that was why Stevens wanted a new ship. But it's spreading very quickly, as I found out in Barbados, where I made a complete above-water examination and reported to the Captain. That was the first time I found out how bad it was."

Ramage guessed that by a bitter irony it was probably Much's report that made Stevens decide to break his promise to the Mate: knowledge of how fast the rot was spreading meant it would need only slight pressure from Farrell to make Stevens surrender the ship at the first opportunity.

"Supposing he hadn't known the stern was rotten," Ramage mused. "I wonder what he'd have done about the *Rossignol*."

"I'd only be guessing," Much admitted, "but I think he might have run. Farrell *might* have been able to persuade him not to fight if he couldn't get away, but I think he'd have made a more effective attempt to escape." The Mate thought for a few moments and then added wearily, "I'm not sure, though. I begin to wonder."

"Of course," Yorke said casually, "One mustn't forget Stevens does own the ship; up to a point, he can decide what he does."

"I'm not disputing that," Ramage said grimly, guessing Yorke was leading up to something else. "He could own a bank or an abbey as well, but he doesn't own the bags of mail, and treason is still treason."

"Don't pick on him alone," Yorke advised. "Don't forget the other commanders. They surrendered simply because of insurance on the ventures, not because their ships had rotten sterns. Incidentally, Much my dear fellow, bearing in mind we'd all like to stay afloat, were you exaggerating a few minutes ago about the extent of the rot?"

"No, I wasn't. I told Captain Stevens we ought to get some precautionary work done before we left Kingston: doubling some frames for example, and making sure the gudgeons and pintles were held in good wood, in case we lost the rudder. But there wasn't time: the Agent wanted us to sail almost at once, and naturally the Captain didn't want to tell him about it. He wants to get full value for a sound ship."

"So our chances of reaching anywhere safely would make a professional gambler go pale?"

"Faint clean away," Much said, in the most cheerful tone of voice Ramage had yet heard him use.

"The rot," Ramage said. "Presumably it's very obvious?"

"Some of it – if you start looking. I had some lining ripped out. But from on deck, no; that was all painted over again a'fore we reached Kingston, in case we shipped some nosy passengers."

"Like Mr Yorke and me."

"Exactly, sir."

Bowen said: "When will you tackle Kerguelen, sir?"

"After breakfast."

"Why not wait a day or two?" Yorke asked. "After all, you said yourself the chances of this packet being recaptured increase every day."

"I'm not a gambler," Ramage said. "Not unless I have to be. And if Kerguelen meets a British frigate he'll try to make a bolt for it. Firing those stern-chasers might be fatal – for all of us."

"Yes, you're right," Yorke conceded. "The sooner he puts his helm down – gently! – the better."

"We'll ask to see him when they bring breakfast," Ramage said.

Kerguelen sat down on the bunk as though paying a social call and ran a hand almost apologetically over the stubble on his face. "You gentlemen are so freshly shaven ... You asked to see me."

"We have a business proposal to make," Ramage said bluntly.

"So?" Kerguelen's eyebrows lifted, and he smiled ironically as he glanced round the cabin. "Banking ... shipping ... armaments...?"

"Shipping," Ramage said.

"It's an interesting business. Banking is dull, and armaments so noisy. What is the proposal?"

Ramage picked up one of the chessmen left on the board and tapped the table with it. "I'm gambling on this voyage, and so are you. I'm betting the *Arabella* will be recaptured before we reach St Malo; you're wagering you'll be able to dodge any

176

British ships. What do you reckon the odds are?"

"Even," Kerguelen said promptly. "Perhaps slightly in your favour."

"But neither of us wants to lose."

Kerguelen shrugged his shoulders. "But one of us has to!"

"No," Ramage said. "That's why we asked to see you."

"A moment," Kerguelen said warily, glancing at the door, "if you have any trick in mind, I warn you..."

Ramage shook his head. "No tricks, I promise you. Our proposal is this: instead of taking the *Arabella* to France from Lisbon and selling her in St Malo for whatever you can get, will you sell her to us in Lisbon for an agreed price?"

Kerguelen's jaw dropped. "Do you have money with you?"

The Britons burst out laughing, and Kerguelen said sheepishly, "Well, how do you pay if you have no money?"

The Frenchman was showing interest; Ramage was sure of that. French money was not a popular currency these days – particularly with privateers trying to use it to buy timber and rope from Baltic or Portuguese merchants.

"You're already bound for a neutral port," Ramage said. "If we can't raise the money in Lisbon we can have it sent out from London."

"Oh no! You aren't going to be allowed on shore: it would be too easy for you to escape."

"We would give our parole," Ramage said stiffly. "Anyway, only one of us need go on shore for a couple of hours to arrange it. You keep us on board until you get the money, then you hand the ship over to us."

Kerguelen frowned and Ramage realized that he was still looking for the trap. He hoped Much would remember his instructions.

"What sort of price had you in mind?" the Frenchman asked.

"What price would you get in St Malo?"

"You can't expect me to show the cards in *my* hand," the Frenchman said. "You make an offer."

Ramage hated bargaining: having no experience of business, it embarrassed him. He glanced helplessly at Yorke.

"We offer £2,500 for the ship and our freedom, paid to you in cash at Lisbon."

Kerguelen made a mental calculation and then shook his head.

"I'm sorry, because the idea appeals to me, but I can get a lot more in St Malo; enough to make me take a chance with your cruisers."

Yorke said, "Don't make any mistake, *M'sieur*: the money comes out of our own pockets."

"Have you no influence?"

"It takes more than influence to prise money out of a government!"

Kerguelen nodded, but Ramage thought the Frenchman feared a trap and was going to turn down the proposal. The moment had come to show his hand.

"Before you refuse our offer, go and inspect the transom of this vessel. It won't take long: you can poke around with a knife or punch with your fist."

"What are you saying?" Kerguelen demanded as Ramage glanced at the Mate.

"He's saying," Much interrupted suddenly, "that you'll be lucky to make Lisbon, let alone St Malo, before the stern drops off. It's all rotten. And don't risk firing one o' the stern-chasers, either!"

"Parbleu!" Kerguelen exclaimed and hurriedly left the cabin. The door shut and once again the key turned in the lock.

"We may get a bargain yet," Yorke said. "I think we've set the right price, and Much's bombshell about the rot was perfectly timed."

"I'd even settle for St Malo if someone'd give me a guarantee we'd get there," Much muttered, "what with the rot and these cut-throats."

They had to wait for more than half an hour before Kerguelen returned, looking worried and nervous. He sat down on the bunk again, his fingers drumming on his knees. "It's bad. This man wasn't exaggerating."

"Wish I had been," Much said.

"But why did you sail from Kingston? She's not safe. And

178

why are you offering to buy a rotten ship?" asked Kerguelen.

"Our offer isn't for the ship alone: we want our freedom as well," Ramage said.

"There's no precedent," Kerguelen said, half to himself. "But it's like a ransom."

"Exactly like a ransom," Ramage said, and wondered what argument he could use to tip the scales. "But when you get two beautiful women and two men who want to marry" – he gestured at Yorke and himself – "they get a little desperate..."

Kerguelen looked at Ramage. "You are going to get married?"

Ramage nodded. It was at worst only a white lie; he'd marry Gianna one day if she accepted him, and Kerguelen was not asking when.

"You poor fellows!" Kerguelen said bitterly. "My wife decided I was away too long at sea." It was said with so much hatred there was no need to wonder whether she had found solace in another man's arms.

"Our proposition?" Ramage prompted.

"I'll do it for £3,000."

Yorke said, "We don't have it." Ramage glanced up in alarm.

"Your families will raise it."

"They certainly won't! They can't. Each of us has put up all he has – including the Surgeon here."

Kerguelen looked at each of the men in turn. Each of them thought of the rotten wood in the transom, and they held his eyes.

"All right, I'll do it for £2,500 and the *agent* will agree. I talked with him. He's grateful to you, Mr Bowen, for your treatment," Kerguelen said. "But I need the parole of each of you."

"You shall have it. In writing."

"How long will it take to arrange, once we get to Lisbon?"

"A month at the most. Time for a packet to reach England, and another to get to Lisbon with a reply and the money."

"Supposing the money does not come?"

"It will, but even if it didn't, you'll have waited a month,"

Ramage reminded him, "and by then the Channel Fleet will have returned to Plymouth..."

"Lost a month," Kerguelen said.

"You'd wait a month to make sure the Channel Fleet's in harbour again. But if the money didn't come we'd lose – how long? A year? Three years? Five? Would you like to be a prisoner that long?"

Kerguelen reflected a minute or two. He saw that once the *Arabella* arrived safely in Lisbon he had nothing to lose and everything to gain, while the odds were against the Englishmen.

"Very well," he said, and held out his hand to Ramage, who shook it, and was followed by the other three men. Kerguelen said, "If you give your parole that you won't try and interfere with the running of the ship, three of you can be on deck at any one time."

Ramage agreed at once: there was no chance of them re-taking the ship – so far they had been exercised three at a time and covered by a dozen muskets – and nothing was to be gained by refusing. Also Kerguelen was probably trying them out; applying a little test to see if the British were acting in good faith.

Chapter
Thirteen

The *Lady Arabella* made her landfall at Figueira da Foz, where the River Mondego flows into the sea just south of Cape Mondego and some eighty miles north of Lisbon. For an hour as they approached the coast Ramage listened to a spasmodic argument between Kerguelen and his second-in-command, who swore he recognized the Burling Islands, a group of small islets half a dozen miles from the next headland south.

Finally, he asked Kerguelen for the use of the telescope. There was no mistaking the Cape, although its rugged rocks gave the impression of separate islets because of the high mountains behind it. But southward towards Lisbon the land was flatter, the coast lined by sand dunes backed with pine forests and dozens of little white windmills, many with the canvas of their blades reefed against the strong west wind.

"Cabo Mondego," he told Kerguelen as he gave back the telescope.

"You're sure? All these damned headlands look alike along this coast!"

Ramage nodded. "They do, but I remember Mondego: coming down from the north it's easy to mistake it for the Burling Islands."

With that Kerguelen snapped out a stream of orders that brought the brig round to the south, steering parallel with the coast but out of sight from anyone but sharp-eyed lookouts on the headlands.

Soon after noon the packet was reaching down towards Os

181

Farilhões, a group of islets ten miles north-west of Cabo Carvoeiro and which, because many of them were jutting triangles of rocks, looked as if a fleet of small vessels were sailing among them. Closer inshore was Burling Island, flat-topped and over three hundred feet high, its sides precipitous cliffs which shot spray high into the air as the Atlantic swell hit them.

As he walked the deck with Yorke, Southwick and Wilson, Ramage saw several ships making their way north and south inshore of Burling Island, but they were coasting vessels, probably carrying local cargoes between Lisbon and the places to the north, like Porto, at the mouth of the Douro.

Southwick gestured towards Os Farilhões and Burling Island, the scattering of rocks between them now showing clearly. "They're no trouble in this sort of weather, but beating up here with a north-west gale and heavy rain..." He shuddered at the memory of the times he had done it. "I don't like to think of how many ships have hit one of them in a blinding squall with only a moment's warning."

As night fell, with no British ship of war having been sighted, Kerguelen had the *Arabella* jogging along under reefed topsails, ensuring they did not arrive off Cabo da Roca, just north of the wide entrance of the River Tagus, until after dawn. It was half an hour after sunrise when Ramage came up on deck to find the packet three miles off the great cape, the westernmost point of the continent of Europe. More than five hundred feet high, the cape was a series of almost precipitous layers of rock, and inland it merged into the Serra de Sintra, a range of spiky mountains. For the time being the peaks were hidden by thin layers of cloud which clung to them as though each wore a white wig. Ramage remembered the palace built on the summit of one of them, Castelo da Pena, and shivered at the thought of how cold it would be: he was still used to the Tropics...

An hour later the *Arabella* rounded Cabo Raso – which, with Cabo Espichel twenty-one miles south, were guardians of the great bay into which the Tagus flowed – and was soon passing the Santa Marta Fort perched on the headland sheltering the fishing villages of Cascais and Estoril.

182

"You know the entrance to Lisbon?" Kerguelen asked suddenly. When Ramage nodded, the Frenchman said, "I've not been here before, and we have no charts..."

"I know it well enough," Ramage said, and pointed. "You can see Forte de São Julião on the north side, and that's Bico da Calha on the southern side. It's three miles across, but the channel is only a mile wide and goes close to the Fort."

He moved to the starboard side to get a clearer view. "Now, you see that long yellow bank of sand in the middle there, with breakers on it?" Quickly he described the entrance channel, pointed out several forts lining the entrance of the estuary, and ended up with a warning: "The tidal stream reaches four knots out there – more if there's been much rain in the mountains, because the Tagus starts five hundred miles inland – and sets right across the shoals. So if you lose the wind in the channel you'll have to anchor in a hurry."

With a steady west wind the *Arabella* crossed the bar, ran in past Forte de São Julião and, as she hugged the north shore, Ramage saw the curious Torre de Belém guarding the approach to Lisbon itself and pointed it out to Kerguelen.

The Frenchman sniffed. "Looks as if a Portuguese designed the main part and let an Indian add the ornamentation."

Half an hour later Ramage was hustled below as the packet, flying the tricolour, anchored off Trafaria, on the south side of the river and close to the quarantine station. After Kerguelen had dealt with the Customs and port authorities, the brig got under way again and Ramage was allowed on deck to pilot the ship for the last four miles up to the city itself, finally recommending an anchorage in front of the main square, almost in the shadow of São Jorge Castle.

Yorke, who had seen it before, commented, "One of the finest capitals that's also a port. Venice gets the prize, then Copenhagen. Lisbon comes third."

Southwick grunted, "Stockholm?" When Yorke admitted he had not been there, Southwick said, "In summer it's pretty enough. No tide, of course; not like here."

The three men went to the bulwarks, where they were joined

183

by Wilson. The muddy water of the Tagus was swirling past at a good four knots. Then they watched several fregatas working their way out of the various docks.

"Loveliest working vessels I've ever seen," Yorke said. "Just look at the fancy paintwork on the bow of that one!"

Lisbon's equivalent of the Thames barge was a graceful vessel with a heavily raked mast, a plump, apple-cheeked bow and a sweeping sheer. Almost the entire bow was covered in a gaily painted design, belying the sacks of grain with which she was laden. Two British frigates were anchored upstream of the *Arabella*, while a Post Office packet and a dozen more merchant ships, mostly British, were alongside the docks lining the city side of the river. Ramage was pointing out various landmarks in the city, which is built over the slopes of several hills, when Kerguelen came up to him.

"If you're ready to go on shore, I'll have the boat lowered. You and Yorke?"

Ramage nodded and grinned, "You have enough hostages to make sure we come back."

Kerguelen, not realizing Ramage was joking, said simply, "I have your parole; that's enough for me."

Half an hour later, during which time the eight privateersmen at the oars of the *Lady Arabella*'s boat had had a hard struggle to reach the shore against the current, Ramage and Yorke were walking carefully up the slippery, weed-coated steps of one of the quays. At the top both of them stopped to get their bearings. As they turned away from the river, a green-painted carriage which was clattering over the cobblestones towards them suddenly stopped and a man, poking his head out of the window, called, "Are you gentlemen English, by any chance?"

"Yes," Ramage said warily.

"From that Post Office packet?"

"From that former packet: she's prize to a French privateer."

The man's attitude changed immediately. "What are you doing?" he demanded brusquely.

"What business is it of yours, pray?" Ramage asked icily.

"I am the Post Office Agent here," the man announced pompously.

"Indeed? We've just come on shore to find you," Ramage said, his voice deliberately neutral.

With that the man flung open the door, kicked down the steps and scrambled down, introducing himself as Henry Chamberlain, adding, "I couldn't believe it when word came from the signal station that they'd sighted a Post Office packet coming in with a Tricolour flying. I've been waiting here hours," he complained pettishly.

Ramage looked up at the coachman, an unshaven and gaunt individual in a faded green livery who was leaning over as far as he dare, trying not to miss a word that was spoken. "Can we go to your office?"

Chamberlain gestured to the carriage door. "My house. It's not far."

As the carriage rattled away, Ramage introduced himself and Yorke and tried to remember the details he had read in the *Royal Kalendar*. Four or five packets had been listed for Lisbon, but all he could recall was that Chamberlain was paid £150 a year. After heading towards Belém along quiet streets the carriage finally stopped outside a small house set back from the road within a walled garden. The coachman jumped down, opened the gate and walked the horse through.

Chamberlain led them into the house, and after introducing them to his wife – a woman with a shrewish face and wearing a dress that would have been unfashionable even a decade earlier, and who treated them with what she probably thought was suitable condescension – took them to his study.

Once he had ushered them to comfortable chairs and sat down behind his desk, Chamberlain became the man of affairs. Although he looked unprepossessing, with small eyes set far apart and a receding chin, his manner was brisk. He picked up a pen and dipped it in an inkwell, and was clearly going to take notes of their conversation until Ramage motioned to him to put the pen down, remembering the eavesdropping coachman, and asked, "First, Mr Chamberlain, when does the next packet sail for England?"

185

"Why do you want to know? The exact time is secret, of course."

His tone was that of the squire questioning a couple of poachers, and Yorke looked at Ramage, who said, "I have to write an urgent dispatch which must go to the First Lord of the Admiralty, Mr Chamberlain. As soon as I've written it I intend placing it in your custody, and it will then be your responsibility to have it delivered safely."

"Oh by jingo, no!" Chamberlain exclaimed, putting his hands flat on the desk in front of him and pressing down, as though pushing away any responsibility. "Anything like that you'd better put on board a ship of war; I'm not responsible for the Navy's business."

Ramage was beginning to dislike the man: he was revealing all the brisk bumptiousness of a jack-in-office; the kind of man who could spend two hours talking a string of clichés, quoting whole paragraphs of regulations, and taking enormous delight in thwarting other people without once taking any responsibility.

"Mr Chamberlain, this is Post Office business," Ramage said quietly and patiently. "Before you decide what you will and won't do, wouldn't it be wiser to inquire why a naval officer and a shipowner land on the quay here from a French prize?"

"Very well," Chamberlain said grudgingly, "tell me."

He said nothing as Ramage briefly described the capture of the *Lady Arabella* and the offer he had made to Kerguelen. Ramage made no mention of Stevens' behaviour, nor of the information given him by Much. Originally he had intended to make a complete report to the Agent, but having met him he was less sure; his manner, the way he sat at his desk, the expression on his face implied automatic disbelief.

As he finished his account he suddenly noticed that Chamberlain's eyes were gleaming. The man was perhaps fifty years old and his thin face was a Gilray cartoon of someone who, bullied and nagged by his wife, in turn bullied and nagged any staff he might have.

Chamberlain smirked as he asked: "Well, Mr Ramage, how

do you propose paying your – ah, debt – to this French scoundrel?"

"I hope the Post Office will provide the money."

"And if not?"

"We shall have to raise it privately, although I hope it won't come to that."

"Why not, pray?"

"Because for something like half what they would have to pay out to the commander for the loss, the Postmasters-General can get back a packet." He suddenly remembered the rot in the transom. *Caveat Emptor!*

"Do you and Mr Yorke fancy being hanged, drawn and quartered at Tyburn?" Chamberlain asked with a sneer.

"Not much."

"Well, if you give that French scoundrel so much as a penny, you'll be guilty of high treason."

Chamberlain had dealt his ace; his thin lips were pressed together in a chilly smile of triumph. Yorke glanced quickly at Ramage, who was rubbing the scar on his brow. There was no doubt Chamberlain was right; he could probably quote the regulation verbatim.

"Explain yourself, please," Ramage said with a calm he did not feel.

Chamberlain stood up and sauntered over to a row of shelves which lined one side of the room. He shuffled through some folders, took out several pages and brought them back to the desk, sorted through them until he had the one he wanted at the top, then looked up at Ramage as a judge might glare at a murderer before he pronounced the death sentence. "I won't bother to give you all the references, but this is a copy of a recent Act of Parliament. The part that concerns you declares it to be treason for any British subject to remit money to anyone owing obedience to the French Government."

He tapped the paper for emphasis as he added, "The phrase 'owing obedience' does not mean just being a French citizen. It includes paying money to someone here, for example, who is acting as agent for the French, even though he might be a Portuguese."

187

Ramage looked at Yorke, who said tactfully, "Perhaps Mr Chamberlain has some suggestion to make."

The Agent shook his head. "I can have nothing to do with it: as a servant of the King I can have no cognizance of treason," he said pompously, savouring every word.

Ramage flushed. "I suggest you choose your words more carefully."

"Don't threaten me," Chamberlain said loftily. "And I'd like to hear from the packet commander how much assistance he received from his passengers in trying to defend his ship against the privateer."

Yorke, seeing Ramage had gone white and was once again rubbing the scar over his brow, said quickly, "Mr Chamberlain, it would be unwise of you to assume that *your* attitude towards us – particularly towards Lieutenant Ramage – might not eventually be construed as something close to treason. We knew nothing of this new Act and you know nothing of how the packet was captured. In the meantime, it is only fair to warn you that as Agent for the Post Office you, of all people, should be careful with the word 'treason'."

"He means," Ramage said heavily, "that I have by no means told you the whole story."

"Why not? Why not, I say? I have every right to know!"

"Because I don't trust you," Ramage snapped. "My report is secret and for the First Lord's eyes only. He will pass on to Lord Auckland and the Cabinet what he sees fit. In the meantime I have told you all *you* need to know. Now, I must go and write my report. When does the next packet sail?"

"Tomorrow. It came in last night," Chamberlain said truculently. "What are you going to say?"

Ramage stared unbelievingly at the man. "I've just said my report is secret. Are you an Agent of the Post Office or the French Government?" he asked, making little effort to hide the contempt in his voice.

"How dare you," Chamberlain yelped. "Calling me a spy! Why, I'll –"

"I'm not calling you a spy: I am asking you."

"I don't mind telling you I have been here for seven years,

188

and I have been a faithful servant of the Post Office for nineteen altogether. I –"

"Please!" Ramage said wearily, "we'll accept your word for it that you are an honest clerk, and you'll have to take my word for it that I have special orders concerning the whole operation of the foreign mails. Just tell me, yes or no, whether you will make sure that when I send my report from the packet, it is forwarded directly to London."

"From the packet? You mean the *Lady Arabella*?"

"Yes, of course."

"You mean you are going back on board?"

"Naturally."

"But she's a French prize! They'll –"

"We are on parole, Mr Chamberlain!"

"But no one would expect you –"

"*No* one, Mr Chamberlain? Neither Mr Yorke nor myself is interested in what other people expect. We've given our word."

"But ... I warn you, I shall make a full report to Lombard Street!"

"Please do," Ramage said heavily, "it would help me if Lord Auckland could read your own description of your behaviour. Now, please make sure that when the reply comes from London it is sent out to me immediately. May we have the use of your carriage to return to the quay?"

Neither man spoke as the Agent's carriage took them to where the *Lady Arabella*'s boat, with the privateer crew, was waiting.

Kerguelen met them as they climbed back on board.

"You had a successful visit?"

Ramage nodded. "The regular packet leaves for England tomorrow. I have to write a letter and have it delivered to the Post Office Agent. If I could have paper, pen and ink ..."

"Of course."

Kerguelen seemed about to say something else, and Ramage waited.

The Frenchman said, in a rush, "It seems silly to keep you on board while we are here at anchor waiting for the money.

But" – he waved towards the skyline of Lisbon – "if you broke your parole..."

Ramage could see the man's dilemma: the Frenchman might well think he'd just arranged for a boat to hang around tonight to pick them up if they manage to escape and leap overboard! Kerguelen needed to be convinced. Ramage knew the Admiralty had no time for an officer-prisoner who escaped by breaking parole, but in this case they might be equally harsh with him for not breaking it to make sure the information now in his possession reached Whitehall as swiftly as possible.

Well, he thought to himself, the Admiralty will have to be satisfied that so far I've staved off a French prison. He had already given Kerguelen his word, and that was the end of it; whatever the Admiralty might say, keeping his word concerned no one but himself. But, having given his word, Ramage found himself getting impatient with a man who hesitated about how to treat it. So he grinned at the Frenchman and pointed to the two British frigates anchored farther up the Tagus.

"We could have arranged for boats to drop down on the ebb tonight and cut your anchor cable and board you as soon as you get out to sea."

"But this is a neutral port," Kerguelen protested.

"And who is to say your cable didn't chafe through? That it wasn't worn and parted with the strain?"

"But ... but you gave your word!"

"Exactly." Ramage laughed. "I gave my word. You and I have to trust each other: we've no choice. You have to trust me to get the money; I have to trust you to free us when the money arrives. I could hand over the money and have you just cut our throats and sail..."

Kerguelen held out his hand and Ramage shook it.

When Yorke and Ramage went down below they found that Much had gone to the cabin he shared with Wilson and South-wick was back, playing chess with Bowen. Both men looked up expectantly as they came in.

"Did you have any success, sir?" Bowen asked.

Yorke stood by the open door, guarding against eaves-droppers, as Ramage described their meeting with Chamberlain, and when he told them about the new Act of Parliament, both men groaned. "So we have to call it off, sir?" Southwick asked.

"If the Admiralty won't allow it."

"But you'll be able to pass the word to Their Lordships about – about the matter that Much told us?"

"I hope so; it depends –"

Yorke gestured from the door and a minute later Kerguelen came in, handing Ramage paper, pen and ink.

"A moment," he said and put his hand in his pocket. He brought out a stick of wax. "When you want to seal the letter, one of my men will bring a lighted candle. It's not that I don't trust you," he said hastily. "It is just that I have a great fear of fire. I was once in a ship that burned..."

The other four men murmured sympathetically: fire, not storms or reefs, was the greatest danger that a ship faced every day of the year, whether at sea or at anchor.

"Write a persuasive letter," Kerguelen said with a grin, and left the cabin.

Ramage turned to Southwick and Bowen: "Since our parole gives us the run of the ship, why don't you two take a turn on deck and give Yorke and me room enough to compose an ode to the First Lord? Tell Wilson what's going on, and Much, too."

When they had gone, Yorke said, "Supposing your report gets intercepted by the French? Stolen from Chamberlain's house, perhaps, or the Falmouth packet is caught and the mails opened? Is it safe to give Lord Spencer *all* the details?"

Ramage inspected the pen and smoothed the feather of the quill. "That's what I wanted to talk to you about: I was wondering the same thing."

"Then you'd better just give the broad outline and tell him the details when you get to London."

"But will he believe the story and persuade the Cabinet to pay the 'ransom' without the details? Without names and facts and dates?"

Yorke shrugged his shoulders. "Write it down and see how it reads!"

An hour later Ramage put down his pen, gathered up seven sheets of paper that he had covered with his first draft, and sat on the bunk to read it. When he had finished he looked up at Yorke and shook his head. "He'll never believe it."

"Why not?" Yorke demanded.

"It sounds bizarre; he'll never believe the ventures part."

"Nonsense," Yorke said brusquely.

He sat in the opposite bunk and scanned the draft, occasionally turning back a page and reading it again. Then he put it down on the table.

"You've met Lord Spencer. Is he shrewd? – I have an idea he is."

"He's shrewd enough!"

"Then he won't find it bizarre. He'll send a copy to the Post Office and they'll pay up!"

"It'd need an Act of Parliament!"

"Small price to pay for finding out what's happening to the mails!"

"But will they *believe* it? I'm really asking them to pay up before they get all the details."

"You are exasperating at times," Yorke said patiently. "Can't you see they already have most of the facts in their possession this minute without realizing it – mostly Falmouth-bound packets lost, the men carrying ventures, and so on? It won't take long to check up on the insurance frauds. Your report shows how all the facts fit together into this – well, this conspiracy. You've just withheld the details of how you found out – and you've explained why you're doing that."

"I suppose so," Ramage muttered lamely. "But even if they believe me, I can't see them either putting up the money to pay Kerguelen, or allowing us to use our own. It's a new Act; to make an exception almost immediately ..."

"You're a miserable fellow," Yorke said. "If you don't have anything to worry about, you very soon manufacture something. Come now, we want a fair copy of the draft. Do you want me to sign as well?"

Ramage shook his head. "But I'll add a line saying you concur with my report, if you're agreeable."

192

Chapter
Fourteen

"What did Mr Ramage say?" Stafford demanded of Jackson as soon as the sentry had herded them below again after their morning exercise.

"Said he hoped to have some news for us when the packet arrived from England in about four weeks' time."

Stafford sniffed. "'Ave to be patient, don't we."

"Perhaps you'd sooner wait in a French prison," Jackson said unsympathetically. "For a year or two."

"I'd sooner be on shore wiv the señoritas."

"Italy," Rossi said, "that would be better. In fact Genova: there the women understand."

"Understand what?" Stafford asked innocently.

"Understand what to do with young and innocent sailors like you when they come on shore with much money in their pockets."

"What do they do?"

"Oh, take them by the hand for a walk along the street and feed them sweet cakes!"

Jackson waved them to be quiet as he turned round to face the rest of the *Arabella*'s crew.

"Listen, all of you: a message from Mr Ramage. No cheering or yelling after I've told you because we don't want to alarm the Frog guards. Now, Mr Ramage has made some sort of bargain with the French prizemaster to pay a ransom, so there's a chance we'll all be freed. And the *Arabella*, too. It'll be a month before he hears from London whether the Admiralty agree to paying."

193

Suddenly Jackson realized that only eleven men – the former Tritons – were grinning; the packetsmen had long faces. Not only long faces: he thought they were suddenly suspicious and hostile. The Tritons had worked hard to restore good relations after the packetsmen had been killed as a result of Captain Stevens' order to cut the sheets and braces, but obviously that had all gone by the board.

The Bosun pushed his way through the crowd of men and stood in front of Jackson.

"How does a Jonathan come to be in the Navy, eh?" he demanded aggressively.

Jackson laughed cheerfully. "Thought I'd give you chaps a hand!"

"That's a damned Yankee sort of answer," the Bosun sneered. "And what's this Mister Ramage mean to all you people anyway?"

Jackson thought for a moment. "We served with him once."

"Where?"

"At sea," Jackson said, "and what's it mean to *you*?" He thought quickly. These men would never be friendly: there was some gulf that he didn't understand. But the Tritons had to have the upper hand. His eyes narrowed. "You're the fellow that tried to kill Mr Ramage. We're the fellows that'd die for him. Just remember that – you *and* your shipmates."

Suddenly the Bosun, a swarthy and heavily built man, stepped forward and grabbed the front of Jackson's shirt with both hands.

"What's going on?" he bellowed, shaking Jackson. "What are you and that meddling lieutenant planning with –"

He broke off with a yelp of pain, hurriedly pushing Jackson away, and the American saw Rossi's grinning face over the Bosun's shoulder.

"Not to move, Bosun," he said, "otherwise..."

"You damned dago, you'll cut open my back!"

A moment later Rossi's hand, holding a knife, came round the Bosun to hold the point against the man's stomach. "And the front too, if you make the move."

Jackson waited a full minute, watching the Bosun's face

beading with perspiration, the eyes flickering fearfully from side to side, trying to see Rossi but not daring to move.

"All right, Rosey," Jackson said, waving the Italian away. "I think he understands now."

The Bosun stepped nimbly to one side, wiping his face with the back of his hand. "Where the hell did you get that knife? The Frogs searched us!"

"*Si*, they make the search," Rossi said calmly and, putting his left hand into his pocket, took out another knife which he handed to Jackson. The Bosun watched fascinated as the Italian put his hand back into the pocket and took out two more knives, giving one to Stafford and the other to Maxton.

"Is magic," Rossi said nonchalantly fetching out four watches, several gold rings and a small medallion. He gave the rings and watches to Jackson. "You can give them back to Mr Ramage when you see him."

Jackson took them without a word. He had hidden them with the knives in the packet's belfry just before the privateersmen boarded, and had been trying to retrieve them ever since the ship anchored in the Tagus. Yet he had not noticed Rossi anywhere near the belfry when they were on deck exercising.

Their silence showed the packetsmen were impressed, but Jackson tried to guess why the mention of freedom had made them surly. He had expected cheers, but instead...

"What's bothering you all?" he asked the Bosun. "You seem upset at the idea of getting freed!"

"Did you mean the Frogs take money and give us back the ship?"

"Yes. We'll be able to sail her back to Falmouth."

"So the insurance won't pay out?"

"For the ship?"

"For everything."

"Damned if I know," Jackson admitted, "but I can't see anyone paying out for the ship if she hasn't been lost."

"Our ventures," the Bosun said. "What about them?"

"Have the Frogs taken 'em?"

"Yes, but they're still on board."

"Then you haven't lost them, have you?"

"So the insurance won't pay out?"

Jackson stared at the man. Was he being deliberately stupid? "I don't know what you're driving at, but you know dam' well that insurers don't pay unless something's lost."

The packetsmen began muttering among themselves and Rossi had moved closer to hear what they were saying. Stafford looked at Jackson questioningly and Maxton moved so he stood with his back against the bulkhead.

As the tension in the cabin increased, Jackson realized that the packetsmen were becoming the enemy; that he and the eleven Tritons – and Mr Ramage of course – were slowly being pushed over on to the side of the French privateersmen. A glance at Rossi, Stafford, Maxton and several of the more perceptive Tritons showed that they too were conscious of strange currents. And almost at once Jackson sniffed danger. Should they make a show of strength right now, in the hope of deterring the packetsmen from trying anything silly?

The more he thought about it, the more sure he was that for some strange reason the packetsmen had expected the insurance underwriters to pay out for a total loss. Now they knew that Mr Ramage had arranged something that could free both ship and crew, they were angry. And, Jackson thought, that means they will probably try to do something to wreck Mr Ramage's negotiations; something that would force the French prizemaster to take the ship to a French port...

By now the packetsmen were grouped round the Bosun at the far end of the cabin, and Jackson waved to the Tritons. "Here, lads!"

They grouped round him, all muttering the same question: "What are they up to, Jacko?"

"What are they up to?" Jackson repeated loudly. "I don't know for sure, lads, but it smells to me like treachery!"

The Bosun turned to listen and the packetsmen stopped talking.

"Their captain didn't want to escape from the privateer – you all saw that," Jackson continued. "You saw the two men at the wheel dropping the ship off to leeward. And you saw the Bosun try to kill Mr Ramage. Well, lads, in London they'd call

196

that treason, and they'd march 'em off to Tyburn and string
'em up. At first I thought it was just those four – and maybe
the Surgeon as well – but perhaps the rest of them can be
bought for a guinea as well.

"But," he said, speaking very clearly, "they don't stand a
chance, whatever they're up to. The French prizemaster wants
to sell the ship to Mr Ramage, instead of risking being recaptured on the way back to France. So he won't take too kindly
to anyone trying to interfere. Nor will the privateersmen, since
they'll share the ransom money. And none of us wants to end
up in a French prison. So that leaves these packetsmen on their
own."

"What are you going to do about it?" one of the packetsmen
jeered.

Jackson turned to face them. "Do?" he asked quietly.
"Why, everyone knows what to do about treason and treachery,
don't they? And apart from that, although the French exchange packetsmen in a few weeks, there are plenty of Navy
seamen captured at the beginning of the war who are still in
French prison camps. Five years, some of them. Five years,"
Jackson repeated, "not five weeks, like a packetsman, but five
years. And maybe another five years before they're freed. Ten
years. A baby is grown up in ten years. A woman's forgotten
she had a husband in ten years. I'm not going into a French
prison for ten years because of treachery..."

The Bosun banged his hand against the bulkhead and bellowed: "You listen to –"

He broke off, his head jerking to one side and his eyes wide
open with fear. Rossi had barely moved, but a knife was now
vibrating in the bulkhead only a couple of inches from where
the Bosun's hand was pressed against the woodwork.

In the complete silence that followed, Rossi sauntered over
and pulled out the knife. He put out his left hand, the index
finger extended, and tickled the Bosun's stomach. The white-
faced Bosun stood stock-still, pressed against the bulkhead,
afraid that even the slightest movement might be dangerous.
Rossi, still smiling, once again tickled his stomach before turning to rejoin Jackson.

The American, left hand on his hip, looked contemptuously at the packetsmen.

"I hope you can all take a hint," he said. "Most of us can do that trick."

His right arm moved suddenly and a knife thudded into the bulkhead on the other side of the Bosun, and a moment later Stafford and Maxwell made slight movements and two more knives vibrated a few inches above the Bosun's head.

Rossi sauntered back, collected the knives and returned them. "You move your arm too much," he chided the Cockney. "And not to throw so hard. The blade doesn't have to go right through the man: three or four inches into the flesh is enough."

As the days passed, Kerguelen made a habit of visiting Ramage's cabin in the late afternoon and staying for an hour or more. Sometimes the five men had an animated discussion about a diversity of subjects; sometimes the Frenchman sat watching Bowen playing chess with one or other of them.

Ramage noticed that the Frenchman followed every move without ever making a comment. Occasionally, after some move by Bowen, Ramage saw Kerguelen's eyes move across the board and invariably it showed he had spotted a trap being set by the Surgeon: sometimes a trap that would not be sprung until a few moves later.

Slowly they came to know him. He was a curious mixture, and at heart probably a royalist. He was contemptuous of many aspects of the Revolution and also contemptuous of his men, and he cared little for their welfare. To him each seemed simply a machine, like the lock of a gun. You offered them money, and they fought. Money, Kerguelen had once commented bitterly, was their fuel: with enough fuel, they gave you heat or light; without fuel, they were nothing.

Although he did not say it, Kerguelen's attitude provided a corollary: without money, there was no loyalty. It was obvious that, as the *Lady Arabella* swung at anchor in the Tagus, Kerguelen was more concerned with the possibility of treachery among his own men than the prisoners. Ramage realized that the Frenchman's contempt for his men was based on a cold assessment of their worth, rather than a lack of leadership.

It was equally obvious that Kerguelen and his brother came from an old family: one that might well have had trouble keeping the guillotine at a distance during the early days of the Revolution. That might explain how a cultured man – and Ramage assumed the brother was the same – was involved in privateering.

Bowen had finally provided a key to the visits. After Kerguelen left the cabin one day, the Surgeon commented, "It's ironic to think a man can be so desperately lonely that he seeks the company of his enemies."

"Enemies?" Yorke echoed.

"We're hardly his allies," Bowen said ironically. "You forget we're his prisoners."

"I fancy he forgets it, too."

"He does: he's becoming more and more worried about his own men."

Ramage nodded. "I've noticed that; as if he's their prisoner in a way – at least until the money arrives."

"He's their prisoner," Yorke said, "and we're his guests."

Southwick grunted and ruffled his hair. "I still don't trust *any* of 'em," he said stolidly. "No good ever came out of trusting a foreigner."

Bowen laughed, moving one of the pawns on the chessboard. "I don't entirely agree, but the idea of this ship anchored in the Tagus with the captors as captive as the captives intrigues me!"

Southwick asked Ramage, "Any more news from Jackson, sir?"

"Nothing. There's still a sort of armed truce between the Tritons and the packetsmen. Apparently Rossi's knives continue to scare the packetsmen."

"Those knives! Well, I'm glad to have my watch back," Southwick said.

"Just be sure these damned privateersmen don't see it," Ramage said. "They'll search again and strip us of everything."

"Aye, Kerguelen has no control."

"He wouldn't do anything, even if he had," Ramage said soberly. "He's a privateersman, not a philanthropist. Don't forget his men signed on for 'share of the profits'. He has a duty to them."

Yorke yawned noisily. "Oh for the delights of Lisbon ... I'd welcome an evening on shore, even if I had to spend it listening to those miserable *fado* singers and watching an elegant lady drive her *cicisbeo* to distraction by staring at a handsome fellow like me!"

Fado, Ramage thought to himself; the Portuguese were a far from sad people, but those sad, sad songs ... always about the broken-hearted woman left at home while her loved one departed, whether for some distant shore or the gates of Heaven. If one judged the country by the song, the nation comprised only women who'd been spurned, jilted, widowed or whose lover had disappeared over the horizon, and every dam' one of them wailing about it to the accompaniment of musical instruments obviously invented by gloomy men for use at funerals.

Was Gianna singing *fado* as she walked or drove around St Kew? Ramage almost laughed at the idea. She might slash at nettles with a stick, she might get angry with her horse, she might lose her temper with her maid, and all because her Nicholas was away at sea (was he being conceited? He thought not), but wailing *fado* in any language: no, Gianna was pure Tuscan in that respect!

Here at anchor in the Tagus, with the hills rolling beyond the city of Lisbon, it was easy to think of Tuscany: of Gianna's Tuscany, and her little hilltop kingdom of Volterra, now overrun by the French. Would she ever be able to go back there to resume her rule? Would this war ever end? He found it hard to remember peacetime. Had he been fifteen or sixteen when the war began? It didn't matter; he could only remember war. Naval service in peacetime must be very boring: going into foreign ports to fire salutes to governors and leave visiting cards, instead of sending in armed boats to cut out prizes from under the nose of the batteries.

Yorke broke into his thoughts. "You look wistful, my friend: your mind was over the hills and far away!"

Ramage nodded. "In Tuscany!"

"Ah – the fair Gianna; I look forward to meeting her."

"You will," Ramage said. "If we ever get to London I'll give an enormous ball and you'll be allowed one dance with her."

"You're not very generous."

"She's very beautiful!"

Southwick slapped his knee. "She is that, Mr Yorke, and I know Mr Ramage won't mind me saying she's a little wild, too. Headstrong, really."

"Uses a pistol instead of a bell to summon a servant, eh?" Yorke said banteringly.

Southwick and Ramage looked at each other and burst out laughing. Yorke said, "Come on, what have I said?"

"Nothing," Ramage said. "It's just that the first time I met her, she was aiming a pistol at me. It was like staring into the muzzle of a 32-pounder!"

"She wouldn't be flattered at the comparison," Yorke said, deliberately misunderstanding Ramage. "I know you can be irritating, but what drove her to such extremes? I mean, a pistol at your *first* meeting!"

"I was supposed to be rescuing her. She and her family bolted from Volterra as the French troops arrived. I was picking them up at dead of night from a small lookout tower along the coast. It was all very mysterious – or romantic, or obvious, depending on how much romance you have in your soul – and she feared a trap because the French were close. So she suddenly arrived in a black cloak that hid her face and kept her pistol aimed at my stomach until she was sure I wasn't a Frenchman."

"Mysterious perhaps," Yorke said, "but hardly romantic as far as I'm concerned."

Bowen, sitting at the table with a chess problem set out in front of him, began clearing the pieces from the board. "What do you propose doing if the Government won't allow us to pay Kerguelen the money, sir?" he asked.

Ramage had been expecting one of them to ask the question eventually. "There's not much choice: withdraw our parole and brush up our French. If the packetsmen come to their

201

senses, we'd stand a chance of retaking the ship. Or we might meet a British frigate..."

"Those two frigates anchored here," Yorke said. "They've done nothing..."

"Nor will they," Ramage said. "The French Government is probably just waiting for a chance to invade Portugal. The British seizing a French ship – for that's what the *Arabella* is now as far as the French are concerned – right in front of Lisbon might be just the excuse they need."

Yorke shrugged his shoulders. "Surely you'd have expected some word from them, though?"

"No. Chamberlain might have told one of the captains that we're prisoners, but he hasn't told them what I'm doing because he doesn't know himself. You can't expect a frigate captain to get excited over some lieutenant held prisoner on board an enemy ship in a neutral port."

"I can," Yorke said, "but it wouldn't be justified! Let's hope the Government pays up!"

From the time his report to the First Lord had been taken on shore to the Agent, Ramage had tried – without much success – to shut his mind to the question. It was easy enough during the day, but at night it always sneaked in, nagging and probing and swirling like spasms of toothache. He would deliberately contrive erotic thoughts of Gianna, but they would be jostled out...

To pay or not to pay ... The answers he gave himself never varied. Having just passed an Act of Parliament, the Government certainly would not allow the bargain to be carried out ... Yet, knowing what was at stake the First Lord and the Joint Postmasters-General would persuade the Cabinet ... No, because the First Lord will not be persuaded that Lieutenant Ramage has really discovered what happens to the packets ... Yes, because the First Lord will guess from the bizarre situation outlined in his report that Lieutenant Ramage has been forced to take unusual steps ... No, because the First Lord is away in Dorset, confined to bed with gout and a high fever, and another one of their Lordships dealt with his report (a dam' dull dog) – and refused the request without bothering to refer to either of the Postmasters-General.

Perhaps the Lisbon packet had been captured before it reached Falmouth and sank the bags of mail. Or failed to sink them, so that the French, having slowly read their way through the captured mail, had found his secret report and knew that the meddling Lieutenant Ramage was prisoner on board a French prize in Lisbon ... Word would soon reach the French Consul, or the French agents in Lisbon – the city must be teeming with them – that a throat needed cutting. Perhaps even Kerguelen's as well, if he had a royalist background...

Yorke was repeating the question: "Do you think they will?"

And Southwick and Bowen were staring at him as if he was a stranger. Why? What had happened? Were they...

"You need a rest, sir," Bowen said, getting up and walking over to him. Ramage suddenly felt unutterably weary; a weariness no sleep could ever satisfy. Weary and full of a sense of futility, that even if something was worth doing – which was so unlikely – he hadn't the energy to do it anyway. Neither the energy nor the wish. The three men seemed to be floating ... Bowen's face was enormous and peering down at him.

Chapter
Fifteen

The days passed slowly. Much usually stayed in his cabin, reading his Bible, while Wilson sat with him studying military manuals. Bowen and Southwick played chess steadily with quiet desperation and Ramage and Yorke, who spent hours pacing the deck, were now so familiar with Lisbon's skyline that they rarely looked at it. They had invented various games – betting against each other how many tacks one of the gaudily painted and heavily laden fregatas would take to reach them; how many times gulls would dive into the water between the *Arabella* and the shore in the next ten minutes. They bet on how many butts there were in the *Arabella*'s deck planking, and halfway through counting them found a startled Kerguelen watching them. He was so intrigued that they persuaded him to join a lottery on how many knots there were in the king plank. When he won, he was quick to think of more objects about which they could bet.

Finally it was the day before the packet was due and Yorke, walking on deck with Ramage, said, "Shall we ask Kerguelen if we can go and see that Agent fellow, Chamberlain?"

Ramage grimaced and shrugged his shoulders. "No point, unless you want a run on shore." He thought about it again, conscious that for the past few days he had had little energy and initiative.

Yorke was obviously thinking the same thing, and said, "You're sure of that?"

"Yes, he can't have any news yet. Anyway, if the Government agrees to pay up, Chamberlain will be so impressed he'll rush to let us know. If it refuses, he'll be so damned pleased he'll still rush to tell us."

Yorke walked over to the bulwark and looked over at the city. When Ramage joined him, he tapped his arm. "When this is over, you must take a rest. You've had a bad time in the Caribbean, and now this. Everything has to have a rest, you know. Like my razors."

"Your razors?" Ramage exclaimed.

"Haven't you seen them? How many do you have?"

"A set of two."

"And you use them alternate days?"

"Of course," Ramage said.

"But you don't get a good shave."

"Oh yes I do!"

"By your standards! Try having seven razors, like me. Each has a day of the week engraved on the back."

"But what's the point? Just more razors to strop!"

"Yes – but each has six days' rest. I don't know why, but good steel honed really sharp needs a regular rest to keep a fine cutting edge."

"You're a good man lost to the Church," Ramage said sourly. "Or maybe you should have been a barber."

"Church or barber, eh?" Yorke said amiably. "You're the one with the sharp tongue!"

Suddenly he pointed westward, towards the broad entrance of the Tagus. Running in before a fresh westerly wind was a small brig similar to the *Lady Arabella*.

"Not only the Lisbon packet safe and sound, but a day early!" he exclaimed. "Did she find good weather, or did they send her out a day early to bring the glad news?"

If Ramage was honest with himself, Yorke's matter-of-fact acceptance that the Post Office might have sailed the packet a day early because of his efforts was the first time he had thought of the possibility, yet it was an obvious one, given the Government's position.

Certainly he had listened when Sir Pilcher Skinner had described how dispatches from admirals, generals and governors

205

were being lost along with the Government's orders for new and secret operations. But with an almost frightening detachment he realized that it was not until this very moment, as he watched the distant packet coming in under all plain sail, that he fully appreciated how one continent was cut off from another by the packet losses.

Previously it was a fascinating problem in which he was closely involved. Now he seemed to be standing back aloof, looking at an invisible barrier, like a *cheval de frise*, running north and south down the centre of the Western Ocean and cutting it in half. A barrier with gaps here and there, since occasional packets got through, but still a massive barrier.

The Government in London was like an admiral on board a flagship unable to signal to his Fleet; a regimental sergeant major struck dumb on a parade ground. The Prime Minister in Downing Street, the War Minister at the Horse Guards, the First Lord at the Admiralty, the Foreign Secretary also in Downing Street – and not one of them certain he could pass even the most trifling order beyond the shores of Britain...

As the packet drew closer, the long days of waiting began to recede. Southwick, Bowen, Wilson and Much came up on deck and Kerguelen joined them. Soon the brig was near enough for them to see a crowd of people on her deck, but clearly her captain was not going to get too close to the *Arabella*.

"Carrying a lot of passengers," Southwick commented.

Ramage stared moodily at the packet. Locked up in a drawer on board that ship was the letter which was going to tell him if he was a free man with a future or a discredited lieutenant doomed to spend the next few years in a French prison. The next couple of hours were going to be worse than the past month...

Almost exactly two hours after the packet had gone alongside the quay, a boat came out to the *Lady Arabella* and Kerguelen sent for Ramage. In the boat was a messenger from the Post Office Agent who, after making sure it was indeed Lieutenant Ramage to whom he was speaking, handed over a heavily sealed letter. He would wait for the reply, he said.

As Ramage turned to go down to his cabin he saw that every privateersman was on deck watching him. Kerguelen glanced away to avoid Ramage's eye. Every one of those men, Ramage realized, knew that the letter he was holding might represent a great deal of money; money to be handed over to Kerguelen and shared out among them.

Yorke was sprawled on one of the bunks, ostentatiously reading a book; Bowen was demonstrating some complicated chess defence to an obviously bewildered Southwick. All three were making a great effort to avoid showing any curiosity about the letter.

He broke the brittle green wax of the seals and found it contained not a letter from Lord Spencer but a note from the Agent. "My Lord," Chamberlain had written, "I have this moment received an urgent communication from Lord Auckland concerning the *Lady Arabella* packet, and with it is a letter from the Admiralty addressed to you which I dare not risk having delivered to you on board the prize. I shall be at my house if you can leave the ship; otherwise would you be kind enough to give written and sealed instructions which the messenger will bring to me without delay."

Hmm ... Mr Chamberlain's attitude has undergone a lot of modification, Ramage thought wryly, but there is no mention of the ransom money. What did "concerning the *Lady Arabella* packet" mean? Was Chamberlain being discreet, afraid the letter might fall into the wrong hands?

"From Chamberlain," he told them. "He wants me to go and see him."

"Kerguelen will agree," Yorke said. "May I come?"

Ramage nodded, and Yorke swung himself from the bunk and reached for his hat and cloak.

Southwick still looked worried, and Ramage said, "I'm afraid I don't know what's been decided; the Agent doesn't give a hint."

Yorke followed him up on deck, where Kerguelen was pacing up and down, head bowed, hands clasped behind his back. The Frenchman walked over to Ramage and asked abruptly, "The money – it is arranged?"

"The Post Office Agent wants me to go to his house: he has dispatches from London." Ramage held out the letter for him to read, but Kerguelen waved it aside with a gesture showing he accepted Ramage's word. "You'd better use our boat – the messenger can dismiss his." He shouted orders to a group of seamen.

"You think everything will be all right?" he asked, once he made sure the men were working quickly.

Ramage gave the best imitation of a Gallic shrug that he could muster, and waved the letter. "The Agent makes no mention of difficulties."

Suddenly he wanted Kerguelen to come with him to see the Agent. The Frenchman had behaved honourably so far: he had agreed to the bargain, accepted their parole, and done his best to make their stay on board the *Lady Arabella* as comfortable as possible.

But, Ramage thought sourly, all of them had now passed well beyond the point where the word of honour of honest men necessarily influenced what would happen: they were now in the shadowy world of politics. What Lord Auckland – the Cabinet, rather, since it was obviously involved – decided might well be based on political expediency: ministers always had a wary eye fixed on Parliament and a highly sensitive ear cocked which could detect a rumble, let alone a howl, from the Opposition Front Bench. If Lieutenant Ramage's word of honour or freedom had to be sacrificed to quieten that rumble ...

Yes, Ramage decided, Kerguelen deserved not only to know exactly what was happening, but to be present while it was happening. "I hope you will allow Mr Yorke to come with me."

"Of course."

"And yourself."

"Me? *Pourquoi?*" Kerguelen did not try to hide his astonishment.

"I would prefer it," Ramage said simply.

Kerguelen seemed to sense that whatever reason Ramage

208

had was straightforward but not to be explained or debated. "Give me a minute to change," he said.

When the three men arrived at Chamberlain's house they were met by a Portuguese manservant who, after taking their hats and cloaks, gestured towards chairs in the large hall. Ramage looked gloomily at Yorke and made a face. The Agent was playing the childish game, so beloved by petty officials and minor diplomats, of keeping visitors waiting as the only way of proving – to themselves, if no one else – their importance. So childish, Ramage reflected; so unnecessary, since it revealed the man's unimportance. And, perhaps the most unforgivable thing of all, so predictable and obvious: it had all the subtlety of a caulker's maul.

After twenty minutes, the manservant returned and indicated that they should follow him into the large cool room the Agent used as an office. Chamberlain, sitting at his desk, kept his head bent over some papers in front of him until Ramage was half-way across the room. Then he gave a carefully timed start, glanced up, arranged a thin smile on his face and came round the desk with his hand outstretched.

"Ah, Lieutenant, I'm glad to see you. And you, Mr Yorke ..."

His voice tailed off as he saw Kerguelen.

Ramage took the Agent's arm and said in a deceptively quiet voice, "You must meet Captain Kerguelen, the prizemaster of the *Lady Arabella*. Captain – this is the Post Office Agent, Mr Chamberlain."

The Frenchman bowed but the Agent looked dumbfounded. "Lieutenant! I can't allow –"

"Let's resume our talk out in the street then," Ramage said, his voice ominously quiet. "Then we'll be on neutral ground."

"But I ..."

"I want you to tell us if you are ready to pay the money to Captain Kerguelen."

"Indeed I am not!" Chamberlain exclaimed. "I will neither provide the money nor allow you and Mr Yorke to pay it."

Ramage looked at Kerguelen. The Frenchman's face was

209

impassive. It was impossible to guess his thoughts.

"Perhaps you would be kind enough to tell the Captain why," Ramage said.

"I most certainly will not!" Chamberlain said angrily, sitting down in his chair with a thump. "I don't have to explain my decisions to enemy privateersmen – to pirates!"

Ramage turned to look down at Chamberlain and said, his voice little more than a whisper, "You weren't being asked to explain *your* decisions; you don't have the power to make any that matter a damn. You were being asked to explain the recent Act of Parliament. However, before I withdraw my parole I'll explain."

With that Ramage described to Kerguelen the Act, explaining that it was newly passed, and the first he knew of it was when the Agent told him. As Ramage spoke, Kerguelen occasionally nodded his head and, at the end of it, after Ramage described his application to the Admiralty for an exception to be made, he shrugged his shoulders expressively.

"So," Ramage concluded, "I withdraw my parole."

"Me, too," Yorke said. "We are your prisoners again."

Chamberlain gasped. "Lieutenant! You can't do that!"

Ramage just stared at him but Yorke said contemptuously, "You count your mailbags! Leave a matter of honour to people who understand it!"

"But there's a letter for you," Chamberlain wailed helplessly to Ramage. "From the First Lord of the Admiralty. And there's the letter from the Postmaster-General – from Lord Auckland himself."

Kerguelen was quicker than Ramage to grasp what the Agent had done and said: "Revoke your parole when we get back to the ship. I'll wait in the hall until you are ready." With that he left the room, carefully shutting the door behind him.

Ramage turned to Chamberlain and, still speaking quietly and rubbing the scars over his brow, said, "Give me Lord Spencer's letter."

Chamberlain was about to speak, but Yorke saw that Ramage's face had gone white and he knew what the unconscious rubbing of the scars meant. He also knew that Ramage was one

210

of the few men whose voice became quieter as he grew more angry. Ramage at this moment was a spring under enormous tension: at a certain point it needed only a fraction more strain to release it. Chamberlain had been so objectionable that Yorke knew it was a miracle that Ramage had kept his temper up to now. But the Agent was far too stupid to be warned by the drawn face, the narrowed eyes and the hard line of the lips.

"Mr Chamberlain," Yorke said hurriedly, "you're in much deeper water than you realize. Stop playing silly games with Mr Ramage because there's nothing to discuss. You have two letters to deliver, and that's your only function. You are the Post Office Agent; merely a clerk in this affair. Mr Ramage and I gave our word of honour to Captain Kerguelen – you forget that long before we reached Lisbon we agreed to buy back the ship and our freedom for £2,500, and we gave our parole until the money came from England.

"Then you told us of the new Act and Mr Ramage wrote to the First Lord," Yorke continued, as though explaining to a child. "From what you say, apparently the Government will not honour our agreement, but that doesn't mean to say *we* don't honour our parole. So from the moment that you told us the Government had disavowed us," Yorke continued, speaking very distinctly, "we reverted to being prisoners of war, and the *Lady Arabella* remains a French prize."

"But you can't do that! You must stop him!" Chamberlain gabbled excitedly. "You can't go back on board and let that pirate escape with the *Lady Arabella*!"

"Can't we?" Ramage interrupted coldly. "Write to Lord Auckland and explain how you tried to prevent two British gentlemen from keeping their parole! Now, give me that letter from the Admiralty!"

Chastened, Chamberlain unlocked a drawer in his desk and handed Ramage a packet on the back of which was the familiar anchor seal of the Admiralty. Ramage took it and put it in his pocket.

"Aren't you going to read it?" the Agent asked incredulously.

"Yes, but not now."

"But supposing it contains orders?"

"You've told me the money is not here, and Mr Yorke and myself are not allowed to pay it privately. That's all that matters for the moment."

"But Lord Auckland..." Chamberlain broke off nervously, as though at a loss what to do next, and Ramage saw he was fingering another letter, the seal of which was broken.

"What about Lord Auckland?"

"Well, he says that although..."

Again he broke off. Instinctively both Yorke and Ramage moved closer to him: obviously the Agent was holding something back.

"Why don't you read your orders from Lord Spencer, Lieutenant?"

"We are dealing with Post Office business, Mr Chamberlain. You, as the Post Office Agent, have already told us – and I include Captain Kerguelen – officially that the Government will neither provide nor allow us to provide the money. The moment you told us that, we were Captain Kerguelen's prisoners again. He's freed of any undertaking he gave us."

Yorke was watching Chamberlain closely as Ramage spoke, and the Agent's manner had become nervous and jerky, almost like a trapped animal. When they had first come into the room, Chamberlain had been pompous, almost bombastic, though his attempted snubbing of Kerguelen had fizzled out like a damp fuse. Although he had obviously not understood the parole business, he had condescendingly accepted it as being something that eccentric men involved themselves in, to the detriment of the Post Office.

Yorke began to wonder exactly what were Lord Auckland's instructions to the Agent. He had more than a suspicion that something underhand was going on. A quick glance told Yorke that Ramage thought so too and would probably offer the wretched Agent a way out.

Ramage said quietly, "I think you had better give us some idea of what Lord Auckland says."

Chamberlain was struggling to recover some of his poise. "It's confidential," he said, looking significantly at Yorke. "I'm

212

prepared to impart it to you, Lieutenant, as a King's officer, but..."

"Then keep it to yourself," Ramage said abruptly. "Mr Yorke was as much a party to the agreement as I was and has every right to know. Moreover he knows a great deal more about all this than you do. However, we are taking up your time. You can mention in your next report that since the money is not forthcoming we have withdrawn our parole. Now, if you'll excuse us..."

As Ramage abruptly turned away, Yorke saw the desperate look in Chamberlain's eyes: the paralysed stare of a frightened rabbit. The Agent's hands were clenched, perspiration suddenly beaded his forehead and the tip of his tongue wetted his lips.

Yorke put his hands on the desk and leaned slightly towards the Agent. "You are *quite* sure there's nothing more we should know, Mr Chamberlain?"

"I ... well, his Lordship has ... I have certain powers delegated to me ... in certain circumstances ... I –"

Ramage swung round and said savagely, "Give me Lord Auckland's letter!"

In a complete reflex action, Chamberlain handed it over.

Yorke knew that the moment Ramage read the letter and discovered whatever complex game it was that Chamberlain had been trying to play, he might lose control of himself and possibly strike the Agent.

"Mr Chamberlain," he said quietly, "if you had some other business to attend to for five minutes, so that Lieutenant Ramage and I could..."

"Oh, certainly, certainly!" the Agent said thankfully and fled the room.

Ramage read the letter standing and then slumped in a chair. He held it out to Yorke. "It's just as well you got that scoundrel out of the room. Did you guess?"

Yorke did not reply and began reading quickly. "... absolutely essential that Lieutenant Ramage's freedom be arranged ... Act forbids the Government to permit payment ... However, if you can arrange his release by any means..."

213

At that point Yorke nearly stopped reading but, realizing Ramage had read to the end, he carried on. The second page began, "In view of the importance of obtaining Lieutenant Ramage's freedom, and in case you are unable to arrange this, the Government are drafting a special Act to allow the payment to the French prizemaster in this particular instance, and it is confidently expected that this will be passed by both Houses of Parliament within a matter of days. The next packet, I anticipate, will bring you authority to carry out the terms of the agreement, should you have failed to obtain his prior release in some other manner. Lord Spencer is writing to Lieutenant Ramage by the same mail giving him fresh instructions and you will use your best endeavours to ensure that Lieutenant Ramage receives Lord Spencer's letter..."

"What on earth was Chamberlain trying to do?" Yorke asked incredulously.

"I'm damned if I know," Ramage said wearily. "That phrase 'by any means' at the beginning of the letter: perhaps he thought we'd agree to cheat Kerguelen and it'd be a feather in his cap. A letter of congratulation from Lord Auckland for saving them money..."

Yorke nodded. "It'd seem so simple to anyone with a mind like Chamberlain's: neutral port, British ships of war near by ... we're safely on shore in his office so Kerguelen couldn't take us prisoner again ... Leave Kerguelen to get out of the Tagus as best as he could, and arrange for a frigate to be waiting for him."

"Exactly what I'd guessed," Ramage said. "Yet there's nothing in Lord Auckland's letter even suggesting anything underhand."

"Oh come," Yorke said chidingly, opening the letter again and reading aloud: " 'release *by any means* ... should you have failed to have obtained his release *in some other manner*...' That's the way a politician words it – and you've seen how a clerk interprets it!"

"I begin to wonder if Chamberlain doesn't fit into the disappearing packets business..."

"No, I'm sure he doesn't," Yorke said firmly. "He's not dishonest. The phrase that frightened him was Lord Auckland's *'should you have failed...'* He's scared stiff of what his Lordship would do if he fails – and dreaming of glory if he succeeds. Just imagine the way he'd report that he'd freed you and got the packet back without paying any money. And it's certainly the first – and probably only – time in his life he's been concerned in matters involving the Cabinet."

"It's the first time for me, too," Ramage said ruefully.

"I won't flatter you by pointing out the differences in personality," Yorke said. "But what are we going to do about Kerguelen? I wouldn't blame him if he calls the whole thing off, thanks to Chamberlain's play-acting."

"I think he's been damned decent up to now. It was a mistake to bring him though."

"Oh no," Yorke said emphatically. "Going back on board and telling him he has to wait another couple of weeks would make him suspect some trickery. Why not just haul Chamberlain back, and make him explain it to Kerguelen? Make him sign a letter to Kerguelen, if necessary."

"Chamberlain would refuse; he'd end up insulting Kerguelen again."

"Threaten him," Yorke said flatly. "Tell him you'll report to Lord Spencer exactly what has happened."

"We can't prove it."

"We certainly can! Your word and mine – on oath, if need be – against Chamberlain's."

"All right, I'll try it," Ramage said reluctantly. "But I'm so damned angry it's as much as I can do to keep my hands off him!"

"I guessed that," Yorke grinned. "But don't worry – pride is his weak point, and you've just about blunted that!"

Yorke went to the door and shouted peremptorily for the Agent, who came into the room looking as frightened as a schoolboy reporting to the headmaster for a well-deserved and long-anticipated beating.

"Sit down," Ramage said brusquely. "Now, pick up that letter – Lord Auckland's. Adjust your spectacles and read it aloud slowly, from beginning to end."

Sheepishly the Agent did so, rushing the final paragraph. Ramage waved a hand. "Too fast; let's have that last paragraph again."

The Agent took out a handkerchief and mopped his face, and then read it once more.

He glanced up to find Ramage and Yorke staring at him. He looked down and folded the letter, and then arranged the inkwell squarely in front of him. Still neither man spoke, and Chamberlain wriggled in his chair and shut the drawer beside him. He put the letter under a paperweight and rearranged the position of the inkwell. Then he looked up again and found both men still watching him. He tried to smile, but the muscles of his face were frozen.

Then Ramage said, in little more than a whisper, "What were you trying to do, Mr Chamberlain?"

"I thought ... it seemed to be best that..."

His voice trailed off and he stared at the heavy inkwell.

Damn the man, Ramage thought; but since he'll never be punished officially for this day's work it'll be worth frightening him. "Curious, Mr Chamberlain, how Lord Auckland seems so concerned about my freedom, isn't it? A mere lieutenant..."

"I haven't thought about it, I must admit."

"Why don't you, then?"

"Well, I suppose ... your father ... The Earl of Blazey. A friend of Lord Auckland, perhaps?"

"Of no significance. For months the Prime Minister's nephew was a prisoner in French hands," Ramage said evenly. "There was no special act of Parliament for him ... just a routine exchange."

"I don't know, then," the Agent said helplessly.

"Think, then!" Ramage snapped.

Suddenly Chamberlain looked alarmed. "You aren't really concerned with secret Post Office business, are you?"

Ramage just held the man's eyes without speaking, and saw the look of horror spreading over his face. Chamberlain looked away, to find Yorke watching him. He swallowed convulsively as though a hard crust was stuck in his throat.

"How ... how was I to know?"

"Because I told you the very first time I came here, but you were so puffed up with your own importance you took no notice. Anyway, there's no excuse for juggling with your orders. Were you expecting me to break my parole, so you could put the money in your own pocket when it arrived and claim the French bolted with it?"

Ramage knew he was being cruel, but the man's meddling might even now result in Kerguelen being too suspicious to wait, so that instead of Ramage reporting to Lord Spencer by word of mouth he'd end up silent in a French prison.

"How dare you!" Chamberlain spluttered. "What a terrible thing to say!"

"But it's a question Lord Auckland might well ask you," Ramage said relentlessly and, realizing he had frightened the man enough, decided Kerguelen was the next problem. "Well, Mr Chamberlain, you've probably wrecked everything by now: I can't blame Captain Kerguelen if he's decided – thanks to your behaviour – that he's dealing with tricksters and insists we go back on board so that he can sail for France at once."

"I don't see how you can blame me for –"

"It's irrelevant what I think; Lord Auckland will be the man who sacks you," Ramage said harshly. "At the moment my only concern is to give you a chance of repairing some of the damage you've done. You are the only one who can."

"How? In what way?" the Agent asked anxiously, not far from tears.

"Persuade Captain Kerguelen that the money will be forthcoming in a week or two, and that what you said earlier was entirely your own warped invention."

"How can I?" Chamberlain wailed. "He won't believe anything I say!"

"Very well, then Mr Yorke and I will have to leave as his prisoners: you can inform Lord Auckland that thanks to your handiwork we'll be in France in about ten days' time, and ask him to pass the word to the Admiralty."

Chamberlain suddenly stood up and scurried to the door. "I'll try," he muttered, as if talking to himself, and Ramage noticed he had snatched up Lord Auckland's letter.

217

As soon as the door closed, Ramage asked Yorke, "Am I being too hard on him?"

Yorke sniffed. "I could wring his neck. But what if he can't persuade Kerguelen?"

"We'd better brush up our French. But if he reads him extracts from that letter, it might do the trick."

"D'you really think so?"

"The letter and perhaps some help from us – if he trusts us an inch, which I doubt. Still, he'll see what a state Chamberlain is in; he's no fool."

No fool, Ramage reflected. The £2,500 they had offered him must have represented a substantial profit for the Frenchman; a profit without risk. At this moment he was probably trying to balance the unknown risk of staying for £2,500 in sterling against the known risk of making a bolt for France.

The door opened and a worried and perspiring Chamberlain hurried in. "He wants to speak to you."

"Bring him in, then."

Kerguelen came in and Ramage gestured him to sit at Chamberlain's desk. The Frenchman looked bewildered but not suspicious.

"I'm sorry about this," Ramage said. "I hope Mr Chamberlain has explained."

Kerguelen nodded. "This Lord Auckland..."

"You've seen the letter?"

"This man read from it. Extracts."

"Very well. Lord Auckland is one of the two Ministers in charge of the Post Office. He has written that after passing an Act of Parliament, the Government will pay the money, and –"

"But when we first arrived here this man" – Kerguelen pointed at Chamberlain – "said he would not pay."

"This man," Ramage said contemptuously, "is a clerk who has exceeded his authority and was trying to curry favour with the Minister. He will probably be punished. He misled me, too, until I insisted on seeing Lord Auckland's letter to him. That showed me what this man had done. If you wish to read Lord Auckland's letter, you may do so. Chamberlain, put it on the desk."

218

The Agent put it in front of Kerguelen, who pushed it to one side. "Mr Ramage," he said quietly, "will you give me your word that you truly believe the money will come and I'll be paid without any traps being set?"

"I give you my word," Ramage said, and gestured to Yorke.

"You have mine, too," Yorke said.

"And mine," Chamberlain added eagerly. "In writing, if you wish."

No one spoke, and Chamberlain flushed.

Ramage stood up. "If we may renew our parole, perhaps we could dine out before returning to the ship. Would you be our guest, Captain?"

"It would be a pity to ignore the delights of Lisbon, but until your new Act of Parliament is passed, I think you'd better be my guests!"

Chamberlain said hurriedly: "Please make use of my carriage. Keep it for the day, if you wish to see the sights of Lisbon..."

Back in his cabin on board the *Lady Arabella* Ramage sat on the bunk and finally opened the letter from the Admiralty. All through dinner, and for an hour's drive round the city, he was so conscious of the unopened letter in his pocket that it might have been a piece of red-hot shot, but he had been determined not to read it until he was on board again. A childish test of willpower, he told himself, but whether he read it then or a week later it would still say the same thing. As far as the ship and their freedom was concerned, the Postmaster-General's letter to the Agent was the only one that mattered.

As he read he found he had denied himself very little. The letter was, of course, signed by the Secretary to the Board of Admiralty, Evan Nepean, who began with the customary phrases and then said, "I am commanded by my Lords Commissioners of the Admiralty to inform you that they give qualified approval of your actions concerning negotiations with the French prizemaster as described in your report to them of the tenth ultimo."

Nepean went on to describe how a recent Act of Parliament

made it a criminal offence to transfer funds to someone owing allegiance to an enemy country, but added, "In view of all the special circumstances, which had not been visualized when the present Act was drafted, Their Lordships have recommended to His Majesty's Government that a special Act be passed authorizing the transfer in this particular instance...

"Their Lordships further command me to express their displeasure that your report is written in such general terms and contains no specific details enabling them to advise the Post Office what course to take to avoid further losses of packets, nor recommend specific legal action, if any, against any of its employees alleged by you to be guilty of unspecified crimes or misdemeanours.

"You are hereby directed to forward by the quickest means available a second report giving these details, regardless of the risk of such report falling into unauthorized or enemy hands. Their Lordships further direct me to acquaint you that the reasons for not giving such details in your first report are sufficiently vague as to warrant a further expression of their displeasure."

Ramage folded the letter and put it back in his pocket. A single expression of Their Lordships' displeasure was often sufficient to blast the career of a post-captain, let alone a lieutenant. Maybe, he thought wryly, the "qualified approval" cancelled out the first "displeasure", so he would be debited with only the second.

Still, to be fair to the Admiralty, sitting back on his bunk here in the Tagus, the ship rolling slightly at anchor, the ebbing tide sluicing past the hull like a running tap, the whole capture of the *Lady Arabella* now seemed remote; something that had happened to other people. He thought of Lord Spencer reading his report and then pictured himself sitting in the First Lord's quiet, remote office in Whitehall, trying to persuade him that it was all real: that the frauds had happened, were still going on, and would continue...

Lord Spencer would listen attentively – he always did. And then – judging by the tone of this letter – he would probably shake his head politely, without saying anything. Yet it would be clear that he thought Ramage was being melodramatic, imagining much of it and guessing the rest.

Much of it! Much, the Mate, would corroborate everything. But his Lordship would probably say – or think, anyway – that Much was a man with a grudge and consider that he had hoodwinked Ramage. The Bosun's attack with a cutlass? The poor fellow was overwrought ... The packetsmen slashing the rigging? Captain Stevens' way of making sure the French could not get the ship under way ... There was no way of describing the dozens of little episodes, each one trifling and apparently meaningless, but which taken all together, like thousands of strokes of an artist's brush, made a clear picture. A look on Stevens' face, a remark of Our Ned's, items of information passed on by Jackson. Probably none of it was evidence acceptable in a court of law – or acceptable to the First Lord either.

Yet how *could* it be proved in a way that would satisfy a judge and a jury? A judge would ask if the packetsmen insured their ventures and deliberately found a French privateer and surrendered to her. If the answer was no, he would dismiss everything as the chance of war. Would a judge accept that meeting a privateer was simply a bonus; something that happened perhaps once a year? Would a judge – the First Lord, anyway – accept that for men being paid £12 a year, the chance of a profit of £400 was enough for them to surrender their ship – commit treason, in fact?

Well, one thing was certain: lying here fretting would achieve nothing: they just had to wait for the money to arrive ...

Chapter
Sixteen

It was a fortnight before the next packet arrived from Falmouth: fourteen days spent mostly on shore in Lisbon. Kerguelen, intrigued with the city after their excursion in the Agent's carriage, insisted that Ramage, Yorke, Bowen and Southwick accompany him on visits to various towns near by, where he showed a lively interest and a surprising knowledge of Manueline Gothic architecture.

On the fourteenth day after the arrival of the last packet – a fortnight of settled weather with a stiff breeze between north and west, just the wind to give the packet a fast passage – Kerguelen joined Ramage and Yorke on deck shortly after dawn, and carrying his telescope.

After greeting them he used the glass to search the river to seaward. Finally he shut it with a snap. "What is it you say in England? 'Watch a pot and it never boils'!"

"Something like that," Yorke said. "No sign of her, eh?"

Kerguelen shook his head. "Give her a day or two." Then he added with a grin, "Perhaps your Government is having trouble finding the money."

"They'll just increase the taxes," Yorke said cheerfully.

Up to that moment Ramage had tried to keep the whole question of the Act of Parliament at the back of his mind. Now, standing on the *Lady Arabella*'s foredeck and watching the fregatas drifting down the Tagus on the ebb tide and finding no sign of the packet's sails on the horizon, the doubts began to flood in. Supposing Opposition Members of Parliament had seized the opportunity to embarrass the Government by opposing the Bill?

Any defeat of a Government bill, however unimportant the actual subject, was regarded as a major triumph for the Opposition. Party politics were supreme; each party was a veritable Moloch frequently demanding the sacrifice of honour and decency – and certainly the fate of a Post Office packet and a miserable lieutenant – if it brought votes.

He turned from watching the skyline of Lisbon. Just along the coast was Cape St Vincent, where he'd lost the *Kathleen* cutter in the battle that took its name from the Cape. Farther south the coast swung eastward in to a great bight round to the Spanish border and Cadiz, where the Spanish fleet was blockaded. And then Gibraltar, and across the Gut the shore of Africa, lined by the great mass of the Atlas Mountains.

Sailing into the Strait from the Atlantic as dawn broke never ceased to fascinate him. The dark mountains of Spain to larboard would be heavily shadowed, and because a ship usually kept close in to avoid the current, the distant land sounds carried across the water. The insane, agonized braying of donkeys; the occasional heavy thud of a mason chipping stone; the tinny clangour of a village church's tiny bell ... The heavy smell of herbs borne seaward by a gentle offshore breeze, and always the mountains of Africa, powder blue in the early light and mysterious like veiled Arab women watching from curtained windows in the narrow streets of Tangier.

How remote London seemed. Whitehall running northward from the Houses of Parliament, with a short turning off it called Downing Street, where the Prime Minister lived in a nondescript house. Five minutes' walk along Whitehall to the Admiralty building set back from the road behind a high screen wall, with a cobbled courtyard in between. And a mile away, in the City itself, the Post Office headquarters at Lombard Street. In four buildings – Parliament itself, the house in Downing Street, the Admiralty building and the one in Lombard Street – men had discussed the *Lady Arabella*.

By now Government lawyers and Parliament's legal draftsmen would have drawn up a short Act, dipping deep into their enormous store of clichés and redundant phrases. The Act would have been printed and gone through various stages in the House of Commons and the House of Lords. There would have been divisions, with the Members faithfully trooping into the "Ayes" and "Noes" lobbies like flocks of sheep driven into pens to be sheared of their votes. The sheepdogs would be the party whippers-in and the shepherds the party leaders. Should one sheep stray by accident or design into the wrong lobby to cast a vote against his party, then his fleece would be nailed up in one of the whips' offices, a warning to all others.

They were having dinner later the same day when Kerguelen came into the saloon to report that the packet had been sighted running up the Tagus with the flood tide under her. Half an hour later she passed the *Lady Arabella*, heading for the packet berth a mile farther up the river. The name *Princess Louise* was picked out in gilt across her transom, and beneath it her port of registry, Falmouth.

"Are you going to see Chamberlain this evening?" Yorke asked.

Ramage shook his head. "We'll wait to hear from him. By the time they've cleared Customs it'll be nearly dark, and I doubt if he'll get the mails off tonight."

"But surely the commander will have the things we're interested in under lock and key in his cabin, won't he?"

Ramage grinned. "Yes, but I don't see any need to give Chamberlain the chance to play 'I'm King of the Castle'. If we go along to his house tonight he can tell us to come back in the morning."

"Hadn't thought of that," Yorke admitted. "You seem to read the minds of these people like a book!"

"Bitter experience. When you're in the Navy you learn quickly enough that the sailors' worst enemies are not the French but the quill-pushers in Government offices like the Navy Board and the Sick and Hurt Board ... It's straightforward dealing with the French – they're only trying to kill you. But the clerks are trying to cheat you or make your life a misery by abusing their authority. Great fun for the clerks, who

224

never think of wives and mothers and children starving because seamen can't send them money. Have you ever seen a man who lost a leg in action hobbling round trying to get the pension to which he's entitled? Sent from one office to another, from Plymouth to London and on to Portsmouth. Ninety per cent of the clerks are stupid or corrupt or lazy. Some are all three."

"And the remaining ten per cent?"

"They run the Navy. To be fair you'll find the percentage is the same elsewhere, at the Horse Guards, the Post Office, the Treasury – in every damned office listed in the *Royal Kalendar*!"

"Faro," Yorke said, opening a drawer and taking out a pack of cards. "At this point let's drag Bowen and Southwick from the chessboard and play faro."

As Bowen dealt the cards, he said idly, "I wonder what happened to Stevens?"

"Still a prisoner in the *Rossignol*, I suppose," Yorke said.

"And that damned Surgeon," Southwick growled. "I hope he has the gravel, or something just as painful."

"Ah, an interesting man," Bowen said. "But in no need of medical attention."

"Pity," Southwick commented.

"He's a man with an appointment, eh, Mr Ramage?"

"An appointment?" Ramage echoed. "With whom?"

"With what," Bowen corrected. "The hangman's noose at Tyburn, I was thinking."

"Aye, and Stevens, too."

"Stevens is a weak man," Bowen said quietly, as though giving a diagnosis to a relative. "I had the impression he was completely under the Surgeon's influence."

Yorke nodded his head in agreement. "That was the impression Much gave."

"They'll both escape the rope," Ramage said sourly, picking up his cards.

"How so?" asked Yorke. "Surely there's enough evidence against them?"

"Plenty of evidence, most of which we can provide. But how much admissible in a court of law? Even if all of it is, I think

225

the Government will keep it quiet. Can you imagine the uproar in Parliament if it was revealed that most of the packets lost for the last year or two were captured because of the treachery of their officers and men?"

"Can't see how they can keep it quiet," Southwick said complacently.

"The only way the news could get out," Ramage said, "would be if you or I told an Opposition Member of Parliament. And that would mean a quick end to our naval careers. But you" – he waved his cards at Yorke and grinned – "could earn yourself the undying gratitude of the Opposition by telling them. You'd get the next safe Parliamentary seat that fell vacant and a baronetcy if they won the next election. Why, it could be the making of you!"

"If you call that being made! But are you serious in saying the pair of them will get away with it?"

"Well, the chances of my report being believed in detail are slender enough – though the broad terms might be accepted. But they'll dodge Tyburn all right. Assuming I'm believed, Stevens will be sacked. He'll get his ship back, of course, since he's the owner, but his Post Office contract will be cancelled. He'll have to pay for a new stern to replace the present rotten one. The Surgeon – he'll set up in practice in Falmouth, no doubt, and the old ladies will be thrilled when they hear his stirring tales of adventure on the high seas..."

"Let's concentrate on faro," Yorke said, sorting his cards. "The Devil take the mails; we seem to talk of nothing else."

A boat arrived alongside with Chamberlain's messenger early next morning. The letter he brought was brief: would Lieutenant Ramage, Mr Yorke and Captain Kerguelen call at the Agent's house at their convenience? There would be a carriage waiting at the quay at whatever time Lieutenant Ramage told the messenger.

When the three of them arrived at Chamberlain's house there was no waiting in the hall: they were hurried through to the office, where Chamberlain jumped up from his desk and shook hands with all the enthusiasm and vigour of a penniless

226

uncle hoping for an allowance from three rich nephews.

"Aha! You saw the packet come in, I trust?"

"Yes," Ramage said. "Looks as though she could do with a new maintopsail."

"They will cut the foot so flat, man-o'-war fashion, that it chafes," Yorke said conversationally. "Means so much patching."

Kerguelen was quick to join the conversation. "I was surprised how few spare sails the packets carry. Privateers usually have at least one extra suit."

"They can afford it," Chamberlain said, hurriedly trying to contribute something and then going red at his tactlessness. "By the way," he added, making a great effort to sound casual, "I have a letter from the Postmaster-General."

"Indeed! And how is his Lordship?" Ramage asked politely, and before the Agent could answer, said to Yorke, "Didn't you have some question for Mr Chamberlain about the origins of *fado*?"

Yorke shuddered. "I did, but it's too sunny a morning to discuss such a mournful subject. And Lady Auckland?" he asked Chamberlain. "I trust she is in the best of health?"

"His Lordship does not say," the Agent said unhappily. "I expect he would if she wasn't," he added lamely but with little conviction.

Kerguelen thumped his chest. "Ah, but that English winter will soon be here, with all the rain and fog and coughs and fevers..."

"Quite," Chamberlain said. "Well, gentlemen, if you'd care to sit down..." He gestured to the chairs and unlocked a drawer in his desk with what he clearly hoped was a significant movement.

However, Kerguelen had thoroughly entered into the game that Ramage and Yorke had been playing, and commented to the Agent, with a lewd wink, "You leave your wife in England to brave that atrocious climate, eh, while you have your 'establishment' here in Lisbon?"

"Indeed I do not!" The Agent was shocked. "Mrs Chamberlain is here with me!"

"Ah, but things can be arranged more easily in Lisbon," Kerguelen said knowingly. His voice was amiable and Ramage decided it was his turn to add to the Agent's discomfort.

"Well now, I'm sure we're all very pleased to hear about Mrs Chamberlain," he said, his voice implying reproach that the Agent should waste time discussing his marital affairs when matters of state had to be decided, "but I do think you should tell us what his Lordship has to say."

Chamberlain's hands were pressed flat on the desk, the whitened nails revealing the pressure he was exerting in an effort to control himself.

"Certainly, Lieutenant, my apologies!" He reached into the drawer and took out a letter.

"His Lordship says the Act has been passed without a division – without having to put it to a vote," he explained in an aside to Kerguelen. "He has empowered me to pay the agreed sum, against a properly notarized receipt. A decision has been made concerning the ship after the prize crew has left her." He gave Ramage an appealing look, as if imploring him not to ask any further questions in front of Kerguelen. "He also says that Lord Spencer's orders to you are being sent under separate cover. In fact I have them here."

He took two packets from the drawer and passed them to Ramage. "Perhaps you would care to peruse them while Captain Kerguelen and I discuss the details of the payment?"

Only someone like Chamberlain would use a word like "peruse", Ramage thought, and took the letters. "I'll be in the hall." He left the room knowing Yorke would make sure the Agent made no slip.

Sitting down in the most comfortable chair, Ramage saw that the two packets were numbered and opened the first. Again his instructions were signed by Evan Nepean. After the usual "I am commanded by my Lords Commissioners..." the Secretary went on to mention the passing of the Act and that, although the Post Office agent would be dealing with the payment, he had been instructed to "act in concert" with Ramage concerning the exact time the French prize crew left the ship.

This time should be noted with precision, Nepean emphasized, because from that moment the *Lady Arabella* would be under Admiralty orders, not Post Office, and Ramage would be in command, his commission being contained in the packet marked "Number 2", which also contained the private signals and a copy of the Signal Book.

Any passengers on board should be brought home, Nepean continued. The original ship's company would be under Ramage's orders, and these instructions constituted authority to waive their Protections. Lord Auckland had sent instructions to the Agent covering this point, and should any difficulties arise, Ramage should apply to the senior British naval officer in Lisbon and show him the orders. Their Lordships were most concerned that Ramage should sail for Plymouth at the first possible opportunity, and forthwith report to them in London.

Ramage found his hands trembling with excitement as he broke the seal on the second packet and read the commission. He had a ship once again! It would be a brief command, and he tried not to read too much into the appointment – he was still smarting under their Lordships' "displeasure" of a fortnight earlier. He had been given the command simply because he was available to bring the ship home. No, that could not be entirely true; the senior of the captains commanding the two frigates could have been told to provide a lieutenant. Stop fretting, he told himself and be thankful that, unknown to Their Lordships, he had a dozen Tritons to stiffen up the packetsmen.

He went back into the Agent's office and found himself sufficiently cheerful to look on Chamberlain with favour, if not affection. Kerguelen, too, looked cheerful: obviously there had been no hitches so far. The Frenchman was sitting close to the desk holding some papers, and Chamberlain was smiling.

"Ah, Lieutenant, the Captain has read the receipt and approved the wording; we've agreed on the mode of payment; and the transaction will take place here at four o'clock this afternoon, when I have arranged for a notary to be present. It only remains for you and the Captain to arrange the details of handing over the ship – handing back the ship," he corrected himself. "It is agreed that any, ah, pillaging will not be the subject of claims on our side, nor will the Captain, nor his agents, heirs or assigns, make any claims relating to any injuries wounds or fatalities –"

"I'm glad to hear all that," Ramage interrupted grimly. "It would make for some strange litigation! Well, Captain, when do you propose giving us back the *Lady Arabella*?"

Kerguelen's brow wrinkled; he was obviously torn between wanting to make sure of receiving the money before handing over the ship, and not wanting to appear distrustful.

Ramage said, "Supposing we settle for midnight? By then all this" – he gestured towards the papers – "will have been completed."

Kerguelen nodded vigorously, and Chamberlain said, "Very well, gentlemen, I'll have that written into the receipt." He rubbed his hands together and looked questioningly at Ramage. "I think that concludes everything – I'll look forward to seeing M. Kerguelen later."

Once again Chamberlain offered them the use of his carriage for the rest of the day, and as they were leaving the room the Agent called to Ramage and followed him with a letter in his hand.

"I nearly forgot to give you this," he said. "One of the passengers in the packet gave it to me yesterday to pass on to you."

"Thank you," Ramage said absently, and followed Yorke and Kerguelen to the front door. While the coachman unfolded the steps of the carriage Ramage glanced at the letter. He stared unbelievingly at the handwriting. What had Chamberlain said? One of the passengers had given it to him? He relaxed, disappointed. The passenger was probably acting as a messenger, since the ship arrived last night.

"Anything wrong?" Yorke asked.

"No – just give me a moment to read this."

He broke the seal and began reading, and slowly the garden and the house and the carriage seem to sway and start to spin, and a moment later Yorke and Kerguelen were holding him.

"I'm all right," he muttered, "just a shock." He smiled weakly. "Everyone's getting shocks today. If you'll just drop me off at the Embassy – I'll join you on board later."

He tucked the letter in his pocket, took several deep breaths and climbed into the carriage. Once the other two men had joined him and the coachman had whipped up the horses, Ramage told them what the letter said.

Chapter Seventeen

At the residence of His Britannic Majesty's Envoy Extra-
ordinary and Minister Plenipotentiary to the Court of Portugal,
the two liveried and bewigged attendants in the hall were obviously expecting Lord Ramage; but equally obviously they
were not expecting him to be a naval officer whose uniform
had not received the loving care of a steward for many weeks
and who was not wearing a sword: part of the regular dress of
an officer visiting the Embassy.

When Ramage gave his name both men were too well
trained to show surprise, and the elder smiled. "There has been
some – er, concern, my Lord; you were expected earlier."

Ramage nodded and sat down while the younger attendant
disappeared along a corridor to announce his arrival.

"His Excellency has been inquiring every half an hour, sir, to
see if you had arrived."

Ramage nodded. Too many thoughts were racing through
his mind to allow for small talk, though it was reassuring that
Mr Hookham Frere was a conscientious Ambassador.

Damn this waiting: it was all he had done since leaving
Jamaica. Waiting for weeks for the sight of a privateer; waiting
to see if Kerguelen would agree to ransom the *Arabella*; waiting to see if the Government would agree to paying. Now, just
when the ransom was about to be paid and all the waiting
seemed to be over, here he was sitting in the hall of the Embassy, once again waiting.

He was too jumpy to sit still but, not wanting to fidget in

front of the attendant – who had more than an inkling of why he was here – he took the letter from his pocket, unfolded it, smoothed the paper, and read it again. There were few words, carefully chosen and neatly written. They told him a lot, yet left a lot unsaid. They raised more questions than they answered and left his heart thudding.

"Hmm ... sir ... if you'll follow my colleague..."

A startled Ramage glanced up to find the older attendant looking down at him anxiously, as though he had said the same thing several times.

Folding the letter and tucking it back in his pocket, Ramage stood up. "I was daydreaming. Thank you." The attendant smiled understandingly and bowed.

Ramage found his heels jarred unpleasantly on the hard, polished mosaic of the floor: for months he had been used to the forgiving wood of a ship's deck. The corridors were cool from windows opening on to a central courtyard, but he was hot, his shirt sticking to him. Hot, nervous and puzzled; excited yet apprehensive. The story of my life for the past few weeks, he thought sourly.

He followed the attendant up a wide staircase and along another corridor. Suddenly the man stopped, knocked gently on a door and entered.

"The Lord Ramage," he announced quietly, and stepped aside to let Ramage pass.

It was a large, high-ceilinged room with pale blue walls on which hung portraits in heavy gilded frames. Several walnut chairs with caned seats and backs, and a long day-bed. Two bookcases and a matching secretaire. Thick rugs on the mosaic floor and the curtains of heavy blue velvet drawn back to let the sunlight stream in.

She was standing by one of the windows, a tiny motionless figure watching him uncertainly with large brown eyes, hand now reaching up nervously to brush back a stray strand of hair that seemed as blue-black as a raven's wing. The door clicked shut and she ran towards him without a word. Her kiss spun back the clock: the past year vanished and he had no sense of time or space – just Gianna in his arms, a dream suddenly become improbable reality in an upstairs room in a British Embassy.

"You were so long," she finally whispered, "we were afraid of treachery..."

"The Post Office Agent gave me your letter only a few minutes ago."

"Mr Frere – he was worried in case the French took the money and killed you: he is writing orders for one of the frigates to – oh Nico!" She clung to him, half laughing, half weeping. "That fool of an Agent said he would give you my letter at once."

"Well, I'm here," Ramage said lightly, trying to kiss away the tears, "and so are you. But how – I mean why..." He broke off as she kissed him again.

"I wanted to see you," she said. "So I went on board the packet at Falmouth and here I am. You" – she looked at him, suddenly alarmed – "you aren't angry with me?"

Ramage shook his head. "Of course not! But we sail for England tomorrow night." Suddenly he recalled her reference to the Ambassador. "What did you say Mr Frere was doing?"

"Oh, telling one of the frigates to rescue you all, or some such thing."

Ramage recognized the imperious ruler of the little state of Volterra: the wilful young Machesa for ever hiding behind the golden-skinned Gianna.

"Quick," Ramage snapped, "I must see him at once! My God! This could wreck everything."

"In a moment, Nico," she protested.

"Come on," he said hurriedly, grabbing her hand and pulling her to the door. "My men could get killed because of this!"

The Ambassador had been as affable as he was efficient. By the time Ramage and Gianna had arrived in his office one messenger had already been dispatched with orders to the frigate captain cancelling his earlier instructions; a second messenger was on his way to the Post Office Agent demanding to know why the Ambassador had not been informed immediately the ransom arrangements had been concluded. And Frere had commented sourly that the Agent could be thankful the attendant in the Embassy hall had reported Ramage's arrival.

After politely refusing Frere's invitation to stay at the Embassy for a few days or, failing that, dine with him, Ramage had explained that he planned to sail for England with the *Arabella* in a few hours, and there was much to be done before then. Frere had nodded sympathetically and shot a questioning glance at Gianna.

Much to Ramage's surprise she had formally thanked Frere for his hospitality and told him she would be leaving the Embassy within the hour. Ramage had been about to suggest she would be more comfortable at the Embassy than waiting in a hotel for the next Falmouth packet to sail in ten days or so, but he decided against it. Gianna must have her reasons.

They walked back to the first-floor room. Gianna chattered cheerfully, giving him fond messages from his father and mother. She was so excited she did not notice Ramage's silence. Why, he wondered, isn't she going to stay here? He did not like the idea of her staying in one of the hotels without a chaperone. Without a guard, for that matter: the French had made one desperate attempt to capture her in Italy, and the moment they discovered she was alone in Lisbon they might try to kidnap her.

Ramage shut the door and pointed to a chair. "Sit down for a moment; I've some questions!"

"They can wait," she pouted. "So *serioso*, Nico! I came all this way ... Did you forget me in the West Indies? Don't you love –"

"I love you!" he said almost savagely. "That's why I'm worried. Love and war don't mix!"

"If that Bonaparte hadn't driven me out of Volterra, you'd never have met me," she reminded him. "So you're wrong, *caro mio* ..."

"*Accidente!* Tell me, what made you take the packet from Falmouth?"

"Nico! Shall I say I have a lover waiting in Lisbon, and I thought I'd see you at the same time?"

That smile, Ramage thought to himself; and that body, and

as always he remembered Ghiberti's beautiful carving of "The Creation of Eve" on the east door of the Baptistry in Florence. Eve's bold and slim body with the small, jutting breasts; the small, finely chiselled face (Gianna's was fuller, more sensuous). He glanced at the body hidden by the white dress: the flat belly and rounded thighs, the long, slim legs.

"I know what you are thinking," she said.

"Indeed you don't," he said, flushing.

"I do!" she said furiously. "You are thinking this Gianna is a nuisance, and why didn't she stay at St Kew, out of the way, and – and –"

Ramage stood helplessly as she searched for words: they'd been together ten minutes and were already quarrelling. Why the devil couldn't she understand what he meant?

"Listen," he said, "let's get it over with –"

"There you are! You *don't* love me!"

"No – oh darling –"

"So you don't love me, you just said so!"

"No – I mean I was saying 'No' because you said that I said I . . ."

They both burst out laughing. She stood up, pushed him to a chair, and as soon as he sat she curled up on the floor at his feet, her head resting on his knee.

"Ask all the questions you want, sir!"

"Very well, *signorina*: tell me how you got here. From the beginning. From breakfast the day you had the idea!"

"Not breakfast," she said promptly, "Your father always complains I don't eat enough breakfast. That porridge – ough! I'd get fat like a fishwife. Well, Lord Spencair wrote –"

"Spencer," he corrected.

She sniffed. "– 'Spencair', then. He wrote to your father describing all the trouble out here, and a silly new Act of Parliament they had to pass. Your father laughed," she added as an afterthought. "He thought it very funny that you were the cause of a special Act of Parliament. He made me cross."

"Why? I hadn't thought of it like that, but it is amusing."

"Amusing? But supposing those cretins in Parliament hadn't passed it? What then, eh?"

236

Ramage laughed: the "eh?" and the upraised palms was so typically Italian.

"You laugh," she protested, "but if you get put in a French prison for years it is me – it is I," she corrected herself, "who has to wait at home and grow old and wrinkled and when you come back I am too ugly for you and you – oh, don't think a quick kiss on the head will silence me," she said furiously. "A shrivelled old walnut, that's how I'll look; all my youth wasted waiting for you and you are faithless –"

"Steady on," Ramage interrupted mildly, "the French haven't caught me yet and you're a long way from your twentieth birthday!"

"Now you mock me," she snapped. "If it wasn't for your father I'd forget all about you."

"My father's already married."

"Oh, *cretino*!" she pummelled him with her fists, her eyes blazing with anger, and he gripped her wrists and twisted her arms until she was facing him, and then he kissed her.

"Stop shaking with indignation," he said, "it makes our teeth click together."

She jerked away from him. "I don't love you. I inform you officially." She frowned, her lips pressed into a thin line.

"I'll make a note of it in the log," he said. "Anyway, what happened after Lord 'Spencair' wrote?"

"I told your father and mother that if the Act was not passed, I would go to Lisbon with the money and pay for the ship myself, and –"

"But –"

"But nothing: the law says no *British* subject can pay money to a Frenchman. It doesn't say anything about foreigners paying. Anyway," she said arrogantly, "it would be my own money, and am I not the Marchesa di Volterra?"

He nodded numbly, overwhelmed by both her logic and her generosity. "What ... what did Father say?"

"At first he was very angry – he has a worse temper than you," she said reproachfully. "Then your mother said it was a silly law anyway because obviously it was supposed to stop traitors paying spies and things like that, but Parliament was so

237

stupid it didn't word it properly. That made your father change his mind. He finally agreed with her that it was the intention of the law, not the wording, that should concern us."

"And then?"

"Well, I made him angry again because I said I didn't care about intention, wording or law; that I was going to stop you being put in a French prison."

"What did he do?"

"At that moment? Well, I walked out and your mother got angry with *him*, but by the time I came back he'd found out when the next packet sailed for Lisbon and was arranging a guard for me."

"Guard?" Ramage exclaimed.

"Yes – one of the men on the estate. He came out as a passenger in the *Princess Louise* with me."

"Where is he now?"

Gianna shrugged her shoulders. "On board the ship. I do not need him in Lisbon – it was in case of trouble on board the packet."

Ramage froze for a moment. "But the *Princess Louise* sails at noon. It's" – he pulled out his watch – "hell, it's past noon! There's not another packet for two weeks!"

"Why are you worrying? The guard went back in the packet. He stayed on board."

"But I'm sailing tomorrow. You'll be on your own. Look, you'd better stay on here at the Embassy."

She looked puzzled. "But we both sail tomorrow. I come with you. The packet has plenty of room for passengers. A whole week with you," she said excitedly. "It'll be like the old days in the Mediterranean!"

"You can't," he said firmly. "I'm sorry. It would be wonderful, but –"

"Why not?" she interrupted angrily.

"Because the *Arabella* is no longer a packet. Once the French have handed her over, she comes under Admiralty orders and I'm in command."

"*Alora*, then all is well."

"It's not; far from it. The ship is in a dangerous state – most

238

of the wood in the stern is rotten. She's not safe."

"Then you mustn't sail with her," Gianna said promptly. "Tell the Admiralty and wait for the next packet."

"But I *can't* wait that long! Anyway, I have my orders. Besides, half the crew are likely to mutiny."

"Mutiny?" She almost screamed the word. "Supposing they seize the ship and sail to France? You'll be a prisoner – *Madonna*! After all the trouble so far!"

"Don't worry," he said comfortingly. "I have Southwick and Jackson with me. And Stafford and Rossi – you remember them. We can hold down a mutiny."

"Well, if there's nothing to worry about, then I can come with you."

"But a King's ship can't carry passengers," he said lamely, and then remembered the phrase in his orders, written in specially by Nepean to cover people like Yorke who were passengers from Jamaica.

She sensed he was only making excuses and stood up. "I'm going to see Mr Frere. I shall tell him to *order* you to take me. Ah – you didn't know I knew about that, did you. But when he decided to tell that frigate to get ready, he explained to me that an ambassador can give orders to the captain of a ship. He says the task of the Navy and the Army is to carry out the policies of the Secretary of State for Foreign Affairs. Is he correct, Lieutenant?"

He was, and Ramage knew he would be wise to agree now, rather than force an issue she was bound to win.

"Darling – it will be dangerous."

She shrugged and pointed to her left shoulder. "The French shot me once – remember?"

"Of course I remember. I'll never forget the night in that damned boat. I thought you were going to die."

"Did you?" She sounded surprised. "Oh, Nico, you shouldn't have worried. Anyway, you hadn't fallen in love with me then," she said matter-of-factly.

"How do you know? I nearly went crazy. Why I –"

"When did you fall in love with me, then?" she asked curiously. "It was still dark. You saw me for the first time – oh, about midnight, and I was shot soon after."

"What does it matter?" Ramage snapped, thoroughly exasperated.

"Oh! You say you love me and grumble because you worried about me one night – one night," she repeated, her voice rising, "when I worry about you *every* night of the year. How can you love me when you can't even remember when it happened?"

"I'll look it up in the ship's log," Ramage said angrily. "Now, get packed and let's go on board, otherwise you can wait for the next packet."

"Ha, listen to him," she said furiously. "You bully – oh, to think I wanted to rescue you! I wish they hadn't passed the Act. I'd have stayed in England and you'd have rotted in a French prison for years and years–"

He put his arms round her and kissed her. "And you'd have slowly turned into an old walnut..."

The two burly boatmen groaned and swore as they lowered Gianna's trunk so that it rested on the centre thwarts. "You told me you had very little luggage," Ramage said mildly. "I don't think these two fellows would believe you."

"It's only *one* trunk," Gianna protested crossly. "I'd have had more if your mother hadn't interfered."

Knowing that his mother did not believe in travelling with the minimum of luggage, Ramage shuddered at the thought of what Gianna had intended to bring.

Finally the trunk was lashed down and the boatmen looked at each other in bewilderment. There was now little room left for two passengers in the small boat, which made up with brightly coloured paintwork what it now lacked in stability.

Ramage pointed to the forward thwart, and when the men protested that Gianna would get splashed by spray he held up his boat cloak.

Five minutes later, with the two of them wrapped in the cloak, the lugsail hoisted and drawing, and the two men aft, one handling the sheet and the other at the tiller, the boat was heading for the *Arabella*.

240

The French mate is going to be puzzled, Ramage thought: instead of Kerguelen and the two Britons returning, there's only one Briton with a strange lady and an enormous trunk ...

As the boat tacked for the last board that would bring her down to the *Arabella*, Ramage noticed that the packet's boat was secured astern by its painter. Perhaps Kerguelen had sent it back, with orders to the crew to return later when he and Yorke had sampled enough of what Lisbon had to offer.

Ramage pictured Southwick's face when he looked down into the boat ... The Master's attitude towards Gianna was a curious mixture of awe, respect and affection: Ramage had the feeling the old man had never quite reconciled the ruler of Volterra with the tomboy of the voyage from Corsica to Gibraltar; the occasionally cold and imperious Marchesa with the laughing girl he hoped his captain would marry. The attitude of Jackson, Rossi, Stafford and the other Tritons who had helped rescue her a couple of years ago was both simple and straightforward: they worshipped her. Every letter Ramage had ever received from her always mentioned their names, and when he told them that the Marchesa was inquiring about them their delight was both spontaneous and genuine.

The privateersmen weren't keeping a very good lookout: not a man in sight on deck. Well, once the boatmen hooked on he would be able to rouse out a couple of seamen to help with the trunk.

The *Arabella* was a pretty ship: nice sheer, graceful yet powerful. Sad to think of all that rot aft, hidden under the paint. I hope that damned rudder holds, he thought to himself ...

Forty yards to go. He turned to Gianna and grinned. "Soon be home!" She squeezed his hand and smoothed her hair.

Suddenly there was a deep bellow: "What ship?"

"*Triton!*" A startled Ramage shouted in an automatic answer to the time-honoured challenge from a King's ship; a reply indicating the captain was in the boat. He realized his mistake just as Gianna nudged him and as he shouted, "Belay that – *Lady Arabella!*" a couple of dozen faces suddenly appeared along the bulwark: grinning and freshly shaven faces topped by hats carefully squared and hair neatly combed: the faces of Tritons – and Frenchmen. And Southwick, Kerguelen, Yorke, Bowen and Wilson looking down at them from the gangway...

As he helped Gianna on board, whispering that Yorke and Kerguelen must have hurried back to prepare a surprise, a bosun's call trilled and a moment later Kerguelen stepped forward, sweeping off his hat in a graceful bow: "M'selle – welcome on board the *Lady Arabella*!"

Ramage introduced the Frenchman, and then Yorke, Bowen, Much and Wilson, and Gianna was very much the cool Marchesa. When she saw there were no more strangers to meet she turned to Southwick and as the Master stood awkwardly, obviously uncertain whether or not to salute, she stepped up to him, put her hands on his shoulders and kissed him on the cheek.

The privateersmen, delighted onlookers, cheered heartily and a moment later the Tritons joined in.

"Mr Souswick," she said, and Ramage remembered she always had trouble pronouncing the name, "you look five years younger!"

"Thrive on trouble, ma'am, and I want to say how glad we are to see you."

"Because I am more trouble, eh, Mr Souswick?" The Master went red as Gianna laughed, and she cut short his explanation. "I don't believe a word you say – Nicholas has spent half the morning telling me what a nuisance women are on board a ship."

She looked round. "Jackson! Stafford! And you Rossi! *Sta bene? Piu grasso* – you eat too well in the Royal Navy!"

Within a minute or two Gianna's tiny figure was hidden by a throng of former Tritons, all eager to add their quota to the welcome she received, and as Ramage turned to speak to Kerguelen he was startled to see three burly Frenchmen hoisting the trunk on board, cheerfully cursing and speculating in their broad Breton accents how many yards of smuggled French lace had gone into making the gowns inside.

Kerguelen slapped him on the shoulder. "You never expected to see a crowd of French cut-throats acting as Cupid's assistants, eh?"

"And you never pictured yourself as Cupid," Ramage said with a grin, "but thanks. Whose idea was the reception committee?"

Kerguelen shrugged his shoulders. "Yorke and I decided to come back early and have a cabin tidied up ready. I freed all your men, incidentally. Then –"

"How did you know she would be sailing with us?"

"Even an Englishman couldn't be so unromantic as to let her return in the *Princess Louise*," Kerguelen said sarcastically. "Anyway, by the time the cabin was ready, Southwick and that American were so excited they started holystoning the decks, and then my men asked what was going on. When I explained that your – ah, fiancée – was coming on board, they joined in, and as soon as the ship looked tidy they all vanished below, and half an hour later they were shaven, hair tidied and rigged in clean shirts and trousers."

Kerguelen moved closer and lowered his voice. "All except the original packetsmen. You've noticed they're not on deck?" When Ramage nodded, the Frenchman said, "Keep your eye on them, my friend; I saw more than you give me credit for when we captured this ship..."

With that he went down to his cabin, saying he had to get ready to return to Chamberlain's house to collect the money.

Ramage saw Yorke, Bowen and Much watching him.

"Haven't seen you look so happy for months," Yorke said.

"Wouldn't you?" Bowen exclaimed. "She's the most beautiful woman I've ever seen!"

"All of that," Much said. "Acts like a real queen," he added. "Is it true she's a queen, sir?"

"Not exactly," Ramage said. "She's the ruler of Volterra – that's a small state in Italy. Or she was, until the French invaded. She escaped just in time."

"Southwick was telling us about that," Bowen said. "You had a romantic meeting!"

"She was pointing a pistol at him," Yorke commented for

Much's benefit, remembering Ramage's reference a few days earlier.

"Nothing would frighten that lass," Much said emphatically.

She finally left the group of Tritons. "Ah, it's like old times! I hope we have some excitement on the way back!"

"Let me show you your cabin," Ramage said hurriedly. "Oh, leave the trunk to the French fellows, Jackson; they hoisted it up and I think they'd like to finish the job!"

Gianna's arrival made the *Lady Arabella*'s last few hours in Lisbon a bizarre and festive occasion. It began with Yorke's suggestion that they invite Kerguelen to dinner, whereupon Gianna demanded that Rossi be allowed to help her prepare the meal. While the two of them were busy in the galley, Kerguelen returned from his visit to Chamberlain, but his privateersmen seemed far more interested in the barrels he brought with him than the canvas bag which obviously held the money. The Frenchman explained that he had brought some wine for his men to celebrate with, and a case of champagne as a present for Ramage.

By midnight, when the *Arabella* was officially handed over, former Tritons and privateersmen were toasting each other with mugs of wine and singing raucous songs on the foredeck while Ramage and Kerguelen toasted each other with champagne on the quarterdeck, watched by Gianna, Yorke, Southwick, Bowen, Wilson and Much.

"A speech, a speech!" Wilson insisted drunkenly. "Got to have a speech!"

"Let's hear the Marchesa," Yorke said enthusiastically. "I'm so tipsy I can see three of her, an' I don't know which one's the loveliest!"

Kerguelen took out his watch and held it close to the lantern. "Two minutes past midnight," he said solemnly, "and the *Lady Arabella* begins a new life. What more appropriate than a few words from you, Mademoiselle?"

Gianna nodded and put her glass on the binnacle. "Yes, I will make a speech. The last time I saw a Frenchman, he shot me in the shoulder. I had hoped never to see another one until long after this hateful war ends. But I was curious to meet the Frenchman that Nicholas respected, and pleased to find when I met him that he respected Nicholas. I shall pray," she lowered her voice and spoke slowly, so that they should not miss the significance of what she was saying, "that you will never meet again until after the war is over..."

Then she looked round and said gaily, "But I am jealous of all you men: you have had Nicholas's company for so long, while I have been waiting for him in England."

"You haven't missed anything, ma'am," Southwick said unexpectedly. "Very snappish he's been most of the time, an' all because he missed you."

"Well spoken," Yorke said. "I wasn't going to say anything, but..."

At that moment they heard the bells of Lisbon's churches as they struck midnight. Kerguelen took out his watch and looked at it ruefully. "Well, now I can afford to buy a new one!" He stood still for a moment, his stance indicating a change of mood. "Everything is yours, Lieutenant," he said softly. "Will you all wait a moment?" With that he went below.

Yorke glanced at Ramage, who shrugged his shoulders. There was little Kerguelen could do: most of his men were drunk on the foredeck. The Frenchman returned in a minute or two with three swords under his arm. "A ceremony," he said, glancing round to make sure Southwick and Captain Wilson were present.

"Lieutenant Ramage – it gives me great pleasure to return your sword!"

With a flourish he extracted Ramage's and presented it to him. "Mr Southwick – I believe this is yours. And Captain Wilson..."

It was a gracious gesture, and Ramage felt he ought to say something.

"On behalf of your former prisoners, Captain, I want to thank you for being such an amiable captor, and..." Ramage broke off: Kerguelen knew what he was trying to say, and the two men shook hands.

By dawn, with the last of the privateersmen taken on shore, the *Arabella*'s boat was hoisted up and Ramage, having moved into the captain's cabin, sent for Much and Southwick to discuss the merits of the various packetsmen before Southwick drew up a quarters, watch and station bill. Ramage's first surprise was Much's warning that no trust should be put in his own son, Our Ned.

"No father would like to admit it," the Mate said apologetically, "but though Our Ned's a smart seaman he's a bad lad. I'm going to warn him, Mr Ramage, just as soon as you give me the word; but he's not to be trusted, no more than the Bosun, nor *any* of the *Arabella*'s men!"

Ramage stared at him. "*Any* of them?"

"Mebbe one or two, but ignore 'em. Best rely on the Navy men. Your own men."

"But I can't keep the packetsmen prisoners!"

"No, but if 'twas me, I'd make sure each Navy man was told to keep an eye on a particular packetsman. Just in case."

Ramage felt his elation at the prospect of commanding the *Lady Arabella* slowly vanishing like sugar dissolving in warm water. Would anything in his life ever be straightforward? With Stevens out of the way and the packet back in British hands was it asking too much that the voyage home would be free of complications?

"As bad as that, Mr Much?" he asked.

"As bad as that, Mr Ramage."

"Will you work with Southwick to draw up a new quarters, watch and station bill?"

The Mate nodded. "What about your men, sir?"

"Jackson could have been rated Bosun, but that'd cause more trouble with the present one. For the rest – my men are all steady and handpicked: I've taken them into action several times."

The answer seemed to satisfy Much, who said, "What is my position now, sir?"

"Well, now the *Lady Arabella* is a King's ship – or she will be within the hour – I shall be in command, Mr Southwick the Master, and Bowen the Surgeon. You, Mr Yorke and Captain

Wilson will be passengers – along with the Marchesa, of course – but I'd appreciate any help you can give. The packetsmen will be mustered as part of the ship's company: their Protections are withdrawn."

After Much and Southwick left to draw up the watch bill, Ramage relaxed for a few minutes to finish a cup of lukewarm coffee. Well, the packet was almost ready to sail. Kerguelen had kept his men busy during the last few days filling water casks, and according to Much there were enough provisions. Damn, there was the rot in the transom to be examined. As soon as Southwick and Much had finished their present task, they could survey it and draw up a detailed report. It wouldn't affect the *Arabella* leaving Lisbon as soon as possible; but it might be important later, since the Admiralty was taking over the ship.

Was taking over? *Had* taken over at midnight, to be exact, and it was high time he read himself in: at the moment he had no legal authority in the ship, and although Southwick and Much would not appreciate being interrupted while doing the watch bill, it was high time he completed that formality.

He stood up, more than conscious he had a nasty headache, and went out to tap on Southwick's door. "Muster the ship's company aft, if you please, Mr Southwick."

Back in his cabin he washed his face again in the hope that it would freshen him up, and as soon as he heard the men assembling on deck, put on his sword, set his hat square on his head and picked up the Commission he had received from Nepean.

By the time he emerged on deck the ship's company was drawn up fore and aft, a dozen on each side of the binnacle, with Southwick, Bowen, Yorke, Much and Wilson by the taffrail. He was thankful Gianna was probably still asleep: her presence at the moment would be an unnecessary distraction. Yet, he noted grimly, just about everyone – particularly Wilson – looked so bleary-eyed that they might well not notice if a pasha marched on board with a dozen dancing girls. Well, what he had to tell them would soon wake the packetsmen...

Automatically he noted the wind was light from the north-east, the ship was beginning to swing as the tide turned, the sun was weak but had some warmth in it and the clouds told of fairly settled weather – for a day or two, anyway. Patches of smoke over the city showed its inhabitants were awake and lighting fires while wives were probably filling pots to prepare their husbands' favourite food. For a moment he envied those husbands; they knew what would be happening to them tomorrow, and next week, and next month ... There would be no sudden alarms and dangers for them...

He looked round at the men. His new command. The first had been the *Kathleen* cutter, and he had lost her as she was smashed under the forefoot of a Spanish ship of the line at the Battle of Cape St Vincent; then he had been given the *Triton* brig, now wrecked on a reef east of Puerto Rico, pounded by the waves and slowly rotting, her battered bulwarks a perch for pelicans. Now the *Lady Arabella* ... He hoped he would hand her over to the Commander-in-Chief at Plymouth without the need for writing anything in the log and his journal apart from the usual navigational and weather entries and such descriptions of the regular daily routine as "ship's company employed as the service required".

The packetsmen, standing sloppily (or was it insolently?) were watching him curiously, not knowing what was going to happen. The dozen Tritons were standing to attention; all but one of them had gone through this ritual with him twice before, and would have seen it many times in other ships. For any captain it was a memorable day, no matter how often it was repeated. Few captains – and Ramage knew he was not one of them – cared to hurry it. And today there was a particular reason for giving the ritual as much drama as possible.

Southwick marched up, head erect, left hand clasping the scabbard of his sword.

"Ship's company all present and correct, sir."

"Very well, Mr Southwick!"

The Master marched back to rejoin the group of passengers.

Blast! The Colours! In all the flurry of Kerguelen leaving the ship, the Ensign had not been hoisted. Well, let us add it to the ritual – the packetsmen would not know any better.

"Have the Colours hoisted, if you please Mr Southwick."

Just a slight stiffening – which Ramage knew only he had noticed – betrayed the Master's annoyance at not having noticed the omission.

Jackson suddenly took one pace forward, turned aft and marched to the halyard. Ramage saw he had a large bundle under his arm. That damned American, he thought to himself, he doesn't miss a thing! Jackson had also realized the need for ritual. He secured the upper toggle of the Ensign to the halyard, then the lower. Then he stood to attention, facing Southwick.

"Hoist away!" The Master bellowed.

The flag caught the breeze and Ramage wished there had been a drummer on board to strike up a ruffle or two. With the halyard secured Jackson marched back to his place.

To anyone unfamiliar with naval routine, it appeared the correct procedure. And, Ramage thought wryly, there is no routine laid down anyway since the circumstances are unusual. He took the Commission from his pocket, unfolded it and, after glancing at the two ranks of men, began reading in a loud and firm voice.

"By the Commissioners for Executing the Office of Lord High Admiral of the United Kingdom and Ireland ... to Lieutenant the Lord Ramage ... His Majesty's packet brig *Lady Arabella* ... willing and requiring you forthwith to go on board and take upon you the charge and command of captain in her accordingly..."

Ramage paused for a full minute. The wording of the commission was archaic and unfamiliar to the packetsmen and he wanted the full significance of it to sink in: that the ship was now under the command of a lieutenant in the Royal Navy; that the ship was now controlled by the Admiralty, instead of being under charter to the Post Office.

Although looking directly in front of him, Ramage could see out of the corner of his eye that the packetsmen were glancing at each other, and he wished he could also see the expressions on their faces – but he would know about that soon enough since Southwick, Yorke and Bowen would be watching like hawks.

He glanced down at the Commission again and continued reading:

"... strictly charging and commanding all the officers and company of the said packet brig to behave themselves jointly and severally in their respective appointments, with all due respect to you, their said Captain..."

Again he paused long enough for the men to absorb the words, and he detected some shuffling of feet, as though uneasiness caused movement.

"... you will carry out the General Printed Instructions and any orders and instructions you may receive..."

Again he paused. The next phrase was the one he wanted to ram home. He looked slowly and deliberately from man to man along the file to his left, and then did the same on his right. He had their attention all right! He held up the Commission.

"... hereof, nor you nor any of you may fail as you will answer to the contrary at your peril..."

He finished reading the remaining sentences and then folded the Commission slowly and deliberately. The Regulations and Instructions had been obeyed; by reading aloud to the officers of the ship the Commission appointing him captain, he had "read himself in". Now he was lawfully established as the captain of the ship, responsible for everything about her, from the behaviour of the crew in battle to the chafe on a sail in a gale of wind.

He had more power over the men, he mused in the silence that followed, than the King: he could order a seaman to be flogged – but the King could not. He could order them aloft in a storm, and punish any man that refused. He could order them into a battle from which none would return alive. And, if he was a good captain, he was also now the father of a large family. Although the Articles of War allowed him to have a wrongdoer flogged until he screamed for mercy, the obligations of leadership also meant a man could – and should – come to him for help and advice.

It was usual for a new captain to make a brief speech: apart from giving the men a chance to size him up, it allowed him to sound a keynote.

"Several of you men," he said, "have never heard a Commission read before. So that there'll be no misunderstanding, I'll explain that the Post Office and the Admiralty have jointly decided that I take command of the packet and take her back to England. You are all under naval discipline. All Protections have been withdrawn, and you are subject to the Articles of War. Those of you who don't know what that means can find out from those who do.

"Since this ship left Jamaica, we have all shared some strange adventures. The First Lord of the Admiralty and the Postmaster-General have read my report about it – and indeed it was a very *full* report." He decided exaggeration was pardonable; it should convince the packetsmen – particularly that villainous Bosun – that it was too late to silence him. But he must be careful not to scare them too much: he daren't risk them refusing to sail the ship back for fear of being arrested. A little bit of reassurance, then.

"They have approved my negotiations to secure the release of the ship. The result is that instead of ending up in a French prison, we'll all be back with our families in England in a few days.

"While I am in command of the ship, Mr Southwick will be the Master. The Surgeon is Mr Bowen. Mr Much will have a well-earned rest, but will stand watch if needed, as will Mr Yorke."

He looked round again. He had every packetsman's attention, that much was sure. Whether he had their loyalty was a different matter.

Ventures! He suddenly realized that was what the packetsmen wanted to hear about. Hellfire, ventures were forbidden by the Post Office, so he could hardly mention them as such. But there was an easy way out of it.

"If any of you men had any of your property taken and kept by the privateersmen, give me a written list before we arrive in England. Apart from that, keep your possessions stowed away tidily, just as you would on a normal voyage."

"We are sailing within an hour. There'll be a guinea for the first man to sight the English coast."

He turned and with a curt "Carry on, Mr Southwick!" strode to his cabin, where Yorke joined him, after politely knocking on the door in a tacit acknowledgement that, now Ramage commanded the ship, their official relationship had changed.

"I wouldn't bet on it," he said, "but I think you've got 'em!"

"I thought I heard some shuffling of feet and sucking of teeth," Ramage said doubtfully.

"There was at the beginning, but the '*at your peril*' stopped that: I saw at least two men glance up at the fore yardarm, as though they already saw a noose hanging there..."

Ramage laughed grimly. "Well, the sooner we get 'em to sea the better: a month at anchor rots any but the best of men."

He unbuckled his sword and put it in the rack, then took his Commission and locked it in a drawer. He was – from force of habit – just going to call to the Marine sentry to pass the word for Southwick when he realized that he was commanding little more than a cosmopolitan bumboat: no Marine, no steward ... Well, until he knew more about the mood of the packetsmen, there would have to be an armed Triton at his own cabin door and also Southwick's. A thought struck him and he said to Yorke, "Would you mind continuing to share a cabin with Southwick?"

"No, of course not. Hadn't occurred to me I wouldn't, though now I think of it we do have plenty of accommodation."

"Sentries," Ramage explained tersely. "The same man can guard you and Southwick in one cabin, and Bowen and Wilson in the next, and the Marchesa too."

"Don't forget Much: doubt if he's very popular among the packetsmen..."

"I had forgotten him," Ramage admitted. "But yes, the same sentry could see that fourth cabin – Much had better move in there."

"Nasty feeling, isn't it, when you aren't sure of all the men."

Ramage nodded. "We have the Tritons," he said simply.

He walked to the door and called for Southwick and Much, and when they arrived he quickly gave them their instructions

252

concerning accommodation and sentries. Then he added, "You should all sleep with a brace of loaded pistols close at hand – warn Wilson and Bowen, too. And only packetsmen at the wheel."

The Mate looked puzzled.

"Men at the wheel are helpless, Mr Much, and it's easy to keep an eye on them!"

Much grinned, "Yes, indeed, sir; the Devil makes work for idle hands!"

Ramage looked at Southwick. "Very well, we'll get under way as soon as you've finished the watch bill. I don't want to lose the ebb."

An hour later the anchor had been weighed and catted, and the *Lady Arabella* was reaching down the Tagus towards the open sea, Southwick giving occasional orders to the men at the wheel to avoid fregatas beating up against the ebb. The clouds were clearing and as they approached the bar the wind veered slightly.

Gianna had come up on deck as soon as the ship was under way, walking aft and standing at the taffrail, out of the way of the bustling seamen yet in a position to see everything that was going on. She caught Ramage's eye and he knew she was happy; content to be left on her own until he had time to be with her. She had his big boatcloak over her shoulders, the hem nearly touching the deck; a silk scarf of blue and gold – Ramage recalled they were the national colours of Volterra – held her hair against the tug of the wind and the downdraught of the sails.

Yorke walked up to him and said quietly, "I don't think I've ever seen such a beautiful picture."

And Ramage did not have to turn to look: Gianna was standing against a background of the pale blue sky and the city of Lisbon spread over rounded hills, the hard vertical lines of its monastery and church towers softened and tinted oyster pink by the early sun. He was taking her back again – to his home, not hers. A home she had left without hesitation because she thought she might be able to help him in Lisbon. It was a humbling thought that a woman such as this would cold-bloodedly risk her life for him.

253

Yorke, as if reading his thoughts, said softly, "She took a fearful risk coming out here." When Ramage nodded he added, "What would the French do if they got their hands on her?"

"Murder her, I imagine. While she's alive she's a threat to them. She could rouse three-quarters of Tuscany if the people knew she was in the hills waiting to lead them."

"It'd be a massacre, though," Yorke said. "Peasants with pitchforks against Bonaparte's Army of Italy."

"A massacre now," Ramage said. "But maybe not in a few years' time. The French fighting troops being used elsewhere, and the garrison troops grown soft and slack by inactivity ... Curious place, Italy: it rots the weak and inspires the strong."

The familiar thumping footsteps warned them Wilson was approaching. "Morning, Captain," he said almost shyly, as though unsure how he should treat Ramage in his new role. "Just going to take my exercise. Wondered if the Marchesa might care to join me. Permission to ask her, as it were?"

Ramage stared at him blankly for a moment, and then grinned. "Of course. She probably heard you," he said with gentle irony, since the soldier's confidential whisper was probably audible on the foredeck.

Gianna gathered up the folds of the boatcloak. "How thoughtful of you, Captain Wilson: I was feeling cold and the exercise will do us good."

"A mile before dinner, Ma'am," Wilson said as he fell in step beside her. "Have to you know; it's the porter. Drink too much of it and it makes..."

Yorke winked at Ramage. "Seems half a lifetime ago we first heard him say that. I say," he said suddenly, "how long is it really?"

Ramage shrugged his shoulders. "Seven or eight weeks, I suppose, but it isn't the sort of time you can measure with a calendar."

"I wonder what's happened to Stevens and Farrell?"

"I was thinking about them last night. Probably in a French prison by now. I expect the *Rossignol* put them on board her next prize."

Yorke gave a bitter laugh. "While we were prisoners in

Lisbon, the French may have exchanged the pair of them by now..."

"I've thought of that too," Ramage said firmly, "and in case your imagination is sluggish this morning, I've thought of them making an official protest against me to the Inspector of Packets, and I've tried to guess what Lord Auckland says to the First Lord of the Admiralty when he reads their version."

"Stranger things have happened," Yorke commented. "But the *Rossignol* may have been caught by one of our frigates, and a British roundshot may have knocked both their heads off."

Southwick came up. "With your permission, sir, I'd like to get on with that survey of the stern. If I could have Much to help me, too."

"Carry on," Ramage said. "Make it detailed!"

The *Arabella* was making good time: the village of Estoril had dropped out of sight behind Punta de Salmodo, and the Citadel at Cascais, with Fort Santa Marta on the point, would soon be hidden by Cabo Raso as he headed the packet north for the long slog almost the length of the Peninsula. For once the wind was being helpful, veering as the *Arabella* rounded each headland so that it stayed just abaft the beam.

By mid-afternoon Much took the conn to allow Southwick an opportunity to give Ramage his written survey. As the Master sat down in the Captain's cabin, groaning and complaining of aching muscles after crawling round down below and reaching into almost inaccessible places to test the hardness of the wood, he was shaking his head. He held out several sheets of paper. "My written report, sir."

Ramage took it. "Just tell me the worst of it."

Southwick sniffed. "If we were in England, the dockyard people wouldn't have let us sail. The sternson knee, wing transom knee on the starboard side, several cant frames and the deck transom are all spongy. The sternpost – where I could get at it – was soft. Like cheese in some places. It's all in the report, sir," he said miserably. "Unsettles me to talk about it, specially since we can't do anything about it."

Ramage reached over and patted the old Master's knee.

"Cheer up; if it was action damage you wouldn't let it worry you!"

"That's true," he admitted cautiously. "But roundshot just breaks the wood up: you can see the extent of the damage. Rot – it's insidious: you can't measure how far it goes or how much the ship's weakened."

"As long as she'll get us to Falmouth..."

"Aye – well, as long as the sternpost holds, the rudder will hang on. Just remember we can't fire the stern-chasers – not that we're likely to forget that."

"Forget about the rot, then," Ramage said cheerfully. "I've just remembered I forgot to clear Customs in Lisbon. That damned Agent will think that's far more serious!"

Immediately after the mid-day meal, Ramage told Gianna to stay in her cabin and had the whole ship's company mustered aft. As he looked around at the men he could see that the resentment was there all right: the packetsmen's sullen stance was emphasized by the cheerful bearing of the former Tritons.

"The decks look a little better," he said harshly, "but in the time you've taken you could have sanded half an inch off the planks. Well, now you have a meal inside you, we'll have some exercises at the guns – I trust you packetsmen can remember the drill. Just to refresh your memories, you'll be shown how it should be done."

He took the key of the magazine from his pocket, and his watch.

"I want the packetsmen over there, by the mainmast: the former Tritons stand fast."

As soon as the ship's company was divided into two groups, Ramage called for the two ship's boys. "Do you two lads know what powder monkeys are?"

Crimson with shyness and embarrassment, the two boys said they did.

"Very well, you're going to have to take those charges and run twice as fast as you ever thought possible. Mr Much!" The Mate stepped forward and Ramage handed him the key to the magazine. "Will you stand by to take over below?"

Ramage turned to the former Tritons. "Jackson, Rossi, Stafford and Maxton. You will be the crew of number one gun on the starboard side. You're captain, Jackson; Stafford you'd better be second captain. Rossi, you are sponger and Maxton rammer. But leave the gun secure and you four men and the boys stand fast. The rest of you Tritons hoist up the tubs, fill them with water and get the decks wetted and sanded."

Quickly two small, low tubs were brought up from below, put one each side of the gun, and filled with water. Half a dozen buckets of water were swilled across the deck round the gun and between it and the hatch from which the boys would emerge with the powder charges, so there would be no chance of stray grains of gunpowder igniting as the wide wooden wheels of the carriage spun back with the recoil. A man then hurried across sprinkling sand so that feet should not slip on the wet planking.

With the gun still secured to the ship's side, the tackles were tight and seized so that it could not move no matter how much the ship rolled in heavy weather. The sponge – in effect a large mop fitted to a short wooden handle – and the rammer, a similar handle with a round wooden plug at one end only slightly smaller than the bore of the gun, were still lashed along the bulwark. Two handspikes – long wooden levers with wedge-shaped iron tips, used for levering the gun round to train it – were lashed near them.

Half a dozen roundshot nested like black oranges in semicircular depressions cut in a piece of timber bolted to the bulwark on each side of the gunport. Ramage had inspected the shot earlier. They had been painted within the past few months, but he had wondered idly when they had last been passed through a shot gauge to check whether several coats of paint over small bulges of rust meant they were no longer spherical, so they would jam in the bore of the gun or, when fired, would not fly true. There was no shot gauge on board, so he could do nothing about it.

He looked at his watch and held up a hand. Much and Jackson watched him closely. Suddenly he snapped, "Load and run out number one gun, starboard side. Roundshot!"

257

It was not an order from the drill books – such as they were – but it was a good exercise. Much, after almost diving down the hatch, followed by the two boys, would now be unlocking the magazine and unrolling the fire-screens, the rolls of heavy material which hung down like curtains to ensure that neither flash nor flame could enter the magazine to ignite the powder stored inside.

Much would have kicked off his shoes by now and be fishing around in the darkness down there. He would be cursing the fact that he had forgotten (as Ramage guessed he would) a fighting lanthorn to put in the V-shaped double window which ensured a light shining into the magazine from the outside without an actual flame anywhere near the powder. And he would be trying to find a pair of felt slippers that anyone working in the magazine was supposed to wear – again as a precaution against accidents from grains of powder.

If he had any sense he would work in his bare feet. He'd grab some empty cartridge boxes and pass them out to the boys, who would slide up the lids on the cylindrical boxes. Then he would pass out a powder charge, a boy would grab it and put it in his box, slide the lid down on the rope handle and head for the ladder clutching the box.

Now the men working under Jackson had cast off the lashings, overhauled the train tackles, thrown the lashings off the sponge, rammer and handspikes and run the gun in. Maxton was just removing the tompion from the muzzle of the gun when a boy arrived breathless with the charge.

Ramage wondered how long it would be before Jackson realized his two – no, three – mistakes so far.

They snatched the charge from the boy and eased it into the muzzle. Maxton slid the rammer in to push it right home, then gave it two smart thumps. Suddenly one of the former Tritons was standing by Jackson and passing several things to him. And Ramage knew he had underestimated the American – Rossi had slipped below unnoticed and brought up wads, pricker and powder horn, all of which were kept in the magazine. Rossi grabbed a wad and that was rammed home; a shot followed a moment later.

258

In the meantime Jackson, who had earlier checked the spark from the flint in the lock, jammed the long, thin metal pricker into the touch hole and made sure it had penetrated the covering of the powder charge, then shook powder from the powder horn into the pan and made sure it filled the touch hole. The long trigger lanyard to the lock was already coiled up on the breech.

At a word from Jackson, the gun was run out and Maxton and Rossi leapt back, each grabbing a handspike, ready to train the gun. Jackson stepped back smartly, uncoiling the lanyard and Stafford stood with his hand over the lock, ready to cock it. Jackson gave the word and the Cockney cocked it and jumped sideways out of the way.

Jackson dropped to his right knee, his left leg outstretched to the side, and called "Number one gun ready, sir!"

Ramage glanced at his watch and said: "Fire!"

Jackson took the strain on the lanyard. Suddenly the gun gave a sharp, almost bronchitic cough, and leapt back in recoil, the trucks rumbling until brought to a stop by the thick rope breeching secured to the bulwark each side and passing through the big ring on the breech.

One and three-quarter minutes from the moment he had given them the word. Not bad, not particularly good.

"Secure the gun and return equipment to the magazine," Ramage ordered.

Southwick walked across and muttered crossly, "They've got rusty . . . this soft life they've been leading for the last month or so. If you'll give me half an hour with them, sir . . ."

"Just wait," Ramage grinned. "If you think that's slow, we'll see what the packetsmen do."

The sponge, rammer and handspikes had been lashed against the bulwark, and the little canvas bonnet protecting the lock mechanism and flint against spray had been tied in position when Ramage turned to the packetsmen. He had no wish to humiliate them; he just wanted them to demonstrate themselves.

"Bosun – pick your four best men for that gun's crew. Pick a

259

fifth man to collect wads, pricker and powder horn from the magazine."

Four packetsmen shambled up to the gun. A fifth man stood by the hatch and the two boys joined him. Ramage glanced round and held up his hand.

"Is everyone ready?"

The men muttered and Ramage said loudly, "Load and run out number one gun, starboard side. Roundshot!"

As the fifth man and the boys ran below, the four packetsmen began casting off the gun, but Ramage noticed they did not overhaul the tackles. That meant the ropes would almost certainly kink and curl and jam in the blocks. They undid the lashings holding the rammer and sponge and tossed both down on the same side of the gun – that would waste time because the rammer worked on one side and the sponger on the other. The two handspikes followed, and were kicked out of the way as a man grabbed a roundshot and in his haste dropped it.

Southwick raised an eyebrow – there was no need for anyone to touch a shot at that point since the first boy had not yet arrived with powder. The fifth man appeared with wads, pricker and powder horn, but as the gun captain snatched the powder horn the fifth man in his excitement dropped the wads, which rolled aft. He was so flustered that he scampered round picking them all up, instead of grabbing the nearest and passing it to one of the two men at the muzzle of the gun.

By then a boy had arrived with the cartridge, which a seaman snatched and thrust into the muzzle. Then he looked round hurriedly for the rammer – and realized that it was on the other side of the gun.

Ramage looked at his watch. Two and a quarter minutes.

They all had to wait while the man with the wads came back in response to the gun captain's shouts. In went the wad and was rammed home. The sponger had a shot ready in his hands and tried to cram it in the muzzle. He was so clumsy that it dropped and rolled aft along the deck. Finally a shot was in and rammed home, priming powder was in the pan, and the gun ready to run out for firing. The men were hauling on the tackles to run it out before Ramage realized that the gun captain was holding the trigger lanyard taut and, even as he watched, the second captain cocked the lock without waiting for an order. If the gun moved a few more inches its own travel would tighten the lanyard and fire it – and probably kill the gun captain as it recoiled.

"Belay!" bellowed Ramage at the top of his voice, and fortunately the men froze.

Even as he strode across to the gun he saw the gun captain had not realized what he was doing. Ramage stopped right beside him and took the lanyard from his hand.

"You fool!" he said coldly. "The lock is cocked – if they'd run out another couple of inches the gun would have fired and you'd have been killed by the recoil – and some of the others too. And you" – he turned to the second captain – "don't you *ever* touch a lock until the gun captain gives the order. Now, carry on!"

He walked back aft, seething, and looked at his watch. Nearly four and a half minutes. Finally the gun captain called, "Number one gun ready, sir."

"Fire!"

And he looked at his watch yet again.

As the smoke drifted way he looked at the packetsmen. "Bosun!" he snapped. "The first crew took one and three-quarter minutes. Guess how long yours took."

"Three minutes, sir?" the man asked nervously.

"I wish they had. Six and a quarter minutes. They are your best men, but you saw how they nearly killed themselves. Right, secure the gun. You and your men," he told the Bosun harshly, "are going to exercise at the guns until you wish gunpowder had never been invented."

He turned to the Master, who commented gloomily, "And that was the leeward side..."

The fact the packet was heeled to leeward meant that when running the gun out ready to fire, its own weight helped the men at the tackles. If they had been using a gun on the other side they would have had to haul it up the inclined deck.

"Exercises start now," Ramage told Southwick angrily, "and

261

continue for two hours. No live firing, but the men will ram and sponge as though there was."

He knew he was in a fury, although that was not going to make the men any faster.

"Jackson!" he called. When the American coxswain came running aft, Ramage said, "As soon as the Bosun divides his men into fours, I want you, Stafford, Rossi and Maxton to go through the drill with each crew one by one. Make sure they know what they're trying to do. When you're satisfied they all know the drill, report to me."

An hour had passed before Jackson made his report, and Ramage ordered the three crews to three of the 4-pounder guns. For the remaining hour he had the crews competing against each other, loading, running out, pretending to fire, sponging, ramming and running out again until sweat was pouring from their bodies. At each gun stood Rossi, Stafford or Maxton, bellowing encouragement, instructions and occasionally abuse while Jackson strode from one gun to another, like the conductor of a wayward orchestra.

Every ten minutes Ramage timed a different crew, and to begin with there was a gradual improvement, measured in seconds rather than minutes. But after that the improvement stopped as the men wearied. Very well, he thought to himself, from now on it's punishment, not training.

At five o'clock he ordered the guns secured and the magazine locked. He glanced up at the sails, impatient for the next day, so that he could start exercising the packetsmen aloft.

Chapter Eighteen

By early evening the *Lady Arabella* was making seven knots with a brisk quartering wind. The Os Farilhões islands, their sharp outline caught by the last of the sun's rays and giving the impression of several sails on the eastern horizon, were eight miles away on the starboard beam.

Southwick, responsible for navigation, was already grumbling about the French charts. "These packets," he muttered to Ramage. "They carry just enough charts to get them through to their usual destination. Fancy Stevens not carrying a chart for anywhere south of Brest! Supposing he ran into a week of bad weather on the way home and found himself driven on to the Spanish peninsula, or into the Bay of Biscay? Not that these damned French charts are much better than having nothing. Don't trust 'em."

"Kerguelen was going to – in fact he took us down to Lisbon with them without running ashore!" Ramage said mildly. "He probably brought the French charts on board with him because he didn't trust British ones!"

"Or he guessed that packets don't carry a proper folio of charts. And this business of measuring the prime meridian from Paris," Southwick snorted. "Why not Greenwich, like other civilized people!"

Ramage had forgotten that. "When do we come on to the British charts?"

"Just south of the latitude of Brest. Stevens has a copy made from some other chart. He's left the south-eastern section blank

– probably too damned idle to finish the job."

Ramage began pacing up and down the starboard side of the deck: the strange lassitude that had threatened to overcome him in Lisbon, and which had been given a sharp nudge by Gianna's arrival, had now vanished completely. The *Lady Arabella* was a strange command for him – strange in every sense, from the ship's company to her actual ownership – but at least a command. Sir Pilcher Skinner was the other side of the Western Ocean; the Admiralty and Lombard Street were still a few hundred miles to the north. It was going to be a problem convincing Their Lordships about the fate of the packets, but that was all sufficiently far over the horizon to be left for a day or two so he could enjoy Gianna's company. The devil take it, she'd gone below ten minutes ago to change before the evening meal, and he was already missing her...

He had to write a full report for Their Lordships before they reached Plymouth, and it would be worth having Much write one as well. In fact, Ramage thought, I'm damned if I won't take Much to London with me; Lord Spencer can hear the Mate's story from the man's own lips if he wishes to. Yorke will probably travel to London at the same time, so he will be available too.

He looked slowly round the horizon as he walked. The wind was little more than fifteen knots, and there was the usual evening cloud to the westward, looking dark and menacing with the sun setting behind it.

As he watched several men washing down the deck to clear away the sand, he saw how easy it would be for the most unobservant landlubber to pick out the former Tritons. They were working with a will, not a sloppy eagerness as though trying to please. They had a brisk precision; their complete economy of movement made the least effort do the most work. He had noticed it before, when Stevens was in command, because that had been his first chance of comparing man-o'-war's men working side by side with packetsmen.

There had been scores of occasions when he had seen a crowd of lubberly volunteers or newly pressed men being shown how to do various tasks on board a man-o'-war, and it

264

had taken weeks for them to get into the swing of it all. But here were packetsmen – trained seamen who had spent their life in merchant ships – who made a very poor showing when working alongside men who had spent only a few years in ships of war.

Of course, he had to make allowances for the fact that these packetsmen were sullen; there was no disguising that. They hated exercising at the guns; they would resent being roused out to go to quarters to meet the dawn; they already resented having to scrub the decks daily. Nor did they like the idea of four lookouts, one on each bow and each quarter: Stevens had been content with one at the bow. Well, Ramage thought grimly, they are going to dislike the drill I have planned for them tomorrow even more. They would probably hate him long before they sighted the English coast, but he was going to work the packetsmen until they were ready to drop. And if they did drop, he was going to be sure it was on to scrubbed decks.

Yorke sauntered over and fell into step beside him.

"Feels good, doesn't it?"

"Aye," Ramage said, motioning Yorke to follow him down to the cabin, "I was never a good passenger."

"Nor me," Yorke said ruefully.

"Sorry, I didn't mean it like that!"

"I know you didn't; it just reminded me. Anyway, you've already got her looking more like a ship."

Ramage led the way into the cabin, acknowledging the salute of the seaman on guard at the door, and waved Yorke to a seat. "By sunset tomorrow these packetsmen are going to wish they'd never been born!"

"Oho! What other little treats have you got in store?"

"Four hours' drill at the guns, for a start. And an hour's sail drill. More if they don't look lively!"

"Is it worth it? I mean," Yorke said hurriedly, "you gave them a good run at the guns today and we'll be in Plymouth before you can get a polish on them. If we sight any ships with designs on our virtue, presumably we'll make a bolt for it."

"We most certainly will. No, I'm going to work these

packetsmen until they nearly drop simply because it's the only way to punish them."

"Why not leave it to the courts?" Yorke said mildly.

"Courts?" Ramage snorted. "These scoundrels will never be hauled before a court! And if they were, how can we prove what we've seen with our own eyes? Their word against ours, and a smart lawyer would probably convince a judge that we never saw anything; that we are just nasty troublemakers perjuring ourselves."

"But they'll certainly be arrested, won't they?"

Ramage shook his head. "I can't see it. The Post Office – the Government, rather – are going to handle everything very discreetly, and to a politician 'discreetly' is a polite word for 'secretly'."

"Oh come now!" Yorke chided. "I know you've said all this before, but..."

"All right, m'lad. Who *has* the power in the City of London? Who *really* has their hands on the purse strings?"

"The merchants and the bankers, I suppose."

"Exactly. And of all the merchants, the ones with the loudest voices are the –"

"The West India merchants," Yorke interrupted. "All right, I take the point."

"Very well, they're the most powerful – and they've lost the most because the West Indies packets were vanishing. In fact I'm damned certain it's only their pressure that eventually forced the Government to do something drastic.

"You see, it'd be one thing for the Post Office to report in vague terms in about three months' time that losses have stopped. But it'd be something quite different if the Postmaster-General suddenly announced in Parliament that he'd just discovered the heavy loss of packets had been caused by the treachery and greed of their commanders and crews.

"I can just imagine the overwhelming vote of confidence the Government would fail to get in Parliament! And I can see the Lord Mayor of London leading his cronies in a brisk trot to Downing Street armed with nasty threats. Consols would come down with a crash – and from what I've always heard, the moment they drop ten points or so the ministers start emptying their desk drawers, ready to hand over to their successors."

"So you think these jokers" – Yorke waved a hand to indicate the packetsmen on deck above with scrubbing brushes and buckets of water – "won't be popped on the scales of Justice?"

"No – but by the time I've finished with 'em I hope they'd sooner have taken their chance in a court. In my crude way I don't see why they should escape *any* sort of punishment."

"Bit hard on your fellows, though."

Ramage shook his head. "Oh no – they'd be doing it anyway in a ship-o'-war. You saw them just now; they simply show how fast a thing can be done, then they watch the packetsmen working at it until they can do it as quickly."

"That seems fair," Yorke conceded.

"It's not intended to be fair," Ramage said sourly. "Don't labour the point or I might keep them at it for ten hours a day. Anyway, weary men are less likely to cause trouble!"

The sentry's voice interrupted. "The Marchesa's coming, sir!"

Ramage grinned at Yorke. "The Marines would go mad if they heard that. Still, the poor fellow has been told he's to guard us – from each other, too!"

There was a knock at the door and Gianna walked in. "It's so dark in here, Nicholas. Oh, Mr Yorke – am I interrupting an important conversation?"

"No," Yorke said quickly, "but I have a very important and urgent job."

When he saw Ramage's eyebrows raised questioningly he pointed to the lantern clipped to the bulkhead over the desk. "I was going to get that lit – we can't let such beauty blossom in darkness."

"Nicholas is not as beautiful as all that," she said with a straight face. "Come, sit down again; the Captain's cabin in the twilight is so cosy. That saloon – horrible! Like some cheap inn! Now tell me what you two did in the West Indies."

"Nothing much," Yorke said warily. "Deuced hot, of course."

"Too hot to flirt with beautiful women?"

"Oh, much too hot," Yorke said emphatically.

"That is not what I hear," Gianna said. "The rustling palm trees, the perfume of frangipani, an enormous moon ... is that not romantic, Mr Yorke?"

"Indeed it is. But you can't hear the palms rustling for the buzz of mosquitoes, and you can't stand still long enough to look at the moon for the itching of their bites. Even if you could, you'd be eaten alive by sandflies – 'No-see-'ems' they're called in some of the islands – and their bites are like red-hot needles jabbed in you."

Yorke hoped she was convinced, and looking at her and listening to her talking in that delightfully accented voice that one heard with the loins rather than the ears, he suddenly remembered the many occasions back in the Caribbean when Ramage had not heard him say something. He would give a start and Yorke had guessed he'd suddenly come back from wherever his thoughts had been. For a moment he would look confused; then he'd seem embarrassed. Now Yorke realized what iron control Ramage had. In the isolation of the West Indies, it was a rare man who could have resisted the urge to ease the loneliness by talking of the woman he loved so desperately and who was nearly five thousand miles away. Yet until he met her, the only things Yorke knew about her had been the few admiring anecdotes which Southwick had related like an adoring grandfather describing his favourite grandchild.

Yorke had often heard men describing beautiful women, but when he'd eventually met the women he'd been disappointed. Sometimes a woman's beauty matched the words used to describe her, but usually she proved to be as characterless as a piece of statuary.

In a bitter way – just jealousy, if he was honest with himself – Yorke had pieced together Southwick's occasional descriptions and pictured a beautiful shrew: a young woman who used her beauty to mesmerize men and her power as the ruler of a small state to bully them. Wilful, making everyone rush round for the sake of a whim, sulky when thwarted ... The moment he had heard she was coming back with them in the

268

Arabella, Yorke admitted to himself he half thought of moving over to the *Princess Louise*.

But how wrong he had been: she was all Southwick had said, and more. More because Southwick could not appreciate her love of music, the breadth of her reading, the subtlety of a patrician mind completely free of the restraints normally ingrained in women.

Would Ramage ever be able to marry her? Perhaps not. If she was ever to return to rule Volterra a foreign husband might be too much for those Tuscans to accept. Religion – would that be an obstacle? Ramage a Protestant, and Gianna presumably a Roman Catholic? Obviously they would be the main problems. Apart from that, everything was in his favour: heir to one of the oldest earldoms in the country, he spoke perfect Italian, and from all accounts understood the Italians as well as a non-Italian ever could.

Yet would she be allowed to marry the man she loved? Would she be forced – for political or dynastic reasons – to marry some dreary and corpulent ruler of a neighbouring state? If that ever happened Yorke pitied the poor fellow! How could he compete with the memories she would have of the handsome young Englishman who rescued her from Napoleon's cavalry and took her away in his ship...

"A penny for your thoughts, Mr Yorke..."

Now *he* was daydreaming about her!

"I was thinking about your secret admirers, ma'am."

"And who are they?" she demanded.

"All the former Tritons on board this ship who served in the *Kathleen*, and the worthy Captain Wilson, Much and Bowen..."

"So few?" she teased.

"I'm not including myself because I don't – with the Captain's permission – have to keep it a secret."

Ramage wagged a warning finger. "If you think flattery will get you an extra dance, you're wasting your time."

"A dance?" Gianna asked. "With whom is Mr Yorke going to dance – and when?"

"In a weak moment, when the chances of us ever getting

269

back to England seemed very remote," Ramage explained, "I told him I would give a ball in your honour – and let him have one dance."

"Hmm, you'll be charging people soon. A guinea to dance with the crazy Italian lady," she said with a sniff. "Mr Yorke, I shall give a ball – and you can be my partner as often as you wish. But you must both excuse me now; I must see how Rossi is getting on with our dinner. He's having trouble with that wretched seaman, Nicholas."

"I'm not surprised. Two cooks in one kitchen!"

"Cook!" she exclaimed crossly. "That other man is an assassin!"

With that she left the cabin and the two men sat in almost complete darkness. It was not classical beauty, Yorke mused; it was a great deal more than that. Classical beauty tended to be cold. Her mouth was too wide and her lips too warm, if you measured her by those standards. Her eyes too large – and too lively. Her skin was golden, not the alabaster white and pink that classical beauty dictated. Yet if she walked on to the floor at one of the Prince of Wales's famous grand balls, every woman present would demand to know who she was, and hate her for being there!

"You'll have dinner with us?" Ramage asked.

"No, I'll eat in the saloon with the others. The captain of one of the King's ships dines alone – unless there is a charming passenger on board. You don't need a chaperone for your first evening together!"

The excitement of her first day at sea had left Gianna tired, and as soon as dinner was finished and Rossi had cleared the table she had smiled ruefully at Ramage and said she was going to bed. Ramage took her to her cabin and then went up on deck to have a chat with Southwick, who was on watch.

The Portuguese coast was now a thin black line low and vague on the dark eastern horizon. Ramage had decided quite deliberately not to beat far out into the Atlantic; instead he planned to clear Cabo Finisterra by only a few miles, even though the Spanish bases of Coruña and Ferrol were just a short distance round the Cape to the eastward. British frigates – if not a sizeable squadron – were keeping a close watch on them even as the *Arabella* stretched along the coast, and the packet would probably be safer close in.

After a glance at the slate recording the *Arabella*'s recent courses and speeds, Ramage looked at the two helmsmen, their faces lit faintly by the light in the binnacle box, nodded to Southwick and went below to his cabin again. The Master had been given his night orders, which he would later pass on to Much: orders which covered any likely eventuality. A major wind shift or change in its strength, sighting another vessel, doubt concerning the ship's position – any of these circumstances and many more would result in the captain being called.

In the meantime Ramage was now feeling sleepy and decided he might well spend an hour or two beginning a draft of his report to the Admiralty. He took the lantern from the centre of the cabin's forward bulkhead, where it lit up the table, and hooked it on the bracket on the starboard side of the bulkhead, so that he would see to work at the desk.

For the next hour he wrote and crossed out, tore up complete pages and started again. The *Arabella* was rolling; not heavily, just enough to make it necessary to wedge the inkwell. He was thankful the desk had been built athwartships against the bulkhead, so that he faced forward: it made it less tiring than if he had to face outboard.

The sentry tapped on the door and said quietly, to avoid rousing the occupants of the other cabins, "Mr Yorke, sir."

Ramage glanced up as the door to his left opened in response to his reply.

"Want a game of chess?" he asked mockingly.

"Don't you start," Yorke said wearily. "I've been fighting off Bowen for hours. He seems to think that Southwick standing a watch is a deliberate plot on your part to keep him away from the chessboard."

"I doubt if Southwick minds," Ramage said, getting up from the desk and going to sit in a chair by the table on the other side of the cabin.

271

"Don't be too sure," Yorke said sitting in a chair beyond. "Your Master is getting the disease. He beat Bowen in three consecutive games just before we left Lisbon."

"Oh? I didn't hear about that!"

"I'm not surprised: Bowen was too startled, and Southwick couldn't believe it himself. I think Bowen was getting careless."

"If you'd like a drink..." Ramage gestured to the locker in which bottles sat in racks.

Yorke shook his head. "No, I want to sleep lightly tonight." When Ramage raised his eyebrows questioningly, Yorke said: "The packetsmen ... I don't trust that Bosun an inch."

"I imagine he's borne that cross since he was a baby and first reached out of the crib to pick his father's pocket," Ramage said dryly.

Yorke glanced at Ramage's desk, on which there were several sheets of paper, and the open inkwell. "I shouldn't be interrupting you."

"Plenty of time for that: I was starting a draft of my report to the First Lord."

"I saw Much tickling his chin with a quill."

"I've told him to write a report to me, so that I can enclose it."

"He seems to have as much enthusiasm for quill-pushing as you," Yorke commented, picking up one of the two pistols lying on the settee. "I see you don't follow your own instructions, Captain. This isn't loaded! Mine are loaded and ready!"

Ramage pointed to the box on the settee. "There's powder, wads and shot..."

"Armourer – that's the only job I haven't had since I've been with you," Yorke said caustically. "I'd make a good armourer, you know," he confided. "I love guns. Not as instruments to kill" – he snapped the lock a couple of times to check the spark from the flint – "but just for good craftsmanship. Not one of these Sea Service pistols, of course; but a pair of good duelling pistols by someone like Henry Nock."

He took the powder flask, slid back the rammer and methodically loaded the gun.

"I feel the same way," Ramage said. "A gun is inert; just a

piece of metal with a flint and some wood attached to it. By itself it can't move or kill anything: it can't do a damned thing unless someone picks it up."

"Ah – an interesting point," Yorke commented, beginning to load the second pistol. "Who is the killer – the gun that fires the shot or the man who squeezes the trigger?"

Ramage sat back in his chair and crossed his legs. "That's a fatuous point which isn't worth mentioning, my friend, let alone discussing. No –" He stopped and listened for a moment. The rudder still creaked as the wheel turned a spoke or two this way or that, keeping the ship on course: he could picture the quartermaster checking by the dim light at the compass and muttering something to the men at the wheel. The lookouts were watching in the darkness, and Southwick would be strolling up and down. He had heard the sentry outside the cabin cough once or twice. A sail occasionally flapped as the packet pitched and momentarily spilled the wind. The hull creaked as all hulls did. He was not sure what he had heard: perhaps only a distant seagull giving a squawk of alarm as it sighted the ship.

"No," he continued, idly taking one of the pistols, while the light from the lantern threw the shadow across the cabin, "just take this as an example. Old ladies and parsons regard them as inventions of the Devil: evil contrivances which kill men. Yet it's the man that's evil, not the gun. A gun is no –"

That noise again, and a slight thump which could have been a piece of wreckage bumping the hull, and from the way Yorke glanced towards the door Ramage knew he'd heard it too. When he raised his eyebrows questioningly Yorke turned down the corners of his mouth, shrugging his shoulders. Then a plank creaked.

There were many beams and planks, lodging knees and hanging knees, frames and stringers creaking in the ship at this very moment, but only one particular plank creaked like that.

A butt in one of the planks in the corridor had sprung close to Ramage's door – he remembered stubbing his toe on it and cursing violently, startling the sentry. And as he stood there, his toes tingling with pain, he had pushed down on the plank and it had creaked: a high-pitched creak – more like the squeak of

273

a loose plank in a staircase than the usual deeper creaking made by the ship, which by comparison was a series of groans. He had intended to have the carpenter's mate put in a couple of fastenings to secure it.

Surely the plank would creak like that only if someone stood on it? But the sentry would see anyone there, unless he was leaning with his right shoulder against the bulkhead, facing to starboard. Still, it could be the sentry himself, or Bowen or Wilson going on deck for some fresh air. Ramage knew he was getting jumpy and leaned over to put the pistol back on the settee. At that moment he heard a soft grunt and a gentle thud.

Without realizing it he continued moving upward so that he was on his feet and heading silently for the door, pistol in his hand, almost before registering that the grunt came from a man's throat. Yorke followed him a couple of seconds later.

Ramage gestured to him to stand to the left of the door, where he would be hidden if it was opened, and himself stood the other side, flat against the bulkhead. He watched the handle.

The light was so dim from the lantern over his desk that it was hard to see the wooden latch. Yes! It was lifting slightly ... and anyone wanting to see if he was lying in the cot at the after-end of the cabin or sitting at the desk on the starboard side would have to open the door at least a foot. And men entering a room or cabin tended to look first at the level of their own eyes.

Gently he lowered himself until he was crouching.

A black crack began to show as someone slowly opened the door, careful to do it gently for fear of a creaking hinge. The crack widened ... an inch, two inches ... four ... five ... Whoever it was could see part of the cabin but not the cot or the desk. Eight inches ... nine ... he could probably see the empty chair by the desk now ... eleven ... twelve ... he could see the whole of the desk and must guess the Captain was lying in the cot.

Suddenly the door flung open wide and the Bosun jumped into the cabin, a pistol in each hand, shouting at the cot, "Don't move!"

274

It took him a few moments to realize that there was no one in the heavily shadowed cot, and as he began to look round Ramage shot him in the leg. The flash of the gun blinded him for a second and the noise boomed in the tiny cabin, but as the Bosun pitched forward another man with a pistol took his place, saw Ramage crouching with an empty gun smoking in his hand, and sneered, "Now it's your turn, Mister Captain! We need your help to capture this ship!"

Ramage stood up slowly and glanced down at the Bosun. The man was lying on his face and had let go of both pistols as he tried to clutch the wound just above his knee.

Ramage knew that if he wanted to live he needed time. "Do you, indeed?" he said icily, recognizing the seaman as a man called Harris. "Do you want me to give the officer of the watch a written order? Or would you prefer me to ask the Admiralty?"

"None o' that smooth talk," Harris said harshly. "The shot will have roused that bloody slave-driver Southwick. I'm warning you, if he tries any nonsense, you get yourself shot. You're our *second* hostage, Mister Captain – sir," he added derisively.

Suddenly Ramage realized that there were only two of them: the Bosun and this man Harris. They must have crept from their hammocks – or sneaked from their stations – without the Tritons spotting them, clubbed the sentry at the door and been planning to seize Ramage as a hostage.

By marching him on deck with a pistol at his back, they guessed they could force Southwick to surrender the ship as the price of saving Ramage's life. Then they would head for a Spanish or French port to hand over the ship and get what they expected would be freedom. They had probably – what a terrible irony – thought the gibbet awaited them at home in England, never for a moment ... all at once he realized that Harris had just referred to a "second hostage". Who was the first?

"Come on, Mister Captain, let's get on with the business a'fore the Bosun bleeds to death. Remember, one false step and you're a dead man."

Hoping Yorke would continue to play a waiting game, Ramage decided to try and find out as much as he could. "You're a brave fellow – you and the Bosun. Just two of you taking a ship, eh?"

"Not difficult for packetsmen," Harris sneered. "No, not just two of us: the rest of the lads are ready, waiting for me to pass the word. Then we'll show Mister Bloody Southwick some sail handling – aye, and navigation too. Ever been to Coruña, Mister Captain Ramage? Ever been in a Spanish prison?"

"No. But I imagine you've been in an English one."

"Never – an' there'll never be no risk o' that again; I'll take my oath on it!"

"I'll take my oath that you're wrong," Ramage said conversationally. "Do you know Mr Yorke, by the way?"

"What, the passenger? No, why?"

"I just wondered. You are Harris, aren't you, Bosun's mate?"

"Aye, that's me. Now, let's –"

"Don't turn round, Harris; otherwise you'll be shot dead," Ramage said conversationally. "Mr Yorke is standing right behind you with a loaded pistol in his hand."

The man froze, the white showing all round his eyes. Then he relaxed. "That's a silly trick. You can't catch a packetsman like that. And we've got the Marchesa as well – didn't know that, did you. Got the pair of you, we have!"

At that moment the muzzle of Yorke's pistol pressed into the back of his neck.

"We *can* catch a packetsman, you know," Yorke said jauntily, and cocked the pistol so that Harris felt the metallic click travel down his spine.

Again the man froze and Ramage saw his eyes straining to look behind him. In a swift movement Ramage stepped to one side and seized the man's gun. Outside the door he heard the plank squeak several times and as he turned he saw Southwick peering cautiously through the door, holding a musketoon whose muzzle in the shadows seemed to bell out as large as a cavalryman's trumpet and which a moment later was jammed into Harris's stomach.

Still trying desperately to think what the mutineers could be doing to Gianna, it took him a few moments to snap, "Come

276

in, Southwick! Is the wheel secure? What about the packets-men on watch?"

"All attended to, sir," the Master said calmly. "All three of 'em lying in a row by the binnacle. We knocked 'em out the moment we heard the shot. The Mate's at the wheel."

"Very well. Don't make any move against the rest of them yet: they've got the Marchesa as a hostage. Secure Harris and get Bowen to look at the Bosun."

"Come on," Southwick called to the men behind him, "Rossi, Maxton – this man's under arrest. Put him in irons and guard him well."

"*Accidente!*" the Italian seaman exclaimed, and in a moment he was in the cabin, a knife in each hand and crouching behind Harris while Maxton stood in front, a cutlass pressing against the man's stomach. "Follow me," Maxton hissed, backing to the door, "and just trip once, eh?"

Ramage, rubbing the scar over his brow, saw the Surgeon at the door, with Wilson behind him. "Ah, Bowen, we have a patient for you: a turbulent Bosun."

"The sentry is dead," Bowen said quietly. "Skull crushed in."

The sentry dead and Gianna a hostage. Ramage felt a chill spreading through his body; time was slowing down and the colours in the dimly lit cabin were growing brighter. He knew the symptoms and knew that for the moment his greatest enemy was himself: this cold rage occurred rarely, but when it did there was no fear and no mercy for whoever caused it.

Cursing himself for letting Rossi and Maxton take Harris away before he could force answers out of him, Ramage pushed Bowen aside as the surgeon went to kneel by the Bosun, who was now beginning to groan, apparently having fainted when he fell.

Ramage paused for a moment and asked Bowen, "Who was the sentry?"

"Duncan, sir."

Duncan ... the young Scot who had been with him in every action from the Mediterranean onwards, and now murdered by one of his own countrymen. Murdered because he was looking the other way and did not know the significance of that squeaking plank. Ramage began rubbing the scar over his brow again and knelt beside the Bosun, who was conscious now and groaning softly. He pulled the man's shoulder, rolling him over on his back. The face was grey: he had lost a lot of blood – it was soaking across the deck, seemingly black in the faint light from the lantern.

"Tell me," Ramage said, almost whispering, "what have you done with the Marchesa?"

"Oh, the pain," the Bosun groaned. "For pity's sake, sir, the Surgeon. I'm bleeding to death..."

"Where is the Marchesa?"

"I'm bleeding badly, sir; my leg, it's smashed – ach..." The man's eyes closed as his body moved when the ship gave a more violent roll.

Ramage stood up and, deliberately winking at the Surgeon, said harshly, "Look at him, Bowen, and tell me how bad the bleeding is. I want to know when he'll die."

The Surgeon gestured towards the lantern, and Yorke unhooked it, holding it so light shone on the man's leg.

Quickly Bowen slit the seam of the trousers and rolled back the material. Ramage could see the wound was painful but not dangerous.

"The bleeding," Bowen said with a wink, "I've got to stop it or he'll die."

"Hear that, Bosun?" Ramage said. "You're quite right; you are bleeding to death. Five minutes, from the look of it."

The man groaned again and Ramage said crisply, "Stand back, Bowen. Now, what's happened to the Marchesa?"

"Oh God, I'm dying – the pain, sir ... I've got a wife and two children..."

"The sentry had three children. Who hit him?"

But Bowen was a surgeon with scruples, and he said emphatically, "Sir, I can't be responsible for what happens if –"

"You're not responsible," Ramage snarled as he knelt beside the Bosun again, turning the man's face so he could not avoid Ramage's eyes. "If I'm not mistaken you now have about three minutes before you go. What's happened to the Marchesa?"

278

"You're murdering me ... If I tell ... oh, the pain ... if I tell, will you let the Surgeon..."

"Yes," Ramage said, and added bitterly, "I'll save you for the hangman's noose."

"T'was Harris," the man whispered. "He gagged her and dragged her out and passed her over to the rest of them. They were supposed to take her forward."

"Who killed the sentry?"

"Harris, sir. I just caught him as he fell."

Ramage picked up the two pistols the Bosun had been carrying, checked that they were loaded, and gestured to Bowen. "Carry on."

He waved to Yorke. "I'm going to find out what's happening on deck. Are you coming?"

Yorke picked up Harris's pistol, which Ramage had pitched on to the settee. "Delighted," he said. Captain Wilson, still in his nightshirt and with his moustache drooping, waited cheerfully at the door, a pistol in each hand, and followed them.

At the top of the companionway Ramage paused for a few moments while his eyes adapted to the darkness; then he saw Much and Southwick standing beside a man at the wheel, with another – was it Stafford? – holding a pair of pistols aimed at three bodies sprawled by the binnacle. A group of men waiting at the taffrail were presumably the rest of the Tritons.

Suddenly Jackson was at his elbow. "Mr Southwick said to wait before we winkle out the packetsmen, sir. Says they've kidnapped the Marchesa."

He was speaking in the dull monotone which Ramage had heard only once or twice before but knew was the warning that the American was sufficiently roused to kill without compunction. We are a pair, Ramage thought sourly; maybe it is the quietness that misleads people.

"Stand by me a moment," he said, and did a quick sum. The Bosun, Harris and three men by the binnacle: five accounted for. One of the packetsmen had been killed when the privateer arrived. That left six packetsmen below, and a couple of boys.

One Triton was dead, one was there at the wheel, two were guarding Harris and one guarding the three packetsmen. Two

279

more were needed as lookouts. That left five Tritons plus Yorke and Wilson. He needed Southwick to handle the ship, and Much would have to act as quartermaster and help at the wheel if it became too much for one man.

Seven men against six packetsmen holding Gianna as a hostage. Think, he told himself savagely: a few moments of clear thought now may save her life; the slightest mistake will kill her. He gripped the pistol butts as though trying to crush them.

Very well, try to guess what the packetsmen – the mutineers, rather – planned. Obviously they intended to use Gianna and me as hostages to force Southwick to hand over the ship. Or perhaps, since they could not be sure they could make prisoners of the Tritons, force him to sail the *Arabella* to a Spanish port – only a few hours' sailing from here. Right, now they have lost the Bosun and Harris. Does that leave them without a leader? Probably: with such a small group of comparatively unintelligent men, the leader would carry out the most difficult part of a plan, taking the most reliable man with him. That pointed to Harris, because the Bosun was genuinely terrified of him.

Right, six mutineers are down below holding Gianna. Presumably Harris handed Gianna to them before coming to my cabin. Those six men heard a shot. They still don't know who fired it: all they do know is that Harris and the Bosun haven't returned, and the ship is still under our control.

Their only offensive weapon is Gianna, and Gianna alive. And their only defence, too. If they kill her they know they'll never get control of the ship: we will simply guard the hatch and sail the ship into Plymouth with six mutineers trapped down on the messdeck.

The six of them are probably arguing about that now. Even the most stupid of them must know Gianna has to stay alive to be of any use. Can I be sure of that? I have to be; it's a risk I must take because Harris is the man with the answers and I need ten minutes to make him talk. If I try to loosen the Bosun's tongue, I will have Bowen protesting. Yet the Bosun's tongue will be easier to loosen than Harris's. So I'm going to start with the Bosun, and if Bowen wants to get soft-hearted about it he can go and sit by the belfry for an hour or two: my questions and the Bosun's answers may be the only things that will save Gianna's life.

Have I forgotten anything? Gianna's face keeps getting in the way of the thoughts.

Ramage walked over to the binnacle and gestured to Southwick, Yorke, Much and Wilson to gather round. Quickly he told them what little he guessed and then gave his orders.

"Southwick, you have the conn and keep Much with you and one man at the wheel. I want two lookouts, one forward and one aft. These men" – he motioned to the three packetsmen lying by the binnacle, covered by a Triton with pistols – "put them in irons: we can't spare a man to guard them. I'm taking Jackson and Stafford with me and I want Rossi. Maxton can guard Harris. Pick two men to help Captain Wilson. Keep the rest with you.

"Now, Wilson: I want you to cover the forehatch with a couple of men. Take musketoons but be careful: I don't want any shooting. They may send up someone to talk with us, but don't let more than one man on deck at a time. Is all that clear? Very well, carry on."

He tapped Jackson on the arm. "Fetch Rossi and tell Maxton to keep a close watch on Harris. If he gives any trouble, he can knock him out, but I want that man kept alive..."

Turning to Yorke, Ramage said quietly, "Have I forgotten anything?"

"Not that I've spotted. I reckon you've got half an hour before those mutineers make up their minds what to do next. Shall we go down and have a chat with the Bosun?"

As Ramage hesitated, Yorke thought: he's a cool one. The Marchesa is down on the messdeck, probably with a mutineer's pistol stuck in her ribs, and he's as calm as if she was still in Cornwall. But he's changed in the last few minutes: now he's as cold and supple as a rapier blade.

Then Ramage looked straight at him and said, "I'm taking Rossi and Stafford down with me. Either the Bosun or Harris are going to talk. It might be –"

"A trifle messy," Yorke interrupted. "I should hope so!"

They found the wounded Bosun lying on the table in the saloon, secured by lines across his chest and hips against the rolling of the ship. The big gimballed lamp swung with the roll of the ship and weird shadows slipped back and forth across the saloon. Bowen was standing over the man's leg, the table holding him against the lee roll.

He glanced up as they came in and Ramage saw his face was dripping with perspiration. "Ah – just too late to lend me a hand. I'm about finished. Then perhaps I can have a couple of men to lift him into a cot; he'll be more comfortable swinging; the rolling makes the leg jerk on this table."

" 'Swinging' is the right word," Ramage said sourly. "Have you stitched him up?"

"Yes, both sides."

"*Both* sides?"

"Yes, sir; the shot went right through, of course. Missed the bone and the femoral artery: if that had been severed, he'd have been dead in a few minutes. At first I feared it was – the light is bad in your cabin, sir," he explained.

The Bosun groaned, looking up at Ramage. "A drop o' rum, sir, to take the pain away?"

Yorke sniffed. "I can't see you offering the Captain a tot of rum if you'd fired first."

"Oh, I would, sir," the Bosun protested. "And you too, sir."

"Thanks," Yorke said dryly. "But as far as you're concerned, dead men tell no tales, and they don't drink either."

"But I'm not dead, sir."

"Not yet," Yorke said ominously, "and neither are we."

Ramage grinned to himself: he would have given the Bosun a tot, and he realized Yorke had guessed that. But Yorke was right; giving a murderous mutineer a tot made little sense, and from what Bowen said it was only a flesh wound. At that moment there was a knock on the door and Jackson came in with Rossi and Stafford.

Ramage moved to stand over the Bosun. "Some more questions," he said. "You might as well answer them now."

282

The Bosun gave a heart-rending groan. "I'm not in a fit state..."

"You're alive," Ramage said. "That's enough, and be thankful. Now, whose idea was the mutiny?"

The man's eyes darted from side to side of the saloon; his hands gripped the edge of the table. Then he watched the lantern as it swung with the ship's roll. He swallowed several times but said nothing.

Ramage said, "The mutiny has failed. There's nothing to stop you talking."

"I ... I daren't, sir, an' that's the honest truth."

"Why not?"

"They'd do for me!"

Ramage was certain that the man was both terrified and telling the truth. But terrified of whom? Certainly not the ship's officers, since with them he felt safe enough to ask for a tot. Ramage made a quick guess. "Harris is in irons."

"He'll find a way, though," the Bosun muttered. "I know he will."

Ramage nodded significantly to Yorke: they had a definite answer to one question.

"What did Harris intend to do once he had the Marchesa and me as hostages?"

The Bosun just watched the swinging lamp. Perspiration was pouring down his face and he blinked rapidly as some of it ran into his eyes.

Ramage touched him on the shoulder. "Don't forget you're not a packetsman now: you are in the Navy. You're subject to the Articles of War. They lay down the death penalty for threatening a superior officer. They lay down the death penalty for mutiny. They lay down the death penalty for murder. Just think, Bosun: murder, mutiny, attacking a superior officer. You're guilty of all three, Bosun."

He paused for several moments, fighting back the driving sense of urgency as he thought of Gianna in the mutineers' hands. Then, speaking slowly and quietly he went on, "You'll hang, Bosun; you'll be run up at the fore yardarm of one of the King's ships. As far as the Articles of War are concerned,

Bosun, you're already a dead man. There's only one thing that might possibly keep your neck out of the noose, Bosun, and that's if the court let you turn King's evidence. That means you tell the court all you know. Do you understand?"

The man said nothing.

"I think you do," Ramage said. "But you don't understand *me*. The rest of your mutineers have kidnapped the Marchesa. She's your hostage. Let me tell you something about her. You see Jackson, Rossi and Stafford here? They were with me when we rescued the Marchesa from French cavalry in Italy. All my men on board – except Maxton, who joined me later – have sailed with the Marchesa in the Mediterranean. I don't think I'm exaggerating Bosun, when I say that every one of them – and that includes Mr Southwick and me – would give his life for her."

The three seamen growled their agreement, and Ramage's voice dropped to little more than a whisper when he said, "So as a mutineer, you're already dead as far as the Navy's concerned. If you don't tell me what the mutineers intended to do, you'll be dead as far as you are concerned, and within the next couple of minutes..."

"You'd never kill a wounded man," the Bosun muttered.

"*Accidente!*" Rossi hissed, leaping forward with a knife in his hand. "If the Marchesa is hurt, I killing you even if it make *me* a mutineer!"

Ramage's startled reaction and hurried, "Steady, Rossi!" was not lost on the Bosun, whose eyes were fixed on the knife blade.

"Let me have him, sir," Rossi pleaded. "Two minutes and he say everything!"

The Bosun's mouth was slack and trembling; the flesh of his face sagged as though every muscle had let go. A faint smell of urine told them the man had almost completely lost control of himself.

Ramage pressed his foot against Rossi's. "I think I will, Rossi: tell me, how will you start?"

"Testicles!" Rossi said eagerly. "First one, then the other. I

284

show him them, sir. Then I cut the ligaments, so he can't move the legs or the arms. Then –"

"I'll tell you, sir," the Bosun said hoarsely, "only just keep that madman away from me!"

"He's not mad," Ramage said viciously, "he's just unimaginative. What I planned would have had you screaming for an hour. Now, talk!"

"T'was Harris's idea, sir. Seize you an' the Marchesa and get you both forward before Southwick realized what was happening. Then we'd hold you both and force Southwick to sail the ship to a Spanish port. Coruña or Ferrol. Just before we got there he was going to shoot the lot of you."

The man paused for breath. "That's about all, sir, so help me."

"What will the mutineers do now, with Harris in irons and only the Marchesa?"

"Dunno, sir. Probably carry on with the plan. Don't make no difference that I'm wounded and Harris in irons," he said. "They've still got the Marchesa. And don't make any mistake, sir," he added, his voice becoming ingratiating, as if the idea of turning King's evidence had at last sunk in, "they're desperate men. They'll kill her if you don't do what they say."

"If they do, they'll all hang."

"If you won't take the ship to a Spanish port, they're dead men anyway," the Bosun muttered, "so they've nothing to lose by killing the Marchesa."

"Nothing to gain, either," Ramage pointed out.

"Revenge, sir. They'll have settled their score with you. They hate you: you've ruined their lives."

Ramage looked across at Bowen. "You'd better be ready for more casualties. Don't waste too much time on this one."

Gesturing to Yorke and the seamen he strode out of the saloon and went to his own cabin. "You three go and join Captain Wilson," he told Jackson. "You'll be hearing from the mutineers soon: they don't know whether I'm alive or dead, and don't tell 'em. Pretend you have to report to Mr Yorke, but pass the word to me. Warn Captain Wilson about that."

"Supposing they try to rush me, sir?"

285

"I'm certain they won't, but if they do, don't open fire. Use belaying pins or handspikes. We've got to safeguard the Marchesa. The sound of shots might panic any of them left below..."

As Jackson left, Ramage sank into a chair. The large bloodstain on the deck was black in the lantern light, as though a caulker had spilled hot tar.

"Want a drink?" Yorke asked.

Ramage shook his head. "I've got to think clearly, and spirits won't help."

Yorke sat down. "This is where we were when it all started," he said miserably.

Ramage grunted. "I should have made her take the next regular packet."

"Don't talk nonsense. No one could have made her do that," Yorke said severely. "Stop blaming yourself: keep your mind clear to work on how to free her."

"Any ideas?" Ramage asked bitterly.

"Why not go and shout down the hatch – she may answer. That'll set your mind at rest that she's not been harmed."

"Why the devil do you think I'm sitting here?" Ramage demanded angrily. "I'm here just to make damned sure I *don't* shout to her. Those bloody mutineers would probably knock her out to stop her answering."

Yorke nodded, slowly realizing that Ramage was right and knowing the strain had sharpened his tongue. "We just wait," he said. "The next move is up to the mutineers."

"I know damned well what they'll do: the Bosun confirmed that. They'll demand we go to Coruña, and if we don't –" He broke off, as if unwilling to put the rest into words. "It's getting her out..." He paused and jumped to his feet as he heard Jackson calling as he came down the companionway.

"They're asking for the Captain, sir," Jackson reported grimly. "Mr Wilson told 'em he'll pass the word. They didn't ask for you by name."

Yorke turned to Ramage and said slowly, as though thinking aloud, "Let me talk to them. Better they think you're dead – or wounded, maybe, so the Marchesa isn't upset and doesn't do

286

anything rash. I can tell 'em I'm in command. They won't think about Southwick."

Ramage thought for a moment. "That's a good idea. But even if she thinks I'm only wounded, Gianna might . . ."

"She will sir," Jackson said anxiously. "Perhaps Rossi . . ."

"Right, belay the talk and listen," Ramage said crisply, and quickly gave Yorke and Jackson their instructions. The three men then hurried up the companionway, Yorke and Jackson going forward while Ramage went aft to tell Southwick what was happening. The Master was sceptical at first but admitted, after a few moments' thought, that there was little choice.

Ramage hurried forward, where he could see the hatchway lit up by a lantern. Yorke was standing a yard or so to one side, the thick coaming shielding him in case a shot was fired from below. Wilson had placed his men forward of the hatch, so that any mutineers coming up the ladder would have to step into the ring of light from the lantern and be a perfect target. Jackson was whispering to Rossi, who was nodding vigorously.

After glancing round the deck for a place to hide out of sight but within earshot, Ramage finally ducked down on the after-side of the forward 4-pounder gun on the lee side.

Rossi went over to join Yorke while Jackson walked to the breech of the gun and whispered, "Everything's ready, sir. Do you think you'll be able to hear what's said?"

"I think so, but you can repeat it if necessary."

Then he heard Yorke call, "Send up your spokesman. One man, unarmed."

There was a pause as the mutineer replied.

Jackson whispered, "Didn't hear that, sir."

"This is Mr Yorke: I'm in command of the *Arabella* now, thanks to the Bosun and Harris."

Again Jackson could not hear the mutineers' reply.

Yorke called down the hatch, "You've *no* guarantee we won't seize your spokesman, but you're holding the Marchesa: she's enough security . . . Very well, one man, and he stops at the top of the ladder."

A minute later Yorke said, "Right, stand there. Now, why did you want to see the Captain?"

"To give our orders!" said the mutineer.

"Go on, then," Yorke said mildly.

"You alter course immediately for Coruña. That's the first order."

"We are already on course for Coruña. The course for Falmouth and Coruña is the same until we get to Cabo Finisterra. Then we turn east to Coruña."

"Very well, see you do that."

"I didn't say we would," Yorke said sharply.

"We'll see about that in a minute," the mutineer sneered. "The second order is that you don't try to interfere with us."

"Go on."

"The third is you release Harris and the Bosun."

For a moment Ramage cursed himself: he hadn't anticipated that demand. What would Yorke do?

"You can have the Bosun this minute," Yorke said quietly.

"Right, send him here."

"He'll have to be carried. He'll be dead before you get him to the bottom of the ladder, though."

"How so?" the mutineer demanded.

"The surgeon's working hard this very moment to save his life."

"Wait," the mutineer said, and Jackson whispered to Ramage that he'd gone down the ladder. For a moment Ramage wondered whether to risk having Jackson pass a message to Yorke about Harris, then decided against it: Yorke was capable of dealing with that.

"Mutineer's back," Jackson whispered.

"Well, Mr Yorke, your orders from the mutineers are that the Bosun's life must be saved."

"I'm no surgeon and I can't perform miracles. Mr Bowen's doing his best, so don't be absurd."

"What about Harris, then?"

"Harris!" Yorke said with a sniff. "No surgeon can do anything for him!"

"Oh Gawd," the mutineer exclaimed. "We heard only one shot..."

"It only needs one," Yorke said crisply. "Now, you mutin-

288

neers are trapped down on the messdeck; why the devil do you think I'm going to take any notice of so-called orders from you?"

"Because if you don't, we'll cut the Marchesa's throat."

"Whose idea is it to threaten to murder a helpless woman?" Yorke asked casually.

"'Twas Harris's, God rest his soul; he was the one what planned to get us our liberty."

"Very well, what guarantee can you give that if I sail the ship to Coruña you'll free the Marchesa unharmed when we get there?"

The mutineer was silent for several moments, then went below again to consult with his shipmates.

"That was smart of Mr Yorke," Jackson whispered. "Everything he said was true but the fellow believes Harris is dead. Pity he isn't."

Two minutes passed before they heard Yorke ask, "Well? What have you got to offer."

"You've got our word of honour."

Yorke roared with laughter. "Do you think anyone in the world would accept the word of men who are guilty of murder, mutiny, kidnapping and blackmail? Are you drunk?" he asked suspiciously.

"But ... but we didn't do no murdering!"

"Oh yes you did! Eleven of you – I'll ignore the two boys – planned mutiny and kidnapping. If people get murdered in the process you're all equally guilty. Ask any judge."

Once again the mutineer was silent, and Yorke said, "You've got the Marchesa as a hostage. Very well, if I sail this ship to Coruña I want hostages from you. You hand over the Marchesa to me unharmed in Coruña, and I'll hand over my hostages unharmed."

"I'll have to ask my mates."

"Two hostages," Yorke said as the man went below.

Ramage knew the next two or three minutes were critical. If the six mutineers agreed, it would leave only four of them and the two cabin boys down on the messdeck: four men and the boys to guard both the hatch and Gianna. They might insist on one, and Yorke would have to agree, but it still left them weaker – and even one mutineer as a hostage for Gianna's safety was better than nothing. Would they insist on the release of the three packetsmen he had in irons?

Then Yorke was speaking to the mutineer again.

"One hostage, you say? One of you murderers as security for the life of the Marchesa? Don't be absurd," he said contemptuously.

"But what about the three of our mates who were on watch?" the mutineer asked lamely.

"In irons and lucky to be alive."

"Well, sir, you've got four hostages, then . . ."

"*Four?* Those three are prisoners, not hostages!"

"Well, if anything happens to them," the mutineer said stubbornly, "it'll be too bad for the Marchesa. My shipmates say one more is enough."

"Very well, send him up."

"I'm the one."

"Step out on deck, then, and let's have a look at you," Yorke said, moving clear of the hatch and at the same time clearing the field of fire for Wilson.

As soon as the man emerged from the hatch Yorke said sharply, "Now, I want proof that the Marchesa is safe."

"You can't go down there," the mutineer said doggedly.

"If you've harmed her –"

"No, no, she's safe," the man said hurriedly. "One of the Tritons can call down to her."

Ramage just managed to stop himself giving an audible sigh of relief.

Yorke signalled to Rossi, who promptly shouted a stream of Italian down the hatch. Before the startled mutineer could intervene, Ramage heard Gianna replying. He could not distinguish what she said, but her tone of voice told him she was not only alive but in good spirits.

Rossi shouted back and as the mutineer stepped forward, protesting that he'd not given permission for a long conversation, Yorke was laughing. "My dear fellow, you know Italians;

they couldn't say anything briefly if they tried. He asked her if she wants her toilet things and clothes – you surely don't expect her to stay in her nightdress all the way to Coruña!"

"Well, no," the mutineer said uncomfortably as he heard Gianna answering again, "but–"

"Hairbrush, comb, shoes. You really don't expect the Marchesa to wear a sailor's shirt and tie her hair in a queue?"

"No, but–"

"Well then, just be patient and give Rossi time to find out what she wants."

"But that's the third–"

"Are you married? Have you ever met a woman who could decide in a minute what she needs when she goes away for a week?"

"Well–"

"Have you?" Yorke insisted, hoping Rossi would hurry. "Come on, yes or no!"

"But–"

"Goes away for a week, I said. But the Marchesa has just been kidnapped, so obviously she needs more time. Anyway, your mates down there can stop the conversation whenever they want."

"Yes, but they'll think I've given permission for–"

"And so you have," Yorke said heartily, noting the man had revealed his role among them, "and very civil of you, too. I'm sure the Marchesa appreciates it–" He broke off, seeing Rossi turning away from the hatch. "Is she all right?" he asked the Italian.

"Yes, sir; is bruised in the arms by these *banditi*, but..."

"Very well," Yorke turned and waved to Jackson. "This man is our hostage. Take him away and secure him."

"But you're not going to put me in irons–"

"What do you expect? You've got the Marchesa locked up below–"

"In irons, sir," Rossi interjected.

"In irons? Well, I'm damned if I'm going to dress you up as Father Neptune and let you strut around the ship," he told the mutineer.

Jackson and Stafford led the man away, and as Yorke walked aft Ramage joined him.

"How was that?" Yorke muttered.

"Masterly! I liked the touch about Harris. But let's get hold of Rossi; I couldn't hear what Gianna said."

Yorke called the Italian seaman and followed Ramage down to the Captain's cabin. Rossi reported that apart from bruises the Marchesa was all right. She had a leg-iron round one ankle, with the other part secured to an eye-bolt, but her hands were not tied.

The mutineers were nervous of her tongue, Rossi said proudly, and all of them were very frightened of what Harris had done. When they presumed from what Mr Yorke said that Harris was dead, one of them wanted to surrender and would have persuaded the others had the man who was now the hostage not come down and argued against it. Yes, he said in reply to the question from Ramage, he had passed both sets of instructions to the Marchesa, and by now she should be weeping and wailing and accusing the mutineers of killing the *Arabella*'s Captain. "She said to tell you, sir," Rossi added with a grin, "that you make the trouble for her every time she goes to sea."

Rossi had no sooner left the cabin than Southwick arrived, reporting that Much had the conn, and asking if the Marchesa was safe. Ramage brought him up to date, and then the old Master ran a hand through his white hair. "Now what, sir?"

"We wait for daylight. Get some sleep. Early breakfast..."

"I'll stand a watch if you like," Yorke said. "Otherwise neither of you is going to get much rest."

Ramage nodded. "Much, too. Highly irregular, of course; the Admiralty would not approve. But we seem to be in a highly irregular ship!"

"Aye," Southwick said heavily, "this ship is one of the bad ones. People can laugh at the idea, but some ships are just bad: they get bad men on board, and bad things happen to them. I felt it the moment I came on board in Kingston."

Chapter
Nineteen

By daylight next morning the *Arabella* was stretching north-wards along the Portuguese coast in a fresh south-westerly wind, with Porto broad on the starboard beam and forty miles away and Cabo Finisterra some 130 miles ahead. The cloud was well broken and, Ramage noted thankfully, the glass was steady.

By now Gianna and the mutineers would have eaten the breakfast Ramage had arranged to be passed down to them. The Tritons had received their orders, and Jackson, after inspecting the prisoners and the hostage, reported that Harris, locked in one of the cabins, had pleaded that Maxton should not guard him again. Apparently the West Indian had reduced the man to a state of gibbering terror before being relieved by another Triton.

Although thankful that settled weather meant he did not have to keep his meagre crew busy reefing or furling sails, Ramage was far from pleased that this late in the season it was going to be a sunny day. The mutineers had only to look up the hatch or skylight to see the sun's direction and know immediately which way the *Arabella* was heading, so there was no chance for slowly bearing away and running up the River Douro to Porto, or turning back for Lisbon, telling the mutineers the wind had shifted. But for the sun, it would have worked, though there was the risk that running into a neutral port would make the mutineers panic when they suddenly discovered what had happened.

If those five men down on the messdeck panicked, there was no telling what would happen to Gianna: men in a panic ceased to be human. Ramage had spent a good five minutes drumming the point into the Tritons that the only hope of rescuing the Marchesa was to apply a steady but mounting pressure on the mutineers. A gradual pressure, which would lead them to surrender; not a sudden pressure that would make them behave like rats in a trap. It was only a fine distinction; one he knew he would never dare to make unless the alternative was – he forced himself to face it – the murder of Gianna.

As he paced up and down the weather side of the after-deck – after listening to Yorke conduct a brief funeral service for the dead sentry Duncan – Ramage tried to drive away the depression, doubts and fears by telling himself that if he had ever been asked to name the dozen or so men he would want with him in a situation such as this, he would have named those he had. Even Wilson, with his staccato speech and love of porter, was proving reliable, and the Tritons liked working with him.

And in the Admiralty at this moment the First Lord considered Lieutenant Ramage had made wild allegations about the Post Office packets which he would never be able to prove. Well, he thought bitterly, I may not live long enough to get the word to Lord Spencer, but there will be proof enough if just one of the Tritons or the *Arabella*'s passengers survive.

Southwick interrupted his thoughts. "Not a sail in sight, sir. What time do you want to make a start?"

Ramage took out his watch. Three minutes to seven o'clock. The horizon is clear, the wind is steady … There's no excuse for putting it off any longer.

"At seven o'clock, Mr Southwick. Pass the word quietly."

As the Master strode away, shoulders braced back, hat jammed square on his head and a picture of confidence, Ramage wondered if he dare call him back and cancel it all. It was a damnably desperate attempt. Yet Yorke was right: if it did not work, they were no worse off – unless the mutineers panicked.

Yorke joined him. "By now you're scared stiff."

"Does it show?" a startled Ramage demanded.

"No, on the contrary, you look your usual arrogant and assured self," Yorke said lightly, "but you'd hardly be human if you weren't scared!"

"What about you?"

"The same. Does it show?"

Ramage laughed. "No, you look your usual debonair self, the idol of –"

"Deck there! Sail ho!" came a shout from the foremast, and Ramage recognized Stafford's voice.

"Deck here – where away?" Much hailed.

"Four points on the larboard bow, sir, just on the 'orizon."

"What can you make of it?"

"Too far off, sir."

"Keep a sharp lookout."

Ramage nodded approvingly: Much was doing well.

"Pass the word for Captain Yorke!" the Mate shouted.

A seaman took up the cry at the companionway leading to the Captain's cabin.

Yorke hurried over, waited a minute, and then called, as though he had just come up the ladder, "What is it, Mr Much?"

"Strange sail, sir, on the larboard bow. Wouldn't expect to see anyone out there unless she was up to mischief."

Ramage knew that at least one of the mutineers would be crouched on the ladder, listening carefully.

"Well, send a man up with a telescope, Mr Much: we don't want to get taken by another French privateer, do we."

"Indeed not! We've enough trouble already."

That, Ramage thought, is the Machiavelli touch: to raise the mutineers' hopes of rescue with the idea that a French ship was on the horizon.

While Much ordered one of the Tritons to take up a telescope, Stafford called again. "May be fairly big, sir, an' I think she's steering east."

Two minutes later the man with the telescope hailed, "Deck there! She's bigger than a privateer an' – oh, there she goes: she's letting fall her royals, sir."

"Very well," Yorke shouted, "let me know the moment you have an idea what she is."

Much had walked forward to the foremast, as though to be nearer the lookouts overhead, and called back to Yorke nervously, "I don't like it, Captain; seems to me anyone out there and on that course *must* be a ship-o'-war or a privateer."

"Let's hope she's one of ours, then."

"Aye – but could be French or Spanish, hovering off the coast to pick up someone like us."

"You think I ought to send the men to quarters?"

"'Taint for me to say," Much answered, though the tone of his voice belied the words.

There was an excited yell from the lookout with the telescope. "Deck there! Reckon she's a frigate, an' she looks like a Frenchman."

"Can't you make out her colours?" Yorke demanded anxiously.

"No, sir, she's almost bows-on; but her sheer don't look English."

"You hear that, Mr Much?" Yorke called.

"Course I do, sir," Much said crossly.

"Well then – well, I think we must send the men to quarters! Where the deuce is Mr Southwick? He's supposed to know all about this sort of thing. Hey, you men; pass the word for the Master!"

Yorke turned and winked at Ramage and gave Much a reassuring wave.

Southwick came up the companionway. "You sent for me, sir."

"Of course I did! Are you deaf? Didn't you hear the lookouts hailing?"

"Yes, sir, but you're the Captain," Southwick said sulkily, "and I'm off watch."

"Well, send the men to quarters! Aloft there – what can you see?"

"She's a frigate all right, sir."

"French or British, blast you?"

"Can't rightly say yet, sir."

Southwick began bellowing at the men to go to quarters, and Ramage pictured the mutineers grinning to themselves. And

296

Gianna – if she had followed the instructions passed by Rossi she should be weeping by now...

"I say, Mr Southwick," Yorke said loudly, "I think we should bear away for Porto, you know."

"Never a chance, Mr Yorke. Forty miles to go. Yon frigate will be up with us in half an hour, probably less."

"But we can't fight a frigate!"

"Nor can we run from this one, Mr Yorke." Southwick said sarcastically.

"But if we can't fight and we can't run, what shall we do?"

"Haul down our colours in good time! Won't be the first time for this ship!"

"Oh dear me! Then we'll all be taken prisoner."

"Aye, we'll be prisoners, and our prisoners will become free men, guzzling red wine and pretending they're all heroes."

By now the Tritons had cast the lashings from the guns, tubs of water were in place and Jackson reported to Yorke from abaft the foremast, asking loudly whether the guns should be loaded with roundshot or grape. Yorke told him roundshot, then changed his mind twice before the lookout interrupted by hailing, "Deck there! – the frigate's hauling her wind."

Yorke glanced over the weather side. "We can just see her from the deck now. Send down that blasted telescope!"

Yorke had just the right amount of petulance in his voice, Ramage noted; the uncertain impatience of a badly frightened man who was being overwhelmed by events.

Yorke called to Much, who was still by the foremast. "What do you make of her?"

"She's a frigate right enough."

"French or British?"

"Wouldn't rightly know. But she's coming round to the north a bit so we should make out her colours soon."

"But she's closing fast!"

"We can't do any more'n we're doing, sir, so it don't matter what flag she's flying until we're in range of her guns!"

"I expect a more helpful attitude, Mr Much," Yorke said sharply.

The Tritons had broad grins on their faces: they were enjoying the various exchanges. Ramage looked at his watch, tapped Yorke on the shoulder and waved to Much, who promptly shouted to the lookout above him, "You sure she's French? From the cut of these topsails she looks British to me!"

"The other chap's just gorn down wiv the telescope," Stafford's Cockney voice complained. "I never said nuthing right from the time I got up 'ere about 'er being French. It was 'im. Took the telescope, he did; never let me 'ave a look, he didn't, and now you—"

"Belay it!" Much shouted angrily. "You think she's British?"

"Yus, an' if I 'ad the bring-'em-near I could say for sure."

At that moment Southwick's voice boomed along the deck. "She's British all right: I can't make out her colours yet, but I recognize her."

"Very well," Yorke said loudly, "*now* what do we do? We don't want her rushing down and shooting at us! Supposing she doesn't see our colours? What then, Mr Southwick, what then, eh?"

"Hoist the private signal."

"What private signal?"

"Mr Ramage had the list in his desk: special one for each day of the month, the challenge and reply."

"Well, go and find it – here are the keys to the desk."

Ramage could imagine the mutineers, at first elated at the thought of a French frigate rescuing them, now terrified at the picture of a British frigate hove-to to windward ... a picture which included them eventually hanging by the neck from a noose at the yardarm. The grim warning contained in the Commission that Ramage read aloud at Lisbon might come to mind, and the reference to the Articles of War. Now the pressure was being slowly applied; pressure that – if everyone kept to the plan – would increase steadily over the next fifteen minutes ...

The private signal was hoisted; a few Tritons near the forehatch speculated in bloodcurdling detail about the imminent fate of the mutineers below.

Ramage saw one of the Tritons suddenly go to the hatch,

listen a few moments and then wave urgently to Much, who was standing a few feet away. The Mate called something down to the mutineers, listened, then hurried aft.

"The mutineers, sir," he reported to Ramage. "They're asking to see the Captain: they say it's urgent!"

"Tell them the Captain is coming, but their spokesman is to stay at the bottom of the ladder. If he got a chance to look round the horizon..."

Much went forward as Yorke came over to Ramage and asked, "They want to bargain?"

"Perhaps. They might offer to free Gianna now in return for their freedom and immunity from arrest. That's their best plan."

"And we accept?"

Ramage nodded. "We accept anything that gets Gianna out of there safely."

"Anything?"

"Look, we argued about the ethics of all this last night," Ramage said quietly. "So go and hear what they have to say."

Ramage followed Yorke and crouched down behind the gun, where he could hear one side of the dialogue. Yorke stood close to the hatch to make sure the mutineers' spokesman stayed at the foot of the ladder.

"Well, what d'you want?" he demanded in an uncompromising voice. "Bargain? You think I'm going to bargain with a bunch of mutineers when there's one of our frigates up to windward?"

Ramage peered round the breech of the gun. From the beginning he had known there was only one move the mutineers might make that would wreck his plan. He had tried to increase the odds against them thinking of it by pretending a French frigate was closing in, but he dared not keep that up for too long because of the danger that they would panic if the frigate's identity changed at the very last moment. Had he applied the pressure too soon? Given them a few extra minutes to recognize that they still had a weapon?

Yorke was tense as he stood listening; then he took a step forward, as though angry enough to want to seize the man at the foot of the ladder. He spoke slowly and distinctly, as though determined the mutineers should not misunderstand him.

"You are threatening cold-blooded murder. A completely pointless murder. A murder that can gain you nothing. The moment you committed such a foul act we would be down there and I swear that within thirty seconds not one of you would be left alive."

And as Yorke listened to the mutineer's reply, Ramage knew he had lost the gamble: it had been a ten to one chance that they would think of it. Reasonable odds. But when you gambled you needed luck or a big purse, and his purse contained only Gianna's life. Yet perhaps he was wrong: perhaps they were demanding something else. Yorke's reply would –

"I can't stop that frigate coming down to us!" Yorke said angrily. "What do you expect me to do? Shout a couple of miles? For all I know the Admiralty has sent her out to escort us to England. What do I do then? Tell her captain we don't need him? He'll want to know where Mr Ramage is. What do I say? How do I explain why I'm in command? Dammit," Yorke exploded, "he'll probably think *I'm* a mutineer!"

He paused as the mutineer said something, then declared abruptly, "I'm going to talk it over with Mr Southwick. Stay there; the sentry up here has orders to shoot anyone who sticks his head over the coaming."

Ramage got up and hurried aft, where Yorke joined him and asked wrathfully, "You heard all that?"

"Only your side of it."

"They say they'll kill the Marchesa if I let the frigate approach."

"What good to they think that'll do them?" Ramage asked quietly.

"They say if the frigate sends a boarding party they'll be shot or hanged anyway, so they've nothing more to lose if they kill the Marchesa as well. The scoundrel reminded me they couldn't be killed twice."

Ramage nodded. "I hoped they'd be too scared to think of

forcing us to keep the frigate away. Or if they did, they'd decide it would be impossible."

He rubbed the scars over his brow and saw Southwick shaking his head, occupied in his own thoughts. Then the old Master came over to him and said quietly, "Don't chance anything, sir; they're desperate men. I'd sooner go into Coruña and hand myself over to the Spanish than risk the Marchesa being harmed."

"Me too," Yorke said, "and the Devil take the report to the First Lord. Anyway, even if this horse won't start, you've still got another in the stable."

"Aye," Southwick said, "we can pretend the frigate is satisfied with the private signal and goes about her business. It gives us a bit more time. We can't risk calling their bluff, sir..."

And Ramage knew both men were right; his gamble had failed but, as Yorke had said, there was still one more chance. "Very well," he told Yorke, "tell them you and Southwick will try to reassure the frigate. Say you can't make any promises – and remind 'em we have the Bosun and some mutineers up here in irons..."

"They've thought about that," Yorke said. "The fellow said they were all in the same position, whether they were down on the messdeck or in irons. He's right, too," he added ruefully.

Twenty minutes later, with the imaginary frigate dropping astern on its way to Lisbon, apparently reassured by the *Arabella*'s private signal, Yorke came back after reporting the fact to the mutineers.

"They say that someone can talk to the Marchesa this afternoon," he told Ramage. "They refused to agree to Rossi at first, but I said she might want some woman's things that she'd be too embarrassed to shout about in front of a lot of strangers, whereas speaking in her own language to Rossi..."

"Thanks," Ramage said. "Let's go down to my cabin; I'm so damned depressed."

Sitting in the same chairs, with the carpet still damp where a couple of seamen had tried to scrub away the stains of the Bosun's blood, Yorke said, "It looks as though we've no choice but to head for Coruña."

301

"You don't think the second plan will work?"

"I'm afraid not. They're really desperate down there. If you'd seen that bloody man's eyes..." He shuddered at the thought.

"But you realize that now we can't risk going into Coruña, don't you?" Ramage asked quietly.

"It's our only chance of saving the Marchesa's life," Yorke said bluntly.

Ramage shook his head. "On the contrary, it's a sure way of having them kill her. Their reaction to our 'frigate' shows that. Why do you suppose I said I was depressed? Look, the Navy's blockading both Coruña and Ferrol. There's probably a squadron of our 74-gun ships in the offing; certainly two or three of our frigates within a few miles. Their job is to prevent *any* vessel getting in or out, whether a ship of the line or a fishing boat. They'll see us trying to get in and we'll be boarded. There's no way we can prevent it. And we know the mutineers will kill Gianna the moment a British ship gets within hail. Signal to our hearts' content, send a boat over with a letter of explanation ... the fact is no frigate captain would believe our story and certainly wouldn't let us go in to surrender the ship to the Dons."

"Supposing you went over and spoke to him?"

"He'd probably put me under arrest because he'd think I was deserting to the enemy. Wouldn't you, in his position?"

"He could come on board and see for himself."

Ramage stared at him. "That's the point! If you were one of those mutineers, what would you do the moment you knew the frigate captain had come on board?"

Yorke held his hands out, palms upwards, in a gesture of despair.

"What in God's name can we do then? They'll kill her if we don't go to Coruña; yet they'll kill her if we do and get intercepted. Are you absolutely sure our blockade is as close as that?" he asked.

"Certain. Ask Southwick. No," he said when Yorke shook his head, "I'd be glad if you did, because I will if you don't. I want to be certain."

302

"Very well," Yorke said, and left the cabin, to return almost immediately. "He agrees with you. Close blockade, summer and winter. Says he hadn't realized the position we are in now. The old fellow is almost in tears. He worships her, you know."

"I know," Ramage said soberly.

"What the devil are we to do? We'll be off Cabo Finisterra by tomorrow. We daren't go into Coruña and we daren't stay out. It's almost unbelievable."

Ramage suddenly stood up, thumping his forehead with the back of his hand. "We're damn fools!" he exclaimed. "We can go into a Spanish port that isn't blockaded. Some fishing village, or even an open anchorage." He began walking up and down the cabin, picturing the coastline to the northwards. "Yes, there's Corcubion, right in the lee of Cabo Finisterra. Difficult entrance without a chart, though. Camarinas Bay – that's it! Ten miles or so beyond the Cape, and we can get in easily. No patrolling frigates – it's our one hope!"

Yorke looked doubtful. "Don't risk it without the mutineers agreeing," he advised.

"Why?"

"Because these men don't know the Spanish coast. They've picked on Coruña because they've heard of it. If you go in somewhere else they might suspect a trick."

"Go and talk to them," Ramage said impatiently. "Point out Camarinas is nearer and – hellfire, what difference does it make to them? It's Spanish – they get what they want and we're made prisoner!"

Yorke got up. "I'll try it," he said, leaving the cabin. "I'll tell 'em about the blockade, eh?"

"Yes, warn them we're certain to be intercepted and boarded. A squadron of seventy-fours, frigate patrols – even Spanish ships."

"You stay here," Yorke said. "You make me nervous, crouching behind that damned gun, listening to every word I say."

But when he returned to the cabin five minutes later Ramage knew as he came through the door that he had failed to persuade them.

303

"They won't hear of it. Coruña or Ferrol, or else..."

"You explained about the blockade?"

"Of course I did," Yorke said impatiently. "They say it's up to me to keep frigates away. They said I did it once less than an hour ago, and I can do it again."

"But why not Camarinas?"

Yorke shook his head wearily. "They've a good enough reason, and I suppose we should have thought of it. They say how are they to know I won't take the *Arabella* into a Portuguese port and tell them it's Spanish. They know Cabo Finisterra isn't far north of the border between Portugal and Spain."

"How will they know it is Coruña or Ferrol, then?"

"I asked them that. Apparently one of the men has been to both: says he'll recognize them at once."

Ramage sprawled on the settee, drained of all energy and hope. "So we've no choice," he said, almost to himself. "We have to try the second plan."

"It puts the very devil of a responsibility on the Marchesa," Yorke protested.

"Of course it does," Ramage said harshly, "and if she'd gone home in the other packet as I asked her this would never have happened."

He buried his head in his hands. "I suppose I don't really mean it like that."

"It's true, but you tried to persuade her," Yorke said sympathetically. "It's helping no one to blame yourself, though. It's happened, and we've got to sort it out."

Ramage sat up straight in the chair and rubbed his eyes with his knuckles. "I'll give Rossi his orders. He can give Gianna her new instructions this afternoon. We'll time it for breakfast tomorrow – when the food is passed down the hatch. It'll mean a couple of the mutineers are at the foot of the ladder, and we have a good reason why a couple of our fellows are at the top."

Yorke nodded slowly. "It's going to be a damned long night."

"If only they'd got me as a hostage, instead of Gianna," Ramage said miserably.

304

"Don't be absurd," Yorke snapped. "It wasn't your fault the frigate business failed. I'd never have thought of anything as ingenious. Better they'd taken me, or Bowen, or Wilson. Or all three of us. Stop blaming yourself, for God's sake!"

He paused for a moment and then said savagely, "I blame myself for one thing, though."

When Ramage raised his eyebrows, Yorke said, "Harris thought of all this. I should have ignored you and shot him dead as he stood here. I'll regret that for the rest of my days."

That evening Ramage sat at his desk and wrote up his journal. He had never before filled it in with so much detail. Although he knew there was a chance it would never be sent on to the Admiralty, just putting all the events on paper helped pass the time.

As he described how he – as the future commanding officer of the *Lady Arabella* – met the Marchesa di Volterra at the British Embassy in Lisbon, and how she had subsequently taken passage for England in the packet brig, he thought bitterly how the bare words, true as they were, bore no resemblance to what actually happened. Not, he admitted, that he was anxious to try to explain it in detail! But fortunately captains' journals were by tradition written in a sparse, impersonal style. Courses, speeds, distances, positions, wind strengths and direction when at sea; when in port a notation of official visitors and official visits made, weather, anchorage position, the way the ship's company was employed...

For the tenth time that night he took out his watch: an hour past midnight. He wished he was standing a watch, but both Yorke and Southwick had been insistent that the risk was too great. A sudden squall or an unexpected emergency needing shouted commands would immediately reveal to the mutineers that he was alive.

Yet even the idea of pretending to be dead had misfired: the mutineers had not relaxed into a false sense of security after finding they were (apparently, anyway) dealing not with the ruthless Lieutenant Ramage but with a passenger about whom they knew nothing. They hadn't made one mistake, blast them.

Yorke reckoned their leader – after they lost Harris – had been the first spokesman, the man who agreed to be a hostage, but Ramage now doubted that. Someone down there on the mess-deck was shrewd and cool. Was it Our Ned? The Mate's son had the brains, and probably the cunning. It made sense: Harris and the Bosun led the kidnapping party; Our Ned stayed behind ready to secure and guard them. Or maybe Our Ned had been with Harris, one of the men who somehow bundled Gianna forward in the darkness without Southwick or any of the Tritons spotting them. Perhaps the three mutineers who were on watch did something to divert the Master's attention at the critical moment.

That was more like it: Our Ned and one or two others took Gianna; Harris and the Bosun were supposed to lead the merci-less Lieutenant Ramage on deck at pistol point, or – at last he was feeling sleepy, and the details blurred. Thankfully he stood up and walked aft to the cot, trying not to rouse himself. He pulled off his coat, loosened the stock, kicked off his shoes and lowered himself into the cot. Almost immediately he drifted into a deep sleep.

He began dreaming wild dreams of what he wished would happen. That in the dim light of the lantern a shadowy Gianna was bending over him, whispering urgently. In the dream he could neither understand her words nor say anything in reply. He wanted desperately to tell her he loved her, and if anything happened to her he did not want to go on living, but the words would not come.

A sudden slap on his face woke him with a convulsive jerk, his head ringing.

"*Mama mia*, will you never wake up?"

He lay in the cot rubbing his eyes, trying to focus them on the shadowy figure.

"Nicholas," the figure said crossly, "I've escaped! While you've been sleeping like a pig, I've been getting myself free!"

He leapt from the cot in a completely reflex movement, grabbed the two pistols from the settee and cocked them; then, watching the door swinging to and fro on its hinges with the ship's roll and expecting mutineers to burst in any moment, he snapped, "What happened?"

Gianna, startled by his unexpected leap, said furiously. "You aren't at all pleased to see me!"

"Of course I am!" he hissed. "What happened to the damned sentry?" He went to the door to find a seaman standing there with a musket. "What the hell are you grinning at?" he demanded angrily. "Pass the word for Mr Southwick – and Mr Yorke, too!"

"Oh, Nicholas," Gianna was complaining. "What's wrong with you?"

"Oh shut up, woman!"

She slapped his face so hard his eyes watered.

"*Senta*," she said angrily. "Our Ned and the two ship's boys are waiting out there in the corridor. Don't let your clumsy sailors shoot them!"

Ramage had to hold both pistols in one hand as he used the other to wipe his watering eyes. Two slaps in two minutes, he thought irrelevantly, were not his idea of a happy reunion.

"All right, now tell me what happened," he said with as much patience as he could muster. "I want to make sure those blasted mutineers up forward are secured: they'll go crazy when they find you've gone."

"It's all taken care of," Gianna said with a chilly dignity spoiled at the last moment by an uncontrollable giggle. "Stafford and Rossi are guarding the top of the hatch with those big muskets. Musketoons. They were the sentries. I whispered to them as we crept up the ladder."

"*We?*"

"Oh, you don't *listen*. We – Our Ned, the two boys and me."

At that moment Yorke hurried into the cabin, saw Gianna, said, "My God!" weakly, and sank into a chair. He was followed by Southwick holding a pistol. The Master stopped suddenly as if he had walked into a wall.

Gianna went up to him and kissed his cheek. "Have you missed me, Mr Souswick? No one else seems very pleased to see me. Nicholas told me to shut up and Mr Yorke just said 'My God' and flopped into the chair."

"Can't blame 'em, ma'am," a confused Southwick mumbled. "Bit of a shock, you know. A very nice shock," he added hurriedly, "but you vanished in the middle of the night and now you've –"

"Vanished in the middle of the night again, only this time from that horrible place forward!"

Ramage said suddenly, "Where are Our Ned and the boys?"

"With the sentry," Southwick said. "The minute I saw Our Ned I got worried about you, sir. The sentry has him covered."

"Very well," Ramage said. "You'd better get back on deck."

"Jackson went to rouse Much," Southwick said. "He'll be all right. But I'd better get more men covering that forehatch."

"Don't worry," Ramage said heavily, "the Marchesa has already arranged that."

He took her arm and led her to the settee. "Sit down and tell us what happened. You're not cold?" he asked anxiously. "We're not singing songs of joy simply because – well," he said lamely, "it's such a shock; we hadn't much hope of saving your life..."

She looked up at Ramage wide-eyed and smiling. "You haven't kissed me yet!"

As he bent to kiss her he said shakily, "I'm having trouble getting things in the right order. You still seem part of a dream."

Gianna brushed back her hair, arranged her skirt and said, "Let's have Our Ned and the boys in here. It's their story more than mine. I'd never have escaped without their help."

"No, tell us your story first," Ramage said firmly. "We can hear what they have to say afterwards."

"Oh, don't be so irritating, Nicholas. I don't know what Our Ned was thinking. I've only whispered to him."

Reluctantly Ramage nodded to Southwick, who went to the door and called Our Ned.

Unshaven, his thin face haggard from weariness and his usually furtive eyes now constantly flickering from side to side to reveal nervousness, Our Ned looked like an unsuccessful poacher just hauled before a magistrate with a ferret still in his pocket.

"Evenin', gentlemen."

Ramage nodded. "The Marchesa says you helped her escape. I want to thank you." He held out his hand and Our Ned stared at it for a moment, and then grasped it in a surge of embarrassment.

"We all helped each other, sir," he muttered.

Turning to Gianna, Ramage said, "Now – at long last – please tell us what happened."

"Our Ned had better start," she said, smiling impishly. "He can probably tell you how it began."

"Can you?" Ramage asked. "Will you, rather?"

"Aye, sir. I'll incrimulate meself, or whatever you call it, but I'll have to take me chance on it. Where shall I begin?"

"From the time I took command of the ship?" Ramage suggested. "I can guess what happened before that."

"Yes, well, sir, we packetsmen got scared when you read your Commission and found we were under naval discipline, like we was pressed. The Tritons told us what the Articles of War said, and we guessed you knew all about ventures, and Captain Stevens surrendering the *Arabella* for the insurance money.

"Well, sir, Harris reckoned you were taking us home to have us all court-martialled and hanged. You might still be, for all I know..." He paused and wiped his mouth with the back of his hand. "That's why I said about incrimulating myself.

"Anyway, Harris got this idea of seizing the ship and taking her to Coruña and handing her over to the Spanish. He reckoned we'd escape being hanged, get a big reward from the Dons, and would have plenty of money to live on after the war ends. The Bosun said Harris was right and we all agreed.

"There weren't enough of us to seize the *Arabella* openly, as you might say, so Harris suggested we took the Marchesa and you as hostages: seize the lady and get her for'ard, and take you up on deck and threaten to shoot you unless Mr Southwick and the Tritons did as we said. The Marchesa was to be a sort of insurance in case Mr Southwick wouldn't cooperate."

He wiped his mouth again. "Well, I didn't want the Marchesa touched. I agreed with what Harris was saying about going to Coruña, mind you; just that it was wrong to lay hands on a foreign lady who had nothing to do with the Post Office or the Navy. Harris and me had a bit of a falling out over it, and he and the Bosun decided I couldn't be trusted. The two boys – they was scared and whimpering, so Harris and the rest of them kept us out of it. Out of the planning, I mean: made us stay the other end of the messdeck while they talked.

"I found out later the plan was that with all the Tritons on watch, Harris and the Bosun went aft, knocked out the sentry and seized you, sir, and a couple of the other lads took the Marchesa. The two packetsmen at the wheel were to keep a sharp eye open and when the third one on watch – he was to keep an eye on the companionway – reckoned the lads were ready to bring the Marchesa up, he'd give a signal and the helmsmen would get off course. Harris reckoned that'd keep Mr Southwick busy cussing and distract the Tritons on watch and they could sneak her forward. She was to be gagged, of course."

"And I was, too!" Gianna said crossly.

"Yes, Ma'am. Well, off they went, and the next thing I heard was a shot, and a minute later the two men bundled the Marchesa down the hatch. After that, we heard you'd been killed, sir," he said, turning to Ramage, "and that Harris was dead too and the Bosun badly wounded. I got a shock just now when the Marchesa came into the cabin and I heard your voice."

Gianna explained, "I didn't tell him that Rossi said yesterday you were safe."

"Now we get to the incrimulating bit, sir. With Harris dead, the Bosun wounded, the three men who'd been on watch made prisoner, and one man gone as hostage, there weren't many of us left on the messdeck, so everyone had to take it in turns to guard the Marchesa.

"Things were looking bad, sir, and the lads were scared. I was afraid they'd do me in if they decided they couldn't trust me, so I helped them. Then the frigate was sighted. We knew if she was French we were safe, but when she turned out to be one of ours we knew we'd be caught. One of the lads said we'd hang and swore he'd kill the Marchesa first."

"He was *horrible*," Gianna shuddered. "He meant it."

Our Ned nodded in agreement. "When they told Mr Yorke they'd kill her if the frigate came close I – well, I ain't trying to save my neck, sir, but murdering a lady in cold blood was more than I can stomach –"

"What did you do?" Ramage asked.

"I argued with them, sir, but it didn't do no good. Then the frigate didn't board us anyway. Then Mr Yorke came along and said about Coruña being blockaded, and us not being able to get in without being intercepted. Seemed to me we couldn't avoid a frigate catching us and that meant the Marchesa would be murdered and we'd still be taken prisoner.

"I tried to persuade them to agree to Mr Yorke's proposal for a smaller port that wasn't blockaded, but they wouldn't have none of it; they'd set their hearts on Coruña. One of 'em had been there and said he could recognize it. Well, that was a sort of turning point for me. I thought about it all over again and decided I wanted none of it – murdering the Marchesa *or* handing the ship over to the Dons. So when it was my spell to guard the Marchesa tonight I waited until the man I relieved was asleep and freed her, and we all crept out."

Gianna was shaking her head as he concluded. "Nicholas – it was much more dangerous for him than that. And the boys – they were terrified, but Our Ned reassured them – all in a whisper so the rest of the men didn't wake up, and then they were really brave."

"How did you get the key to the leg-irons holding the Marchesa?" Yorke asked the seaman.

"It was kept on a hook, sir."

Ramage held the man's arm. "Will the mutineers bear out your story that you didn't help?"

Our Ned grimaced. "They'll kill me if they get the chance."

"They won't," Ramage said. "Don't worry about a court-martial. If you've told the truth you'll be safe enough, I guarantee that. This night's work more than makes up for the past. Now, we'll have those two boys in here and thank them; then you'd all better get some sleep."

He turned to Southwick. "We'll leave sentries on the fore-hatch for the rest of the night. We don't want to risk any more bloodshed. By the way," he said to Our Ned, "Harris isn't dead: he's in irons, along with the Bosun, who was only slightly wounded."

Our Ned's jaw dropped. "Phew, I hope you've got some good men guarding him, sir!"

"Don't worry; Maxton has turned him into a lamb."

Our Ned shuddered and for a moment his eyes remained fixed, as if staring at some terrifying picture. "Yes," he muttered, "Maxton could do that ..."

Gianna stood up and put her arms round Ramage. "Darling, I'm glad we didn't have to try out your other plan!"

"Would it have worked?"

"I don't think so," she said soberly. "I was going to try it, but that crazy man Our Ned told you about – I think he would have killed me, and you'd have never known."

Our Ned looked puzzled, and Ramage was curious to know if the man agreed with Gianna.

"When Rossi spoke to the Marchesa this afternoon – yester-day afternoon, I mean – he told her to pretend she had gone off her head and start screaming. I hoped that –"

But Our Ned was shaking his head. He drew a finger across his throat in an unmistakable gesture.

"It was our only hope," Ramage said lamely, "we'll be off Cabo Finisterra in a few hours."

"I know that, sir; that's why I got the Marchesa out to-night."

Chapter Twenty

The first person to sight the English coast four days later was Rossi, and his hail from the masthead that he could just make out land broad on the larboard bow secured him the guinea Ramage had offered earlier in Lisbon. It also confirmed Southwick's latitude sight at noon, when his calculations put the ship thirty-five miles south-west of the Lizard.

Two hours later, as the *Lady Arabella* surged along before a brisk west wind, with a scattering of cloud, they could see enough from the deck to recognize the high land of the Lizard, now slowly drawing abeam as the packet headed for Plymouth.

"Probably the first time she's not rounded the Manacles and slipped into Falmouth," Yorke commented. "Could probably find her own way in."

And every mile up the River Fal would have taken Ramage closer to St Kew, to Blazey Hall, where his father and mother would be waiting, anxious to know what had happened in Lisbon; whether he and Gianna were safe. Suddenly he felt an almost overpowering nostalgia for his home, mingling with a deep love for Gianna, who even now was standing beside him at the taffrail.

More than a year had passed since he had looked astern over the taffrail of the *Triton* brig at the Lizard dropping below the horizon. Since then, he blushed at the recollection, he had had a couple of affairs, ones which left no nostalgia, only pleasant memories – and been nearly killed four times. Five, if you included the Bosun's attempt. And he had lost the *Triton* after a

313

hurricane. Yes, it had been a busy time and the months had passed quickly. But the next few days would pass slowly enough to make up for it.

So now, although off the Portuguese coast he had despaired of ever doing so, he was looking at the Lizard again, and with him were Southwick, Jackson, Stafford, Rossi, Maxton and a few more of the *Triton*'s original crew.

The Lizard meant all things to all men. The last sight of England for many great sailors – and pirates and smugglers and scallywags too. Drake had looked back on it at the beginning of his last voyage – and had been buried at sea off Portobello, thousands of miles away on the Spanish Main. Henry Morgan, freed from arrest after ingratiating himself with Charles II, who had then made him a knight, looked back on it as he returned to Jamaica to become its governor and continue as the most successful pirate the Caribbean had ever seen.

It had been the last sight of an oppressive country – countries rather, since many on board were Dutch – for those in the *Mayflower*; the first sight of the country he was supposed to conquer for the Duke of Medina Sidonia and the troops embarked in the Spanish Armada.

And, he grinned to himself, a welcome sight for Lieutenant Ramage and for the Marchesa di Volterra, otherwise Gianna, otherwise a small and black-haired girl with a mouth slightly too large for classical beauty, and deep brown eyes, and bosoms whose promise kept him awake at night, and a temper which could be imperious or flare like Etna on a dark night, and a love which knew no limits...

He suddenly realized Southwick was standing in front of him.

"Sorry sir," the Master said, guessing that the sight of the Lizard was stirring up memories, "but we can bear away, to north-east by east, and if the wind holds we'll pick up the Eddystone an hour after daybreak."

"Very well," Ramage said, "and I'd better get below and start preparing the paperwork."

Plymouth ... the Commander-in-Chief, if he was there, otherwise the Port Admiral, would be waiting for a sheaf of

314

returns, since the *Lady Arabella* was sailing under Admiralty, not Post Office orders. Ramage cursed because he did not have the necessary stationery. Now he had to try to remember the headings on the dozen and one standard forms he was expected to have filled in and ready on arrival.

Anyway, the worst of the paperwork was done: the most important was the report for Lord Spencer. The mutiny had simplified everything, Yorke pointed out: Ramage had written half the report before it started and had been sitting at his desk preparing to complete it only a few minutes before the *Lady Arabella*'s Bosun sneaked in with a pistol in each hand. The mutiny should convince the First Lord that there was treachery in the Packet Service.

What he now had to do was to prepare a report for the Commander-in-Chief, or the Port Admiral, which revealed nothing! Enough to satisfy his curiosity, but not enough to endanger secrecy. The List of Prisoners was complete – not often a ship commanded by a naval officer arrived at Plymouth with prisoners all of whom were British. A list with a hundred French or Spanish names, yes, that was a commonplace, and boats would soon take them over under Marine guard to the prison hulks lying in the Hamoaze. But a list of British prisoners, all accused of mutiny, one of murder and another of attempted murder – that was rare.

He went to his cabin, sat at the desk and unscrewed the cap of the inkwell, lodging the wide-based bottle between two books against the rolling of the packet. After trying unsuccessfully to recall what he had read in the slim volume of the printed 'Plymouth Port Orders', he thought of the 'Portsmouth Port Orders' which he had more recently read, since that was the port from which he had sailed with the *Triton*.

His mind was still a blank ... "... a correct statement of their defects, deficiencies of sails, rigging and stores, specifying every particular ..." The phrase came to him, though he could not remember from which port orders.

He took a sheet of paper from a drawer and in the top right-hand corner wrote, "His Majesty's packet brig *Lady Arabella*." If it had been his own ship – one he would continue to com-

315

mand – he would have discussed the report carefully with Southwick, because the list of defects and deficiencies meant that a survey would be held and – if the penny-pinching dockyard agreed to them – they would be put right. But any defects and deficiencies found after the survey would not exist, as far as the dockyard was concerned: all port admirals and dockyard commissioners sang the same chorus: after that survey, "no second survey will be allowed ..."

In the case of the *Lady Arabella*, though, the Port Admiral would probably forward the report to the Post Office, and there it would grow dusty on some shelf.

He scribbled a few lines, mentioning the rot found in the ship, and referring to Southwick's attached survey – he must remember to attach it! Much had already given him a list of stores remaining, and he had Stevens' original lists. The lists of sails and rigging were routine.

Although if the dockyard felt the packet was its concern the survey would give the master shipwright plenty of work, there was nothing wrong with the rigging for the surveying master to fuss about, apart from "fair wear and tear". Ramage only hoped the commissioner would not want the sails taken on shore for survey; he had too few men for that, and commissioners begrudged even a moment of their time, let alone that of a dozen of their men...

Leave of absence. He had to make an application to the Admiral before going up to the Admiralty; admirals were almost as harsh with commanding officers leaving their ships without written permission as with seamen who deserted by swimming on shore at dead of night.

"List of prisoners to be transferred to the prison ship." He took the list from a drawer and put it with the survey. "List of invalids to be transferred to hospital." Well, the Bosun would not need the sick ticket normally given to a genuinely sick or wounded seaman: he needed only a Marine guard.

Weekly accounts, "specifying the numbers borne or petty and able, separately...". He took out his muster book and copied out the details normally entered on a special form. He had made out a paybook that would end up in the Navy Office in London, where the clerks would have a fit because the entries were not on the usual printed forms. Well, by the time their complaints had filtered back to Plymouth, Ramage hoped he would be at sea again.

Finally he wiped the pen and screwed the cap back on the inkwell, putting them both in a drawer with the reports and lists. Then, cursing himself, he remembered he had not done the most important one of all, the report to the Admiral in Plymouth: the one explaining why a Post Office packet anchored in the Hamoaze was manned by eleven navy seamen, commanded by a naval officer, and with nine of its original ship's company in irons and a tenth wounded.

One way and another, he thought grimly, the Admiralty's lawyers – perhaps even the law officers of the Crown, now no doubt sitting comfortably in their offices in London – were going to be scratching their heads in a few days' time.

It took him half an hour to write a ten-line report to the Admiral, and to save himself writing yet another letter he included in the last paragraph a request for leave to go to London to report to the First Lord "according to orders previously received".

Picking up his hat, he made his way on deck to find a frigate coming up fast astern, but he knew her captain would have recognized the *Lady Arabella* as a Post Office packet as her hull started lifting over the horizon, even though he would be wondering why she was passing Falmouth. In such a position, the correct answer to the private signal would be enough.

By nightfall the *Lady Arabella* was under top sails only, deliberately slowing down so that two hours before dawn Rame Head would be fifteen to twenty miles ahead. At midnight Mr Much, who was on watch, turned up all hands until a good deal of shouting from the darkness revealed that the packet was in the midst of a small fishing fleet out of Fowey. By six o'clock next morning Rame Head was fine on the larboard bow and the Eddystone Rock was on the starboard beam, Mr Smeaton's great lighthouse standing up stark in the early light, a hundred feet high.

The Tritons were allowed to go below for fifteen minutes,

three at a time, to shave and smarten themselves up for entering harbour, and at nine o'clock the *Lady Arabella* rounded Penlee Point to reach across Cawsand Bay and into the Sound.

The Commander-in-Chief of the Channel Fleet was at sea: that much was obvious to Ramage since his flagship was not at anchor and the port was almost empty. That made things a lot easier. Port admirals were usually busy enough not to want to bother with anything that did not directly involve them, whereas commanders-in-chief seemed to take a malicious delight in badgering any ship not under their direct command.

No sooner had the *Lady Arabella* anchored than Jackson identified the Port Admiral's flagship – an old vessel acting in effect as a floating signal station, since the Admiral had an office in the Dockyard. A moment later Southwick was pointing out that they did not have enough men to guard the prisoners and at the same time row Ramage in the packet's boat to the Admiral's office. The old Master seemed to regard hiring a local boat for such a task as an insult to the ship, and because the local boats usually waited at the West Pier he had to hail a frigate's boat that was passing and ask the lieutenant in it to send a boat out.

Although it had been a long time since Ramage was in Plymouth, he vaguely remembered that the coach usually left for London at half past six in the evening. However, since Yorke and Much would be travelling with him, he would have to hire a carriage: there was no hope of getting three seats on the London coach at such short notice, and anyway he wanted to get to London without stopping. He was thankful that Gianna was anxious to go to St Kew to reassure his parents that they were both safe: he had expected to have to persuade her not to accompany them to London.

He saw Yorke and asked, "You're all packed, I hope?"

"All ready. Just waiting for the Customs before I strap my trunk."

"Well, I'm going to report to the Admiral as soon as I've dealt with the Customs officers. Then I'd like to hire a 'chaise and be on our way."

"That suits me. Much is coming with us, I presume?"

Ramage nodded, but warned, "Providing we can get horses, I want to stop only for meals."

"Is that wise?" Yorke asked. "There's no point in you arriving at the Admiralty so tired you can't think straight. An extra day for the journey won't hurt. After all, we spent weeks waiting in Lisbon..."

Yorke was right, of course. The Port Admiral would report to the Admiralty that they had arrived, and the nightly messenger would take the report to London on horseback. If they arrived at the Admiralty two or three days later, that would be time enough. A night's sleep before they set off from Plymouth would be good for all of them.

Two hours later, having said goodbye to Gianna, who intended spending the night on board, giving Southwick a chance to hire a carriage to take her to St Kew next day, Ramage reported at the Port Admiral's office.

The portly and jovial owner of the King's Arms came up to Ramage's table and gave a slight bow – a lieutenant's bow, Ramage suspected; it would be six inches lower for captains and twelve or more for admirals – and said, "The carriage is ready, sir, and the baggage has been loaded."

Ramage looked round at his guests, Yorke and Much. "Has anyone an appetite left?" When both men shook their heads, he said to the innkeeper, "That was an excellent breakfast: now, if you'll bring me the bill..."

Fifteen minutes later the door of the carriage slammed shut, the coachman cracked his whip and yelled, "Hup, hup, hup now!" and in the darkness before dawn the coach clattered along the cobbled street in Briton Side heading for the Exeter Road. They had, Ramage thought gloomily, another 250 miles to travel before they reached the Admiralty: they would change horses a couple of dozen times, and stop to pay the toll at twice as many turnpikes.

They reached the turnpike at Ivybridge by daybreak and Much gave a sigh of relief. "Always wanted to see the road to London," he said cheerfully.

"You've never been to London?" Yorke asked incredulously.

"Never farther than Plymouth," he said. "And then only once, when an uncle was took ill. My wife's father's brother, it was. Had a small tavern in North Corner Street, in Plymouth Dock. Just by the Gun Wharf. Took ill and died, and I had to go and bury him and settle everything with the lawyers. A pack of rascals *they* were," he said crossly.

Chapter
Twenty-one

As the carriage clattered over the cobbles of Sloane Street with the London air still crisply fresh and the rising sun sparkling off the dew drops clinging to the last of the autumn leaves, Ramage was thankful that Yorke had suggested they stay the night at the Star and Garter at Turnham Green. All three of them were now freshly shaven; their clothes were newly pressed, and by the time they arrived at the Admiralty they would still look reasonably presentable. Equally important, they would arrive at the Admiralty early enough to make sure the First Lord would be in his office.

Yorke continued to act as Much's unofficial guide – a task begun shortly after leaving Plymouth – by pointing out buildings and streets of interest. The Mate badly wanted to see St James's Palace. It seemed that the high point of Much's visit to London would not be a visit to the Admiralty and perhaps an interview with the First Lord or a visit to Lombard Street: Much simply wanted to walk down the Mall and see where the King lived.

"Hyde Park Corner," Yorke announced for Much's benefit. "More than two hundred and fifty miles from Falmouth – according to the coachman's tariff."

Much was impressed: he had sailed from Falmouth for the West Indies more than a couple of dozen times in his life, and each time had left on a voyage of thousands of miles with less excitement than setting off for London from Plymouth.

The coach swung right at Hyde Park and then along the edge

of St James's Park, and Yorke told the coachman to stop for a moment as they arrived in Parliament Square. He motioned to Much to get out and followed him to point out the Houses of Parliament. But this time Much was unimpressed, and Ramage guessed he did not appreciate the power that Members of Parliament wielded over his life – and over the whole country. He could see no connection between decisions made in that greystone building and, say, a fleet carrying a small army to capture Martinique.

Much climbed back into the carriage with Yorke, and the coachman whipped up the horses, which were still fresh since they had come only from Turnham Green. The carriage turned into Whitehall. "Downing Street," Yorke said unenthusiastically, pointing to the narrow, short road to their left. "The Prime Minister lives there."

"Doesn't pay any rent, I'll be bound," Much commented.

A little farther on Yorke said, "That's the Horse Guards – the headquarters of the Army."

"Does the Duke of York live there?" Much asked.

"No, he works there," Yorke said, wearying of his role as guide.

Ramage said, "The Admiralty is just ahead..."

Because the Admiralty building stood back from the street behind a high screen wall, the carriage swung into the middle of the road to make the sharp turn through the archway in the centre, and a moment later the clatter of the horses' hooves echoed across the cobbled courtyard. As the carriage stopped in front of the four thick columns at the entrance door, two porters hurried out. They opened the door and swung down the hinged steps, already warned by the carriage's travel-stained appearance that it had come a long way.

He climbed out, careful that his sword did not catch in the steps, and the look of interest in the porters' faces faded: they were expecting an admiral and found a lieutenant accompanied by someone who was not even a naval officer and a person who was clearly the mate of some merchantman. Without a word they retreated up the steps and into the large entrance hall.

322

After telling the coachman where to deliver their luggage, Ramage strode into the hall. Even though it was only late autumn, there was a big fire burning in the large fireplace on his left; the great six-sided glass lantern hanging from the ceiling had not been cleaned after its night's work and the glass was sooty. A messenger – the term used to describe the attendants – was lounging in one of the big, black-leather armchairs which had a canopy over the top, like a poke bonnet. Another messenger was standing at the table, glancing at a newspaper, while the two porters gossiped in a corner.

Ramage knew that, clasping the crudely sewn canvas bag containing his reports, he looked an unprepossessing figure as far as the messengers were concerned. And he had no appointment. Dozens of naval officers came into this hall in the course of a week, all trying to see one of the Board members or someone else who might have sufficient interest or influence to get them appointments. Admirals were kept waiting in this hall, and Ramage knew only too well that mere lieutenants without appointments might well die of old age in the waiting-room on his left.

He knew from past experience that if the messenger tried the usual blackmail of knowing nothing and doing nothing until a guinea had changed hands he would get angry, and he knew equally well that he was likely to need all the patience he could muster if the First Lord did not believe his report.

It was time, he decided, to make use of his title.

"Lieutenant Lord Ramage to see the First Lord. I have no appointment for a particular time but his Lordship ordered me to come to London and report to him as soon as possible."

The messenger – probably out of habit – picked up a list and read it. "Your name isn't on the list of appointments, my Lord."

"I said I had no appointment. I've posted from Plymouth. I am under orders from the First Lord."

The messenger, without his guinea, was unimpressed: he had obviously waved away too many impoverished captains and outmanoeuvred too many junior admirals to be intimidated by mere lieutenants, however urgent they might proclaim their business to be.

The messenger snapped his fingers at one of the porters. "Tell the First Lord's secretary there is a Lieutenant Lord Damage asking to see him."

Ramage tapped the table with his fingers. " 'Ramage', and to see the First Lord, not his secretary."

"If you'd care to state your business, sir, I might be able..."

"Pass the word to the First Lord's secretary," Ramage said icily, "otherwise I'll go up to Lord Spencer's office unannounced."

The man gestured to the porter, who went out of the hall along the corridor leading off to the left.

Yorke looked round the hall nonchalantly and said to Ramage in a bored voice, "Damned poor class of servants they have here, what?"

"It's the war," Ramage said, with equal nonchalance. "All the men with any brains or ability are sent to sea. Just the dregs left. You notice it in the seaports, too; the only fellows lounging around are those even the press gangs turn down."

The messenger in the chair straightened himself up; his colleague at the desk was now standing stiffly, his face a bright red. The porter left in the corner sniggered with embarrassment.

The porter came scurrying back to say that Lord Spencer would see Lord Ramage at once.

"Show these two gentlemen to the waiting-room," Ramage told the messenger at the desk, and followed the porter along the corridor and up two flights of narrow stairs. The porter knocked on the door of the Board Room, walked in and announced Ramage.

Lord Spencer was at the far end of the long table, sitting in the only chair with arms: the other four chairs down each side and the single one at the other end, occupied by Their Lordships when the full Board was meeting, were straight-backed and uncomfortable.

Ramage knew that the First Lord's habit of using the Board Room as his own office reflected the way the Admiralty functioned. Most people thought of the Lords Commissioners meeting formally, seated at this table, and listening solemnly to matters raised by Nepean, the Secretary – who usually sat on Lord Spencer's right, at the corner of the table – and then, even more solemnly, discussing and deciding what was to be done. Then orders or instructions would be sent out by Nepean, duly recording that "I am directed..." (or required or commanded – the theme had several variations) "... by my Lords Commissioners of the Admiralty..."

More usually, though, Nepean would come into the Board Room, with his pile of papers and letters just received, and sit comfortably at the table instead of being crowded in the corner. Next to him would be the second secretary, William Marsden, who would keep the rough minutes recording what questions had been raised and what had been decided. The First Lord would be present and perhaps one other. Much of the Board's business was dealt with by a single member, although as far as the recipient of an order was concerned it seemed that at least three or more of Their Lordships were involved. Ramage knew that Nepean's routine with letters was quite simple: the bottom left-hand corner of the letter was folded over and up, and the gist of the intended reply scribbled on the blank triangle.

Three long windows overlooking a stable lit the room on the south side; beside the door on the north side was a large fireplace which still bore the arms of Charles II.

"A moment, Ramage," the First Lord said without glancing up. He dipped his pen into a heavy silver inkwell, scribbled a signature on the document he had been reading, and put down the pen carefully before looking up.

"I was expecting you tomorrow," he said, making it obvious his usual greeting, shaking hands, was going to be omitted.

"I posted, sir," Ramage explained.

"Don't expect the Admiralty to pay for it," Spencer said abruptly, waving Ramage to a chair on his left. It meant Ramage had to walk right round the long table, and seemed a piece of petty irritation suited to the First Lord's icy manner.

"Well, what more have you to tell me that justifies you posting to London?"

Lord Spencer's hostility was an anticlimax for Ramage. Up to that moment the information contained in the long and carefully written report in his canvas bag, with the corroboration of Yorke and Much, had seemed of great significance; worth risking his life to ensure its safe delivery. His discoveries were to put the Government, the Horse Guards, the Admiralty and Downing Street back in communication with the rest of the world.

Certainly he had anticipated some trouble over his first guarded report to Lord Spencer from Lisbon, but his Lordship was not just chilly but downright frigid; not only uninterested in hearing more details but apparently anxious to get back to signing his letters.

"You received my preliminary report from Lisbon, sir?" That was a damned silly remark, he realized, since the ransom had been paid.

Lord Spencer nodded casually and gestured to a closed folder to his right. "Mr Nepean brought it in to refresh my memory."

"Was there confirmation from the underwriters about insuring the ventures, sir?"

"They have not been asked," Spencer said shortly.

Ramage was too slow to hide his surprise, and the First Lord added sharply, "The Cabinet were not very pleased with your attempt to blame the Post Office men, Ramage."

"I imagine not, sir," Ramage said bleakly.

So they did not believe him. They had paid to have the packet released, and that was all. A good bargain, no doubt: they would have had to pay out £4,000 to Stevens if the ship was lost to the enemy; but by paying the ransom they had got it back with the ship's company for £2,500 . . .

"Am I to take it that my first report is not believed, sir?"

Spencer nodded, glancing down impatiently at the papers awaiting his signature.

Ramage looked at the wall to his left on which was something like an enormous clock with a circular map of Europe on its face and the points of the compass round the edge. A pointer with its axis where London was on the map was oscillating slightly, showing the wind direction and moved by a cunning system of rods and cams which linked it to a windvane on the Admiralty roof.

"I have a second and very full report here, sir, giving all the details of insurance frauds and so on," Ramage said, indicating the canvas bag on the chair beside him.

"You'd better leave it," Spencer said, picking up his pen, his voice still distant. "I take it the report doesn't indicate any change of mind on your part about what happened?"

"No, sir."

"All you lacked in your first report was proof, my dear Ramage – as Lord Auckland was quick to point out at a Cabinet meeting. And the only thing you aren't likely to get – as the Prime Minister was equally quick to point out – is proof."

Ramage thought of the dead sentry, the kidnapping of Gianna, the Bosun pointing the pistol in the darkness, the boom of his own pistol going off in the *Arabella*'s tiny cabin. And the mutineers in irons...

The Port Admiral's report from Plymouth must have merely reported that Lieutenant Ramage was coming to London, and not mentioned that the *Lady Arabella* had arrived with a dozen packetsmen in irons ... The Port Admiral had wisely decided to keep his nose out of something he did not understand.

Tiredness from the long journey up from Plymouth – and perhaps the strain of the past weeks – was fast catching up with Ramage. The few hours' rest snatched at the Star and Garter at Turnham Green had not been enough. It was not just physical tiredness either: he was tired of men who tried to dodge responsibility, starting with Sir Pilcher Skinner in Jamaica and including the Post Office Agent in Lisbon. He was tired, too, of cynical, worldly, yet utterly naïve politicians who thought the world's axis was between the Ayes and Noes lobbies of Parliament, and regarded service to the country solely in terms of service to the party. They genuinely rewarded someone who manoeuvred a successful Parliamentary vote of confidence on a critical issue because they could recognize it as a valuable service which deserved recognition, but they were always puzzled about what to do with a general or admiral who won a great victory in battle: that was something beyond their real comprehension. They had to fall back on precedent – so and so received an earldom fifty years ago for a similar sort of thing ... no mention of hundreds or thousands of men who had lost limbs, eyes or life, who were buried in unmarked graves in some distant land or put over the side of ships, sewn up in hammocks with a shot at their feet, or condemned to spend the rest of their lives begging in the streets with sightless eyes or standing on crutches, their futures lost under piles of fruitless applications for pensions...

Ramage lifted the canvas bag on to the table and, rather perversely, wished it had dried fish scales on it, or even white crusted salt from dried seawater: anything that would leave a temporary mark on this highly polished mahogany table to remind Their Lordships of the broad oceans and fighting ships, and take their minds from the stuffy, almost incestuous, atmosphere of the Houses of Parliament.

He unlaced the bag, removed his report and Much's, and put them both down on the table, then glanced over at the Langley Bradley clock in the corner by the door. A quarter past ten. That clock, he remembered Spencer telling him during a happier visit to the Board Room more than a year ago, had told Their Lordships the time for nearly three-quarters of a century, while the wind vane had told Their Lordships if the wind would serve to let the French Fleet escape from Brest. The mirror on the front of the clock had reflected Board meetings that had sent Vernon to Cartagena, and Anson on his great voyage round the world. And given Byng a tiny squadron and sent him too late to save the Balearic Islands from the Duc de Richelieu and Admiral Galisonniere. Port Mahon had fallen, Byng had been blamed for what was the Government's slowness and stupidity and unpreparedness, and as their scapegoat he had been shot.

And out of that shameful episode had come a delight for gluttons – the new sauce the Duc de Richelieu's chef had

328

created to celebrate the fall of Mahon and named *mahonnaise*, and which was becoming very popular these days...

Suddenly Ramage noticed that his Lordship had made no move to pick up the reports; in fact he had returned to reading and signing his letters. Was he indicating that the report was politically unacceptable? Was he telling Ramage not only that he had failed, but that he had earned everyone's contempt by trying to blame the poor defenceless packetsmen?

It was one or the other, and Ramage no longer cared which, even though the mutiny in the *Arabella* had been the final proof he needed. He wanted to be with Gianna again: he wanted to see his mother and father and wander through Blazey Hall, see the portraits of his forebears watching him from the walls. Perhaps they would approve of what he had done. He would walk through the gardens and the fields and forget the Navy, the Post Office and politicians. He wanted to walk through the fields holding Gianna's hand like some rustic with a milkmaid.

"This is my final report, sir: it contains all the proof you could want."

Lord Spencer nodded without looking up. "I'll look at it when I have the time."

"May I have leave, sir?"

"You have no ship," Lord Spencer said, "so you're on half pay. Your time is your own..."

It was true, of course; but the voice was still as friendly as cold steel. It said, without uttering the actual words, you are on half pay now, and that is how you will end your days, because you were given a splendid chance and your first report went all the way up to the Cabinet, and all along the way it was disbelieved.

One grunt of disapproval from the Prime Minister over a lieutenant's activities, and the lieutenant might wish he had died nobly as an enemy shot knocked his head off. The alternative was rotting on the beach on half pay...

"Thank you, sir," Ramage said and stood up. He moved the report so the bottoms of the two packets were parallel with the edge of the table.

329

Spencer nodded curtly, still without looking up or saying any more, and Ramage, his now empty canvas bag tucked under his arm, left the Board Room and made his way down to the entrance hall. Yorke and Much sprang from their chairs in the waiting-room as he entered, but Ramage shook his head, indicating that he wanted to say nothing within hearing of the messengers, and gestured towards Whitehall.

The two men followed him out of the waiting-room, across the entrance hall and out through the doors. They strode down the wide steps and across the cobbled courtyard. The two stone beasts over the top of the archway that Ramage had never been able to identify – they comprised the head, shoulders and wings of an eagle grafted to the tail of a sea serpent – seemed to ignore them, as usual, as they emerged into Whitehall.

Ramage looked up and down the street for a carriage. On the opposite side a tinker was busy hammering at the bottom of a pot, while next to him an upholsterer patiently mended the padding of a chair. There were the usual carts and wagons – one laden high with cords of firewood was passing a brewer's dray loaded with a pyramid of puncheons, more than enough weight for a pair of horses to haul.

"What happened?" Yorke finally asked.

"He didn't believe the first report from Lisbon, and the Cabinet agreed with him. They all criticize me for putting the blame on the Post Office men. I gather it doesn't fit in with Government policy."

"But what about the last report – the one you've just delivered?" Yorke asked incredulously.

"I was told to leave it," Ramage said flatly.

"He didn't read it?"

"No."

"But you told him –"

"I told him it contained all the proof he needed."

"So he doesn't know anything about the mutiny and the kidnapping of the Marchesa, then?"

"I assume not; but it won't make any difference. The policy had already been laid down in Downing Street; that's obvious, even if it means they go on losing packets."

330

"Perhaps it'll be different when Lord Spencer reads the report," Much commented hopefully.

Ramage snorted, then said, "Anyway, here's a carriage."

"Well, I'd better say goodbye, sir," Much said.

"Why? Aren't you coming with us?" Ramage asked in surprise.

"Where are you going, sir?"

"My family have a house in Palace Street. It's about half a mile beyond the Houses of Parliament. You're coming, aren't you Yorke?"

The young shipowner nodded. "Many thanks; I don't keep a town house and don't want to take another carriage down to Bexley for the time being; I've had enough of travelling..."

By then the carriage had stopped. The coachman, leaping down to unfold the steps, was standing with the door open.

Ramage motioned Much in, taking his acceptance of the invitation for granted, and followed Yorke. "Palace Street," he told the coachman. "Blazey House."

The coach smelled dusty and gave the impression there was heavy mildew under the cushions, but the springs had been greased and the coachman controlled the horses without the usual noisy flourishes that they seemed to think necessary to increase the size of the tip.

The three men sat in silence as they passed the Houses of Parliament: Ramage felt that Yorke was not going to try to get Much interested in them again.

"The Abbey," Yorke said suddenly. "That's Westminster Abbey."

Much nodded, but was not impressed, and Yorke sat back in his seat.

Suddenly there was the clatter of a horse's hooves right beside them and a hand was banging on the window. Much jumped up with a warning yell of "Highwaymen, by God!" and, banging his head on the roof, sank back to his seat glassy-eyed and almost stupefied.

Yorke, sitting in the forward seat and looking back, said to Ramage quickly, "It's one of those messengers from the Admiralty!"

331

The carriage stopped before they could call out to the coachman, and, as he opened the door, Ramage heard the urgent call, "Lieutenant! Lieutenant!"

Ramage stared at the messenger on horseback. As far as he was concerned he had made his last visit to the Admiralty; in the brief carriage drive he had decided to resign his commission and ask Gianna to marry him...

"What do you want?"

"Lieutenant Ramage, sir! Will you return to the Admiralty at once, sir? First Lord's orders, sir, at once sir, it's urgent sir, no delay his Lordship said, it's urgent –"

"Belay it," Ramage snapped, although the last "urgent" would have been the final one for a few moments since the man was now taking a painful gasp of breath.

Yorke muttered, "He's just read your report!"

"Yes, you'd both better come back with me."

He called to the coachman to return to the Admiralty, and a small group of passers-by, peddlars and hucksters who had stopped to watch, moved out of the way as the coachman reined the horses round with a flourish.

Fifteen minutes later Ramage was sitting in the same chair in the Board Room.

"Are you trying to make a fool of me?" Lord Spencer asked furiously.

"No, sir! Why?" Ramage exclaimed.

"Your report! Why the devil didn't you mention the mutiny, the attempt to murder you and the kidnapping of the Marchesa di Volterra – though God knows what she was doing on board?"

Ramage decided that, for all the anger, nothing had really changed. "I referred to it in my report, sir."

"I know that! But why the devil didn't you mention it when you were sitting there?"

"I said the report contained all the proof you needed, sir – although I didn't think it would make much difference..."

"Difference to what?"

"Difference to the Government's decision."

"*What* Government decision?" Lord Spencer asked angrily.

332

"That the packetsmen aren't to be blamed for anything, sir."

"Well – that wasn't exactly a decision," the First Lord said, obviously taken aback.

"You said that my first report was not believed, sir – by the Postmaster-General or the Prime Minister."

"Well, yes; but that was before this mutiny, which is just the proof we needed."

"I had all the proof *I* needed long before we reached Lisbon. Still, I suppose the fact that they tried to murder me and kidnapped the Marchesa does prove I'm not a liar!"

The bitter comment was spoken before Ramage realized he had even thought it, and he waited, red-faced and angry, for the First Lord's wrath.

Instead Lord Spencer said calmly, "It proves you're not a politician."

Ramage sat staring in front of him, determined to guard his tongue.

"Lord Auckland will be here in a few minutes," Spencer said. "Fortunately he hasn't gone down to his place in Bromley."

"The underwriters," Ramage said. "There are three men from the *Lady Arabella* for instance: the Commander, the Surgeon and the Bosun's mate. We need to know how many times they have collected insurance on total loss claims. And how many times they've been captured and exchanged, too. Sir," he added as an afterthought.

The First Lord picked up a small silver bell and rang it violently. Almost immediately a secretary hurried into the room. "Ah, Jeffries," the First Lord said, "Take a list of packetsmen that Lieutenant Ramage will give you. Check with the Navy Board to see who deals with the exchange of Post Office prisoners, and then find out how often these men have been captured and exchanged. And at the same time – at the *same* time, mind you, because we're in a hurry – ask the Committee of Lloyds to find out what policies these same Post Office packetsmen have taken out since the beginning of the war, and what claims they've made – all on personal freight between Falmouth and the West Indies."

333

Ramage wrote the names on a sheet of paper and gave it to Jeffries, who was obviously the First Lord's secretary.

As soon as they were alone again, the First Lord said, "Well, what answers shall I get?"

Ramage shrugged his shoulders. "All of them have been captured at least twice. The Surgeon has probably been making nearly £4,000 a year from private cargoes and insurance claims, and many of the seamen £500 or more. The claims are quite legal, sir – or, rather, claims the underwriters never questioned since they were for goods in a packet captured by the French."

"Why didn't the underwriters ever query the claims?"

"Because the Post Office was authenticating every loss by paying out the full value to the owner of the packet. If the Government is satisfied and pays out, sir, how can underwriters avoid following suit?"

"I follow what you mean. But see here, Ramage, when Lord Auckland arrives, you watch your tongue. I'll do the talking: it's very delicate when one department has to tell another that some of its people have committed treason..."

"And murder, attempted murder, mutiny and kidnapping," Ramage said, picturing the sentry's body sprawled on the deck, and Gianna held prisoner.

"Yes, quite. I appreciate that you, as an intended victim, have a proprietary interest in the attempt, but nevertheless ... By the way, you shot the Boatswain in the leg. You could have killed him. Why didn't you?"

"There was no point in killing for the sake of it, sir, and anyway I needed live evidence."

"There'll be no court case, Ramage; I'd better warn you of that now. And don't start –"

His Lordship broke off when he saw that far from getting angry, Ramage was gently laughing. "What is so funny, Ramage?"

"I'm not quite sure, sir; it's got very mixed up. I never thought for a minute there'd be a trial –"

"Why?" Spencer snapped.

Ramage managed to stop the blunt answer he was about to

make, and rephrased it. "I assumed that the exigencies of the Government's political situation would have made it inadvisable," he said in a bored monotone.

"Excellent. If you go on like that, Ramage, you'll be offered a safe Parliamentary seat somewhere. Yes, you're quite right, although I still don't see what there is to laugh at."

"I'm not really laughing, sir. I had – er, anticipated the problems relating to a trial..." He paused for a moment, reflecting on his words: yes, he could see himself standing with his hands clasping his lapels, his head slightly inclined forward, and an utterly false smile on his face, and facing the Opposition Benches. "I took the liberty of administering a little punishment to one or two of the men."

Spencer nodded understandingly. "That might be thought by some to have been a wise precaution."

At that moment there was a knock at the door and when Spencer answered a messenger came in and whispered something. Spencer said, "Show him in at once – I gave instructions that he was not to be kept hanging about in the hall." As the messenger hurried out the First Lord said, "Lord Auckland has arrived."

The Postmaster-General's first words when Lord Spencer introduced him were biting: "So this is the young man who sees treason the length and breadth of the Post Office, eh?"

Instead of defending him, Ramage was surprised to find Lord Spencer agreeing. "The same young man, and he's just posted up from Plymouth at his own expense to bring me another report."

"I trust it makes more sense than the one he wrote from Lisbon."

"Well, William, it may not make more sense, but it's certainly more interesting. Care to read it?"

"I hope you haven't dragged me all the way over here for that," the Postmaster-General said sourly.

The First Lord slid the report across the polished table as though dealing a card and, for that matter, Ramage thought, the Postmaster-General opened the report with the same wary interest that a player picks up and looks at his cards.

He read it through slowly without any expression showing on his face. Then he looked up at Lord Spencer and raised an eyebrow. "The Mate's report?"

When Spencer skimmed it across he read it slowly with the same concentration. Finally he put it down on the table and looked at Ramage. "So you found the proof." The voice was almost bitter, but Ramage sensed it was not bitterness over him. "You knew you'd find it even when you wrote from Lisbon, didn't you?" He made his question sound like an accusation.

"No, sir," Ramage said flatly. "I'd already found all I needed."

"Why didn't you mention it in your first report, then?"

"I don't think you understood quite what Ramage meant, William," the First Lord said quickly. "I think he means he didn't know what the *final* proof would eventually be, but he knew he had only to bide his time before finding it. Proof, that is, which would stand up in a court of law."

"I've given him credit for *that*," Lord Auckland said testily. "What I was asking Ramage was this: did he suspect the packetsmen would mutiny before they arrived in Falmouth?"

The First Lord looked questioningly at Ramage, who nodded.

"And tell me, George," Lord Auckland asked the First Lord, "don't you find it odd that there are a dozen of your seamen on board the *Lady Arabella*? I hope you don't mind me asking young Ramage about it?"

George John Eden, first Earl Spencer, shook his head. "Carry on, William. I assume it is something arranged with the Commander-in-Chief in Jamaica. Was that so, Ramage?"

Keep up a united front with strangers present, Ramage thought to himself. "Quite so, sir; it gave us a nucleus of" – he just stopped himself saying "reliable men", and substituted – "men I'd sailed with before."

"The Commander," Auckland said. "What is your private impression of Stevens?"

"Under the thumb of the Surgeon, sir. I don't mean blackmail; it might have been just the gift of the blarney. Apart from

336

that, sir, with all that rot in the transom he had a good enough reason for wanting the Post Office to buy him a new ship."

"I can see that quite clearly, thank you," Lord Auckland said sarcastically. "I'm trying to see what characteristics this particular commander has that might be common to other commanders who surrendered at one time or another."

Lord Spencer said, "Your report is excellent, Ramage, but now tell us what happened and what you thought from the time the privateer came in sight."

Briefly, but without leaving out any important detail he could remember, Ramage described the scene. When he had finished, Spencer asked, "What made you think of the exchange – the ransom, as it were?"

"I don't remember what gave me the immediate idea, sir; but my main concern was to avoid being made prisoner so that I could get the word to you as soon as possible about what was happening."

"Those damned ventures!" Auckland said suddenly. "I suspected it all along." He turned to Lord Spencer, as if seeking reassurance, and the First Lord nodded. "You've tried to get the Cabinet to agree to banning them often enough, William, but the strike of packetsmen last year frightened them. Yet you were right."

Ramage thought of Much sitting out in the waiting-room. Here was the chance of the Mate receiving a reward, if only praise from his minister, but the request had better go through the First Lord. "Mr Much, the Mate who wrote the other report you have, sir . . . I brought him to London with me in case he was needed for questioning. Perhaps his Lordship . . . ?"

Spencer caught on immediately. "He's your man, William; we all owe him a vote of thanks. By the way, Ramage, when is this Sidney Yorke due in London?"

"He's in the waiting-room with the Mate, sir. I thought you might want . . . that he'd be needed a a witness, perhaps," Ramage said lamely.

"Why should you think you'd need a witness?" Lord Auckland asked, watching Ramage closely.

"If there was any question that . . ."

337

"The fact is, William," Lord Spencer interrupted, "that Mr Ramage has a poor opinion of the probity and intelligence of politicians, so he mustered all his guns..."

Auckland's eyebrows raised as he looked at Spencer. "He's a lucky young man; the fact the Mate and this fellow Yorke are still out in the waiting-room without you having seen them means he persuaded you without difficulty, eh? Well, let's have a word with this Mate now."

"Without difficulty..." Ramage thought to himself. As he went to the door to call a messenger, he saw the First Lord's face was red.

Both Lord Auckland and the First Lord were excellent in the way they handled Much. Surprised at the extent of the detail in the Mate's report that they had absorbed, Ramage noticed how both were quick to ask Much for further information they both needed not so much for further inquiries, but to answer critics in the Cabinet or Parliament. Indeed, he thought to himself, the political mind works very differently from any other.

After Much, they invited Yorke to the Board Room, and within five minutes or so the young shipowner was, in his own nonchalant manner, having both ministers admit that at first they had disbelieved Ramage's report from Lisbon and had doubts about payment of the ransom to free the *Lady Arabella*.

Lord Spencer's face was going red again, and Ramage feared Yorke might go too far. Lord Auckland gave a dry laugh. "But please remember, Mr Yorke, that Cabinet decisions are always collective – and secret – and that we did pay out."

Yorke turned to the First Lord. "Would it be impertinent, my Lord, to ask the result of the inquiries into insurance on the packetmen's ventures?"

"Er – well, not impertinent, but perhaps premature. I was telling Ramage that inquiries are being made. We haven't received the answer from the Committee of Lloyds yet."

And, Ramage thought sourly, that was hardly surprising, since the First Lord's private secretary hasn't been gone with the list of names for more than half an hour...

338

Yorke was shaking his head and Spencer's eyebrows raised questioningly.

"The official approach, my Lord," Yorke explained. "I was wondering if it was the best way, if there is any urgency..."

"There's no real urgency now, Mr Yorke," Lord Auckland said, but to Ramage it seemed his voice lacked conviction.

Yorke apologized hastily, and for a moment Ramage thought he had overdone it. But no, it hooked Lord Auckland, who said, "Well, my dear Yorke, I wouldn't say we have all the time in the world, but a week or two..."

"The Plymouth and Falmouth newspapers," Yorke said vaguely, as if thinking aloud, "and the mutinous packetsmen ... they've got to be charged before a magistrate pretty soon, or else lawyers will be rushing round shouting ... I think these packetsmen are well organized, and Cornishmen stick together ... A reference in the London press ... one feels – at least I do, personally, but of course I'm only a layman in such things – that if Parliament suddenly asks for explanations..."

"We won't have all the answers ready," Spencer said abruptly. "You're wasted at sea, young man; you ought to think of joining Ramage here in a career of politics."

Yorke waved his hand vaguely and muttered something about "leave it to the rest of the family", and then said, "I could pass the details of the insurance claims to Mr Ramage by first thing in the morning, if that would help: I have some friends in that line of country."

Ramage appreciated what Yorke was proposing. It was the most acceptable method for both ministers: unofficial, more remote and politically safer – and yet providing quick answers.

Lord Auckland answered, since it was his ministry involved. "Any assistance, Mr Yorke ... with discretion of course..."

"Of course, my Lord," Yorke said with a smile, and Ramage suddenly saw why Spencer had mentioned a career in politics. But Spencer had not seen Yorke at sea; he could never realize the enormous gap...

"By the way," Lord Auckland said, "I must warn you young men that the whole of this inquiry is secret. I doubt if the packetsmen will be brought to trial – except for the Bosun's

339

mate, who will be charged with murder – because we have no wish to advertise our defects to the French."

"Although I was the intended victim each time in the two attempted murder charges against the Bosun, and the Marchesa di Volterra the actual victim of kidnapping," Ramage said bluntly, deliberately ignoring the First Lord's warning glance, "the French have been well aware of the defects in the Packet Service for a year or more, sir."

"Quite so," Lord Auckland said smoothly, "I was using the phrase 'the French' in a metaphorical sense. But one has to take the broader view."

"Quite surprising how broad the muzzle of a pistol seems when someone's threatening to shoot you," Yorke said conversationally, "or how sharp a cutlass blade when a man tries to cleave your skull with it..."

"I can imagine," Lord Auckland said, "and I realize how Ramage must feel over the death of one of his men. The murderer will be brought to trial, but the others..."

"Their Protections, sir," Ramage said. "Supposing the Admiralty cancels them entirely."

Spencer slapped the table top. "That's it, William! Let 'em spend a few years in the naval service!"

The Postmaster-General nodded at Ramage. "An excellent suggestion." He turned to Lord Spencer. "I shall be writing to you officially to thank you for Mr Ramage's efforts. I will make myself responsible for Mr Much's future. As for you, Mr Yorke" – he stood up and held out his hand – "it is lucky for the Post Office that Mr Ramage has such friends."

Next morning at the family house in Palace Street, Ramage was having a late breakfast with Yorke and Much when the ancient servant who looked after the house while the family was in Cornwall came to the table.

"A man called, my Lord," he said lugubriously.

"When, Hanson?"

"A minute or two ago, my Lord; he left this packet."

Ramage took it and then saw the superscription. He gestured across the table. "It's for Mr Yorke."

"I'm sorry sir, I must clean my spectacles."

"Clean them? You haven't got them on!"

"Oh dear," the old man said petulantly, "I wonder where I left them?"

Yorke opened the packet and took out several sheets of paper.

"This is what we were waiting for," he said, clearing plates and cutlery away to make a space in front of him, then spreading out the papers.

"Stevens. Looks as though this last voyage was the first time he ever carried ventures. Eight hundred pounds worth of insurance for the round trip.

"Now for that surgeon, Farrell. He's taken out policies on seven occasions – seven separate round trip voyages. The underwriters have paid out several thousand pounds on four occasions for cargoes lost owing to enemy action. Add that to the profit normally made on freights and you'll find that Mr Farrell is one of the wealthiest men in Falmouth.

"Now for the Bosun's mate. Insured on nine round trips and he's claimed on three." He glanced through the other papers. "Same story for the rest of them. I notice the amounts they insured for have increased fifty per cent each voyage. They were getting more and more confident..."

He picked up and handed the papers across the table to Ramage. "You'll want to pass them on to the Admiralty ..."

An hour later Ramage was sitting in the same chair in the Board Room of the Admiralty and surprised to find that the First Lord and Lord Auckland were again discussing the packet problem. There was a third man present who was introduced as Mr Francis Freeling, and Ramage thought he remembered seeing the name in the *Royal Kalendar* as being the Secretary of the General Post Office. Freeling was a man of about forty, energetic, greying hair and yet oddly precise.

The two ministers read quickly through the lists from the underwriters.

"So the commander was a comparative new boy to this business," Lord Spencer commented.

"But the stern of his ship was rotten," Lord Auckland said bitterly.

"He could not have been absolutely sure he'd get the opportunity of surrendering to a privateer this voyage, my Lord," Freeling said.

"But from what Much and Mr Ramage say, he was determined to surrender at the first opportunity."

Freeling nodded, but repeated his point. "He could only surrender if he found a captor, my Lord."

"Quite so," Auckland said testily, "there's no need to state the obvious. Tell me, Ramage, you felt things were reaching a climax even before the privateer showed up. Why?"

"That rotten stern, sir; it was a bit frightening. I think Stevens meant to do everything he could to make sure he was captured, even if we hadn't sighted that privateer."

"How could he do that?" asked Freeling. "You appreciate I am a layman, of course."

"Simply by making for the areas where privateers are known to be thickest, and sailing at a reduced speed – as he was doing. Obviously the longer you take to sail through a danger area, the longer you are in danger..."

"What would you do to eradicate the whole problem – put a stop to all this surrendering?" Auckland asked Ramage abruptly – so abruptly that both Lord Spencer and Freeling glanced up in surprise.

Ramage's mind went back to the conversations he had had with Yorke and Much. "Three things would cover it, sir – in my opinion," he added politely. "Put a fresh prohibition on anyone carrying ventures and enforce it strictly: you now have a perfect reason and opportunity for banning it once and for all, and giving no option but jail for any wrongdoers. The second thing would be to make every commander face a strict court of inquiry after the loss of his ship – a court of inquiry held here in London, not among his friends in Falmouth. One of the Elder Brethren of Trinity House, someone representing the underwriters, a naval officer, perhaps a representative of the West India merchants ... a court formed of such men. The third thing would be to sack every Post Office official in Falmouth, and the Inspector of Packets in London..."

As Ramage mentioned his third proposal he watched the three men. Lord Auckland gave a curiously mild snort that was lost halfway in his nostrils, the First Lord glanced up at the Postmaster-General, but Freeling simply nodded. Nodded three times, to be exact; three firm nods, as though it was part of a ritual. Lord Auckland had noticed this and said, "Tell us, Mr Secretary, what do you think of Mr Ramage's Draconian measures?"

"Excellent, my Lord. He is quite right in saying it gives us a perfect opportunity to get rid of ventures. The stricter court of inquiry – you will recall that I've been suggesting that for two years. As for sacking the men at Falmouth ... some might be retired with advantage, others might be given the opportunity to transfer to some other station..."

"Better not antagonize too many people, you mean?" Auckland said.

Freeling nodded. "If we keep Falmouth as the packet port, we have to work with the local people there, my Lord, and they're all related to each other."

"Quite – we don't want to use Plymouth!" The minister coloured slightly and added hurriedly, "Bad holding ground for ships, they tell me, George; nothing against your people."

Lord Spencer nodded and said ironically: "You can also get into Falmouth in any weather, William; that's something you can't do at Plymouth. It's your strongest argument for continuing to use Falmouth..."

"Quite so, quite so," Lord Auckland said. "Well, no doubt Mr Ramage wants to make up for his long absence from the London social scene, and Freeling and I had better knock some sort of shape into the report to the Cabinet..."

He stood up and held his hand out to Ramage. "Thank you," he said simply, "much obliged to you and your men."

It was a sunny though chilly morning, and Ramage decided to walk back to Palace Street, trying to summon up the energy to face the journey down to St Kew. Much had gone off shopping before catching the coach back to Falmouth that night. He was impatient to be back with his family. Yorke was spending the rest of the day in Leadenhall Street at his office – seeing, as he told Ramage before leaving, "how many ships the hurricanes and the French have left me".

As he swung round into Palace Street and idly glanced along the short road, Ramage saw there was a large carriage outside his house. The carriage was blue and gold, and the coat of arms on the open door was familiar. Hanson was bent almost double over some luggage.

He found himself walking faster. Windows upstairs were being flung open, as if to air the house and someone was looking out of one of them; a young woman with black hair and a small, heart-shaped face. She was waving wildly to him and calling in a language the passers-by could not understand, and now at last free of mutineers and politicians and bureaucrats, he was holding his sword in his left hand and his hat in his right, and his heart was beating hard as if he'd run all the way from the Admiralty. He almost knocked Hanson over as he ran into the house, only vaguely hearing the old man's hasty, "The family, sir, and the Marchesa – they've just arrived!"